> Celeste
> The Xo is one books that - concept of playing the game while reading was easy for me ~ and I so badly want to play it! My usual love of Brother/Sister-In-Arms, Duty, Sacrifice, and Honor shine through.

EFL
- Expeditionary Foreign Legion -
The Xo

Ad Legionem

G. Van Wallace

G. VAN WALLACE

Technical Contributor

W. S. Smith

G. VAN WALLACE

Cross The Rubicon Publishing

Copyright © 2022 G. Van Wallace
All right reserved
First Edition

All rights reserved. No part of this publication may be reproduced, distributed, or transmitted in any form or by any means, including photocopying, recording, or other electronic or mechanical methods without the prior written permission of the author. For permission requests, solicit the author at nnpfleetmarine@gmail.com.

TABLE OF CONTENTS

Table of Contents
Author's Forward
Prologue – History...6
Chapter 1 – Draft Day..9
Chapter 2 – Graduation..21
Chapter 3 – Reconnoiter..24
Chapter 4 – Oasis...32
Chapter 5 – Return to Nahil...39
Chapter 6 – Jungle Warfare Training School.....................44
Chapter 7 – Senior Legionnaire..55
Chapter 8 – Top of the World..66
Chapter 9 – Another New Beginning..................................87
Chapter 10 – Rough Days...113
Chapter 11 – Homecoming..150
Chapter 12 – Delta 1/107th II Corps..................................165
Chapter 13 – Juno Company Sand Fleas........................202
Chapter 14 – Bravo Company...229
Chapter 15 – Hard Decision..258
Chapter 16 – An Old, New Beginning..............................304
Chapter 17 – The Middle Years..357
Rank Chart..382
Organizational Chart...384
About the Author...386
Cross The Rubicon Publishing...387
About the Book..388

AUTHOR'S FORWARD

You are about to immerse yourself into the life of *EFL Cassum* D. Baker, a newly conscripted member of the Expeditionary Foreign Legion. You will not just follow the character, but you will become Legionnaire Baker. You will soon ask yourself: *"Does this book read like a computer game, or is it a computer game that plays like a book?"*

EFL – Expeditionary Foreign Legion is laid out peculiarly for the average reader. Don't let that hamper your assimilation of the story. For the average computer gamer, don't let the excessive words dampen your enjoyment. To give the effect of a game, various repetitive boiler-plate *Level Ups*, *Mission Objective Scenarios*, *Scene Setup*, and *After-Action Summaries* are provided throughout the game; I mean book. Even with multiple decision options, the intent is to read straight through, not jump from one choice to another. However, in your mind, you decide, *"Which way would I go? What would I do?"* Chapters continue the flow of the story like any other book. Occasionally Legionnaire Baker may make poor decisions, that may even result in death, and the directive to *Restart* may be given. It is up to you, the reader, to decide whether to forge ahead or flip back to the beginning.

Every decision, great or small, affects what happens to Baker. Life is not a game and is much more complicated than a book. We have all made choices, decisions, that have impacted our lives from that point onward. Such is the adventure you will experience once beginning *EFL*.

The great American 19th Century Poet Robert Frost best put it when he wrote:

> *Two Roads diverged in a yellow wood,*
> *And sorry I could not travel both…*
>
> *…I shall be telling this with a sigh*
> *somewhere ages and ages hence:*
>
> *Two Roads diverged in a wood, and I -*
> *I took the one less traveled by,*
> *And that has made all the difference*
>
> "The Road Not Taken" Robert Frost

Adventure awaits in this uniquely-written book style. The story will keep you entertained and involved. Carry on, Cassum!

PROLOGUE

History

The world is enormous, so large it is said that near a quarter is not even known to the many civilizations that have fought over it for millennia. It has two moons, one medium and one smaller one. Almost 100 years ago, a country endeavored to land on the most promising one, *Hella*. The landing mission was a success, but the orbiter crashed into the lander on the return connection. The two crafts were helpless, orbiting the planet for almost two weeks before being pulled into the gravitational zone and burned up. Another mission was planned shortly after, but sabotage of the launch ended the program.

Scientists believe the planet experienced its last great worldwide Ice Age 25,000 years ago. It ended when a mammoth solar flare burned everything and melted the ice instantly, causing epic flooding over most of the planet. Life returned, flourished, and was destroyed two times more. It has been 4700 years of this current civilizational period.

Scientists worldwide report they have found not only evidence of past civilizations but also time capsules from them as well. Your country's capsule is available for viewing at the capital city of Dubuque, but it is only a replica; the real one is kept in a safe place. The planet's predecessors passed on many great and wonderful advances and technologies, which assisted present societies in growing rapidly and flourishing where previous ones took thousands of years to advance. One of the many projects participated in by nearly all advanced civilizations is to locate seed safes in widespread fashion so that after the next catastrophe, the world will once again re-bloom. Human life continuation has also been planned for, but those plans are held at the highest level of secrecy.

Wars have been waged endlessly, even with past civilizations before their destruction: regional wars, civil wars, world wars, territorial wars, wars for wealth. The current world war has been raging, off and on, for nearly 200 years. The planet's population is estimated to be close to 10 billion inhabitants in a world with nearly 800 million square miles of surface area. It's staggering. Vast resources are claimed and fought over even though there is plenty for everyone to have. Enormous oceans, freshwater rivers and lakes abound, timber, minerals, food, animals of wonderful origin roam on millions of acres of unpopulated areas. Oil is the commodity of war. The empty deserts contain the most easily accessible reservoirs, laying only 5000 feet under the sand. It shows that the deserts weren't always deserts. Thousands of years ago, they were magnificent forests, but the climate changed, as it does every thousand years or so, and a new cycle is coming around again. Increased numbers of hurricanes and deep snows are inching out of the areas where they have been experienced for hundreds of years. Heatwaves are stretching far into the intermediate season of winter. The planet is about to shift again, the fate of life unknown.

The country you were lucky enough to be born into enjoys a level of lifestyle above many other societies. This country is rich in resources, population, and landmass. Every citizen knows the cost of wealth and prosperity, the ability to live free without an overbearing, dictatorial government yoking its citizens for its own increased wealth. Every citizen born for over a thousand years has been required to serve a three-year military or civil service obligation. The sacrifice of life, at times, is necessary for the freedom of others. That is the mantra. However, it has recently been brought to light that citizens with government or other high power connections serve disproportionately in low-risk, civil servant capacities rather than in military service. For you, there are many options to choose from. You are smart, with an above-average level of education, healthy and strong; you are more than willing to perform your service obligation.

The National Navy and correlating Army offers a wide range of after-service skill-related positions. The Civil Service Branch is not necessarily out of the question. Flight Special Service Branch also seems exciting and achievable with your high aptitude. Your great uncle on your mother's side served in the Expeditionary Foreign Legion and always tells stories of his days in the EFL. Your mother forbids you to even talk to the EFL. She served in the civil service as a secretary to an ambassador to Prangenua in the mountains. She speaks very little of her three years other than to say she was so happy for her contract to be up and start a family and get on with her life. Your father was in the National Army and never left the country, serving as a border guard for his three years.

CHAPTER 1

Level 1 – **Draft Day**

Today is your 17th birthday. And when you arrive home after sports, your mother is waiting for you with a worried expression. You thought, at first, she was waiting to surprise you with a party or a birthday wish, but quickly find the reason for her concern.

"You received your Draft Notice today. Your number was called early! You must not delay. Go to the recruiting station and join the civil service. They will see I had a good record and that you are qualified to enter. They will take you! Please, go now, my baby. Run before they draft you. Go!"

She gives you a kiss that is wet with tears. You turn out the front door and hurry to the town government square. Even in the late afternoon, the square is busier than usual. The new draft numbers are unexpectedly low in the series. You see several of your friends or those you know, roughly the same age with the same series. This is unprecedented. You talk anxiously to your friends as you wait in line. Everyone is excited or scared that they will not get the service branch they want. No one wants to join the EFL; the stories are too troubling.

"No, if it comes down to it, join the National Army," one says.

"Yeah, where at least you can choose your job," adds another. You are next to enter the recruiting office. They are only allowing a few in at a time. Three charter buses drive up the street and park in the municipal lot down the block.

You enter the office.

The senior official inside is a civil servant, a three-year assistant aide to the deputy employment director of the town. He has no personal interest in which branches are explored or signed. He is not shocked at the turnout today, as the draft boards were all notified of a peculiar draw last week. There are only two recruiters in their offices today, one from the National Navy and the other from the EFL, Expeditionary Foreign Legion, or simply the Legion. Taped on the wall beside the door of the EFL office is a handwritten note – *The EFL Infantry Quota Is Full* – and the recruiter sits at his desk drinking coffee. As you enter the outer recruiting office you are given a clipboard with an information sheet to complete and a brochure with a list of available enlistment opportunities.

The sheet asks for: Name, Age/Birthdate, Address, Parents' Enlistment Service Branch, Draft Number, Education Level, MATS (Military Aptitude Test Score – everyone takes that), and preferred enlisting branch.

You browse the brochure. It is different than the ones you have seen before, and you look it over. You are one of four applicants in the office and you are busy reading the flyer and filling out the questions.

The list you have provides a brief description for each available branch. It includes:

__ Civil Servant Branch – Work gaining valuable experience and knowledge in one of the hundreds of skill categories while traveling abroad and being paid a good salary. Many positions include meals and lodging while on official business.

__ Officer Corps – All five military branches require incoming, young officer candidates to fill

EXPEDITIONARY FOREIGN LEGION -The Xo

their ranks. If you qualify, you will attend upper education courses for two years and then serve an additional two years in your chosen service branch. All education is paid plus room and board the entire time of your service and a salary befitting an officer.

__ Flight Special Services – The best pay, rank, and opportunity for after-service job placement of all five branches. Many job specialties including mechanic, medical, finance, legal, and pilot.

__ National Navy – The second oldest duty branch with the most after-service job skill opportunities. No other branch gives the opportunity to visit Ports-O-Call worldwide! The National Navy has produced more national public leaders than each branch combined. Many service members find the National Navy so rewarding that it is the leading volunteer reenlistment branch. Check our list of job specialties to find the one that is the most aligned with your interests. See you in the Navy!

__ National Army – The oldest and largest military branch, joining this service will guarantee you a skill that will carry you onto success in life after your military commitment. Great pay, all benefits of the other branches.

__ Special Operations – Serve with the best! Take your three-year obligation and train hard, fight hard, and play hard. Better pay, better rank, and the best opportunity to see the world. Do you have what it takes?

__ EFL Systems/Intel – If programming and data research is your interest, we have a spot for you.

Let your skills drive you to the job market after your service.

___ EFL Quartermaster – Supply and demand, you have heard that in your school economics class. In the real world, the person with the goods dictates the outcome.

___ EFL Ambassador – Do you have a desire to seek resolutions? The EFL leads the way in diplomacy around the world. Great opportunity to see the world, which will never again be available after you complete your three-year service.

You can choose up to three of the options. You turn in the sheet to the assistant deputy, and he types your information into the computer. He scowls and says, "I can't get you in these two right now. Go speak with the recruiter there." He points down the hall. "You better hurry."

You walk to the office, your last chance.

Level Up – Induction

You are now carried by cut-scene through the office to a waiting bus. The buses drive in a caravan for a time and then separate, heading in different directions. The talk is anxious, excited, frightened. Your friends and others don't know what is happening. The driver ignores your attempts to gain any information as to your destination. You ride through the afternoon into the evening and in the late night. Finally, the bus joins a line on a street with other buses. A large parking lot can barely be seen in the lamplight to the right side. A few buildings here and there are along the street.

The driver idles the engine, the fog on the windows from the air conditioning makes you shiver, the smell of bus diesel is nauseating, the hum and rattle of the bus make you sleepy. The overhead lights suddenly come on, and the door is opened. You smell a hint of dust and feel the heat of an arid summer morning. The bus is too cold. A man dressed in an unfamiliar uniform boards the bus and immediately starts yelling instructions.

"You will keep your mouths shut and listen to what I tell you! Do not speak or ask questions! You will respond to any question or directions by me or any other drill instructor with *Yes Sir*, *No Sir* or *I am unaware Sir!* Do you understand?"

The passengers of the bus respond in a meek and pitiful collection of variations.

The instructor reaches out and grabs the nearest individual by the shirt and pulls him to his feet. The person is shocked by the action and resists. The instructor immediately slaps him in the face while at the same time yelling, "Do you understand!"

The drill instructor lets go and the victim utters a reply. He is again struck and then yells through tears, "Yes Sir!"

The instructor slaps another sitting across from the first, "Do you understand?"

"Yes Sir!"

The instructor then repeats again to the bus, "Do you understand?"

"Yes Sir!" The entire bus responds.

"When I tell you to, you will file off this bus at a full run and line up on the street outside. Do you understand?"

"Yes Sir!"

"You will find a painted set of footprints and place your feet on them. Do you understand?"

"Yes Sir!"

"You will take everything you have with you off this bus and place everything you take off the bus at your feet on the ground. Do you understand?"

"Yes Sir!"

He walks up the row and pulls another to his feet.

"Do you understand the directions so far?"

"Yes Sir!"

"You will have nothing in your hands, everything at your feet. Your hands will be out of your pockets and down along the sides of your legs. Do you understand?"

"Yes Sir!"

"When I tell you to, you will have 10 seconds to un-ass from this bus at a full run. Do you understand?"

"Yes Sir!"

"You will not bump or touch me as you file past or you will regret the day you were born. Do you understand?"

"Yes Sir!"

"Get off my bus! Move! Move! Move! Ten! Nine! Eight! *Sev-si-fi-fo*! Three, two, one!"

EXPEDITIONARY FOREIGN LEGION -The Xo

The bus occupants race to stand and file off the bus as quickly as they can. Someone is bumped by another and falls into the instructor. With a punch and a shove forward, the hapless victim trips down the bus steps, taking several with him. The instructor continues to yell profanities and insults, pushing, and kicking the last few off the bus, then follows, chases, and harasses you as you find a spot.

The instructor is in your face, screaming for you to empty your hands – *Where am I?* – you question yourself. The instructor moves on.

It is early morning, late night, the in-between hours when you really don't quite know how to clarify the day. The buses are all empty and drive away. You look around and see hundreds of males and females, both mixed in together. Some are crying, scared of what is happening; the lack of information is the most terrifying. The drill instructor from your bus is joined by dozens or more of others, all running around the rows, screaming and yelling, shoving, pushing, hitting, slapping, and harassing the formation. It's all very degrading.

Eventually, all the new arrivals are oriented on proper movement, behavior, and expected reaction to the drill instructors' demands. Multiple instructions are reviewed and practiced. With that complete, the large group is advanced to a giant pavilion, but even with its great size, it cannot accommodate the entire formation. Four lines are formed, and you wait your turn for whatever comes next. You are hungry. You have not eaten since breakfast the day before. You are tired, not sleeping on the bus ride other than a few catnaps.

It is your turn.

A combination of cut-scenes gives an overview of various stages of basic training, breaking between required interaction of skills needed to be successful. The first activity is a review of the application followed by the next steps:

    __ Review of Application – Here you enter your game username and password, sex of character desired (the game character is neutral based, but to keep the screamers and gender-baiters quiet a pointless option is given), and play level – Beginner or Advanced. The cut-scene continues with a verbal beat down by a drill instructor of the choices you selected at the recruiter station, belittling you for your lack of ability or education. If, by chance, you selected *EFL Ambassador* you are mocked as a *Hero* but gain 10 Bonus *Promotion Points* if that was your only selection. Advanced player does not receive this Bonus. For each errant selection, you are penalized 10 *PP* which will show as negative *PP* since you have not earned any *PP* as yet.

    __ Med Check – Cut-scenes of shots, blood work, vision, and physical exams.

    __ New ID – You receive an AI-generated EFL Service Number and your name – *013579 Baker, D*. Remember it, you will be required to recite it at various stages.

    __ Swearing In – You are sworn in as a *Cassum* – nothing, hollow, inane – of the *Expeditionary Foreign Legion*. Your draft number was called, and you were selected for service for a three-year obligation. You will be paid 30 *Summa* upon graduation. Prepare for training.

EXPEDITIONARY FOREIGN LEGION -The Xo

Level Up – Basic Training

The following will be practiced and performed to acclimate and familiarize you to commands and skills as well as earn *PP*. Each station of training must be completed with a minimum score in each and overall, in order to graduate from *Basic Training*. Your *PP* – Promotion Points, *E/S* & *H* – Endurance/Stamina and Health, and *I* & *E* – Integrity and Experience are displayed at various times.

Orientation cut-scenes outline your training, introduce your Drill Instructor, Senior Caporal Tollerson and review the importance of your Operational Notebook - *"I will not repeat myself! Is that understood!"* Haircuts follow. All heads are shaved bald including females, which also are bunked and undergo all training with their male counterparts – there is no differentiation, no special treatment, no separate scoring scale. Long ago females demanded to be included in the EFL and got exactly that – full participation.

___ Initial Uniform Issue – 25 PP. A list of your issue is displayed; a section is *Copy* available to your Operational Notebook.

___ Physical Conditioning – 15 PP. Using the *L+Ctrl* and *L+Alt* with right *KB Direction Arrows*, *Space Bar* to Jump, *L+Shift* to Run. Complete the following skills: Jumping Jacks 0-3 PP, Push-ups 0-3 PP, Sit-ups 0-3 PP, Mountain Climbers 0-3 PP, 2K Run 0-3 PP. Required to graduate – 1 PP in each category and overall score 8/12, Beginner/Advanced.

__ Tactical Movements – 15 PP. Using *Space Bar* to Jump, *F* to knee-butt, *L+Alt* Crawl, *EASD* or right *Direction Arrows* for movement, *C* to crouch, *R+Mouse* to uppercut, *L+Mouse* to swing. Required to graduate 8/10 B/A (multiple practices of at least 4 in each category to score the PP, this detail is not revealed).

__ Weapons Orientation – no PP on orientation. *Tab* to select sight On/Off. *1* selects GPS – Gun, Plasma, Standard – the basic issue combat rifle. *2* selects GPC – Gun, Plasma, Compact – the sidearm. *3* GPXR – Gun, Plasma, Extended Range – the sniper rifle. *4* AP Gun – anti-Armor/Personnel gun. *5-7* Grenades, HE-FlashBang-Smoke. *8* Demolition Bag. *Mouse Wheel* also scrolls selection when any number is selected. There is no auto-fire, *L+Mouse* fire guns, *R+Mouse* hold and release to throw a grenade. Magazine capacity for GPS is 15-rounds, GPXR is bolt-action 5-round magazine, GPC magazine is 5-rounds. AP is box/belt-fed with 50-HE/Armor/Penetrating rounds. You are issued EFL GPS serial number *gpsEFL1086531*. Specs list is *Copy* available.

__ O/Course – 20 PP. Run the obstacle course circuit, timed event. 8/15 B/A.

__ Navigation/Special Systems 10 PP. *Cassum* are issued their *BAC*, Body Armor-Combat, and introduced to desert compass course, shoot-house, and desert/urban warfare tactics. Various Map & Compass/Nav skills are *Copy* ready. 6/8 B/A.

EXPEDITIONARY FOREIGN LEGION - The Xo

__ Weapons Qual – 20 PP. *Cassum* shoot to qualify only on the GPS. A minimum score of 8/16 B/A is required. Three levels are achievable 8-15 Marksman, 16-18 Expert, 19-20 Sniper. Only Expert and Sniper Qual Pins are awarded. Award scores are *Copy* ready.

__ Final Exam – 6 PP. This is it! The final exam and you get out of this hellhole and away from that prick Sr. Caporal Tollerson! A 100 score on the exam is required to graduate; if you fail, you repeat BT. *Oh! You cannot endure this again, you have studied, trained hard, and sweated liters.* You stare at the exam sheet of 50 questions and begin...

__ How many handkerchiefs were you issued?

__ What are the score ranges for shooting awards?

__ How do you *Box an Obstacle* while traversing a Nav Course?

__ What rank are you?

__ Why are EFL Legionnaires referred to as *Ambassadors*?

__ What is the serial number of your weapon?

You pass! You graduate from EFL Basic Training! You celebrate with your mates that you have made over the months of rigorous and unimaginable hardships – the pain, suffering, and inhumane treatment of the training company as a whole, not to mention personal ridicule and humiliation – it's over! Now you await your new posting. Everyone hopes that they will remain together.

Advanced players are particularly despised by Sr. Caporal Tollerson. He does not approve of non-team-oriented or conceded *legs*. You are put on report for an infraction in the barracks the night of graduation. You lose all accumulated PP.

CHAPTER 2

Level Up – **Graduation**

You are assigned to the newly reorganized line company, India Company, 4th Battalion, 117th Regiment, IV Corps, or I 4/117 IV. The *Ivy Corps*. The other corps are I Corps or *The One*, II Corps or *The Deuce*, III Corps or *Third Herd*, and V Corps or *Vee Corps*. The Ivy is renowned as the initiation corps, based in the immense Xobian Desert. You have heard stories of the Xobian Desert, even from your great-uncle. It is the most fought-over region in the world. The only other information you know concerning the other corps is that V Corps is designated as the training, administration, and Quartermaster Corps.

The 117th Regiment is based at one of the oil fields somewhere in the midst of the Xobian. The entire training company is now India 4/117 IV. Remnants, veterans from India, and other recently assigned legionnaires now join you, mostly newly promoted *senior gradum* – Sr. legionnaire – and lance caporals. Your former training Sr. caporal is your new senior platoon caporal. He does not like you or any of your mates. A new caporal is your direct leader. His name is Caporal Edmunds. He does not like you either. He presses a wager, your new pay of 30 *Summa*, that you will die on your first mission. What choice do you have? You take the bet!

Level Up – Journey to 117th Regiment Area of Operations, Xobian Desert

You and the others of the company load onto ATCs, armored tracked carriers, at the airfield after your flight lands. You glimpse the large base situated in the seemingly endless expanse of nothing. Nothing but sand, heat, and dust. There is a small town of sorts that you pass through outside of the Regiment HQ. You notice a disproportionate number of bars and brothels mixed in with inns, bazaars, cafes, food vendors, and local herdsmen bringing their goats in for market. The most worrisome observation you note is the small groups of legionnaires, evidently on leave, enjoying the varied pleasures that the stark town provides. Their glances and stares are empty and void of feeling, seemingly that of empty souls. It haunts you.

You arrive at 4th Battalion HQ only to find a similar if not smaller arrangement – tents and sandbagged protected shelters, a ramshackle assortment of buildings, bars, brothels, and cafes adjacent to and even among the battalion area of operations!

Your ATC convoy continues after a brief stop and the accompaniment of several personnel. You are ready to get off this carrier and start your new life. The days have merged into the same long line of boredom. It has been over a week since your graduation. You want these three years to be over with. Three years in this desert? Now you understand the blank and distant stares you observed earlier.

The ATCs rumble on to their next stop – India Company AO, area of operations, your new home.

Level Up – First Mission Brief

    Three choices – Easy – Medium – Difficult.

    __ Easy 10 PP

    __ Medium 15 PP

EXPEDITIONARY FOREIGN LEGION -The Xo

___ Difficult 25 PP

Since you are fresh out of BT and Sr. Caporal Tollerson reports you were the dregs of your training company, it is advised you chose Easy Mission 10 PP. Your PP is ___, you require six missions and a set PP before your promotion to Legionnaire. More than enough time to learn.

Summary:

Physical Characteristics:

    75/100 Endurance/Stamina

    80/100 Health

Mental Characteristics:

    50/100 Integrity

    0/100 Experience

If your Integrity falls below 45 you lose Experience points, if it rises above 55 you gain Experience points.

Endurance/Stamina and Health also affect the other.

Caporal Edmunds is waiting to enter the ops tent for a mission brief. He stares at you and says, "Maybe you should hand over that wager now, *Minus Nobilis*," lower rank.

You respond:

    ___ Screw you, Caporal Edmunds.

    ___ You can collect it off my body.

    ___ I can't wait to take your money.

CHAPTER 3

Level Up – Mission #1 Brief – **Reconnoiter**

__ Easy 10 PP chance of success 95%

__ Medium 15 PP chance of success 80%

__ Difficult 25 PP chance of success 60%

Once a mission is selected, the Mission Summary will pop up. You cannot back out of a mission once it has been selected. This is *Final Death*; if you *die,* you start all over. A *Save* is only for break/walk-away and any previous *Saves* will not be available if you die. It is therefore advisable to use caution and improve skills whenever possible. Completed missions are not available again in the chapter.

You have selected Easy Mission.

Summary:

Your squad is assigned to reconnoiter the area to the NE of the oil fields. Scout out any possible enemy forces, and call in artillery or airstrike. You are not to be detected or engage the enemy. Caporal Edmunds will lead the patrol.

You have selected Medium Mission.

Summary:

Your squad is assigned to support the assault on an enemy fortification that was discovered by another patrol. You are one squad joined by 1st Platoon of India. Follow your orders and eliminate the enemy.

You have selected Difficult Mission.

Summary:

EXPEDITIONARY FOREIGN LEGION -The Xo

Your squad is caught in an ambush by a superior enemy force. With casualties mounting and communication cut off by a well-placed shoulder-fired missile to the Sat-link antenna, Caporal Edmunds orders the squad to dig in. You see an avenue to escape. What will you do?

Each mission will have three to four outcomes based on random AI roll – less than 10% will end in failure to the mission, 80% will end in success, 5% loss of E/I or E/S & H possible death, 2% heroic action. Any time a Difficult Mission is selected in a *new* chapter first, the outcome will be death during the mission.

Level Up – Mission accepted and carried out

Random screenshots, pictures, video, cut-scenes that are associated with the particular mission. AI generation of positions, forces, terrain, reaction/discovery of enemy by you or them. Battles will vary in intensity to which mission level was selected. You control the action to include – running, crawling, crouching, knee-butt, shooting, throwing limited grenades if available. Cut-scenes of animated troop movement and 2-D control of the character.

Level Up – Mission Debrief

You survive and attempt to collect the bet from Caporal Edmunds, who not only refuses to pay up but places you on report for your response earlier. You lose five PP.

In the aftermath of Pass/Fail of mission, your summary is updated. You have gained/lost or no change.

Level Up – Time Off

You wait in the company AO for the next mission brief. Life in the desert is boring, hot, and desolate. The oil fields around you are immense.

You can: (pick 2)

__ Take a shower

__ Go to chow

__ Check out the sights

__ Talk to your mates

__ Play cards

Level Up – Mission #2 Brief – Nahil Pump Station

__ Easy 10 PP 95% success

__ Medium 15 PP 80% success

__ Difficult 25 PP 60 % success

Character Summary:

You have selected Easy Mission.

Summary:

Your platoon is assigned to escort a repair convoy from the wells to the pump station at Nahil – 100 miles away. There are no reports of an enemy in the area, but there is always that chance. Caporal Edmunds leads the escort.

You have selected Medium Mission.

EXPEDITIONARY FOREIGN LEGION - The Xo

Summary:

Your platoon and 1st Platoon will patrol the pump station at Nahil and root out suspected saboteurs of the station. Intel reports only a small group of sappers. Sr. Caporal Tollerson leads the platoon.

You have selected Difficult Mission.

Summary:

With 1st Platoon on the east side of the Nahil Pump Station, Sr. Caporal splits the platoon. You go with Caporal Edmunds and the squad runs into a full platoon of *Xobian Desert Grenadiers* with AA guns, and are too close to the oil pipelines to call in artillery. They are quickly surrounding you and Edmunds orders the squad to dig in. Casualties are mounting. You see a way out between a building. What do you do?

Level Up – Mission Debrief

You survive, Pass/Fail status update.

Level Up – Time Off

You wait in the company AO for the next mission brief. Life in the desert is boring, hot, and desolate. The oil fields around you smell. You have only been here a few weeks and already you hate it. Your mates invite you to join them in the bar.

You can: (pick 2)

    __ Take a shower

    __ Go to chow

___ Go drinking

___ Play cards

___ Review Nav

___ Write letter home

Level Up – Mission #3 Brief – Dust Storm

___ Easy 10 PP 95% success

___ Medium 15 PP 80% success

___ Difficult 25 PP 60% success

Character Summary:

You have selected Easy Mission.

Summary:

Caporal Edmunds is still not impressed with your progress. He has picked out this assignment especially for you! Your mission is to climb the spire of the *#12 Oil Rig* and replace the fuse on the antenna booster. He laughs and says, "I hope you're not afraid of heights!"

You respond:

___ Screw you, Caporal Edmunds.

___ No, but I bet you are.

___ What have I done to you?

You have selected Medium Mission.

Summary:

EXPEDITIONARY FOREIGN LEGION -The Xo

A large dust cloud is observed several miles to the SW but the risk is too great for air reconnaissance. India is sent to ensure the cloud is only a storm and not a major assault. Sr. Caporal Tollerson leads the platoon. Your platoon is separated in the dust cloud and a firefight ensues. You must link up with the platoon to the left or die.

You have selected Difficult Mission.

Summary:

Your platoon is separated in a sandstorm. Caporal Edmunds leads your squad. You are to link up with the platoon to the left, but they are not there! A heavy platoon of *Xobian Desert Regulars* is about to encircle you! You spot a *wadi,* a desert gully, that you can crawl to and escape. What do you do?

Level Up – Mission Debrief

You survive, Pass/Fail status update.

You are placed on report by Caporal Edmunds for your reply earlier/or for missing morning formation, you lose five PP.

Level Up – Time Off

You have been in the Xobian Desert for over three months. Other than gambling and a couple of times visiting the shantytown, you have most of your pay, plus you were just paid again.

The battalion is being rotated back to Regiment HQ, the town of Sandubia. Everyone in the company is excited. You have a week off. When you arrive, you can't believe the barracks you are assigned; it's paradise! The bars, cafes, vendors, bazaars, and dance clubs are calling!

Caporal Edmunds informs you that you have duty tonight. He smiles at you and says, "You weren't going to do anything in town anyway, Baker."

You reply:

    __ Is that so?

    __ At least I have the next few days off.

    __ I'll see you in town, Caporal Edmunds.

You pull CQ and have the rest of the week off.

You spend your time: (pick 2)

    __ Reading in the barracks

    __ Taking in the sights

    __ Playing cards

    __ Joining your mates in the clubs and bars

    __ Catching up with letter writing

    __ Improving your shooting skills

Level Up – India Company returns to the oil fields

You have completed three Missions and this Chapter and your PP score is __. Three more missions and you are eligible for promotion to Legionnaire if you meet the PP level. You may choose to remain and complete the missions in this chapter or move on. Missions will rotate randomly in future chapters. Also, you may elect to complete as many missions in a completed chapter as you wish.

__ Remain in Chapter 3 and complete any number of uncompleted missions and/or

__ Move on to Chapter 4

Remain in Chapter 3 – a repeat of the three mission options minus the completed missions follow, along with a cue in the debrief to move on or to remain for another mission.

Move to Chapter 4 – when the sixth mission is completed and a PP of 150/115 B/A is reached, promotion to Legionnaire is awarded.

CHAPTER 4

Level Up – Mission #4 Brief – **Oasis**

__ Easy 10 PP 95% success

__ Medium 15 PP 80% success

__ Difficult 25 PP 60% success

Character Summary:

You have selected Easy Mission.

Summary:

Caporal Edmunds leads a scout patrol to an oasis that recently appeared out of the desert. There are no trees and very little vegetation, but animal activity is increasing. He tests the water and finds it is good, even though anyone drinking from it still needs to filter and purify it beforehand just to be safe.

You have selected Medium Mission.

Summary:

A group of Bedouins have set up camp near an oasis. The location is too close to the oil fields and they must leave. Only your platoon is sent and soon the Bedouins become agitated and the situation becomes violent. Sr. Caporal Tollerson gives orders for no one to initiate deadly force and a physical altercation ensues.

You have selected Difficult Mission.

Summary:

With 2nd Platoon ordered to evacuate a Bedouin camp from an oasis that recently appeared, your squad is outnumbered and surrounded by suspected hardcore veteran desert militia fighters. Caporal Edmunds orders the use of deadly force. It will be a massacre if he is wrong. You aim your rifle at a Bedouin. What do you do? (If this mission was selected first in the new chapter, player dies.)

Level Up – Mission Debrief

    You survive, Pass/Fail status update.

Level Up – Time Off

    You wait in the company AO for the next mission brief. Life in the desert is boring, hot, and dirty. The oil fields around you have made all your belongings, uniforms, and bedding feel greasy, coated in some substance. You have been here for over half a year and you hate it more than anything you have ever experienced. Your mates invite you to join them in the company's favorite bar.

    You can: (pick 2)

        __ Take a shower

        __ Go to chow

        __ Go drinking

        __ Play cards

        __ Read

        __ Do laundry – again

Level Up – Mission #5 Brief – Kepi blanc

___ Easy 10 PP 95% success

___ Medium 15 PP 80% success

___ Difficult 25 PP 60% success

Character Summary

You have selected Easy Mission.

Summary:

A sister company of 4th Battalion is gearing up for their promotion to Legionnaire and *la marche Kepi blanc,* the march of the white cap. You watch with interest. Sr. Caporal Tollerson catches you neglecting your work detail and orders you to tend to *Colour Sergent's Grass.* Each battalion has an HQ hut with a gravel patch in front, simulating a grass lawn. The small stones are painted green on one side. Stones being stones, some get turned and others slip from the company of the others. You are to ensure the *grass* is green and there are no errant *clippings.* The punishment goes all night.

You have selected Medium Mission.

Summary:

Second Platoon is assigned security flank escort for a sister company of 4th Battalion as they march in the desert for two days. An enemy patrol of *Wahti,* desert fighters known for their near undetectable movement, is discovered. Sr. Caporal Tollerson leads the platoon in the assault.

You have selected Difficult Mission.

Summary:

EXPEDITIONARY FOREIGN LEGION - The Xo

Your squad is suddenly encircled by *Wahti*, near undetectable desert fighters known for their ruthlessness. Several of your mates fall in the skirmish. Caporal Edmunds orders a retreat, but you are all that stands between the Wahti and 12 Legionnaires exhausted from a two-day march in the desert. What do you do?

Level Up – Mission Debrief

You survive, Pass/Fail status update.

Level Up – Time Off

You wait in the company AO for the next mission brief. Life in the desert is numbingly boring, hot, and tiresome. Someone thought it would be a good idea to target practice at goats from a dune west of the company AO. When the goat herder runs towards the sniper nest angrily shouting and waving his arms, the guilty shooters flee, melding into the company. You are not part of the group but know who is. The regiment's *first sergent* is *losing a head-gasket* while the entire company stands in formation in the sun and heat for the next three hours. No one gives up the culprits and the full cost of five goats is ordered to be taken from the pay of every single legionnaire of the company. Later during the night, six men are beaten to death.

You feel like: (pick 2)

　　__ You are guilty of the men's deaths because you did not say anything.

___ Your conscience is clean; they should have spoken up.

___ You are shaking in your boots. You almost joined them!

___ You take a shower and put the event behind you.

___ You join in a toast to the dead legionnaires, they were still your mates.

Level Up – Mission #6 Brief – Sniping

___ Easy 10 PP 95% success

___ Medium 15 PP 80% success

___ Difficult 25 PP 60% success

Character Summary

You have selected Easy Mission.

Summary:

Caporal Edmunds is about to enter the India Company ops hut. He knows you are thinking about a night off, joining your mates in the shantytown. A few minutes later he is standing next to you and says, "Gear up, I have something for you!"

A large population of desert mice have become more of a problem than normal. He is actually allowing you to use a GPXR sniper rifle to hunt them!

You have selected Medium Mission.

EXPEDITIONARY FOREIGN LEGION - The Xo

Summary:

Sr. Caporal is a well-known marksman, having earned the lauded *Sniper Badge*. Your platoon is advancing on an enemy encampment during the early morning. Sr. Caporal is in a good position to cover you. Try to get the enemy commander to move to the open.

You have selected Difficult Mission.

Summary:

Caporal Edmunds has found a good spot on a dune to observe an enemy encampment. For some reason, he picked you to act as his observer/spotter. The enemy commander is in the open. Caporal turns to you and says, "Do you want the shot?"

You reply:

__ Are you kidding?

__ You bet!

__ I'm not ready

The opportunity is yours – one shot; it cannot miss.

Level Up – Mission Debrief

You survive, Pass/Fail status update.

Level Up – Time Off

You have completed six Missions and this Chapter; your PP score is __.

Congratulations on your promotion!

With others of India Company that reached this achievement, you embark on *la marche Kepi blanc*, 37 miles in the desert in two days with full pack and the ceremony to receive the distinctive desert cap of the Legion. You are finally a true Legionnaire. It is a huge accomplishment. Sr. Caporal Tollerson and Caporal Edmunds personally congratulate you and tell you that you needed extra persuasion. They always respected you but will not let up because they know you will make a fine lance caporal one day.

You have earned your first stripe! It is in the shape of a large *V* on the sleeve. You also receive a raise to 35 Summa, your *Kepi blanc*, and a *Regiment Commendation Ribbon* for collective actions, one of only a handful in the company to be awarded one!

CHAPTER 5

Level Up – **Return to Nahil**

India 4/117 IV has taken a high number of casualties in the weeks since returning to the line. Fourth Battalion is rotated to Nahil Pump Station to rest and continue patrols. There will be no replacements for a newly reorganized company such as India. Your company has been to the Nahil Pump Station before. There is not much more here to do than at the oil fields. Time passes slowly and you cannot believe it has been over a year here in the desert.

Now that you are a Legionnaire, a *Leg*, there are more opportunities for you. Well, there will be after you are promoted one more time to a Sr. legionnaire. Your PP is on track and you only have to complete three more missions. It is critical to get the promotion before two years, or the EFL will not invest more training and education on a leg who will EOS, leave the EFL at their *end of service* obligation. If you don't get the promotion, it will mean completing all three years of service here in the Xobian Desert.

You will complete any three remaining Missions from Chapter 3 & 4 for a total of 45 PP or more.

Level Up – Mission #7 Brief

Level Up – Mission Debrief

Level Up – Time Off

There is a rumor that something big is about to happen, but all the Sr. legionnaires and lance caporals say nothing. The boredom is nearly intolerable. You cannot do another year here. Sr. Caporal Tollerson holds a surprise inspection of the barracks and you are caught being lazy with your bed-making this morning. You are punished with watering *Company Sergent's Grass*. You must haul seawater from the desalination tanks, a half-mile away and *water the grass* until the entire lawn is wet. In the desert heat, that is nearly impossible as the water soaks into the sand and dries very quickly. You lose five PP.

Level Up – Mission #8 Brief

Level Up – Mission Debrief

Level Up – Time Off

You have three months left to make Sr. legionnaire or you remain in the desert. You think back to your great-uncle. He never spoke of anywhere else now that you think about it. How did he do it? How does anyone do it? All the NCOs including the lance caporals, have served a tour here and then another posting, then back here. Why would anyone want to come back here?

You look around and notice, not for the first time, that the company numbers are shrinking. But not so much for the Sr. legs and lance caporals. They never take risks on the missions. It is always the legionnaires and minus nobilis that are ordered to advance or maneuver in difficult situations.

Today the lance caporals of the company organize a boxing match. The common and oft fun contest is a break from the monotony of the tireless days watching sand blow. Only the legs that are in contention for the next promotion are suited up with a soft head protection helmet, gloves, groin protector, and mouthguard. The contestants wear exercise shorts and a t-shirt. The Sr. legs also gear up and it is soon apparent the two groups will face off. The excitement fades when two Sr. legs enter the makeshift rink to fight a single leg. The matches are wholly unfair. The Sr. legs completely dominate and beat their opponent to the point of no longer being able to stand.

Caporal Edmunds looks at you and then speaks to Lance Caporal Betwah, gesturing to you. Betwah calls a notoriously violent Sr. leg and also prepares to fight. You are next.

The fight, what you remember, was very painful and from what others said later, longer than most. Betwah was the regiment lightweight champion last year. You fought like a tiger, struggling to your knees two times after being knocked down. Sergent Stepanakert finally put a stop to it, even as you hung onto Betwah, punching with nothing behind it.

You spend a week in the infirmary before being allowed to resume limited duty.

Level Up – Mission #9 Brief

Level Up – Mission Debrief

Level Up – Time Off

You have completed nine Missions and this Chapter; your PP score is __.

Congratulations on your promotion!

Sr. legionnaires with a remaining year of service are eligible for advanced school and a transfer to another theater. You have two choices – 1) Mountain/Cold Weather School with Sniper course or, 2) Jungle Warfare Training School with either Demolitions or AP Gunner courses. Even though you have had enough of the desert, you are unsure if the mountain theater is where you want to go. You like shooting the GPXR though. There is a waiting list for the Sniper course. There is a bonus for Demo, as there is a shortage of qualified legs. In either case, you will be transferred to a new corps – I Corps is mountain and III Corps is jungle. It does not matter to you. There are several of your mates that are going to one or the other, so you will not be alone during whatever school you decide on. Three weeks is the length of either school, followed by the accompanying course if available.

You get a message to report to Colour Sergent Willoughby at battalion. You report and are instructed to *stand at ease,* a relaxed position of attention.

"Congratulations Sr. Legionnaire Baker. I have reviewed your service record. You have good marks and a high recommendation from your Sr. Caporal and Sergent. We need legionnaires like you in the jungle, hard fighters, go-getters, full of spit-n-piss and a don't-quit attitude. You take your last year in the jungle and re-enlist, I guarantee you a fast track to lance caporal. Think about it."

You walk back to your sandbag-fortified hut sticking out of the desert sand. Your mates are all packing, ready to catch the ATC back to regiment. You enter the India Company ops hut and make your decision.

EXPEDITIONARY FOREIGN LEGION -The Xo

You chose:

    __ Mountain Cold/Weather School

    __ Jungle Warfare Training School

If you choose MCWS you lose 25 PP and are sent to JWTS anyway, losing all built-up reputation with higher rank.

CHAPTER 6

Level Up – Jungle Warfare Training School

The school is run by 1st Battalion, 122nd Regiment, V Corps in Jaco, located in the Palanquin Rain Forest 20 miles south of the equator, as if that makes any difference. The Xobian Desert straddles the equator both north and south for a 1000 miles. What makes this location unique is the lush tropical jungle vegetation and the heavily moist, you could say wet, jet stream that passes directly over the jungle region. Rain forest, jungle, it's all the same with similar definitions and minute differences. The EFL-JWTS is a heartbreaker. Anyone that arrives with a notion that the three weeks is a vacation failed to appreciate and understand the reason for the beating by the Sr. legs weeks ago. *Never quit – Fight to live.*

You cannot imagine attending this course having gone to Mountain School first. The heat is bad enough; you are used to that. It is the humidity that sucks the energy from your pores, never allowing you the coolness of evaporation. You are constantly wet, even indoors, which is rare. If it is not raining, you are wading in rivers or swamps, sometimes submerged completely. The *BAC* weighs double or triple its original weight when wet. Your normal combat load is unachievable in this environment and most elect to carry only a *butt-pack* with their meager rations and water purifier, a poncho and liner. Everything else is left in the base tent. In addition to your own full ammo load of six spare mags for the GPS and your BAC, the squad equipment is divided among the class to slug through the thick jungle. This includes four boxes of ammo for the AP gun, two boxes simulating the weight of explosives, two stretchers, and a Sat/link radio.

EXPEDITIONARY FOREIGN LEGION -The Xo

The school covers multiple subject areas including: jungle mobility, waterborne ops, combat tracking, jungle warfare tactics, survival, and illegal drug production practices. All of the topics are rehearsed and practiced in situational conditions, most in a covert operational style.

The school opens with their Credo: *The Free only remain so from the Oppressor by the Strength of the Brave.*

It did not seem that big a deal sitting in the pavilion the first morning after chow, still reasonably dry, rested, and unaware of the coming emotional and physical trauma, absolute fear, and whole-body exhaustion. Unimaginable large ugly spiders, snakes, amphibious reptiles, mammals, and insects were all present and waiting to harm you. In addition to those life-threatening creatures, diseases such as cholera, yellow-fever, malaria, dysentery, and who knows what were everywhere hoping to *jump on*. Childhood fears of darkness were nothing like the fear in the jungle with real monsters right beside you, if not on you. Then there are the *Quepos*, the jungle fighters of *Tamiarindo* where III Corps is based. If the Wahti of the Xobian were undetectable, the Quepos are invisible. The drug lords hire the Quepos and also the local people, who understand that if they are caught the punishment is severe, so they are not caught – alive. They have nothing to lose, everything to gain. An EFL captive is of no value, the Tamiarindos have no *World Convention Prisoners Treatment Agreement*. This is truly hell on Summa.

Three weeks later you are emaciated, losing almost 15 pounds body weight that was not excess to begin with. Covered in hives and rashes, your feet, groin and armpits smell like a combination of soured buttermilk and rotted potatoes, and the pain of the open rash is enough to make you cry. But you graduate and the rest of your class is celebrating, downing shots of a fermented rice beer with the instructors, who seem none the worse for the experience, ready to take their next class cycle.

You sleep off the head-splitting pain and the next morning you are admitted to the school infirmary with the rest of the class for three days to heal, take multiple salt/mineral baths, eat, and dry out.

Level Up – The Jungle Fox

On the fourth morning after JWTS graduation, all of you are discharged and given orders to report to 122nd Regiment HQ for reassignment. You walk together; some of the group is from India 4/117, the majority from other regiments of the IV and I Corps. There is even a female lance caporal from I Corps that came from Minsk, the arctic theater! She was tough, even if the stark environmental change near kicked her butt. Her performance never lacked. She drank all the guys under the table the other night, female body-fat stores and hormones the likely advantage.

There are a dozen caporals waiting at regiment for the group, standing around, laughing, talking, drinking *kaffee* and/or spirited water – seltzer water, lemon, and a hint of alcohol – all to fight *dirty bugs*. One of them calls your name along with Sr. Legionnaire Genghis, one of your mates from India, and you stand-to. Your new assigned unit is 3rd Platoon, Fox Company, 3/114, III Corps. Sr. Caporal Gunderson and Caporal Sieng are your platoon leaders. Sieng has come to collect you and tells you to grab your gear and load up in the *Buggy* – a multi-terrain, five-crew, lightly armored, fast maneuver, AP gun-mounted, low-water level, medium sand dune assault vehicle – that you have seen near every day in the EFL. It is nicely adapted for use in the jungle.

Caporal Sieng talks to you as if you are a human. He laughs when you and Genghis respond with short, curt, direct answers.

"Hey! I know you just came out of *The Xo*, but this is the real world here. BT is long over and you are both Sr. legs now. There are no *noobs* here, only survivors, all vets, all Sr. legs and lances. Okay? You respect me and my experience and knowledge and I'll respect yours. Good?"

"Yes Caporal."

He laughs, nearly running off the trail. He's running the buggy wide open, with mud and rotten vegetation spewing in giant rooster tails from all four wheels, covering us.

"One of you jump on that gun; this is all Indian country, damn Quepos are everywhere. You know how to fire it, right?" He turns to look at us and the buggy slips off the trail again and into the jungle, slapping through the tangle and brush, scattering birds, lizards, butterflies, and monkeys before he pulls back on the trail.

"You two are lucky! You just nabbed the best company in the *Third Herd*, *The Jungle Fox*, baby! We got the best theater stats of any regiment out here. I read over your files. You're sharp. That *One-Seventeen* you came from is a good feeder regiment, that's for sure. Here we are, *The Fox Hole!*"

Level Up – A New Company System

The words of Caporal Sieng are echoed by Sr. Caporal Gunderson and to a degree by Sergent Mopti. It is the same EFL here in the jungle, but you are expected to understand and perform as Sr. legionnaires with certain freedoms of responsibility that are not given to *lower ranks.*

Level Up – Jungle Mission #10 Brief – Palanquin Rain Forest

___ Easy 10 PP 95% success

___ Medium 15 PP 80% success

___ Difficult 25 PP 60% success

Character Summary

You have selected Easy Mission.

Summary:

While Caporal Sieng leads a trail walk in the *Palanquin Rain Forest*, the battalion AO, he breaks down the situation. The platoon structure is different in the jungle. There are currently 35 legionnaires total in 3rd Platoon, including *Adjutant Leftenant* Hue, Sr. Caporal, and Caporal. The two squads are – Weapon Squad/*Bulldog* and Assault Squad/*Run-n-Gun*. Bulldog consists of the AP crew of gunner, AG, and runner; the Demo team of four; two Sat-link operators; and six ammo/stretcher-bearers. Run-n-Gun will be led by Leftenant Hue and either caporal, alternating, giving three teams of five. Unlike in the Xobian, where the AP was not carried by the platoon or large amounts of explosive demolitions required, here it is. The AP eats rounds, therefore additional ammo is carried, up to six or eight boxes of 50 belt-fed rounds weighing almost 35 pounds each box. The boxes are spread around but mostly carried by the stretcher-bearers. The assault squad is free of the duty unless the stretcher-bearers are performing their primary task. The *AP Runner* retrieves the boxes during any battle and feeds the AG, assistant gunner. You are new, you hump two boxes of ammo and serve as the AP Runner.

You have selected Medium Mission.

Summary:

Third Platoon discovers a cocaine processing camp and waits for support. With nightfall, Fox moves in for the kill.

You have selected Difficult Mission.

Summary:

Gunderson fears the camp is about to slip away into the jungle. With a single platoon, he launches the assault. Are you ready for this?

Level Up – Mission Debrief

You survive. Or if Difficult Mission was selected first in the chapter, you die. Pass/Fail status update.

Level Up – Time Off

Over the weeks you have made a new mate, Lance Caporal Obalaho. He gives you advice – *Never stick your neck out*. He's happy that you are here. In a few weeks you will go to *Demo Course* and he can go back to *Run-n-Gun*. He has four more months and then his promotion and back to the desert.

After the last mission, *Bulldog* is inventorying their gear and suddenly there is a giant *Ka-Boom*! Obalaho is dead. You are on your way to *DC*.

Level Up – Demolition Course

You are back with V Corps, the same 122nd Regiment as the JWTS but with a different battalion and closer to the ocean. It's nice. The salty, open air is refreshing. The funny thing is, no one shares too much information about the schools and courses with those who haven't gone. You have overheard a few times the lance caporals laughing and reminiscing, telling tall tales of their experiences.

Demo Course is two weeks long and you thought there was no way it could be nearly as long as JWTS. The days are long, but you get plenty of rest at night and good barracks and food. Alcohol is strictly forbidden during the course.

Daily labs are conducted from the previous day's reading assignments and classroom instruction. The course is much more than *blowing-in-a-door* or destroying a cocaine production tent. You learn about

EXPEDITIONARY FOREIGN LEGION -The Xo

Det-Cord, blasting caps, timers and ignition devices, how to set up a *daisy-chain* sequence, delayed reaction, skip detonations, ambush setup, LZ clearing, types of explosives, and even how to use the chemicals and other materials at a cocaine production site to destroy the operation. Though mentally challenging, it is the best two weeks you have experienced since entering the EFL.

Level Up – Return to the Jungle Fox and resume as part of the demo team in Bulldog. Nothing has changed in your absence, and the company prepares for a new mission.

Level Up - Jungle Mission #11 Brief - LZ

    __ Easy 10 PP 95% success

    __ Medium 15 PP 80% success

    __ Difficult 25 PP 60% success

    Character Summary

You have selected Easy Mission.

    Summary:

    On a routine patrol in the dense jungle, the company locates an elevated knoll and the CO decides it would make a good location for a future LZ. Your demo team joins the other platoons' teams and the area is marked, prepared, and cleared of trees and other potential hazards to incoming helos. The CO is impressed. The felled trees are further cut up, and a rudimentary fortified perimeter is constructed.

You have selected Medium Mission.

    Summary:

    During a routine patrol in the dense jungle, your platoon and 4th Platoon set up an ambush off the trail. The demo teams set out AP mines in an L-shaped kill-zone. You sit and wait during the night for the trap to be set. In the early morning, you catch an enemy platoon-sized patrol and wipe them out.

You have selected Difficult Mission.

    Summary:

    Your platoon, while patrolling a trail in a dense area, is ambushed and prepares to fall back to a rally point. Sr. Caporal Gunderson orders the demo team back to hastily prepare rear-guard booby traps along the escape route. You only have five minutes to rig three mines to cover the retreating platoon, which has received multiple wounded. Your mines must hold back the advance while the platoon evacs at a nearby LZ.

Level Up – Mission Debrief

    You survive, Pass/Fail status update.

Level Up – Time Off

EXPEDITIONARY FOREIGN LEGION -The Xo

The jungle offers even fewer recreational outlets than the Xobian Desert. Swarms of mosquitoes, large black flies, gnats, stinging bees of every possible variety, snakes, grotesque spiders, and flesh-eating fish all contribute to an environment that reduces the even minuscule outlets of relaxation when off duty. The people of the jungle, unlike the tribes in the desert, tend to not extend a level of hospitality, and those that do, offer the wiles of forbidden activity, or at the least, those which can be seen as irresponsible. A trading post of sorts is situated within the secure perimeter of the battalion HQ. A collection of local wares, clothing, foods, spices, alcohol, and various trinkets can be traded for. The battalion EM nightclub is the only available legal spot to unwind with alcohol, dancing, or *arranged company* through a matron, who more or less runs a prostitution racket. A cinema house, large game room, a cafe which portrays itself as an *International Cuisine Destination* but only serves the same assorted menu selections which are found in the chow hall, and a quartermaster store where one can purchase personal items, are all located nearby. To venture out of the battalion AO to a local village is a death wish.

You sit with a few of your platoon mates and play cards and drink a local beer on the giant screen-enclosed pavilion extending over the river. The breeze is not any cooler, just pushes the mosquitoes and flies away from the screen. Lamp-pots spaced every few feet burn with an insect deterrent chemical added to the oil. The smell is no longer bothersome. The ointment you smear over your exposed skin and on your uniform is etched into your olfactory glands. The probable poison is sure to kill you off long before the pests.

The night creeps in and you all play and drink until just before dawn, returning to the barracks for a few hours' sleep before morning muster. Your 24-hour pass of freedom lived to the last possible minute.

CHAPTER 7

Level Up – **Senior Legionnaire**

The next few months wash by along with the wet season. When you arrived, you were unaware that it was the dry season. The *wet* differed from the *dry* in that it *rained every day* and the base camps are flooded with water. Cots are all placed upon stilts and all belongings are hung from every conceivable hook, nail, hanger, looped rope, and cupboard that can be found. With the flooding, the various animals and insects which normally reside on the ground move to higher and drier places. That means mice, rats, snakes, opossums, scorpions, ugly gargantuan spiders and anything else can be found at any time of the day or night in the rack with you. More clinic call-outs occur during the wet season from bites and stings than actual combat wounds. You long to return to the Xobian Desert!

You pass the time while waiting for the next mission by: (pick 2)

    __ Reading

    __ Playing cards

    __ Spending time at the pavilion

    __ Sleeping

    __ Taking a course of study

    __ Writing home

    __ Planning a crazy event to stir up the boredom

Level Up - Jungle Mission #12 Brief – Jungle Mounds

__ Easy 10 PP 95% success

__ Medium 15 PP 80% success

__ Difficult 25 PP 60% success

Character Summary

You have selected Easy Mission.

Summary:

Your platoon is patrolling the central highlands, a change of scenery, taking you above the canopy of the jungle. Rolling hills stretch up into the mist, the rain of the wet season is over and you only have a few months left of your three-year enlistment. The thick humidity is back, sweat replaces the rain-drenched wetness of your uniform. The temperature soars above 100 degrees; there is no relief. Sr. Caporal Gunderson and Caporal Sieng have never been to this area before. Leftenant Hue is calling in reports hourly. The company relocated the week before and this entire area is to be patrolled. Hue discovers what appears to be a mound in an obviously regrown, previously cleared area. The one-time field is larger than what an LZ would require. The demo team is sent in to investigate for possible booby traps.

You advance with caution, sweeping the adjacent area. Vegetation has grown up around and over the mound. It is a wonder it was spotted at all. You look around and determine there are three additional mounds laid out in a square, the mounds setting the corners. The lance corporal in charge of the team decides to split the team of four into two. The team finds no evidence of explosives in the first mound. You move to the far corner. As you approach this mound an explosion occurs and you and your teammate are hurled into the air and back several yards. A thick cloud of particulates and dust blacken the sun, you cannot breathe and cough uncontrollably, hastily donning your chemical mask. When you look up Caporal Sieng is standing over you in the field, laughing.

"Are you okay? Ha-ha, I have never seen that happen before, but have heard stories. You activated a seed bunker."

You are covered, as are the other members of the demo team and the platoons of the patrol, in millions of seeds, inert materiel, and chemical fertilizer.

You have selected Medium Mission.

Summary:

Your platoon, while patrolling a new area in the jungle highlands has discovered what is believed to be seed mounds. The order is to rig them for demolition. You can hardly believe that you are responsible for destroying what is a planned *Planet Regeneration Project* in the event of another world catastrophe. You follow your orders and watch with uncertain dread the explosion and destruction of what ultimately could be part of this planet's future existence.

You have selected Difficult Mission.

Summary:

Your platoon discovers what is believed to be seed mounds. With further exploration, you find a buried door or hatch. The order is given to blow it. You are now exploring the darkened corridor of a control room. Within minutes a laboratory is found.

1) A fire fight commences above you, and you and your team are trapped.

2) You selected this mission first in the chapter and you are knocked out by an explosion. When you awake you find yourself strapped to a table and prepped for cryogenics and deep sleep storage to hopefully awaken in the future and restart a population regeneration. You go to sleep. Restart.

3) Your platoon fends off the enemy force and a cryogenics lab is secured for further study.

Level Up – Mission Debrief

You survive or die if Difficult Mission was selected first in the chapter. Pass/Fail status update.

Level Up – The Push for Reenlistment

Your dislike for the Palanquin Rain Forest is no secret. Even so, your potential leadership, valuable skills, and positive military bearing is noticed by your company sergent. You are summoned by the regiment first sergent to discuss your options for reenlistment.

"Sr. Legionnaire Baker I understand you are interested in reenlistment. You are highly recommended by your company sergent and platoon caporals. That is good. I see you have not enjoyed the jungle, eh?"

"I don't mind the tour First Sergent. It is only a year and almost over."

"What if I were to guarantee you - Ha-ha! You smile at that, huh? I am serious with you now, Sr. Legionnaire. I can guarantee you, if you sign your reenlistment contract, you will not return here during the next enlistment. Eh? I will shake on it. Are you interested in hearing what I propose, huh?"

You ponder his words. Are you really interested in continuing another enlistment? What is waiting back home? You have mostly enjoyed your time in the EFL. Why not hear what First Sergent has to say? He speaks the truth; he would never lie.

"I will listen to what you propose, First Sergent."

"Very good, yes. First, I can offer you no extra summa or promise a promotion before your eligibility. Looking at your record, you should make lance caporal close to on time if you continue to be the legionnaire you are now. You sign the contract today or the next day to think about it. I will send you to the AP course the next cycle, next week. When you complete that, you fly out of here nearly two months early and report to 123rd Regiment, V Corps for Mountain School where you will do an 18-month tour with I Corps. At the end of that tour, you have a choice to join II Corps for Amphib, return to the desert, return here, or remain with the Mountain

Corps. How does that sound? Huh? Good? All written in. The EFL cannot send you anywhere else out of the contract without your approval. Oh, you do not share this arrangement with your mates, this contract is between you and the EFL. Understand?"

You are very interested. The possibility of leaving early itself is worth three more years. From what you have heard, Mountain Corps is nowhere near as miserable as the jungle or the desert. As far as a chance to select the remaining tour with an option to go amphib, that is more than seductive. Yes, yes, you will sign the contract right now so that First Sergent does not change a thing. He scribbles on a ledger pad and rips the sheet from the top handing it to you.

"You report to the regiment recruiter. Have her draft this up, and if she has any problems with anything, you don't sign it and come right back to me. There shouldn't be any problem. Look it over. Is everything we discussed on it?"

You look over the conditions. It is exactly as he said. You exit the office and run to the recruiter's office. Within half an hour the contract is what you agreed to, and you schedule to sign and reenlist with the first sergent at morning reveille, topping off a fantastic stroke of luck.

Level Up – AP, anti-Armor/Personnel, Gunner Course

You rejoin the 122nd Regiment, this time with 5th Battalion. The course stretches an awkward two weeks in length. Armorer skills are included, nighttime firing and qualification as well as familiarization with weapon systems used by other world forces. The course is by far the easiest you have encountered within the EFL. The class even provides time to hone your skills on the GPXR sniper rifle.

On the final day of AP, while waiting for exam scores to come back, the colour sergent of 2nd Battalion walks into the mess hall. First Battalion runs JWTS, 3rd Battalion runs Demo, and 5th Battalion covers the AP Gunner course. You had observed a similar event at the end of Demo. The colour sergent is looking for *volunteers* that have completed both Demo and AP to serve as Red Force for the JWTS class final week.

"Sr. Legionnaire D. Baker..." your name is called along with a few others.

You are all assigned a barracks room and given instructions for reporting in the morning. Your thoughts return to that awful three weeks almost a year ago. You have survived numerous missions in the jungle, the wet season as well as the dry. Your abilities are much improved, so much so that you barely can comprehend how much you have learned and how far you have grown since those days. You look forward to the side mission, even as you frown on the broken promise to fly out of this horrible place once AP was completed.

Level Up – JWTS Rehashed

It is hard to not reach out and throttle the legionnaire that is walking only inches from you as you lay in ambush in the muck. Your camouflage is flawless, the buzzing of a mosquito barely noticed. The legionnaire is third in line of the patrol. You have been assigned to steal the Sat-link if it becomes available during the ambush. The plan is on target and the majority of the small training platoon is in the kill zone. You easily identify the Sat-link operator and focus on him. The ambush is sprung and firing is non-stop, and the total confusion of battle, even if it is a training scenario, is widespread. All of these legionnaires are seasoned veterans of the Xobian or Mountain Corps; they are not noobs and should not be discounted. Still, the jungle robs a person's ability to think and reason, to react as they have been trained.

In absolute darkness the patrol leader is confused, the misery of 18 days in the newness of the jungle is mentally destabilizing. He orders a controlled move-and-cover fallback. Huge mistake. The ambush pushes him right into a small river. The patrol immediately struggles to exit the water and form a defensive front. It is what you have been waiting for. The Sat-link operator removes his pack and assists others from the water. You creep in, unseen, and abscond with the vital equipment.

The next three days are just as enjoyable, heckling and harassing the beleaguered jungle cherries. The Sat-link is returned the next morning, left on the path, monkey dung smeared on the pack straps.

The Red Force group watches as the graduating class celebrates their ordeal; you remember your proud

EXPEDITIONARY FOREIGN LEGION -The Xo

moment of this course. The group of you smile and silently wish them luck and go about your next assignments. You have a plane to catch. There is no opportunity to offer a goodbye to your mates back in the *Fox Hole*. Some of them you will catch up to in the *Eye*. Others, well, some you may never see again.

Level Up – PP and Mission Update

You have completed 12 Missions and a Bonus. Your PP is __. With the conclusion of your first three-year enlistment, you will begin the next three years of service as a *true volunteer*. The next rank you are eligible to make is lance caporal. Lance caporal is achieved between four and six years of service. You are now assigned to 1st Battalion, 123rd Regiment, V Corps for Mountain/Cold Weather School. Due to your contribution and excellent performance during the JWTS Red Force exercise, you have been given a *Commandant's Seat* in the next available Sniper Course following your MCWS completion.

Along with your *Xobian Desert Campaign Ribbon*, you now wear the *Palanquin Campaign Ribbon*, two *Regiment Commendation Ribbons*, and the *JWTS Pin* with *Demo* and *AP Devices* on your dress uniform, topped with your Kepi. You make a connecting flight back to the *Land of the Giant PX*, the EFL headquarters, and main training area. You turned in your field equipment to the quartermaster at III Corps HQ prior to departing, keeping only your main uniform issue and GPS, serial number _____. Your duffle bag has never been this light. You will be issued new field gear once you arrive in

Minsk, the home of I Corps, but until then you are eligible for a reissue of 1-DU-W, dress uniform-winter; 2-DCU-W, duty combat uniform-winter; 2-pair underwear, long, thermal; 1-parka, cold weather; 1-hat, winter, used with DU-W and DCU-W; 1-overcoat, DU-W; 1-pair combat boots, cold weather; and 1-pair dress boots, cold weather. You can hardly believe the weight and thickness of the clothing! You will die in these warm clothes. The quartermaster asks if you want to return and credit your JCUs, jungle combat uniform. You are unsure if you want to give them up. He laughs and finally convinces you that it will save you on the cost. He tells you to keep a set, marking the full exchange anyway. You continue to wear the dress uniform you arrived in, the QM tells you there will be ample time to change over to the winter set during the flight travel. Your duffle bag is now as heavy as ever and you still have not drawn field gear.

There are many other legionnaires in transit to new assignments and duty stations. It's exciting to watch your brothers and sisters come and go; you feel a part of the family now more than ever. You are no longer a draftee. You are a volunteer, a bonafide veteran of two campaign theaters, a Sr. leg. You are invited to join a group sharing a table at the EM club as you all wait for your next flights. There is a mixture of eight of you, including three females. One of the group is a lance corporal heading back to *The Xo*. Three of you are heading to Minsk, three to Palanquin for the first time, and one, a Sr. leg who is about to make lance caporal, is assigned to II Corps for Amphib.

"Yeah, you are going to freeze your nimbies off!" one of the Sr. legs heading to the rain forest, laughs, poking at the three of you heading into the whiteness of never-ending winter.

"Well, that may be true, brother, but I have seen Sr. legs beg and cry to return to *The Xo* during JWTS! Your world is about to become a living nightmare!" You all laugh.

"You pulled Amphib, Lance Caporal?" asks the one on her way to what is rumored to be the best tour the EFL offers.

"Nope, just the hellholes these jokers are praising and *The Xo*. Heading back for my first reunion there. I hear Amphib is paradise compared to the rest though. I can't imagine that much water surrounding me. I was one of those that actually liked the desert the first time around."

"What? Get out!" Several at the table jest.

With a light dinner and a beer or two, the group parts, wishing the others well on their new tours. You join the other two heading the same way. The flight to the most northern base before entering hostile airspace lasts 10 hours. An escort joins you after the flight resumes. Each of you hastily changes into the winter dress uniform, overcoat, and fur hat at the short layover. Your suntanned faces chap from the cold wind. There are another eight hours of flight time before making your destination at the top of the world.

CHAPTER 8

Level Up – **Top Of The World**

There is just no way it can be this cold at this time of the year. Two years in the Xobian Desert and 10-1/2 months in the jungles and you have never experienced it below 73 degrees. When you landed at Paladin Airfield it was 45 degrees! Now inside the AC, a play on both air conditioning and the Arctic Circle, it is 8 degrees and snowing. The Flight Special Services ground crew is laughing at the group of you, a collection of almost 30 EFLs from various unit organizations. Some are returning from other tours, having experienced the AC before, caporals, Sr. caporals, sergents, even a colour sergent. The new ones to the AC are on their way to undergo MCWS, either straight from the Xobian on their second tour, or an enlarged group of the original three, heading to your third tour. All will have to spend a week in a Transition/Conditioning course before proceeding to MCWS. The simple act of breathing has to be relearned. Drinking water to keep from dehydrating is reinforced constantly. The physical stress of shivering and cramping are real threats. Psychological testing to measure mental anguish has to be completed and monitored. Some legionnaires just cannot handle the stress of cold weather, and after all attempts to remedy the problems, will be transferred back to the desert to serve out their remaining enlistments before being discharged.

Daily PT and regular activity are conducted outdoors. Swims in the indoor pool mimic being outdoors with large windows along the length to give a view of the snowy environment only a few feet away. Gradually, the transition is enough to allow the next cycle to advance to MCWS. The misery scale just seems to always top itself in the EFL, somehow always breaking a personal high. The first week is a beefed-up continuation of the Transition/Conditioning week already completed. Why they even differentiate the TC week at all from the MCWS is a matter of great debate. The shock of cold weather training is revealed on the seventh day when the entire class is marched from the barracks where you have spent the first days, to the bivouac site, a cluster of tents set up around a warming hut/dining hall. The details of the march and bivouac were kept unknown until today so as not to cause undue stress.

    Regular duty is established and your first night is spent mostly shivering and awake. The tents have stoves that seem not to put out any heat unless you are sitting right on them. The next morning is unbelievable. Live fire range time, followed by PT, a 5K snowshoe march with full kit, then Navigation. The return to the freezing tents is late in the evening but still light, and that is when the real breakdown begins. Many Legionnaires are to their physical and mental limits, frozen and miserable. Suffering from illusions of failure, these are tried and tested veterans, fully immersed in suffering in the most horrendous conditions. Mentally they are beaten.

    The cadre are used to this and ready, pulling time-tested tricks of their own. No pity, no let-up; the excuses and whining fall on deaf ears. Or, so it seems. There are medical doctors and psychologists mixed in with the trainers, and a careful eye is kept on each participant. Duties, including guard, mess hall, grounds cleanup, latrine, fire watch, all are detailed out, leaving little free time that is not used sleeping. The week trudges by. Daily patrols, ambushes, introduction to *Telemark* skiing, hiking with snowshoes, camouflage, weapons care, hygiene, food prep, physical fitness, all are introduced and accomplished. In the third week, the AC Hike is taken, an 18 mile, 2-day bivouac in personal shelters and an assault on a fortified position.

On graduation day, an option is given for those that want to complete it – a Polar Bear Swim. A jump in and out really, in the near-frozen sea under the ice. A hole is cut and a ladder is dropped in. Each swimmer wears a rope around their waist, so they won't be lost or eaten by a giant shark. The joking causes some to momentarily panic! An actual pin is awarded to wear on the dress uniform of anyone that accomplishes the feat. You are one of a dozen of the 20 in the class to take the plunge, immediately given a warmed blanket and shuffled to the warming hut to redress. Cheers and praise follow each new Polar Bear, the outgoing CO of the school taking her 100th swim with the class. You feel good participating in such a memorable event.

Level Up – Mountain Sniper Course

Six days later you begin the next three-week Mountain Sniper Course after completing and qualifying the prerequisite AC day and night range scores and the PT test, again. Many of the topics from MCWS are reviewed the first week, ensuring that the candidates are able to function in the extremes. The second week delves into the fundamentals of AC camouflage and concealed movement. Range time is every day, at all times, in any

EXPEDITIONARY FOREIGN LEGION -The Xo

condition – snow, high wind, whiteout, darkness, unbearable low temperatures. Telemark skiing and snowshoes are the only means of travel used. The final exam is a three-day movement in teams of two from a drop 25 miles from your target. The first two days are higher distance travel with the last day covering less than two miles to target. Personal cold-weather bivy shelters, high-energy food bars, heating tabs to melt drinking water, a micro Sat-link radio, skis, and the best extreme cold-weather gear available are all you carry besides the GPXR.

Twenty-one began the course, only 12 finish. You earn your Mountain Sniper Badge, the hardest and most difficult thing you have ever accomplished.

Level Up – The White Wolves

You are assigned to 2nd Platoon, Delta Company, 2nd Battalion, 104th Regiment, I Corps, The *White Wolves*. Or D 2/104 I. You meet up with two old mates from India 4/117 that are about to head to the jungle, starting their second three years. You swap stories and have a good laugh at old times in the desert, laughing more at how you all wished you were back! Names of legs long forgotten are brought up, the remembrance of the six that were beaten to death over the goat incident, feeling that it was such a waste now as it was then. You each give the other advice on how to deal with the coming adversity of the new tour. You feel comfortable in what awaits you here, having completed the MCWS and sniper course already, knowing that the JWTS is on a different level of miserable that these two may struggle with. You feel that even though MCWS was beyond normal physical limits, JWTS is abnormal in suffering and pain; the fear of the environment is real.

Your new Sr. caporal is happy to see such a promising, well-versed addition to the platoon. He starts you off immediately shoveling the snow from battalion colour sergent's lawn. You work for hours, the temperature hovering around -2. Colour Sergent steps out of the building and stops to observe you, watching your steady work.

Colour Sergent Willoughby, your old battalion colour sergent from the Xobian asks, "What is your name Legionnaire? Why are you punished today?"

"I am Sr. Legionnaire Baker, Colour Sergent. I am not punished, just welcomed."

"Do I know you? You seem familiar."

"I served with you in the Xobian, Colour Sergent Willoughby, 4/117. I was in India Company. You advised me to go to the jungle first on my next tour. I believe that was a wise decision. Thank you for that insight, Colour Sergent."

"Ha-ha! Right you are! So, I bet you wish you were back in the Xobian now, huh, Sr. Legionnaire?"

"Well, Colour Sergent, I have 18 months still to go, and at least I am not having to water your grass."

This sent the colour sergent into a spasm of laughter that he enjoyed more than anything that happened to him that day. "Carry on, Sr. Legionnaire Baker."

The next day you are summoned to the company sergent. You report.

"Are you happy here, Sr. Legionnaire Baker? Hmm?"

"Yes, Sergent Thomas. I don't know what you mean."

"Why is the colour sergent asking about you? You had a punishment duty already and you have only been here two days. What am I to think of that? What am I to think of the colour sergent asking about you? I thought you were a good legionnaire; your record indicates you have no problems. Yet, here we stand, you and I."

"I was clearing the battalion lawn, Sergent Thomas, and the colour sergent stopped to watch me is all. He thought he recognized me from his old battalion in The Xo. That is all. He probably inquired only to check my service and current posting."

Sergent Thomas looks at you, pondering the information. "Why were you assigned lawn duty?"

You are unsure what to say. You surely do not want your Sr. Caporal to suffer any blowback. You must choose your reply carefully.

___ I failed to respond to Sr. Caporal's directions promptly, Sergent.

___ My reporting to Sr. Caporal was sloppy, Sergent.

__ Sr. Caporal felt I needed to condition in the cold more, Sergent.

__ Sr. Caporal does not like me, Sergent. (You do not care if Sr. Caporal is reprimanded.)

You are dismissed and carry on with preparing to rotate to the battalion's assigned border zone duty. The company is scheduled to deploy in a week. Nothing comes of the episode and Sr. Caporal was only testing your ability to follow orders without question.

Level Up – Mountain Mission #13 Brief – Snow-White Ambush

__ Easy 10 PP 95% success

__ Medium 15 PP 80% success

__ Difficult 25 PP 60% success

Character Summary

You have selected Easy Mission.

Summary:

Delta Company returns to their regular border zone and quickly sets up and relieves the company from 5th Battalion. Two weeks is the normal tour duration out in the icy wastelands. There is very little to offer up here at the top of the world. Some oil, some gold. The main reason for the occupation is a protective buffer from any *over-the-top* southward hostility into the northern regions of various adjoining countries' territories. Radar and listening installations dot the Arctic Circle in opposing semi-circles, each bordering country prepared to defend their northern borders from aggression and put up a fierce counter-offensive if their enemy were to be foolish enough to choose a fight in this theater. Conditions here are harsh, even as every other battleground theater points to their distinctive cruel environments, the AC is completely unforgiving. A legionnaire can die within minutes in the brutal elements from exposure, literally freezing to death, solid. Fingers, toes, ears, nose, any exposed skin can die and be lost before the victim realizes they are in danger.

    Sr. Caporal Conducci recognizes you are a good Sr. leg but that you are new to this theater all the same. He assigns you as a spotter to one of the company's LPs, listening posts. The three-man teams usually include a sniper. This gives you time to adjust and learn from a couple veteran legs that are more dedicated than the average legionnaire. You will begin your second enlistment in a couple weeks and have already achieved the Sniper Badge, earning a class spot right out MCWS – that is impressive. You are expected to perform well above your peers.

    During the next two weeks you rotate to the LP, which is relocated several times, and watch snow fall.

You have selected Medium Mission.

    Summary:

    On patrol using skis, Caporal Toga discovers feint tracks crossing the landscape. Surveying the wide expanse, he concludes it could only be an enemy patrol. The Sat-link is spotty on reception. The direction they are headed is determined and you take up pursuit. An ambush is highly probable and any bumps or disturbed snow is approached with caution. The AP gun is too heavy and difficult to carry in this environment. You only have the ammo you can carry. The squad follows the tracks in single file for two hours and then loses them. Caporal Toga feels the patrol may be searching for one of the radar sites to sabotage it. Finally, after almost six hours on the skis, Caporal turns the platoon back to the base camp. You are totally exhausted from the conditions and exercise, the newness and difficulty of telemark skiing showing.

You have selected Difficult Mission.

Summary:

While on patrol inspecting a radar site, your squad is ambushed by a well-hidden enemy force that must have been in place for at least two days. With the Sat-link in a dead zone, your squad is on its own. You are outnumbered and taken by complete surprise. There were no tracks in the recent snow. Knowing that in an ambush, especially in this environment, to run is almost certain death, the legionnaires around you drop to the snow and form clusters of two and three, fighting for their lives and those beside them. Sr. Caporal Conducci yells out commands. You are not the official sniper of the platoon and only carry your GPS, but you make each of your shots count and after time the situation changes.

With more than half their number killed or wounded, the enemy leader offers to surrender. In the AC, a surrender offer is honored. The *Aleihachu* toss their rifles in the snow and unsteadily stand up, hands raised. The snow surrounding both forces is stained red with blood. Quickly, the captives are searched and stripped of all equipment other than their clothing. The wounded, those that can be, are treated on both sides. The prisoners must carry their own wounded plus yours. The dead from both sides will be left to be retrieved later. You lost two with six wounded, one having to be carried. They lost six with 15 wounded, three to be carried. One of their wounded will no doubt die before reaching base camp.

The *Aleihachu* did not know it, but most of your platoon was down to their last magazine. The fight lasted for two hours, a protracted back-and-forth shootout, with flanking maneuvers and counter maneuvers, grenade barrages, and bold actions taken by several individuals from both sides.

Level Up – Mission Debrief

You survive, or if this was your first mission in the new chapter, you die. Pass/Fail status update.

Level Up – You and two others are recognized for your contribution of successfully thwarting the enemy ambush and keeping the legionnaires around you alive. You are recommended for an *R-Com* and *Legion Cross 3rd Class*.

Level Up – Time Off

Months go by with the same routine. The boredom from inactivity is commonplace. Many stunts are pulled by the Sr. legs and lance caporals – hot water turned off to the NCO showers, water frozen in wide flows inside the mess hall during the night, *fake snow* (baby powder) blown under the doors to the NCO rooms covering everything prior to inspections, beach parties thrown in the lounge, with sand hauled in from somewhere and covering the entire floor! Ha-ha! The penalties and punishment are meted out only as officially required for reprimanding, the minor harmless tricks being the same that have been passed on as tradition for centuries.

Amazingly, there are tribes of indigenous people that inhabit the lower edge of the AC. They are an incredible testament to survivability in the harshest conditions, living in an environment that offers very little. They are treated with respect and claimed by each rival nation intruding into their world as their own population. Small villages can be found in the most isolated areas. They are used as guides occasionally, but mostly remain non-involved, choosing to not pick sides. It is said they have survived all of the depopulation events of the world, living their simple lives atop the world for thousands of generations. Their shamans keep the secrets of the past, present, and future. You are struck by the eerie similarities of these spirit men to their counterparts found in the deep jungles and baked sands of the desert.

Level Up - Mountain Mission #14 Brief – Radar Site

___ Easy 10 PP 95% success

EXPEDITIONARY FOREIGN LEGION - The Xo

__ Medium 15 PP 80% success

__ Difficult 25 PP 60% success

Character Summary

You have selected Easy Mission.

Summary:

You are part of a select patrol made up of legionnaires with a combination of various skills and qualities – skiing, long-distance scouting, electronic sabotage, sniping, and courage. Sr. Caporal Conducci is leading the patrol which is tasked with reprogramming one of the *Aleihachu* radar antennae to rotate 180 degrees and transmit intel to your strategists. The download program is carried by one of the electronic engineer specialists from I Corps HQ and the *blackbox,* which is actually white, needs to be hidden in proximity to the radar control panel. It is a small group, your ability to remain concealed and undetected is the key to success. If you are discovered, your size will allow the enemy to easily defeat and capture you.

You have selected Medium Mission.

Summary:

You are part of a reaction force that has been called to assist a special patrol that has been discovered in the *Aleihachu* military zone. Small actions occur all the time – ambushes, patrols crossing paths, and prodding of enemy defensive lines. With the small force caught inside the *Aleihachu* zone, the reaction force cannot number in excess, or it could be seen as a large-scale invasion or assault, causing a larger military action and opening up a front that nobody wants in this theater. Time is of the essence. A full platoon, 2nd, is sent *full bore* to assist the patrol's withdrawal before they are captured or wiped out.

You have selected Difficult Mission.

Summary:

You are part of a select patrol that was sent to reprogram an *Aleihachu* radar assembly. Most of your team is killed or captured and you and two others are able to slip away. Sr. Caporal Conducci is captured alive. You have the EE specialist, who is not capable of surviving the rigors of the AC on her own, and a respected scout who will have no trouble getting you all back to the safety of your zone. You think you can eliminate three of the *Aleihachu*, and possibly rescue the survivors before more forces show up. Should you 1) send the other two on by themselves and attempt to rescue the others, 2) return with the two.

Level Up – Mission Debrief

You survive or die. Pass/Fail status update.

Level Up –Time Off

For Easy and Medium Missions, you enjoy the quiet late dusk midnight-lit sky while standing looking at the whiteness. A year has passed and it does not seem like it at all. Unlike the desert and the jungle, the solitude here is mesmerizing, tranquil, hypnotic. Boredom is different in the AC, in the mountains. Boredom here is relaxing, restful, safe. You turn to join your mates and enter the mess hall.

For Difficult Mission, 1) you return with the others and report to Sergent Thomas that the patrol was discovered and that three of the group were captured; the rest were killed during the fight. Most of the company wonder to themselves how you made it back.

2) You return several days later with all three of the captured legionnaires, including Sr. Caporal Conducci, who, along with the other two captives, give a report of incredible bravery and self-sacrifice that you displayed in their rescue. You are a hero and the *Legion Cross 1st Class* is talked about.

3) You die during the rescue and the two legionnaires that make it back report that the last time they saw you, you were surrounded by the enemy and beaten to death. The captured men are all shot and left in the snow to be eaten by the wolves and bear.

Upon death, a summary page will generate, ranking your achievement and completion level matched against previous attempts and baseline characters. Do not find yourself a loser sent back to your parent's basement to eat a *turkey pot pie* for dinner before your curfew. You gain points from various stages and achievements during the game. Rank, awards, missions, chapters, and schools all contribute to your score. There are several possible ending scenarios, but only one is the true winner. Are you good enough to take it to the end? Read on, *Cassum*!

Level Up - Mountain Mission #15 Brief

__ Easy 10 PP 95% success

__ Medium 15 PP 80% success

__ Difficult 25 PP 60% success

Character Summary

You have selected Easy Mission.

Summary:

Caporal Toga has departed the AC on his way back to a Xobian *close-down company*, a company that is so low in personnel that it is slated for its colours to be cased and wait for reorganization with a fresh company of new lower ranks from BT. He will then attend DI School, be promoted, and take command of his own BT platoon. A new caporal has taken his place.

Caporal Swarles leads the patrol. You are seeking a good spot to set up for an ambush near a recently installed geothermal data recording station. It's really just a decoy-interest trap, something to lure in the *Aleihachu*. The patrol numbers at 25. Swarles sends the two sniper teams, both shooter and spotter, to their spots. You are the number two shooter. Even with the snow falling, it is advisable to reduce the number of tracks to any predetermined location, only the individual(s) taking that spot should advance to it. Swarles comes right up to your spot and begins to point out his projected plan of assault. Sr. Legionnaire Hyssop, your spotter is speechless. The site is ruined, Swarles ambles on, separate ski marks scoring the path.

Sixteen hours later an enemy scout slowly advances across the field and stops, scanning the area before quickly retreating. You are certain he noticed the telltale signs of your nest. You wait another 10 hours in the frozen snow. Finally, Caporal Swarles calls for a retraction, and the patrol returns to the base camp.

You have selected Medium Mission.

Summary:

Sr. Caporal Conducci leads the patrol towards a new data recording site. There is a high probability that the *Aleihachu* have investigated it and set demolitions to destroy it as a booby trap. With the site farther away than any other, it is difficult to continually keep a watch on it. You arrive just as an enemy patrol is approaching the installation. A firefight ensues. Neither side is prepared in a strategic advantage over the other, and soon the *Aleihachu* fall back in an organized withdrawal. Sr. Caporal Conducci decides to not pursue since the enemy no doubt are setting up booby traps in their retreat. After checking the site to ensure no demolitions have been rigged, the platoon prepares to return to base camp. A Sat-link message instructs Conducci to leave a three-man OP that should be prepared to remain until relieved in 48 hours. Sr. Caporal calls for volunteers and looks at you.

You have selected Difficult Mission.

Summary:

You are *volunteered* as part of a three-strong OP on a data collection site to remain until relieved in two days. Before departing, the rest of the platoon each give up a magazine of 15 rounds. You carry your GPS and the GPXR with 20 rounds plus your GPC sidearm. The three of you decide that it will be better if you watch over the other two from a separate location. They will take turns sleeping and on watch, and you will just have to do the best you can. As a new storm front comes blowing in, you move to the spot you all agree on, 20 yards to their rear left shoulder. You quickly set up your bivy and crawl inside as the snow builds up on top of you. You have your seven mags with 105 rounds, the 20 sniper rounds, and 15 rounds of sidearm ammo. Your mates understand that you will allow them to expend more than half their rounds before engaging, allowing the enemy to think they are an isolated OP about to expend all their reserves.

The shadowy, incomplete darkness of the night arrives with only a couple of hours of twilight before the sun returns in full. A rustle of frozen fabric and the crunch of icy snow alert you to the approach of a scout. He is advancing on an angle from your front right, only yards away from the OP. Too late, he realizes he has walked right up to the OP! The purpose of the OP or LP is to observe or listen without being compromised. It is never the intent to act aggressively or offensively unless confronted. The mission is to report on any activity at the site. With their discovery, and the scout moving to fire upon them, they have no choice but to fire first, killing him and at the same time, giving away their position.

The *Aleihachu* do not know if they have just stumbled into an ambush or not. The three shots ring as a reverberating echo in the cold. The patrol leader orders his men to drop and return fire. The fate of his scout is unknown but presumed to be dead. The location of the hidden shooter is still unknown, slipping back into his hole. *Ah, a scout, or sniper, or an OP maybe?* The patrol fans out, advancing slowly, cautiously. The OP, Sr. Legs Hyssop and Auhto wait patiently for the inevitable, but also for the best targets.

The quiet is ripped apart. They fire in a well-disciplined fashion, taking good shots, yet expending a little more than required. They have an additional 15 mags, 225 more rounds than normal. The leader is confounded at first then sends two flanking teams up the sides. He now reasons, gambles, guesses, that this is only a well-stocked OP, alone. Hyssop and Auhto keep the firepower hot and heavy, handing the *Aleihachu* several casualties quickly, more than an average skirmish. Your spot is completely hidden, a small hole giving a limited frontal view. You cannot allow the flankers on this side to move behind you or you will lose them.

You shoot. Once. Twice. Both men lay face down in the snow, their crawling through the deep snow complete. Your position is still unknown, even your presence may not have been observed, the flankers possibly taken out by the OP. Suddenly the patrol leader sees that two of his men lay dead in the snow.

"Sniper!" he yells, pointing in your general direction, even farther to your left. Good.

The flankers on the right are almost out of your sight, a tough shot, but you need to eliminate them before they encircle the OP. One falls, the other slips, and disappears. Did you get him?

A barrage of firing rips the snow to your left 10 yards away and short. Let them shoot, remain quiet.

Another push forward and they lob grenades at the two legionnaires, falling dangerously close. The shooting stops from the OP.

"Throw out your rifles and stand up and we will let you live," the leader offers.

The reply of both GPS signals their answer. The assault continues. Hyssop and Auhto have fired over 200 rounds, their complete combat load. The *Aleihachu* leader wonders how much they have left. A normal firefight is economical mostly, a few random bursts here and there, but these legionnaires have kept a continuous hail of deadly firepower on his men. How much longer can he keep it up? He gives it one last go, rallying the remaining men, challenging them that they can overtake two, three, weak and stupid and abandoned EFLs in a match of superiority. *Why, they have nearly expended their ammo*, he states, briefly rising to wave them forward, and then he falls back to the snow. You have been waiting for that shot.

Silence. An hour passes and then you see one, then two, and three of the *Aleihachu* crawling backward, keeping in the shallow dips and slight ridges formed by the drifts. There are no grasses, brush, or trees this far north. Nothing grows in this cold. Soon another appears, dragging a comrade. You could hit them, but you let them go.

"Throw down your rifles and pick up your wounded, and we let you walk away," you yell out.

A soldier throws out his rifle and stands, hands in the air.

"Go. Take an injured man with you," Hyssop directs.

Several men stand, throwing away their weapons, grabbing and assisting those that have been shot. Ten men, some wounded themselves, carry six others back to their lines.

Another hour passes. "We can't leave, and we can't move. What if they come back with another force?" Hyssop asks quietly.

"We stay." You respond.

"We have 10 mags left, a 150. Both good." Hyssop gives you a report knowing that you said too much already, possibly giving away your position.

The next day the relief patrol finds you still in place, seven dead frozen *Aleihachu* around you, multiple blood trails, and scattered weapons and grenades in the snow.

Level Up - Mission Debrief

You survive. Pass/Fail status update.

Level Up –Time Off

Congratulations! You are promoted to Lance Caporal, enlisted grade four or E4. This is a tremendous achievement. You are entering the lower level of non-commissioned officer. You have many things to learn yet and several years to go before reaching a full caporal, but you have shown a willingness to accept the ways of the EFL. The company lance caporals and caporals give you a *stepping-in* celebration, a hazing of friendly arm shots, light abdomen punches, and a liter of beer that you must drink at once. Sr. Caporal Conducci walks in and looks at you.

"You have done well in the Arctic, Lance Caporal Baker. How do you only spend a year and a half when I must remain another four months of my two years before I join you at the warm ocean? Your orders came in, pack your gear."

The shouts and congratulations fill the room. Another week and you are off to *Amphib* with II Corps. You can't believe it; the time was not nearly as long as the almost 11 months in the jungle or the two years in the desert. Was the duty that much better, or are you really beginning to fit in with the routine?

CHAPTER 9

Level Up – **Another New Beginning**

This has to be it, you think to yourself. The last theater, the remaining Corps assignment. *Amphib*, or amphibious duty, is the collaboration of two military branches, the National Navy and the EFL, working together on operations involving waterborne, littoral zone infiltration of sea-based offensive forces and their safe retrieval. The National Army at times may be transported by the Navy but disembarks in a mostly non-amphibious assault fashion. It is the role of the EFL to act as the Navy's seaborne assault troops and, to this end, ship security on every vessel over 100 tons. That is a large endeavor, taking near every legionnaire of II Corps in the process.

Once again you find yourself assigned to V Corps, this time with the 124th Regiment, 1st Battalion, for *FATS* or *Fleet Amphibious Training School* in the beautiful southwest coast of Summa. The *Palanquin Rain Forest* is nearly 1000 miles southeast, the Xobian Desert half a world in either direction. The AC, the top of the world, is thousands of miles north. You stare out at the endless ocean, the first time seeing it. The base around you is just as immense, it seems. The National Navy Training Center is here, as well as the western ocean fleets, at least those that are not based on remote islands and archipelagos. The eastern ocean fleets are based on the northeastern coast of the country, and that base is not as large as the western base or the EFL main headquarters and training area, where you experienced BT a lifetime ago. The EFL HQ is located in the southwest desert, several hundred miles from here. Your home, where you grew up, is over two days away, more in the central region of the country.

Many things are different in the National Navy from the EFL, or in all the other branches for that matter. The Navy is strictly and constitutionally bound to only operate in a 50-mile reach of the littoral zones of the continents, or in cases of islands with a landmass of not more than 75 miles across, can reach into the interior from the amphib assault point without having to redeploy to the far side. This basically extends to attack and support helo and fixed-wing air operations and, of course, naval gunnery support.

The Navy operates nine fleets on a five-month cruise, one-month shore deployment rotation. There are four fleets on each coast, with one of those in overhaul at all times. The 9th Fleet is stationed at the sub-tropical isthmus zone adjacent to the *Palanquin* jungles. She operates in a roving, patrolling fashion at less than full strength, with half of her ships in port at any time.

The Flight Special Services Branch is altogether separate and the EFL has little to do with them other than desert air support and transportation between theaters. They and the National Army coordinate and work together as the Navy and EFL do. The EFL and Army have no contact, except for Army artillery support in *The Xo* and occasionally the jungle.

Today, you begin FATS, a three-week immersion into everything Navy. *"Ha-ha"*, you think. *"There can be nothing that will near kill me as what I have been through all ready"*. As usual, it is a three-week orientation/training that teaches *The Navy Way*.

Level Up – FATS

The first week is always the same; you could write an overview of the course just sitting in the small classroom waiting for some hard-nosed, sunburned, or in the case of the MCWS, wind-chapped, over-anxious and hardcore, *"Let's get out there and get dirty!"* Sr. caporal who bursts into the room and begins telling you and your fellow classmates how *"This school/course is harder and more difficult than any you have seen before!"* And to give credit where it belongs, that's mostly the case.

There is a combination of caporals, lance caporals, Sr. legs, and even a dozen or fewer legionnaire E2s. *"How is that possible?"* you wonder. You have to make Sr. leg, E3, before leaving *The Xo*, or so you thought. You have not seen or run across a single *lower rank* leg in two and a half years. The class numbers 35 and everyone sits crowded at six small tables, three on each side, for the most part, the ends oriented to the front and back of the room.

You arrived the day before, reported, and were assigned to a barracks room. Due to your rank, it was a smaller room with only two other *lances*. The three of you shared stories, went to mess, and returned, skipping the lure of visiting the EM Club. You sit together at a table this morning.

The door opens and a fireplug-resembling man in tan/khaki pants and shirt, shiny black ankle-high boondockers, a complete upper-lip-covering bushy mustache, and a saucer, black leather-brim, khaki covered hat under his arm walks in and strides to the front of the room.

"I am *Ship's Mate 2nd Class* Yantitee, and you are about to undergo Fleet Amphibious Training School, but since we all love to shorten everything and give it a name, it's known as FATS. There are 35 of you sitting here this morning. I fully expect 35 of you to be sitting here after each break, waiting on me to continue. We have a full three weeks of orienting the EFL to *The Navy Way* of doing things. I have a list of your names and ranks and I don't care where you've been or how you got here. I do expect, as in any branch of service, that the senior of you keep your under-ranks in line. We go about our work duties aboard ship, I'm sure, in the same manner you go about yours, by *divisions*. These tables are divisions, small workgroups. When we return from our first break, the two caporals in the room will have assigned the divisions properly. For now, let's get started."

He went over the schedule for the first week – Orientation to Navy Life – which included rules and regulations, terminology, fleet life, water testing or *drown proofing*, and gunnery range.

The second week would consist of – Amphibious Assault Introduction – On-ship loading and off-loading, landing, support craft, ship classifications, and General Quarters or GQ assignments.

The third week would be an actual, short, three-day cruise and amphibious assault. The remaining two days would be ship and berthing assignments and orientation or tour. You have the weekends off. You nearly fell out of the chair!

The class begins and a full lexicon of what sounds like foreign terminology follows, a separate language. You had heard some Sr. legs and lance caporals speaking in a strange dialect before, always the Sr. caporals telling them to knock it off. Very little talk or gossip was shared concerning the Amphib tour.

At the first break, the two caporals divide the tables into divisions as instructed, a Sr. legionnaire with her fourth tour is given command of the sixth division. The under-ranks are divided as evenly as possible.

The ship's mate returns with a cup of coffee, "Good. Division commanders take your place at the head of the table. Now then…"

In the afternoon when dismissed, the division heads collect for a brief meeting.

"Okay, I want this thing to run as smoothly as possible. Ship's Mate Yantitee gave me a list of *berthing compartment* assignments of the *divisions*. We are on two separate *decks* and have the responsibility of cleaning the *heads*, wiping down the *hatches and bulkheads,* swabbing the *decks*, and checking all *firefighting equipment* assigned to each *compartment* and *deck*. Basically, clean your AO and look at the fire extinguishers. After PT and morning *Mess*, we have division cleanup and then report to the classroom. This schedule couldn't be any easier, so don't foul it up. I will be *Officer Of the Deck* of third deck and Bendalli will be *OOD* of second deck. Baker, Emmett – you are responsible for third deck, Ammahis and Yoder – second deck. Copy down your legs and their berths," Caporal Urvenetti said as he held the sheet out for you to copy the names of your respective divisions.

At the end of the week, you visit the naval gunnery range or the qualification range. Multiple training platforms of working, ship-mounted AP guns in twin- and quad-configuration are present and being fired. You have seen a twin once or twice but never a quad. None of the others have either. The fact that the under-ranks are allowed to even touch the APs without attending JWTS and AP Course or earning that right sets most of you upside down.

That's when Ship's Mate Yantitee enlightens the class. Since this is obviously your first Amphib tour and everyone's second or third enlistment, you have somehow missed the recurring recruitment effort of the EFL to retain a high percentage of legionnaire E2s that complete their first three years of service. Since the Xobian Desert is the initial starting point of all BT EFLs and the only tour a lot of lower-rank legionnaires will ever experience, not making rank for various reasons, the allure of a promised reenlistment bonus in tropical paradise is offered. A Xobian locked-in E2 or E3 Sr. legionnaire can reenlist and be assigned directly to II Corps for an 18-month tour and then choose either to remain with the fleets or return to the desert, or a second option, serve a one-year tour with the fleet, do a second year where the EFL assigns them and then chose the third year. These legionnaires are known as *Salty Sr. Legs* or *Salt-n-Sand Legs*. Most never rank up past E3 and even less serve another enlistment. Nearly all remain in II Corps until they EOS.

You stand there astounded at the unfair enlistment option, having pulled both the jungle and the AC to get here. The under-ranks laugh realizing they have gotten over on the upper-ranks. That is the line that mostly separates the two groups for the rest of the school and onward.

The week runs without a hitch and the weekend is pleasurable.

Level Up – Swimming

The second week intensifies with more physical and familiar type tactical days. Ship's Mate Yantitee accompanies the class to the docks where a *FACS, Fleet Amphibious Craft Ship* is moored. It is huge! Going aboard, he leads you on a brief tour, basically down the multiple decks to the cargo area of the giant hold which resembles a mammoth parking lot and garage. There are four strange-looking vehicles, but there is room for many more *Amphibious Landing Troop Craft or ALTCs*. The ALTC is similar to the *ATC* that you are familiar with. The ALTC is watertight and used for amphibious assault. The ALTC *swims off* the ramp of the FACS during operations a couple of miles offshore and then moves to the beach. You climb inside the ALTC and familiarize yourselves with the interior. The thought of this hunk of metal slipping off the back end of this massive ship into the ocean and sinking a few feet before popping up and bobbing in the water on its way to shore gives you a mixed feeling of excitement and fear.

In the afternoon you change to full gear for training, running through drills, climbing into and out of the ALTC at a shore-based training site for the rest of the afternoon and into the evening. It then steps up. After a combat meal for dinner, you load up once more into two vehicles and ride for what seems like hours, stuffed in the tightly cramped box. A full squad of 20 legionnaires and their gear is supposed to fit – packs, grenades, the platoon AP, extra ammo cases, stretchers, water canisters, combat meal boxes, and so on. There is no way. The driver, or *helmsman*, sits fully forward on the left through a tight crawlspace. The vehicle commander, the *coxswain*, is positioned on a jump seat, the position left of center, nearly as far forward as the helmsman, but just behind the engine compartment. A gunner for the mounted AP, in a swivel protective canopy or *cupola,* is to the coxswain's right rear. There is a top hatch, which is presently closed, and the back hatch, which is part of the ramp which can be lowered. The helmsman also has a small hatch he can climb in and out from.

At some point during the night, Ship's Mate Yantitee is replaced by another mate. Vehicle crews are also go through training. Suddenly you find yourself swaying roughly, even feeling like you are on a roller-coaster. You are in the water! After another half hour, you feel a violent jarring and the engine revs high. You feel a slip backward and then the rear of the ALTC drops and the front raises up at an alarming if not frightening angle, sending all of you crashing against the back ramp.

Seawater flows in from the gunner's hatch soaking all those trapped inside the steel coffin. Sheer panic grips the squad. You are sinking! The gunner scrambles out of his hatch all the way, disappearing in the dark. After leveling up, the surge happens again. This time the contact is good with the sensation of jolting forward at an increased speed for a moment then a bumpy and jarring motion, a hard stop, not soft as in the water. The gunner slips back down into his hatch soaking wet. The engine stops, and the rear hatch is opened from the outside. An overpowering and nauseating smell of oil, diesel, putrid water, engine exhaust, and salty air, along with thunderous, echoing, banging noises fill the air. You are aboard ship, at sea somewhere.

You are quickly escorted through the hold, after collecting your gear, and led to a compartment. It is hot, stuffy, humid, smelly, loud, dim, and cramped. There are other legs here, and you are directed to a set of unoccupied bunks.

"Get some sleep. I will come for you in two hours," asserts your new, unnamed guide.

Quickly, Caporal Urvenetti assigns bunks, and you all attempt to sleep. It is 0300. As promised, two hours later you are collected, rushed through the passageways and down the ladders to the giant flooded garage. You load up and return in the same manner as you arrived. Hitting the beach, you are ordered out from the dropped ramp and into an assault maneuver. As you lay in the wet sand in the shallow, breaking waves, a voice you recognize from your past yells at you.

"Stand up, *Cassum,* and show me you are ready for more of this training. I cannot believe they promoted a sorry *minus nobilis* like you to lance caporal." You turn and find Caporal Edmunds leering at you.

Caporal Edmunds was your first caporal straight out of BT some four and a half years ago, India 4/117.

He punches you in the shoulder. "They tell me you shot up an entire patrol in the AC, just like shooting desert mice, huh?"

"It's good to see you too, Caporal Edmunds. Still struggling to hold onto those two stripes I see."

Ha-ha, you both laugh.

Level Up – Assignment

Nothing is more exciting than getting new orders, and by the end of the third and last week of FATS, you are ready to get moving and join in this exciting tour. The weather is perfect, the salty air is agreeable, and the mission is straightforward and possibly the most open-faceted theater of all. It's dangerous, no doubt, but the odds are level for a change, or so it seems. In the desert, jungle, and even the AC, the environment was a bigger threat than the enemy. Here you meet the enemy on an open battlefield.

The reunion with Edmunds was advantageous. The two caporals, Urvenetti and Bendalli were standoffish at first, not too open with the lance caporals. The word of your exploits traveled, and you became

EXPEDITIONARY FOREIGN LEGION -The Xo

more respected for your skills and experience. Edmunds was part of the training battalion for 1/124 V.

Friday morning the class reports to the classroom with all their gear and awaits new orders. You are all headed to the 3rd Fleet which is shipping out in 10 days. Two regiments each are split between the three active fleets on each coast. The 110th Regiment is assigned solely to the 9th Fleet. Ship's Mate Yantitee refers to them as the *Puddle Fleet*.

As was learned during the second week, the Navy classifies all their ships into nice little groupings, assigning identification letters and numbers to ease in the listing. The ALTCs are known as TL, troop landing craft, and the larger garage ships, the FACS are LC, landing carriers. Other notable letters are: the HMC, heavy missile cruiser or MC; FLSS, fleet landing support ships or LS; FOTS, fuel oil tanker ships or TS; the AHCS, attack helicopter carrier ship or HC; and the EC, escort corvette or CE. Each of you are given a large envelope which contains copies of your records, orders, and directions to your new ship and how, where, and to whom to report.

Level Up – *JW Nowly*

You are not sure if your orders are correct; most of the class is headed to Fox Company 1/107 assigned to the 3rd Fleet and LC51. Yours say you are *attached* to Charlie 1/107 assigned to 3rd Fleet, ship CE25. One of the under-rank legs is also assigned to CE25. Ship's

Mate 2nd Class Yantitee is standing at the front of the room answering questions. You walk to him.

"Excuse me Ship's Mate, what does this mean? Is this a mistake?"

He laughs, "The Navy doesn't make mistakes Lance Caporal. You have *On Board Security Force*. I went through this last week. Every ship has an EFL security detail. You're basically a *landsman shipman* already! You'll find the *Nowly* on Pier 6, taking on supplies and a radar array upgrade. You'll report directly to her CO."

"Who is my Sr. caporal? It's not listed." Yantitee laughs again, turning the page in your hands.

"I swear, it's like having kids all over again. There, Lance Caporal. You haven't read your orders completely. You are, you're the *OBSF* detail commander. It's your first command. Congratulations." Ha-ha, he laughs and turns to assist another leg. You step back and stare at the orders, still in disbelief.

"What did you find out, Lance Caporal?" The leg, Legionnaire Kemp asks after watching you speak to the mate.

"Grab your gear, Kemp. We have ship's security on a cruiser."

"What?" he says with much dismay and excitement at the same time, realizing that he just dodged amphibious combat.

EXPEDITIONARY FOREIGN LEGION -The Xo

You also make that summation, missing the action on your first tour completely, assigned to some ship as OBSF, not even a troop carrier. You part with your new mates, slightly embarrassed of your new assignment and you head to Pier 6 to find the *JW Nowly*.

Level Up – CE25

With the aid of the directions in the envelope and an inquiry of a passing *shipman 1st class*, you eventually find Pier 6, a long concrete and massive timbered-piling structure that juts out into the protected harbor. Ships of various sizes and classifications are moored along the wide causeway. Vehicles of all sorts, parked or moving, unloading cargo and supplies, some transporting personnel, others involved in repair work, are everywhere. Scaffolding is erected along both sides of ships, work crews busily painting, welding, blasting, repairing all that is required. The noise of hammering, pneumatic drills and sanders, yells, and the din of a 1000 voices mix with engines and whistles and ships bells. There is a large warship tied up on the left side, a missile cruiser. Her decks are teeming with activity. Her forward missile turret is under some sort of maintenance by workers and shipmen. The paint scheme of her hull is a grey, blue, white, and black matte motif, as is her superstructure and bridge. She is a fine-looking ship, more elegant than the FACS you were aboard during training this week. The *JW Nowly* is sleek and deadly, brimming with missile rails, AP mounts, AA mini-guns, forward deck torpedo tubes and depth charge ejectors. She wasn't as large as the FACS, but should be comfortable at over 490 feet and a crew of probably close to 300 officers and enlisted. You give up a smile.

The two of you approach the gangway and before you speak to the shipman posted on the dock end, you notice the name of the ship, *JJ Alexandria MC33*. He stares at you.

"Well? You coming aboard or what, Salty Leg?"

"That's Lance Caporal to you *Blue Pants*," you reply, recalling the lesson on history and traditions from the *ship's mate 2nd class*, referring to the shipmens' work pants of the three lower ranks of shipmen - *landsman, ordinary, and able-bodied* - calling out the lack of due respect for your rank.

"We're looking for the cruiser *JW Nowly*. It's supposed to be on Pier 6. Did it sail already?" You look worried.

The shipman laughs, "Ha-ha! The *Nowly*! A cruiser? Ha-ha! You're a blast Lance Caporal. No, she hasn't sailed yet. She's tied up over there, giving the bumpers a work over. Fair winds." He points to the end of the pier on the right side.

As you near, you gaze upon her deck. The radar and Sat-link array bristle out like small branches of a tree. A couple Sat-dishes and radar arms are spinning atop her stocky, three-deck bridge complex. She has two mounted dual AP turrets, a single quad coaxial mini-gun for air defense, port and starboard depth-charge ejectors, and a single dual-rail missile air defense battery. There are other system controls and equipment you do not recognize or know. She is quite small; that was part of the shipman's fun, you now realize. Your misunderstanding of the difference between a cruiser and an escort corvette is now evident. Her hull couldn't be more than 145 feet long, and her widest part is barely 35 feet. Whatever crew capacity the *JW Nowly* has, it is sure to be cramped. There was simply no room on the main deck; how could there be any below decks? There is a short, forward shack wedged between the converging safety cable banister or guy-lines of the prow, its purpose unknown. A narrow catwalk extends over the gunnels above the open water just below so that whoever was crazy enough to do so could walk to the very front of the ship. The aft or back end has a platform extending past the hull by three feet or so, also fitted with a cable barricade guy-line. The platform is somewhat rounded on the corners. Its function and purpose are also unknown.

A metal railed gangplank extends from the dock to the open cable barricade, most of the deck sides protected by a fully covered metal railing a little over waist high with holes at the bottom for water to drain away. A crane stretches out over the deck from the dock with a pallet of long, large, metal boxes; four shipmen stand to the side waiting to unload it. One individual stands post at the gangplank on the ship.

You check the sign and the name painted on the hull as well as the ID on the superstructure: *JW Nowly CE25*. You step to the gangway and walk several feet to the ship, not stepping aboard until given permission to do so.

"Lance Caporal Baker and Legionnaire Kemp, reporting to the *JW Nowly* as ordered. I was instructed to report to Lt. Ashworth." You perform the ritual as practiced during FATS on how to report to a ship.

The deck duty mate, a *ship's mate 3rd class* asks to see your orders and Kemp's. Satisfied, he hands them back.

"You need to sign in, Lance Caporal, and you too, Legionnaire Kemp. Lance Caporal, welcome aboard. You can find the commander of the ship in the *Weapons Control Room*. Drop your sea bags here. I can watch them as you report. The legionnaire can stand here as well. The commander doesn't need to see him. I take it you're the new OBSF detail leader, that right?"

"That's right, Mate. Where's the *WCR*?"

You find your way up the inner ladder through the hatch off the main deck and up two decks, passing several shipmen busy with some activity. The WCR is situated in the rear of the command or bridge deck, which is partially open to the outside with a linking small observation deck on both port and starboard. The forward section is the bridge proper. The hum and activity of repairmen and ships' crew are everywhere. The hatch to the WCR is closed. You knock, actually pound, on the heavy metal door-hatch and then enter as instructed.

The room is dark except for the green glow of computer screens and monitors of unknown equipment. Two men look up at you from peering over the shoulder of a third man seated at a console.

"Who are you?" One demands, their attention fixed on your presence.

"I'm Lance Caporal Baker, reporting to the captain of the *JW Nowly*."

"Incorrect, Lance Caporal. You will not do well in your assignment here on the *JW Nowly* if you do not learn the correct formalities and customs of the Navy. You are reporting to the commander of the *JW Nowly*, which is me, Lt. Ashworth. I am not to be addressed as captain, even as the title of the third-lowest ranking captain of a *ship-of-the-line* is given to a *corvette captain*, an equivalent of a lieutenant commander in the Navy, or a major in the EFL. I am a Navy lieutenant, equivalent to a captain in the EFL. I am the *commander* of the *JW Nowly*. The *JW Nowly* is an escort corvette, simply the smallest *warship-of-the-line* class, and therefore not meeting the requirements of the title of ship's captain. There are 35 officers and crew plus your OBSF detail of seven, including yourself. That makes 42 individuals sharing a very crowded and small space. In order to get along and do our jobs, each must understand their role and the role of their shipmates. My crew and I have learned the ways of the EFL, and the reciprocal is expected. The next time we meet Lance Caporal, I expect you to be well-versed on this ship and have a good working knowledge of the basic Navy daily ship operations. Your legionnaires represent you, and you represent them. You are solely responsible for them and their actions. A small book is located in the crews' mess, *Navy Traditions and the Citation of the JW Nowly CE25*. I encourage you and your men to read it. The *Mate of the*

Ship will square you away. Senior Mate Oswella, carry on."

The other man standing with Lt. Ashworth replies, "Aye, Aye, Sir," and then steps towards you and gestures with his hand to the hatch but pauses. You are frozen in what to do next; the meeting and summary reprimand leaves you unsure.

"You are dismissed Lance Caporal Baker, and you do what, in the presence of an officer?" Lt. Ashworth jolts you.

"Yes Sir, sorry, Sir. Thank you, Sir." You salute and perform a turn to exit the hatch, as Senior Mate Oswella indicated.

You follow Senior Mate Oswella as he quickly leads you through a maze of passageways and ladders, down a deck, down another deck, through a hatch, up a ladder, through a hatch, and into a very narrow, very tight, dead-end compartment. There are collections of pipes overhead and along the bulkheads, painted in various colours, all different diameters, with clamps, levers, dials, gauges and valves all protruding in every direction. These are, of course, intermingled and adjacent to the four bunks. The bunks are attached on each bulkhead, upper and lower, and are themselves narrow, only about 30 inches wide, and set barely two and a half feet from the lower bunk to the top bunk and about the same for the top bunk to the deck above. That space includes a thin five- or six-inch drawer attached to the underside of each bunk for personal storage. The space between the lower bunk to the deck is 12 inches also, fitted with a drawer. The space between the outside corner edge of the bunk from one side to the other is not even three feet at the hatch bulkhead, and it narrows at the forward, or *fo'ward* end of the compartment. At the head of the bunk on the port side – facing fo'ward – there is a small study desk with a chair with arms tucked under it. There is an open face cabinet or shelves with fronting barrier strips on the opposite bulkhead space to keep items on the shelf from falling out. The fo'ward end of the compartment to the bulkhead is less than three and a half feet wide. The entire compartment is less than 12 feet long, closer to 10. The height is no more than six feet, but that includes the pipes running down the length of the compartment overhead. The entry hatch is an oblong oval with a dog-latch. It closes from the outer, aft compartment, basically sealing whoever occupies this compartment in. A manhole plate on the fo'ward bulkhead with large heavy nuts securely locking it into place covers an obvious crawl space. It must lead to a seldom-used area of the ship. As narrow as the compartment is, you guess it has to be close to the very front end of the ship. There is one other hatch on the overhead deck near the center of the compartment. The hatch has a large wheel that locks it closed. It opens upward. It is painted bright red with yellow caution stripes.

  The entire compartment is a dingy white, but it could be light green. The deck is a cold grey and has the same yellow caution lines around the hatch and on the deck in front of it. A stenciled set of letters and numbers in black on the port side of the hatch reads *2D-FC1-B*. On the same bulkhead in the next aft compartment, the identical stencil is in red above the black stencil *2D-FC2-S.*

"This is your berth, as it indicates there on the bulkhead, *Second Deck, Forward Compartment One, Berth*. The seven of you will share this space with your gear, and nothing will be hung, draped, or fastened to any pipe, hatch, light, or railing. Any clotheslines you rig up must keep the passageway clear and unobstructed. No ship's supplies or materials, including food, water, munitions, clothing, bedding, or tools will be taken, borrowed, adapted, or re-positioned. During General Quarters, this compartment will be sealed from the aft compartment, so it is advisable that anyone sleeping during their off shift quickly evacuate to report to their GQ station. This ship operates on four watches – two six hours on, two six hours off. These are known as port and starboard watches. The crews' mess is 0530 to 0630 going on-going off, 1130 to 1230, and 1730 to 1830.

"Officers' quarters are off-limits other than during GQ or instructed to deliver a message, and they are located on this same deck mid-ship to aft; that is why I took you down two decks from the bridge. The ships' mates' quarters are fo'ward of officer berthing, just one compartment aft of this one. The Head on this deck is not to be used by you or your men. You use the crews' head one deck below. Lance Caporal, you are an enlisted rank 4th level, equivalent to a Navy Ship's Mate 3rd Class, not to be confused with a Shipman 3rd Class. You have the same entitlements, courtesies, standing, and professional respect earned by your proven skills and experience. However, to be recognized by those who rank above and below you on this ship, you must prove to this crew that you are equal to their Ships Mate 3rd Class rank. In case you failed to grasp the information during your FATS, I am a Senior Mate, or enlisted level 7, which is equivalent to an EFL Colour Sergent, not your sergent due to the EFL's additional mid-range of caporal ranks. It is also because the Navy recognizes only nine enlisted ranks to the EFL's 11. You will report directly to Ship's Mate 1st Class DeLargo. He will serve as your liaison on this ship. If you should have any problems with Ship's Mate 1st Class DeLargo, come to me directly.

"As Lt. Ashworth suggested, I highly recommend you thoroughly read the *Ship's Book and Naval History* as soon as possible. You can draw your bedding from the ship's quartermaster in the canteen between 1600 and 2000. I will inform the OOD you can be found in the crews' mess from now to the end of the third watch until all your detail report. There's always coffee on, and you can request a biscuit from the cook while you wait for next mess time. I will tell Ship's Mate DeLargo to find you there. Questions? Those that Ship's Mate 1st Class DeLargo cannot answer?"

Yeah, you had lots of questions. But Senior Mate Oswella made it clear that he was done with you.

"No, Senior Mate; you gave me all I needed for now." You come to attention.

"Stow your gear, secure your weapons, including your sidearm. Dismissed."

He quickly walks out, ducking instinctively and without so much as a thought about it through the hatch and was gone. You stand there, as completely confused and lost on a new assignment as you have ever been. You are nearly utterly alone amid not only strangers but among those that see you as an intruder, a necessary inconvenience to their space and duties. With your rank, you stand between those legionnaires that could be seen as lazy or poor legs, though the five others could be Sr. legs that have seen jungle and AC tours, and the ship's mates, officers, and under-ranks that are watching your performance. Kemp may be the only one that is a *Salt-n-Sand Leg*. You can hope.

You attempt to retrace the course that Senior Mate Oswella took to get to your berth but wind up facing a small compartment with two men sitting at a cramped table. You came up a ladder from the lower deck, the EE Deck as stenciled on the passageway, and through two compartments filled with machinery, electronics, and crates of supplies before you found the ladder. You didn't remember coming through here the first time. This is a different part of the ship than what you have seen. You are lost, which is crazy because the ship is only 140 something feet long!

"You are in the aft engineering space, third deck facing forward into the ship's wardroom or mess. Where are you trying to go, Lance Caporal?" one of the officers asks, his attention drawn to you.

"Excuse me, Sir. I'm trying to get back on the top deck to collect my gear and one of my men."

"You are trying to get *topside*, Lance Caporal. Turn around, go aft through that hatch, you'll find a ladder, take that down to the EE Deck. Then move fo'ward through two compartments to *EE-FC-2S*, take the ladder up a deck where you will find yourself just two compartments fo'ward of here. Take that ladder up two more decks to the Command Deck, which is the enclosed structure sitting attached to the main deck. Find the fo'ward hatch. Be sure to close it back after you. There, you will find yourself standing on the main deck, just aft of the 4-quad AA battery. You came aboard right there. Got it?"

"Yes, Sir. Thank you, Sir."

"What is your name, Lance Caporal? Your assignment?"

"I am Lance Caporal Baker, Charlie Company, 1/107 II Corps. Assigned OBSF to the *JW Nowly*, Sir."

"Ha-ha, Lt. Ashworth is going to eat your lunch, Lance Caporal. No. You are OBSF Detail Commander, *JW Nowly CE25*. I am Mister LaFonte, Warrant Officer-2, Electronics Warfare Officer. Carry on."

You finally make it back on deck, collect Legionnaire Kemp, and return to the fo'ward berth without getting disoriented.

Ship's Book of Naval History & Traditions
Citation Naming of the JW Nowly CE25

Lt. Cmdr (Frocked) JW Nowly served a long, distinguished, and meritorious career with her first distinctive action as a *Shipman Armorer 2nd Class* aboard FACS *Open Seas LC306*. She volunteered to fill in as a turret gunner for an EFL amphibious assault operation in the *Douboo Archipelago*. When the ATLC coxswain was killed, she immediately assumed command and continued to direct the helmsman to support the advancing EFLs. When the ATLC was destroyed, *SA 2nd Class* Nowly continued to give fire support from the burning hull of the ATLC until her ammunition was depleted. Then moving under heavy enemy fire, she worked tirelessly and at great personal risk to pull wounded to safety. She was awarded her first *Seafarers Sail & Anchor* for her heroism and actions under fire.

Her second gallant action took place two days later on the same operation. The #2 Port AA-mini-gun and an FCS dish were destroyed during an aerial attack. She evacuated the gun crew, fought and contained the fires, then worked feverishly with great tenacity under extreme conditions while the ship was still under attack to repair the electrical system of the

EXPEDITIONARY FOREIGN LEGION -The Xo

gun, finally able to give fire support with manual operation. She received her second *Seafarers Sail & Anchor* upgraded to *Admiralty Star* and was promoted to *Ship's Mate 3rd Class*.

The next above-and-beyond-normal duty action occurred in the *Saladevo Sea*, serving as Forward Battery Fire Control Supervisor on the missile frigate *Conavan MF68*. After a series of misfires and autoloader malfunctions, the ship's captain yelled over the ship's PA, *"Dammit Nowly! Load 'em up!"* Under constant aerial strafing, SM 3rd Class Nowly pulled the last two remaining 230-pound *BlueJay Heat-Seeking Missiles* from the AL and single-handedly manually loaded and armed the #3 Forward Missile Battery, which scored two separate kills. The term *'Load the Nowlys!'* given after a miss, or *'Loading the Nowlys!'* when reaching the last salvo of a battery, is believed to have its origins here. Ship's Mate 3rd Class Nowly received her second *Seafarers Sail & Anchor* with *Admiralty Star* for her actions and contribution in saving the ship and crew.

Her fourth *Seafarers S&A*, third with *Admiralty Star*, was as a lieutenant-junior rank commanding the littoral assault boat *Kingfisher LP22* off the light class troop carrier ship *LCS45*. With the main amphibious assault complete, the *LCS45* was disembarking EFLs onto *Goonies*, open-top, lightly armored landing craft. A *Chaloosa* coastal defense *Stingray Class* submarine torpedoed two of the Goonies. Lieutenant-jr Nowly raced into open water ferociously leading the hunt, doggedly chasing the elusive Stingray, even as it torpedoed a third Goonie while that Goonie was performing rescue operations of the drowning EFLs. With every armament she had, Lieutenant-jr Nowly kept up the chase even into rough seas, repeatedly yelling, *"Get away from my Legionnaires!"* whenever the sub turned back to shore. With all munitions expended, she fired her last sub-killer DC, scoring the kill! That action forever solidified the terms *Load the Nowlys!* and *Loading the Nowlys!* into Naval History and Traditions.

At the age of 70, with her trademark fiery-red wispy hair blowing in the slight breeze, retired Lt. Commander (Frocked) JW Nowly laid the keel to her namesake, *Escort Corvette Class, JW Nowly CE25* at Manchester Ship Yard. She passed away two days before the *JW Nowly's* christening, listed in the ship's first log entry as *Honorary Plank Owner*.

Fair Winds and Calm Seas Lt. Commander, 'Captain' Jane Willow Nowly.

CHAPTER 10

Level Up – **Rough Days**

You join the *JW Nowly* 10 days before she and the rest of 3rd Fleet sail with the four mixed battalions of the 106th and 107th Regiments – the 3/106, 6/106, 1/107, and 4/107. Close to 5800 legionnaires. The fleet consists of four ACHS, six missile cruisers, ten missile frigates, four FACS, four LCS, two tender/repair ships, three FLSS, two attack subs, two medium fleet fuel oil tankers, two small fleet fuel oil tankers, and 30 assorted escort class corvettes, escort frigates, and corvettes. Each FACS held five companies totaling 800 EFLs with 26 ALTCs. Each LCS held four companies totaling 640 as reserve forces and eight Goonies. The entire fleet totaled well over 15,000 officers and crew. The giant flotilla was just one of seven active fleets on a rotational, overlapping schedule of regular cruises around the world.

It takes several days for the vessels to arrive and group in the marshaling area from their various ports, harbors, and inlets. The helicopters of the AHCS create a huge covering safety umbrella as the ships cut giant circles and figure-8s in the calm seas 150 miles offshore. The majestic cruisers and frigates form an outer protective screen while the smaller corvettes and escort frigates form an inner picket, racing around in crazy dashes and zigzags, reminding you of little yapping ankle-biting dogs.

Your fears are real. Each of the newly assigned legionnaires to the OBSF is a Salt and Sand re-enlistee, four Sr. legs and another legionnaire to add to Kemp.

Kemp is the only new leg to II Corps, the others having served a mix of six months to their last cruise before EOS. All of them, save Kemp, have experience with fleet life and have pulled at least one Amphib assault cruise. One Sr. leg, Juarez, is a cocky, lazy, and borderline insubordinate pain in the neck. He has done one OBSF cruise prior, and the thought of being assigned to a small escort ship gives him a thrill as he feels that this will be nothing but a five-month vacation.

You read the *Ship's Book* in one sitting while waiting in the mess the first day, quickly recognizing the reason for Lt. Ashworth's scorn for any reference to being addressed as *captain*. He obviously feels a great honor in serving as the commander of the ship named after such a fine officer as Lt. Commander JW Nowly. The book also highlights several customs to the National Navy; some were covered in FATS, others were not. Some of the more pertinent for your knowledge are:

The three lower ranks of *Shipman* 3rd, 2nd, and 1st Class are *Landsman, Ordinary,* and *Able-bodied*. They are referred to casually as *Blue Pants* due to their blue work dungarees. The next three ranks are the *Ship's Mates 3rd, 2nd,* and *1st Class*. They are referred to simply as *mates* or *waist-jackets* from their waist-cut duty uniform jackets. The ranks after that, of course, you have already met *Senior Mate* Oswella, then there is *Captain's Mate* and *Commodore's Mate*. They are called *Bluecoats,* mainly by the shipmen and only among themselves, from their elegant dress uniform. Officers of the National Navy adhere to a long history and tradition of formality and customs, as do the mates, especially aboard ship and while at sea. The captain, or even the commander of a smaller vessel, is pretty much a judge and magistrate, listening to a case against an accused, taking advisement from a representative of the accused, usually an assigned officer of the crew, and passing judgment and punishment. They are absolute rulers over their little floating kingdoms. The officer ranks follow this order *Ensign, Lieutenant-junior rank, Lieutenant, Lt. Commander, Commander, Captain* (not necessarily of a ship), *Rear Admiral, Vice Admiral, Admiral, and Commodore.*

The award earned by Lt. Commander Nowly, the *Seafarers Sail & Anchor,* is the highest award for bravery, courage under fire, or gallantry. The *Admiralty Star* is awarded for a second awarding of the *S&A*, which is rare. The awarding of three is nearly unheard of. For years, the uproar of such a low-ranked officer achieving the ultimate was a sore point. That she came up from the enlisted ranks only served as fodder for her political opponents. The *frocking*, the awarding and wearing of rank before official promotion to Lt. Commander was a further slap as she was then eligible to have a *warship of the line* named in her honor. The plotting to publicly humiliate her with the naming of a newly created *escort corvette class* only turned in her favor, since the escort corvette became synonymous with her style and character – small, tough, a rough and tumble fighter, fast and nimble, highly aggressive. The escort corvette proved to be the dependable screening ship for the slower support craft, the more favorable targets of aircraft, submarines, and attack patrol boats. The EC tore them apart, primarily due to electronic jamming anti-missile radar and the sub-surface sonar scrambler they were fitted with. The single dual-rail AA missile battery, the single quad AA mini-gun, and the two dual AP guns served her well with her incredibly fast speed of 45 knots.

The Navy is the second oldest service branch and has the highest re-enlistment numbers of all branches. You look around and can see why. It is a clean, fairly comfortable, and well-ordered organization. From what you have seen already, the life is pretty set, so much so that the legs that managed to find their way here as opposed to slugging it out in the jungles or freezing their fingers and toes off, literally, are having the time of their lives. You have to fix that. You have to instill some discipline, and quick.

The assigned watches are set, three legs on the watch, while you supervise and assist. One leg each mans the fore and aft AP gun mount, and the third stands on the bridge. The bridge is an honor, and whoever stands that watch has to be sharp and dedicated. That is the problem; none of them, except for Kemp and he is slowly being turned by the others, are sharp and dedicated. How any of them rated OBSF is unclear. Either they were masterful con artists, or their caporals wanted to be clear of them. You believe the latter. You enact a guard inspection to see who will win the bridge, where the sentry does not stand in the sun and weather all day and night. They are each capable of winning the spot over the other. It becomes a *who is less prepared than the rest*. You use the history book as a basis of knowledge along with the EFL's own history, to no avail. They just are not motivated.

"Lance Caporal Baker, join me on the Weather Deck," Lt. Ashworth steps to the observation deck off the bridge.

"You are the most pathetic, ill-prepared, non-rated, poor excuse, no leadership potential, sandbagging, fraudulent and useless EFL NCO I have ever encountered or had the miserable experience to witness! Your detail is no more than a copy and replica of you. Your evident lack of example and poor service standards are a beacon in the night for their disappointing sub-level appearance and duty aboard my ship. If I could, I would toss the lot of you over the side with the rest of the garbage." Lt. Ashworth's face is inches from yours. His voice and the utter and complete brow-beating he is giving you is easily heard by everyone on the bridge and even on the main deck as shipmen pause in their duties to listen to the harsh words offered by their commander.

He abruptly turns and storms back on the bridge, still yelling, "Get this miserable excuse of a legionnaire off my bridge!"

"You are relieved, Sr. Legionnaire Juarez. Return to the compartment and prepare your uniform for next inspection."

"Aye, Lance Caporal." He turns, a shocked and confused expression flashes on his face for a moment, and he starts to exit the bridge.

You stand in his place.

"What are you doing? Get off my bridge too. Senior Mate!" Lt. Ashworth commands.

"Aye, Sir!" Oswella looks just as shocked as the rest of the bridge watch.

"Replace the lance caporal as sentry of the bridge until a suitable replacement from the crew can be called up from their downtime. Additionally, have Ship's Mate DeLargo relieve the OBSF on the fore and aft gun mounts."

"Aye, Aye Sir! Shipman Kerny!"

"Aye, Senior Mate!" A young shipman steps from the opposite O-Deck, a pair of high-power binoculars around his neck.

"Send for Ship's Mate 1st Class DeLargo. Post haste!"

"Aye, Aye Senior Mate!" He dashes off the deck down the slightly angled aft ladder flight that accesses the bridge in addition to the inner ladder.

You stand there in shock. "You are relieved and must immediately remove yourself from the bridge, Lance Caporal." Senior Mate Oswella offers in a not-so-loud voice.

Protocol and regulations flow through your head. Somewhere there is a paragraph relating to being relieved of command. The duties of the bridge security fall to the EFL for a reason. Your men have disgraced you; they have disgraced the honor and prestige of the EFL. You have disgraced your command. You turn and exit the bridge and walk out of the command center. You gaze at the fleet all around you steaming across the ocean, finally headed to some unknown destination.

Thousands of your mates are preparing to go ashore on some island or rocky coastline, and you can't handle six legionnaires on glorified guard duty. You walk to the fantail and look at the water below, thinking.

"If you want to quit, I guess that's about the quickest way to get it done."

You turn to see Warrant Officer LaFonte standing behind you, the wind cutting through his hair. He joins you.

"So, you're going to let him win, huh? Give up like that. Let those clowns run the show? You know, the OBSF detail on a full corvette is a Sr. caporal. The corvette class is the smallest *ship of the line* where the CO is addressed as captain. The escort frigate is a little bigger, usually another 80 tons, and at 190, 200 feet or so. Yep, this boat, she's one of the last of the Nowly class. Fifty were built and commissioned. Most all of them have been sunk. I've served eight years below ranks and six as a warrant officer, and I've never seen a lance caporal on an escort ship as OBSF detail commander. So, either you did something right somewhere, or someone is playing a bad joke on you or Lt. Ashworth."

You stand there. "What can I do? They won't listen; they don't care. I have no upper authority to discipline them. They are experienced enough to know I have nothing to hurt them with."

"You uh, you did a jungle tour?"

"Yes, of course, I did. Sir." You add at the end, realizing you are still speaking with an officer.

"And you pulled a tour up in the AC? I hear that is the worst of all."

"No, I mean yes, yes, I did the AC, but the Palanquin is hands down the worst theater. In my opinion, Sir."

"You go down there and mop the deck with that one that pushed the CO off his meds-cycle. He's all blow. I'm sure you've had a few knockdowns in your tours. A good caporal can put his platoon in line one way or another. I think it's time you went with the other. You do that, and then I got another card for you to play. You put fear with some hard discipline out there, that'll wake 'em up. I got to get back."

He walks back to the command center and disappears inside. You stand there. *Well, here goes the other.*

Level Up – Ship's Discipline

The fight is the catalyst for the next event and showdown. With Sr. Legionnaire Juarez humiliated and out of his position as top dog suffering from a busted lip, sore ribs, and a possible dislocated right thumb, the remaining detail stands in the passageway of the outer compartment while you pace to their front, all but floating in the air as you rail-on about lack of integrity, service, honor, personal pride as well as unit pride; they have brought absolute dishonor upon themselves and the EFL.

"If given even the slightest opportunity to send any of you back to *The Xo*, or even, oh-ho-ho, the possibility of the jungle, I would personally pay all my paybook just to give you a taste of the real EFL and not some playground, water show, amusement park tour that you have somehow managed to secure while brother and sister legionnaires fight and die in unbelievable hellholes. Any of you that thought *The Xo* was a place of pain and suffering have illusions of fairy dust clogging your low-level intelligence!"

Since the detail is kicked off their assignment, they have time to spend together performing drills and conditioning. With that, you chase them through the passageway and down a ladder, through the EE deck aft, and up the aft engineering ladder to the second deck and then back down and fo'ward to midship and up the ladders to the command deck and out onto the main deck, fo'ward, around the *doghouse* or *fo'c'sle,* down the port side all the way aft and back up the starboard side and back down the command ladders and down to the EE and all over again. You repeat this cycle for the next hour, mixing calisthenics on the fantail, until they fall on the deck, soaked in sweat and blood from crushed or skinned fingers from climbing ladders, or ripped shins from dragging on hatches and coamings and even an orange-sized bump on one Sr. leg's head who entirely missed the upper rim of a hatch, nearly laying himself out. The crew watches intently, noticing that one of the detail is especially motivated from a prior scuffle below decks, the scuttlebutt that the lance caporal almost choked him out before releasing him.

With this activity over for the moment, you order the legionnaires to their quarters to retrieve their issue, and to return post-haste for field inspection on the fantail. Weapons cleaning and drill follow, the fading colours of a setting sun along the choppy water of the surrounding ocean falls to darkness. Since this activity causes the detail to miss Ship's mess, you issue combat rations as they sit on their duffle bags, fully combat-fitted and ready as if about to deploy. The midnight watch, the first watch of the new day, begins, and your detail stands at attention facing the bridge, as you have since the middle of the fourth watch. Now you have their attention, and at the start of the second watch, you issue orders to go below and prepare and fallout for formal dress inspection on the fo'c'sle.

With your own uniform carefully packed in its specially designed carrier bag, a protective box to keep the *Kepi blanc* from damage, you quickly dress and are out on the deck awaiting your detail. Years of falling out in rapid, non-excusable fashion for inspection in all conditions make the exercise a non-event. You have ample time to straighten and ensure your ribbons and awards are in the proper place.

The uniformed chests of your detail are surprisingly blank and void of any ribbon other than the *Xobian Desert Campaign Ribbon* and either *Expert* or *Sniper Qual Pins*. Two Sr. legs, Capone and Juarez, have a single *Amphib Cruise Ribbon*, earned for completing two cruises of five months each. Juarez also wears an *R-Com*. By contrast, your ribbons and awards include in order of prominence: *Legion Cross 2nd Class, Legion Cross 3rd Class, Corps Action Recognition*

Ribbon, Sniper Badge, 3-Regiment Commendation Ribbons, Wound Pin–Black, Arctic Circle Theater Campaign Ribbon, Palanquin Jungle Campaign Ribbon, Xobian Desert Campaign Ribbon, JWTS Pin with Demo and AP Devices, MCWS Pin, and Polar Bear Pin. The Legion Cross 2nd Class is worn on the left breast pocket flap. It has a connecting ribbon tucked level at the second buttonhole of the jacket. The 3rd Class is worn beside it on the pocket flap. An *LC 1st Class* would be worn around the neck by a short ribbon over the top button of the dress coat. The Sniper Badge and Wound Pin are worn on the right breast pocket. The Black level signifies one wound, a Bronze would recognize two wounds, and Red would be for three or more wounds suffered in combat operations.

Every leg's Kepi blanc is dirty, stained, or crushed in some way. "Take them off. They are a disgrace, and you befoul the tradition and honor of wearing them. Place them at your feet," you command.

They hesitantly remove them, the implication of humiliation as most of the ship's crew watch. That single act tugs the heartstrings like no other. There was a time in every one of these legs when *la marche Kepi blanc* meant something to them. They stare at your uniform, ashamed now of their meager service contribution. An escort frigate speeds up within 10 yards off the *JW Nowly*, her entire OBSF detail in parade formation, on her foredeck, in duty uniform but with their Kepis on, they look upon you and at once perform an about-face, turning their backs. The ultimate slap. The ship's klaxon and bell rings and sounds. The frigate speeds off.

"Lance Caporal Baker, are you prepared for inspection?" You turn to find Lt. Ashworth standing with Senior Mate Oswella facing your detail.

"My detail is lacking in preparedness and appearance, Lt. Ashworth. I am not fit to command the detail and have embarrassed the honor and legacy of my Expeditionary Foreign Legion. I request reassignment to IV Corps while awaiting my demotion to a lower rank that is more fitting to my ability, Sir." You hold your salute as you remain at attention.

Lt. Ashworth stands facing you, taking in your uniform and bearing.

"I will be the judge of that, Lance Caporal. Dismiss your detail to return to their quarters and change into duty uniform. You will remain and stand for Ship's Inspection in their place."

"Yes, Sir!" You turn and give the order to fall out and prepare for duty.

The inspection begins as Lt. Ashworth proceeds with a visual inspection, paying particular attention to placement and arrangement of your awards, cleanliness and presentation of the proper uniform, by the book; he walks slowly around you. It is the most thorough and intense regulation uniform inspection you have experienced other than during BT.

"What is the difference between a Corvette Class and an Escort Corvette Class ship?"

You answer.

"What action did Lt. Commander JW Nowly receive her first Admiralty Star for the Seafarers Sail & Anchor?"

You answer.

"If the higher rank buys the first round and an E8 EFL Colour Sergent and an E7 Navy Senior Mate enter a bar together, who buys?"

You answer, "The Senior Mate would buy all the drinks, Sir. An EFL Colour Sergent would bust himself down all night for free beer."

Senior Mate Oswella bursts out laughing, and the lieutenant joins him, stepping back, shaking his head pointing his finger at you.

"Stand easy, Lance Caporal. There's scuttlebutt that you struck one of your detail yesterday during a character-building exercise. That sort of physical behavior is frowned upon, and your chain of command will be advised of the situation. Your personal appearance and professional bearing have swayed my earlier opinion of you, regardless of that of your legionnaires, but I feel that with your new inspiration, you will correct those deficiencies in short time. Through your demonstrated leadership and recent actions, I rescind my orders and reconfirm your detail to their assigned posts to commence as soon as possible. Also, Senior Mate Oswella has instructed Ship's Mate 1st Class DeLargo to find you a more suitable berthing assignment representative to your rank equivalent of a *Ship's Mate 3rd Class*. Carry on."

You come to attention and salute. Lt. Ashworth returns the salute and heads to the bridge, followed by Senior Mate. Now, who to put on the bridge?

Level Up – The Wild Card

With some men, a simple message is not clear enough. That was certainly the case with Sr. Legionnaires Juarez and Capone. After some time to reflect on his physical mistreatment, Juarez reports the incident to Ships Mate 1st Class DeLargo who is obligated to pass the report of abuse up the chain of command, and a formal inquiry is initiated. During the process, Warrant Officer LaFonte shows you his next card to play. He is able to make an arrangement for you to use the ship's Sat-phone to make a call.

"Who am I supposed to call Mr. LaFonte?" A warrant officer was not a commissioned officer and is addressed differently.

"I assume with your assignment to this ship as a lance caporal commanding a detail that someone you know had something to do with it. Some old friend or NCO who respects you, someone in some place of connection. Can you think of anyone?"

You think, but no one comes to mind. You didn't know anyone connected. You weren't connected!

Tomorrow you stand *Captain's Mast*. Lt. Ashworth is holding a disciplinary trial of sorts. Your detail has become smug again, encouraged by the looming discipline and punishment you will face for striking a lower rank. Their behavior falls again to nearly the same substandard level as before. You dare not attempt the same approach as earlier in fear of an open mutiny. The problem, one of several, is that these were sub-par legionnaires to begin with.

You now share a compartment with three ship's mates 3rd class. One comments, "Nearly all these guys don't belong here. The Navy is getting tired of it. Then there's legionnaires like you, well-seasoned, experienced, good character. It's almost like the EFL has it backward."

You shoot up like a bolt of electricity hit you, and you run to the command deck.

"I got it. I know what to do, who to call. Can you get me connected to FATS V Corps 1/124? I need to speak with or leave a message for a Caporal Edmunds."

LaFonte looks at you with humor and jests, "A caporal, that's who you know?"

"Well, he will call a colour sergent in the AC, who is pretty close to a regiment confirmation. That should be good enough for what I got in mind."

"Which is what, Lance Caporal?"

"A wake-up call."

You make the call, leading to a return call at 0330 the next morning and another call at 0715. With the whistle of the *bos'n's mate* and the ship's bell ringing in the third watch, the afternoon watch, you oversee the change of your details' watch. They are smiling, confident of your soon relief. You remind them they are EFL legionnaires and have a mission to complete.

At 1400 Lt. Ashworth commences the Captain's Mast in the officers' wardroom off the galley and ship's mess. The proceedings are open for any to observe, and Sr. Legionnaire Juarez begins with his statement. The other five legionnaires of the detail are brought in one at a time and recount their testimony. Several ship's crew that witnessed the altercation also share their testimony. It is not looking good.

You are then able to respond to Lt. Ashworth's questions regarding the incident. You detail the situation of the past six days while underway to the assigned mission of 3rd Fleet – poor morale, lack of discipline, and overall neglect of standards which the EFL OBSF are expected to maintain while embarked upon National Navy warships-of-the-line. You point out that your detail was relieved of their posts due to a condition brought about by what you perceive as a lack of respect for the Navy and its customs, history and traditions. You feel this was compounded by a general misunderstanding among some second tour legionnaires that there are no consequences for their poor behavior. A gulf, it seems, between EFL and Navy jurisdiction. You felt you had no other way to reestablish a level of discipline and motivation than to make an example of the most visible offender. Your actions, though not professional, had some success until the detail realized that you were facing disciplinary action instead of the focus being on the detail's lack of duty standards.

Lt. Ashworth then listens to testimony of several of those on the bridge during the relief incident and from Ship's Mate 1st Class DeLargo, Senior Mate Oswella, and Warrant Officer-2 Lafonte. They all speak highly of your character and professional duty.

Lt. Ashworth deliberates the information and testimony presented by taking a recess to evaluate his response and research the Navy's precedent for disciplinary action involving this unusual non-jurisdictional EFL NCO assault against EFL under-ranks.

He returns an hour later and addresses those in the small room.

"Historical Navy justice and tradition demonstrate the occasional need for ship's crew discipline by a senior ship's mate or officer to instill a level of expected performance in a ship crews' duty and care. The EFL maintains a separate position of supervision and discipline of its assigned personnel while embarked upon National Navy ships. This arrangement of non-conflicting, non-interference between joint mission partners is paramount to successful operations within the scope of mission objectives. However, due to the heightened responsibility of an assigned EFL OBSF detail, which is defined as a naval ship's warfare fighting arm, the OBSF detail falls under the jurisprudence of Navy regulations while aboard a ship under wartime operations. Therefore, it is with confidence that I find that EFL Lance Caporal Baker took appropriate and expected action to reestablish ship's discipline among the OBSF detail while serving aboard *JW Nowly*. Additionally, after further communication with EFL II Corps, the practice of assignment of second tour legionnaires to National Navy operations, especially those assigned to OBSF duties through EFL II Corps, will be reevaluated with a more prudent system of merit. This Captain's Mast finds EFL Lance Caporal Baker not guilty of the charges brought forward, and Lance Caporal Baker will return to assigned duties immediately. This Captain's Mast is closed."

The legionnaires present in the room are stunned.

"Sr. Legionnaire Juarez, Sr. Legionnaire Capone." A voice rings out loudly from the passageway. All heads turn to see a Sr. caporal and sergent standing with two unknown, young, disoriented, obvious newly-assigned legionnaires behind them.

"Collect your gear. You've been reassigned. Your enlistment contracts have been rescinded through your breach of the agreement. You're headed to the Palanquin for an 18-month tour followed by a second tour in the Xobian," the sergent flatly states with no evidence of humor.

"What? That can't be. I only have 20 months left. I'm not going to the Pala…"

As quick as a cat, the Sr. caporal bounds into the room and nearly takes the legionnaire's head off with a shot of a giant fist, body-slamming him against the bulkhead as Juarez crumples. Capone looks on, his face as white as a sheet, the sudden reality of his next three years flashing with every story he has ever heard of the Palanquin.

The two Sr. legionnaires are quickly hustled down the passageway by the Sr. caporal.

"Lance Caporal Baker," the sergent continues.

"Yes, Sergent," you answer, not sure of your own destiny at this point.

"These two are straight from *FATS*. First Sergent Willoughby of 117th IV Corps says he can replace the other four; just give him a shout. I guess you had a favor to call in. I've never seen this happen before, but it sure is time. Real legionnaires out in the mud while these pukes jump the line." He looks at one of the detail who is standing against the wall in shock. "That's right, Salty Leg, the gravy train's over. They're going to love you in the Palanquin."

With that, the sergent turns and joins his Sr. caporal.

The ship's routine returns to normal operation, and you settle in the replacements. Word spreads quickly. The ship's crew and OBSF detail are dumbfounded by the sudden appearance and removal of two legionnaires by a special EFL task force. A memo is sent out to all regiment commanding officers of II Corps that, effective immediately, all OBSF assignments are to contain only those legionnaires that have served in two separate theaters. Additionally, any discipline cases of second tour legs are to be reported to II Corps HQ so that those Salty Legs can be reassigned.

Life returns to monotony, the boredom of daily watches and endless circles. The short-lived mutiny is put down. The remaining original four of the detail are in complete fear that if they step out of line just a breath, they are headed to certain death in the Palanquin.

Level Up – The *Lancaster Reef*

You feel you are missing out, that the legionnaires you watch across the waves preparing for the coming assault are much more courageous than you. You are only standing guard, and that is the major embarrassment. The *JW Nowly's* assignment couldn't be more mundane or lackluster. The *JW Nowly* is one of three escort/picket craft assigned to FOTS *Lancaster Reef TS09*. She was constructed with 8-compartmental, disconnecting, cargo-survivable fuel oil cells or tanks. If struck by a torpedo or missile, the individual fuel cells can be released, set afloat, and completely sealed for retrieval. The skeleton ship can then be more easily repaired or salvaged without the risk of the entire cargo being destroyed, including the ship.

Her slow speed, barely twenty knots, causes her to lag behind the rest of the fleet group, prompting her to vary her zigzagging course to a straighter line. This, of course, annoys Lt. Ashworth, as he feels she is endangering herself, and he constantly moves to the *Lancaster Reef's* bow and darts in and out, playing a massive game of chicken, so that the captain of the tanker hastily reverts to a more defensive course until the next time.

That is the full extent of excitement, wondering if the smaller escort will be rammed this time, cut in half, and sunk. The shipmen all jeer, making gestures at the towering ship above, only for the merchant mariners, the civilian shipmen of the support ships, to in-turn call down and curse, laughing, and threatening to sink the little *puddle boat* under their keel!

Your frustration mounts as you watch the first amphib assault from a safe distance. The legionnaires debark from their FACSs while large cruisers give support; the troop carriers and the ALTCs swim ashore, APs firing away. The action passes you by. You have never looked forward to combat before; this new emotion now causes you concern. Why are you feeling this eagerness to want to join in? It has to be from standing on the ship, watching the action from safety as others are in the lion's den. You continue your circles and crazy maneuvers, darting in and out around the tanker, in endless, non-importance.

One night, several weeks after the first light assault, the *Nowly* is towing a target sled for the tanker gun crews when suddenly, you come under heavy fire by accident, barely evading your destruction. The insults and threats are quite a bit more hostile and yelled more angrily by the shipmen to the apologetic mariners over the waves.

A few weeks later, while screening on another amphib assault in the *Caustuantian Gulf*, a contested territorial fishing area among several allies and the Chaloosa who have fought over it for more than 200 years, the *Lancaster Reef* is put under air attack, her missile batteries holding their own, but barely. The *JW Nowly* drives in with tremendous speed and agility, her missile battery and AA mini-gun showing why she is the *Queen of the Screen*! Her missile jamming radar causes the enemy missiles to track widely, harmlessly exploding into the sea hundreds of yards away. The AP crews of the OBSF at GQ man their assigned guns, relentlessly firing at the fast and deadly swept-wing Marauders, notorious ship killers. Two Marauders fire a dual missile attack at close range; both missiles fail due to the *Nowly's* radar jamming. They loose a string of heavy cannon bursts upon the *Lancaster Reef*, setting her ablaze, and then turn to deal with the pesky escort ship. They swoop across the deck, one after the other, raining a torrent of HE cannon shells. Most miss due to the *Nowly's* slender deck and her own wild and erratic maneuvering. As the bellies of the Marauders pass over, offering their light blue and cloud white heavily-armored undersides, the AA mini-gun and fore and aft AP guns rip them open. A *BlueJay Heat-Seeker* follows each, erupting the pair into balls of fire. The sea is too close for one crew to eject before the impact rips the plane to pieces. The other crew shoots out a millisecond from impact. They will be picked up later, if they are still afloat.

 The *Nowly* suffers light damage and, surprisingly, no casualties. The dual missile rails are loaded quickly by the AL, a vast improvement over the years since their debut. Deck damage control crews attack the fires aft immediately and ferociously, ensuring the ship's magazine one deck below is not compromised. The *JW Nowly* never wavers in her position protecting her charge. The fires on the deck of the *Lancaster Reef* are blazing; a cell has been ruptured. If they cannot put the fires under control in a few more minutes, they will jettison the compartment.

After several hours of relentless attacks from swarms of Marauders, which sink two ALTCs and kill 40+ legs and vehicle crew, the assault is landed, and the night falls. You watch from the deck; the fires of a few ships still light the sky as bright as day. The *Lancaster Reef* is one of them. Her captain is confident he has contained the rupture and that the fires are only burning fuel oil that leaked out. He does not want to jettison the compartment unless the situation changes.

One of your Sr. Legionnaires, Quintes, makes a solemn comment, "I wouldn't want to be on that beach tonight." He has completed one amphib cruise before this one.

The next morning, after standing on GQ into the second watch, the threat is downgraded. The crew of the *Nowly* goes about her operations as though it is another day. On the other hand, you are still coming to grips with the total carnage, feeling sick and horrible and embarrassed for your earlier thoughts. The operation, lasting over 18 hours straight from the day before, is as mentally taxing and stressful as any event you have ever experienced. You check on your men and ensure each is good, especially the two noobs. They performed as well as any Palanquin veteran legionnaire you knew. The weeks leading into this assault gave you ample time to effectively train them and bring them up to speed on the AP and general EFL doctrine. They are taking to the cruise like ducks to water.

The *Lancaster Reef* finally gets the fuel cell fire under control in the early morning, and ships of the line begin refueling operations after the fleet moves further into the gulf, safe from the Marauders. The cruisers and AHCSs split up, half remaining with the FACSs and LTCs still supporting the legionnaires on the landing beaches as they move inland to take control of the newly constructed airfield from which the Marauders are operating. With the two medium tankers taking care of the larger vessels, the two smaller tankers refuel the escorts and ALTCs as they swim off the FACS and then back aboard. The process is slow; only one ship at a time can refuel from a tanker in this environment. The escorts busily patrol the open waters.

Suddenly a ship's klaxon goes off, the wails of other ships immediately join the din. Ships scatter. An explosion rips the aft of the *Lancaster Reef*. Her fantail becomes a mixture of a cascade of falling water, jagged metal debris, fire, and smoke. A torpedo! The *JW Nowly* speeds into action, her deck listing hard to port as she makes a turn at almost 30 knots. The sonar array catches the echo of the sneaky sub who somehow eluded all listeners. The *Nowly's* Electronics Warfare Officer is in hot pursuit now. The sub-surface sonar scrambler takes away all readable target capabilities from the enemy. The water is likened to a frenzied electrical charge, the sound waves so erratic that the enemy sub is basically blind and is forced to send out an echo. That is her downfall. The *Nowly* quickly finds the hapless sub and launches a flurry of depth charges that cripples the sub, crumpling her outer skin in a matter of minutes. The explosion of compressed air erupts from the depths as the enemy sub breaks apart, imploding, sending torn bits of buoyant material to the surface in a boil of air. The *Nowly* slows, ceases the sonar scrambler, and sends out a series of sonar pings. She locates the enemy sub, two pieces laying 110 feet on the bottom. There are no survivors. The *Nowly's* crew has no jubilation from their win; they know they just sent 83 men to their cold, watery death. It was different with the two Marauders the day before. Those were air crews and had it coming. The submariners are seafarers, men and women of the sea, and that is a strong bond no matter what country's flag they sail under.

The propellers of the *Lancaster Reef* are badly damaged. She will have to return to port and have them repaired along with her turbine shafts which are now bent from the imbalanced props. She is out indefinitely. She offloads as much fuel oil as possible to the *Emerald Sea TS11*, the second tanker, and fuels two more ships during the night. Her speed is a crawl at seven knots, sending out a *thumping-whoosh* cavitation to any enemy Chaloosa sub listening within 30 miles. The FLSS *Express Lane LS219* comes alongside and completes a quick resupply of *BlueJay* missiles, depth charges, AP, mini-gun munitions, and ship's stores.

With a *full tank of gas, snacks, and toys for the trip*, the three escort ships and the *Lancaster Reef* set out to return to home port at the National Navy Training Center on the southwest coast of Summa. Every man and woman of the crews know that it is as if they are chumming for sharks. The near two-week trip will undoubtedly be filled with more excitement and action than anyone could possibly want.

Level Up – Smell of Blood

The third day out on the return to port, the *William Fitz EF109*, an escort class frigate, picks up the scent of a trailing sub. The *Fitz*, at 205 feet, turns on her quickly, throwing out a pair of DCs to warn her off, then circles, pinging her loudly. The cat and mouse game continues for two hours with the *Fitz* pelting the sub at irregular intervals. Finally, the *Fitz* chases off the sub which goes to lick her wounds. The *William Fitz* is the larger of the three escorts. The third escort ship is a corvette class attack ship, the *Lanny White CA47*, at an 180 feet. The *William Fitz* catches up to the group in no time, taking her place at the trailing position.

The talk of the crew is that the Chaloosa are tracking the small flotilla, waiting until it is well enough away from either the main fleet or Summa. The attack will come in a couple of days, six at most. The watches are tense, every pair of eyes upon the water. Speculation is that they will try to take out the *JW Nowly* first, believing that her capabilities as a jammer and scrambler are the best defense the flotilla has. The days wear on, the continuous circles with unexpected jaunts.

The *Lancaster Reef* signals for the *JW Nowly* to come alongside, her OBSF detail that is free of the watch lines up waiting. The detail numbers a good 20 or more. Their Sr. caporal stands with them. He yells across the gulf, barely audible, then picks up a megaphone.

"We seem to have run short of *CMTP packets*! We'll trade-up some *Whiz-n-Boards!*"

The laughter from all crews is instantaneous as the ultimate trade negotiation has begun. CMTP packets are the small, personal-size, and never-enough-for-the-job *combat meal toilet paper* packets found in a combat meal. Other staples and treats found in a combat meal include salt-n-pepper packs, gum, canned fruit, jelly, instant coffee-tea-creamer-sugar, cookies or pudding or cake loaf, the main meal of course, and the offer – Whiz-n-Boards – the nearly never traded spread cheese and crackers.

The ships separate, the lighthearted joviality easing stressed nerves and giving a short period of fun.

Darkness falls on the fifth night, and the crews are edgy, having expected the attack the day before. The Chaloosa are toying with them. At the mid-first watch of the new day, at a little after 0200, the first salvo of torpedoes is launched against the *Lancaster Reef*. She deploys her anti-torpedo *fizzlers*, an adapted DC with compressed air and loud pinging to attract the *homing torpedo* that is hopefully after her. If the torpedoes are basic HEs fired on a projected course, she has little chance to evade in the short distance, 800 yards, and closing fast. The *Lancaster Reef* turns as hard as she can to starboard and reverses her starboard engine while pushing the port engine as far open as it will go, the props beating the water to a boil, the blades in real danger of twisting loose due to the previous damage. She comes about in a pivot from the stern and then releases the maneuver before she rolls. She is lighter now, nearly empty of fuel oil. The captain is insane, the large cargo fuel oil tanker screams, every weld and joint feeling the strain. She falls back into the water and stops all engines, becoming quiet, even as her momentum carries her forward.

The *JW Nowly* moves after the sub; evidently, the EWO has the course. The two remaining escorts take a fore and aft, port and starboard screen. The *Lancaster Reef* resumes her heading. Another sub now attacks off the *for' starboard* rail at 15 degrees. It's a pack. They waited until several submarines gathered to hunt the tanker down and possibly the escort frigate. The subs have little chance of sinking the corvette *Lanny White* or the escort corvette *JW Nowly*.

With so much fuel oil transferred before getting underway, the keel of the tanker is at a shallower draft and the torpedoes once again miss, slicing within inches under the keel of the *Lancaster Reef*. The captain of the sub or his Weapons Officers did not utilize a magnetic detonator, thinking the tanker would deploy another fizzler. That's another break. The *William Fitz* launches an anti-sub missile drone, one of her *hole-card* weapon systems. The drone easily catches the signature of the sub and launches its missile. The splash and supersonic speed of the powerful electric motor pulsing through the depths was the last thing the sonarman heard before impact.

A third sub launches a deck-hatch cruise missile, the target the *William Fitz*. The game is afoot! While the *Nowly* locates and sinks her quarry, the *Lanny White* fires her AP and AA guns at the guided missile, but more importantly, she has her radar jammer locked on it. The missile explodes off the port beam in midair. Fragments and explosives rain down on the decks of the *Lancaster*

Reef and the *Lanny White*. The drone from the earlier missile is still in flight and locates the remaining sub from the air, tracking it. The sub dives and goes silent, using every tactic the captain knows to keep his crew and boat alive. She is dark and invisible. The escorts lose her. They don't waste DCs or additional missile drones; however, the hunt is not over.

The following day it begins again. Probably the sub that escaped during the night is trailing the flotilla, waiting, observing, reporting. The four ships are less than halfway home due to the evasive maneuvers. The *JW Nowly* is down on fuel, her capacity smaller than the other two escorts. If she is to refuel, now is the time to do it. The lines are threaded through a lower deck port, and the coxswain directs the helmsman to the two fueling lines draped and alternately submerged in the tanker's wake. A shipsman reaches out with a grappling pole, hooks one of the lines, and pulls it in reach of other crewmen who struggle to pull it on deck. The line is given some play from above, and the giant connector ports of the *Nowly* and the *Lancaster Reef* are locked in place. The task is repeated with the second line. The *Nowly* is now near helpless; the connector ports could damage the ships' fueling ports if tugged on to get underway before properly disconnecting. Additionally, if the *Lancaster Reef* doesn't have time to shut off the pumps, fuel oil could continue to flow out upon the deck. In 20 minutes, the fueling is complete, and the process takes place in reverse.

The watch identifies a ship steaming at high speed from the west-southwest. The Chaloosa have a cluster of islands that have been fought over, back and forth, for over 20 years. Every time the Navy and EFL liberate them and turn them over to the National Army to garrison, they have lost them. That was the case with most of this island-hopping campaign. The EFL is too small in number to fortress every hunk of coral atoll they battle over and take, and the army is too stubborn to allocate the proper forces to secure them. The vessel has to be a heavy cruiser based on her steaming speed. There are probably escorts, but they are not keeping up. As darkness falls, the first wave of cruise missiles rains in.

Level Up – Bloody Night

Almost immediately, the *Lancaster Reef* is hit and set on fire. The captain knows there is no option and jettisons the eight compartments. That gives her a top speed of 12 knots, and she zigzags her way towards home. Her crew are now free to man every gun and battery; the skeletal carcass of the tanker, like that of a roadkill animal laid out for a week, has nothing left but the bones.

The escorts are free to attack the heavy cruiser directly with everything they have. The *William Fitz* draws first blood, striking her with a *Deck-Buster* missile that is more a heavy penetrator than explosive, barreling down through the decks and piercing the bottom of the hull. Taking on water from a difficult if not unreachable position, the cruiser is in trouble. The quicker and faster *Lanny White* waits for the water to reach a level where the cruiser is too slow to maneuver before launching her deck-tube torpedoes. The *JW Nowly* wheels to relocate the sub that has hastened its approach. The Chaloosa have forgotten the *Lancaster Reef* and shift their target to the frigate, *William Fitz*. The fuel oil floats in their compartments to be recovered or destroyed later.

The cruiser's escorts came on the scene after midnight. One was a light assault amphib carrier with a *Seahorse* attack helo. You knew none of this during the night, only that there was a helo in the air for a short time, and then it wasn't, an explosion from any number of sources putting it down. Another escort was a frigate class anti-missile ship, much like the *Nowly*, with her jamming capability. The sea battle raged through the darkness, the missiles on both sides exploding before target or in the water. The battle came down to deck-launched torpedoes, AP and AA mini-guns strafing the decks and sides of ships. The *Nowly* chased the sub and put it out of action. The sub was not fully destroyed but was damaged and probably taking on water in the depths to die alone and *lost on mission*.

With dawn, you observe the full enormity of the battle. The heavy cruiser is listing almost 45 degrees, dead in the water, and all her weapon systems have been destroyed; her crew are in boats awaiting rescue. The anti-missile frigate sunk, a jumble of survivors treading water around the oil slick. The light assault amphib craft carrier, with Imperial Marines aboard, is going down; the crew and her marines are launching their version of ALTCs and Goonies, grouping up and moving to take on survivors in the water.

One small assault craft opens up on the *Lanny White* with her beach assault gun, and the fo'ward AP gun chatters away. Other deck gun crews join in, and the little craft returns fire. The *JW Nowly* is just then *coming about* to the sinking amphib carrier, the *Nowly's* fo'ward and aft APs joining in too.

"Cease fire! Cease Fire! Do not engage those men! They are in the water! Cease fire!" You yell, running the deck to stop the carnage.

Two assault craft are destroyed before the *Lanny White's* OBSF commander gives a similar cease order. The dead, dying, wounded, and drowning crew are everywhere. Lifeboats and *ships' cocks and gigs*, and landing craft take on what they can.

Lt. Ashworth looks on from the bridge. His space aboard is limited. Neither he nor the other escort ships can afford to take on the survivors without the threat that his own crew will be overtaken.

He calls from the O-deck with a bullhorn, "I am Lt. Ashworth of the *JW Nowly*, and I will take on your most seriously wounded. We have noted your position, and relief is on the way."

An officer, drenched in oil and bloody from who knows what occurrence, responds, his voice loud upon the calm water and the cut engines.

"I am Commander Osalia of the *Jymsu Attaki*. Your treachery in firing upon survivors in the open sea will be reported, and a World Order for your punishment will be issued. I refuse your offer. My crew fought bravely and remain together bravely."

"Your craft fired first, and I quelled my guns. But as you wish, Commander. I will put supplies over with half my inflatables for your crews. The names of the other ships in the action?"

"The *Jymsu Attaki* was the cruiser, the *Amorii Satzu* was the brave missile attacker, and the *Sami Harturi* was the troop ship. Let their families know that their marines and sailors fought and died valiantly upon the sea."

"Commander." The lieutenant salutes the officer standing in the nearly swamped lifeboat. The enemy officer returns the salute and then bends down to assist another up. The boat is going to sink. Commander Osalia steps into the water and continues to push the nearly drowned man up into the boat. He then submerges and never comes back up.

The captains of the *Lanny White* and *William Fitz* are also offering the same assistance. Each is refused. The ships' crew dutifully release their lifeboats, to the possible detriment of their own survival in the water, and lower water, food, blankets, and first aid supplies. It is past time to go. Chaloosa ships could be enroute to finish the attack. Hopefully, these crew will be found and rescued. Within hours the three escorts rendezvous with the *Lancaster Reef*.

The rest of the passage to port is uneventful. The overnight battle would become known as the *Tripondorea Sea Battle*, with little significance to the overall scheme of things. One enemy heavy cruiser, one anti-missile frigate, a light amphib troop carrier, three subs, with a loss of well over 2000 lives. Later, the Chaloosa maintained that there were no signs of wreckage or survivors when their relief ships arrived the same day, but wreckage and bodies were found 100 miles away for weeks.

Level Up – A Meeting

Upon reaching port, the immediate task is repair, refueling, and resupply. The *White, Fitz, and Nowly* are expected to cruise back and rejoin the fleet. The thought of having to cruise back is overwhelming, considering what you all went through just to arrive here. One consolation is that there is liberty for the crews and OBSF. You release half of your men for the first day; the other half will have tomorrow. You assign port and starboard watches.

The next evening after being nearly forced off the boat by Senior Mate Oswella, you step ashore to the pier and immediately meet the Sr. caporal from the *Lancaster Reef*, who is waiting for you.

"That was some fine back-channel maneuvering you did at the beginning of the cruise. That shook up the whole fleet and II Corps. I hear you were the one that stopped the turkey shoot."

"Yeah, it wasn't right."

"Uh, huh. You haven't gone ashore yet in an ALTC. That'll change your attitude."

He looks at you with a knowing eye.

"Still wasn't right."

You are both walking down the pier.

"Where're we going? Oh, here. I almost forgot." You reach into your breast pocket and hand something to the Sr. caporal.

"What's this?" he asks.

"You were low," you reply. He laughs, remembering the occasion.

"A Sr. caporal and a lance caporal walk into a bar. Who pays for the beer?" he adds. You both laugh like old mates.

Level Up – The Return

Amazingly, the *Lanny White* requires more extensive repairs than first estimated, and the three escort ships are too small and vulnerable to make the journey alone, so you spend another week in port. Finally, with all repairs completed, the three ships steam straight away to rejoin their fleet assignment. When you arrive, you are shocked to find that the fleet is preparing for the voyage to home port. Third Fleet has been at sea for nearly four months. The crews have been on constant watches, GQ and amphib assault duty without a single liberty. The fleet commander, a rear admiral, had planned for a port-o'-call midway through, but one thing led to another, so a port call is made enroute.

The sunny, warm white sand beaches of *Key Esprada* on the southern side of the equator are a favorite spot for the western fleets of all allied and neutral countries. It is firmly in a protected area on the west coast of the Palanquin Rain Forest region but is not part of that country.

After a week, with each watch having three days liberty and a final day languishing with ship-to-shore duties, the fleet makes her way to Summa and home. The energy of completing your first cruise is overwhelming. The experience of liberty, the sights, smells, and sounds of the ocean are forever-etched in your mind. No wonder anyone who comes here wants to return.

For actions while commanding OBSF detail *JW Nowly CE25*, and her actions while escorting the *Lancaster Reef TS09* and the *Tripondorea Sea Battle*, with your efforts, leadership, strong character, level-headedness, and strong commitment to your mission which assisted in the fulfilling of the *JW Nowly's* mission, you are awarded the *Navy Shipman's Crew Compass*. Additionally, because the *JW Nowly* was awarded a *Battle Star* for her contribution in the *Tripondorea Sea Battle*, each crew member who was part of the engagement is authorized to wear the Battle Star as a personal award, as well as on the left cuff sleeve while serving on the *JW Nowly*.

The fleet sails again in one month. Leave time is authorized for most of the crew. You have two weeks leave and decide it is time to finally go home. It's been five years since you left. The letters from home are always full of praise for your service and prayers for your safety, and a hope that someday you will return. You miss your mother and father, your old friends from school; you can't wait to see your old great-uncle. Yes, you have missed home.

CHAPTER 11

Level Up – **Homecoming**

Military regulations state that service members of all active-duty branches must travel to and from leave in *Class I Formal Dress Uniform*. Additionally, they must be in Class I's while attending any formal functions while on leave, such as sporting events, reunions, weddings, funerals, etc. The intent is clear; the military wants attention. The upside of this regulation is that all travel and event fees are free to the member, and most meals and beverages too! Leave is not usually earned during the first enlistment, so the public doesn't see many poor or standard draftees. Only Sr. legs or enlisted-3 and over, with good records and over four-years' service, are granted leave. This leave does not include short two-day passes and liberty at ports o' call. The downside is that the Class I is rarely worn except for formal inspections and ceremonies and is uncomfortable, hot, and difficult to maintain with frequent wearing.

Because some businesses tend to overcharge the military on reimbursement of charges, the member on leave is required to complete *Chits* and retain a receipt. Some businesses have pre-printed chits with the information already completed – airlines, buses, trains, ferries, larger restaurants, bars, sports arenas, and concert halls. If the business submits a charge and the service member's signed chit does not accompany it, it is not paid. The name, rank, branch and date of leave is included on the chit. Receipts are important. If a business is found submitting a fraudulent reimbursement, one where the service member was not present or did not receive goods or services, the business is in very hot water. Most smaller establishments just waive the reimbursements because of the difficulty in claims; besides, a service member in their bar or restaurant brings in business, and customers offer to buy the meal and drinks anyway!

You prepare for leave and pick up a *chitbook* at the Regiment HQ. Your leave orders are ready; you have settled your *paybook,* drawing out *150 summa*, a little over three-months' pay, and the recommended amount. You have saved most of your pay every month and began contributing 15 summa each month to an *EFL Retirement Fund* when you made Sr. legionnaire, increasing to 18 when you made lance caporal. You have over 350 summa invested with a *guaranteed* monthly payout of 30 summa a month at age 45 if you serve 10 years! That is a bargain. The contribution increases with each promotion to a maximum of 25 and a benefit of 45. But then, at 14 years' service, if you take early retirement, you receive 50% benefits immediately from the military services. If you go the full 20 or special service waiver at 25 years, the retirement is 100% benefits. That is in addition to the EFL Retirement Fund. Your personal savings are over 700.

You have no idea what you could spend a 150 summa on, but you draw it anyway. While serving in *The Xo*, the Palanquin, the AC, and on liberty in *Key Esprada*, you shopped for little gifts for your mother and father, hoping you would be able to present them one day. You have a beautiful native dress, a woven scarf, a wooden carving, and small figurines carved from whalebones. You also have a blowgun from the Palaquin Rain Forest

Quepos - the jungle fighter of Tamiarindo. That almost cost you a week in the brig for possession of illegal native weapon contraband; however, you had a signed certificate by the commander of 3rd Battalion, 114th Regiment, EFL Major DeVaul stating that it was a ceremonial, non-combative trinket. You also have a signed affidavit from 3/114th Colour Sergent Mabry and Fox Company Sergent Mopti that the blowgun was one of several collected from dead Quepos after a protracted engagement on a drug production compound in the Tamiarindo in which Sr. Legionnaire D. Baker assigned to Fox 3/114th Regiment II Corps took part. The second document came with firm instructions and clear threats to keep the affidavit completely separate from the blowgun, folded up in a letter from home. The practice of *authentication* by senior NCOs was sparse, only available to dedicated and trustworthy legionnaires. Your father is going to love it!

You pack your duffle bag with the items you need for a visit, very little other than the gifts and spare dress uniform items. You own only one pair of civilian shorts and two colourful island shirts from Key Esprada. You grab a cab with six other shipmen and ship's mates and head to the airport. The leave-press is on. The surge of thousands of legionnaires and seafarers only diminished slightly due to waiting three days for the first wave of leave-takers to subside while you pulled various duties. Evidently, several thousand others had the same idea. The airport is slammed, the waiting room still packed with personnel awaiting flights that have been delayed or postponed.

"Nuts!" You stand beside a ship's mate 2nd class that shared the cab with you, his sentiment the same as yours.

His whites are starched to perfection, the creases sharp and defined. You notice that he wears a BS, battle star on the left cuff, with a hastily sewn tab that reads in fancy cursive – *William Fitz*.

"Hey Mate, you earn that out this last cruise?" you ask, pointing to the star.

He looks at you, sizing up your awards and rank. The BS you wear is on the right pocket, with no ships' indicator.

"Yeah, that's right. Where'd you earn that? On one of those missile cruisers, six deep?"

The implied retort was that the BS you held was a *gimme*, a lackluster ship awarded for normal duty.

"No, I was right beside you in the *Tripondorea*. We took out the first sub and most probably the third one. But you capped the *Jymsu Attaki*. I crewed on the *JW Nowly*."

"I'll be! You're that *skylarking* lance caporal that upended the apple cart! Ha-ha! Ship's Mate 2nd Class Shannon, nice to make your acquaintance," he thrusts out a paw of a hand; he is massive, 6'5, 230 pounds of muscled brawn.

"Lance Caporal Baker, *JW Nowly*," you proudly respond, as if the *Nowly* were your permanent berth. It suddenly dawns on you that once you return from leave, you will be given a new assignment, in most certainty, an amphib assault EFL company to a FACS. All your gear is stored in a regiment storage unit.

"Where you headed? This jumble cluster is bogged down worse than a fourth-deck Head with a malfunctioning egress valve. I'm going northeast to Halifax, Queensland."

"Is that so? I'm headed home to Haslow, Queensland. How about that."

"We're going to be here for hours, if not days. You wanna go in on a car? We can turn it in at the airport in Greenwich and split up on the trains."

"Where are we going to get a car? There's not going to be a rental anywhere in town."

"Yeah, that's right. It'll cost about 10 summa for a cab to Davis, north of here. It's a good size town, far enough that these jokers haven't walked to it yet. From there, we can head across Summa Mare, into the northwest corner of Del Rio and into Queensland, about two days, maybe a day and a half driving to Greenwich." Ship's Mate Shannon continues his gaze at you.

"I don't know, that's a lot of money. What will the rental cost? Two days and still have a half-day for me and another day for you?"

"What do you spend your summa on? You can't take it with you, and we both know we were almost floating back there in the *Tripondorea Sea*."

"Yeah..." You look around the waiting lounge, shipmen and legionnaires sitting on their duffles and seabags wherever they can find a spot. The boredom in their eyes and expressions tell many stories.

"Alright, let's do it!"

"Alright! Let's get out of here and grab a cab." You head for the entrance.

The conversation is mixed over the next two days in between taking turns driving and napping. Shannon had taken leave once before two years ago. He said he couldn't wait to get out of the house and back aboard ship. He was ready to visit again. You part ways, having become good mates, and wish the other Fair Winds. You catch your train to Haslow feeling as lonely as ever.

You hadn't called or told anyone you were coming home. Hopefully they weren't away on vacation or having visitors. The cab stops in front of the house, and you sit there. An eternity passes. The driver watches you in the mirror.

"How long has it been? They'll still see you as the day you left. Don't worry about it."

"Five years. Didn't seem that long, until now."

You hand the two summa note up, more than enough to cover from the train station.

"Don't worry about it. It's on me. Enjoy your leave."

You thank him and step out. The early afternoon warmth feels good. The neighbors next door see you first; Mrs. Iredell holds her hand to her mouth in complete surprise, not wanting to say anything or call attention to you so that the surprise for your mother will be intact. Mr. Iredell is watering the flower garden under the front windows and waves to you. Your mother is sitting having a lemonade, visiting as usual after lunch on Saturday afternoon. She turns to see what the interest is.

Her shriek of surprise and excitement is only shortened by her sudden outburst of tears. She runs to hold you and kiss your cheek and forehead. "Oh! My baby, my baby! You have grown so big! Are you home for good? Please tell me you are here for good," she holds you tightly.

"No, mother, but I am home now, and we can enjoy that, can't we?"

"Yes, baby. I will take that," her tears streaming.

Your father comes around the house wondering what the commotion is. He stands still when he sees you.

"Dad," you simply say.

"I've missed you. And I want you to know I'm proud of you," he answers.

"I've missed you too." The three of you lock in a hug.

Level Up – Catching Up

The news travels fast. Your mother calls her sister and your father's brother. The Iredells spread the word on the block, and your father needs no excuse to fire up the grill and break out wings, sausages, and a couple of steaks for family. Anyone who shows up brings something, and there is a full banquet set up on the back deck in no time.

Everyone wants to hear stories of where you have been. The Thompson kid down the block had joined the Army and came back in three years. And then there was the Steward boy that had been drafted the same time as you, but you had lost touch with him after *The Xo* and his mother said he never came back home after he got out. The town was full of similar stories, some leaving and never coming home, dying in the wars, or just not returning, and others who served their three came back and began a life. *Why did you stay in? Do you like it? Is it exciting? How many places have you been to? Have you only served in the Xobian Desert?* They have a nephew in the Army that was stationed in the Douboo Archipelago at the airstrip, but that was an Army base, and only the Army and sometimes the Navy visited there. The questions go on, no one asking what they really want to ask – *How many have you killed?* They ask about your awards and ribbons. Your mother puts an end to the inquisition as soon as someone mentions the Sniper Badge.

You ask about Uncle Hab. "Oh, he is in the retirement home and doesn't get out much. He would enjoy a visit from you," your mother replies.

Yes, you would have to make a point to see him. Your father says there's an Arena Game tomorrow in Queensboro, and you agree to take him, your treat. He is instantly excited, naming off the events he has been following over the season, reciting player names, their times and strong events.

You promise to take your mother somewhere special too, her pick, and you know that will be the *Red Trellis*, her favorite restaurant that she hardly ever visits. When everyone leaves, you grab your duffle bag and pull out the things you have brought to give them, some wrapped in brown paper, others just in plastic bags. You take off your dress jacket and hang it on the back of a kitchen chair. Your Kepi blanc sits on the table. Your parents love the gifts. Your mother is already up and looking for the right place to put the little figurines and carving. She is wearing her scarf. She is not sure about the blowgun, even with the signed certificate from Major DeVaul stating that it is only ceremonial. You quietly pass the other certificate to your father, and he reads it. A broad smile crosses his face, and he quickly refolds it and gets up, takes the blowgun and the DeVaul document, walks to his little office, and puts them away.

You change into the shorts and flowered shirt and sit listening to your parents tell you everything that has happened while you were away. Finally, they say goodnight, and you go to your old room and sit thinking about everyone you miss. You go to bed and fall asleep with their names and faces in your dreams.

After breakfast the next morning, you and your dad are off to Queensboro to the Arena Games, the day filled with events and races. There are usually four teams, some from the other regions, each with a 15-person team and three alternates. Each player has to compete in at least three events unless alternated out, in which case they cannot participate further. The events vary by venue but include hurdles, relays, dashes, throwing, jumping, and vaulting. There is always a *hunter* event – running, throwing, and hurdles – and a *cup race*, the final running event with the top five point-earners from each team. That means that the strongest and most limber also have to be able to run, like the throwers and vaulters.

In upper school, you had competed in the long jump, hurdles, some vaulting, and javelin. But you were not even close to the regional level. These are professional athletes. Each region competes within and outside their region, amassing points to make it to the championships. That is the goal of every school kid, to be an Arena Player.

You didn't want to wear your dress uniform, but your father insisted. You just want to enjoy the games. When you arrive, you find several other service members in uniform also. The games open with the National Anthem, a recognition of the service members in attendance, and a prayer. The opening event is the 440 Hurdle Relay. The afternoon is fantastic, the players in top form, few injuries, the coaches all working out their best strategies, and when to substitute an alternate depending on the event order. You go down to the infield to get your dad's picture with the Queensland team at the end of the day. They are runner-up to a North Umber team but soundly beat the Del Rio and Summa Mare teams. Queensland is a solid tier-I team, as is the North Umber team. There are three levels I, II, and III. The final championship will be just the tier-Is for each of the eight regions. Each region has to qualify their championship team, and the season is only halfway through. The final champion will proceed to the World United Games and compete against those countries' champions.

You make it home late after a full day and sit and have a piece of pie with your mother in the kitchen, answering her questions, telling her some of the things you have seen, where you have been, mates you have made. She served in the civil service as a secretary to an ambassador to Prangenua, in the mountains. You know where that is now. It is an arctic zone country bordering Aleihachu on the same continent as the Xobian Empire. They tried to remain neutral years before, but the Aleihachu invaded. Summa fought to liberate Prangenua. The border wars have been going back and forth in the years since. The 105th Regiment of I Corps was on that border, so you never had any contact with any Prangenua, just the Aleihachu. She listens to your descriptions and watches you.

You show her some pictures of the AC, the Xobian Desert, Palanquin, some of your mates, and you in combat gear on the *JW Nowly* after an aerial attack. Later in the night, you hear her silently weeping, your father comforting her.

Two days later, you make arrangements to visit the retirement home.

Uncle Hab served only three years in the EFL, but his stories while you were growing up were always told in a positive and adventurous tone as if he enjoyed the desert and the EFL. It was with some confusion when you ended your first tour of why he never made it out of *The Xo* and on to the Palanquin as a Sr. leg. Mostly only the poorer quality or non-ranking lower ranks remained for their third year. You inquired while you were in the AC with the 104th Regiment at the start of your second enlistment as a Sr. leg. The 120th Regiment Commander and IV Corps Historian, Col. J. Easton, sent you a reply with a public record copy of your great uncle's service. The response blew you away. Sr. Legionnaire T. "Hab" Habbit had served with distinction, earning his upper rank at 22 months, and declined an offer to move on to the Palanquin, wishing to remain with a handful of mates. He earned the Xobian Desert Campaign Ribbon, a Regiment Commendation Ribbon, Legion Reserve Service Ribbon, a Wound Pin-Black, and Expert Qual Pin. Upon returning from his enlistment, he joined the EFL Active Reserve Force and served another three years in the reserves. In his service record, he listed *Marriage* as the reason why he did not reenlist for active duty.

His wife Dot, your Aunt Dottie, passed away when you were young. You remember her as a fun, joyful lady with thick, coal-black hair and a gorgeous smile. You walk up to the retirement home, carrying a small bundle of things. Uncle Hab is in his room reading a book and is quite excited to see you. His granddaughter told him you were home visiting on leave. He gets up and moves to hug you.

"Ooh, I am so glad to see you! I always knew you would like it. Look at you! A lance caporal. What do I see there? A Legion Cross 2nd and 3rd? Is that three R-Coms? And what is that? I don't know that one?" his thin bony and crooked finger pointing to the BS.

"Can we go outside? You want to sit outside?"

"Yes, yes, of course. They want me to stay out of the sun as much as possible, but there are shade trees. Ha, if only the nurses had been in the desert, huh? Ha, telling us to stay out of the sun! Ha-ha!"

You help him walk, his frail body not what you remember of a strong and vibrant man.

He points to a bench under the trees, but you find a padded chair and pull it along so that he can sit on it instead of the hard slats. The conversation is broken, his breathing is not good. He asks questions and listens to you tell the stories, his eyes coming alive with memories of a long-ago young legionnaire.

"I brought you a few things, Uncle Hab. Nothing expensive or dangerous."

"You didn't need to bring me anything. What have you got?" He adds, looking down at the bench beside you with interest and childlike anticipation.

"First, I contacted the 120th, your old Regiment. The recruiting officer of the 6th Battalion says that Gulf Company will re-sign you, but you have to go through BT again."

"Blah! I'll go back, but not as a Cassum again!"

"They found that you should have been promoted to lance caporal before your EOS when you pulled your reserve time. So, they put in the paperwork, and you are now EFL Lance Caporal Habbit." You pull out a framed certificate case that reads *Gulf Company, 6th Battalion, 120th Regiment, IV Corps, Expeditionary Foreign Legion.*

EXPEDITIONARY FOREIGN LEGION - The Xo

For Gallant and Meritorious Service, Sr. Legionnaire T. Habbit is Promoted to Lance Caporal.

He takes it, and his eyes mist as he reads the words and looks at the framed promotion certificate, with a new lance caporal stripe and all his awards arranged under the glass.

"Here, it's not new; it's mine from *The Xo*," you hand him a folded, worn, and faded desert smock, the type that is worn over everything but the equipment harness. It has a high neck gaiter with a drawstring to close it up to keep the blowing sand out and a hood worn under the helmet, usually. The two large slash hand pockets zip close. It's constructed of mid-weight cotton, rayon, and polyester with a desert camouflage pattern. An 117th Regiment patch is on the right mid-sleeve, a name tape *Baker* on the center chest, and a worn lance caporal stripe sewn under the regiment patch.

He takes it and struggles to put it on. You gently help him. Now you have drawn attention from the staff and some of his pals.

"Let me take your picture, Mr. Habbit. Face this way." He turns and pulls you alongside him.

You straighten the smock and place your Kepi blanc on his head and turn the certificate in a better position.

"Hurray! Hurray! Lance Caporals Baker and Habbit! *Ad legionem!*" he shouts.

"*Ad legionem!*" you answer back. *To the legion.*

"We celebrate in customary fashion," you look around. The staff has left you alone again.

You pull out a tin and a thick sealed foil packet. Your uncle watches you. "What is this?"

"You had this, didn't you? Whiz-n-Boards?"

He smiles, the recollection coming slowly. You open the tin and rip the packet, handing him a cheesed cracker. "A fine promotion party it is," he says.

"Ahh, but we wash it down, yes?" You look around again and pull the last item out of the cloth bag.

"How long has it been since you had *King Xobian Beer*?" You open the swing-top bottle. You could never have saved this all this time, but you found a bottle in the PX at the base.

"Not long enough! Does it still taste like saltwater and oil?"

"It's better than the Palanquin Rice Beer."

"Ahh, that's good," he says, taking a drink and handing it back, then taking a bite of his cracker. "Old times."

When it's time to go, you walk him to his room and place the framed case on his dresser beside the picture of Aunt Dottie. "Is this good?"

"Yes. She would have been so happy to see you and what you did. I'm proud of you."

"I'm proud of you too, Uncle Hab." You kiss him goodbye on the cheek and walk out.

CHAPTER 12

Level Up – **Delta (Dog) 1/107th II Corps**

The assault is scheduled for 0525 at the breaking of the dawn. You are assigned to 4th Platoon, Dog Company, 1/107th and are one of two designated company snipers. Your ship, your home for the past two weeks, is the FACS *Andover Hill LC96*. The target is the *Sand Flea Islands*. They are part of a large archipelago group in the North Chaloosa Sea, where the Chaloosa have begun constructing a deep-water port. The port would directly threaten the regiments of I Corps in the AC. The central Summa government has pressed the National Army to maintain the foothold once establishing the beachhead. Second Fleet, with both of the 2nd and 5th battalions of the 106th and 107th, is poised to steam in from the south, where they have been operating in a feint since their deployment over a month ago. The 1st Fleet will sail directly to the *Sand Flea Islands* upon their deployment in two months. That involves the entire 106th and 107th Regiments in a single assault and containment action. That's massive.

The invasion is not going to be easy. The counter-offensive by the Chaloosa is already underway, with shipborne attack helos and land-based fixed wings launching from either the unfinished island airfields or the northern Chaloosa mainland bases and refueled in flight.

You are among many of the soon-to-be landed EFL forces that stand on the decks of the 3rd Fleet, watching the naval and air battle. A large battle is occurring overhead, the heavy missile cruisers, anti-missile frigates, and escort ships all belting it out, scores of erratic air-to-ship missiles falling harmlessly into the sea. Trails of unending streams of AA and AP whip into the sky. You gaze further out to one of several detached battles involving smaller groups of fleet landing support ships and fuel oil tankers. A landing support ship is under an intense barrage, its escorts battling it out. You move to a group of shipmen and ship's mates that are part of the deck damage control teams. GQ is up; DDC is waiting in trepidation for its role if needed.

"Come on now! Give it to 'em!" One of the mates is locked on the distant battle.

One of the escorts takes a hit, and you observe a fire on her deck in the darkening night.

"Keep swinging, Girl!" Another calls out, the attention fixed now on the looming disaster.

Another missile connects; the explosion is heard over the water.

"They got her anti-missile array. That's not good." Another 2nd class mate observes.

A smaller escort charges into the fray, assisting her struggling sister.

"There you go! You got a tomcat by your side now, Girl. Keep your head up! Keep punching away!" The battle has attracted a larger crowd, all rooting for the injured medium escort.

The intensity is fierce, with the smell of blood in the air. Another escort leaves her assigned position to cover the beleaguered warship. The battle rages for more than an hour; the streams of naval AA gunnery glow in the night. An occasional missile finds its way. The jamming from the smaller escort ships allows for the defeat of the Marauders and attack helos. An enemy missile finds its way through and hits the injured ship. Her own defenses never waver during the whole of the attack. A massive explosion rocks the night.

"They got her magazines. Damn." A calm but solemn air comes over the onlookers.

The ship is completely ablaze; no returning air defense is seen now. A second explosion reverberates across the water. "Her fuel tanks. She's gone. Good fight to the end, 'ol Girl. You took it to 'em," the 2nd class mate says with reverence.

Your mood is somber, fearful. You watch as one of the smaller escorts continues her aggressive response and circling of the stricken ship.

"What was that? A cruiser?" A young shipman 3rd class asks, his own fears and inexperience of his first action giving him away.

"No, Landsman, that's probably a frigate or escort frigate by her size and firepower. The other two are corvettes. Mean little shits. You wanna make sure you never get berthed below a frigate, though. A cruiser is the *Double-A* ticket ride. The birds know better than to go after them, even though the action is usually heavy on whatever they are picketing. If you land an escort corvette, look out, all action." The mate instructs his young charge.

After another half-hour and the sound of a muffled explosion, the ship disappears, the fires extinguished by the engulfing waters of the sea. The air attacks subside; the aircraft regroup for the coming morning invasion. You bow your head; you have no idea which ship it was of the numerous fleet group. Your own lack of naval experience and intelligence thwarts your conclusion. You head below decks with the other EFLs, the lure of sleep heavy with the late hour, but the tension and stress give no relief. It is almost 2330; wake-up and breakfast are scheduled for 0300, and loading of ALTCs at 0400. The first wave, which you are a part of, will assemble on the seaward side of the FACS starting at 0430. The beach assault is scheduled to begin at 0525.

The majority of the present battalion has been together for years, training and growing as any standard unit. Naturally, the individual companies took on replacements, seasoned Sr. legs and lance caporals, and Salty Legs for tour after tour, the regular rotation of all regiments. The appearance or arrival of a lone lance caporal is not even noticed. *Here you are – fill in the blank – Sr. Legionnaire/Lance Caporal Nobody. This is your assignment; see you on the beach.* That you began your first cruise on OBSF instead of with an amphib assault company only makes it more difficult. You have no connections to anyone in your company. You know no one. You are assigned as a designated sniper, which also adds to your isolation and mystique. The snipers from the AC are seen as mythical legends by the salt-n-sand legs and as stone-cold killers by those veterans that served in other theaters.

EXPEDITIONARY FOREIGN LEGION -The Xo

Level Up – Dawn, Day One

Amphib Assault Mission #17 Brief

Difficult 25 PP 60% success

Character Summary

Your Assigned Mission Is To Assault the Beach and Stay Alive.

Summary:

You are assigned as a sniper to your company. Assault the beach and seek out and eliminate all targets of opportunity.

The ALTC is bouncing and dipping. You have experienced similar motions on the small escort corvette *JW Nowly* in the fo'ward compartment of 2D-FC1-B. You have no physical discomfort. The others of your squad are nearly all sick, puking out their light breakfast. The caporal of the squad takes great pleasure in the misery of the legs and Sr. legs that are made up predominately of single tour Xo veterans. You have had little interaction with him. Your mission is as separate from the platoon as his interest in you. A few of the legs look at you with wonderment and outright fear. You are an apparition, a ghost of the battlefield, a rumored higher being.

You returned from leave and joined Dog 1/107 a few days before sailing, reporting to the barracks assigned to your FACS *Andover Hill*. You had no extra duties assigned to you, unlike the remainder of the company and battalion. On the sixth day before deployment, the snipers of the battalions from the entire battle group were pulled off separately from the companies and housed in a training area barracks. Range time, concealment technique, review, and practice were the order of the day. Night fire, movement, camouflage, target acquisition, mission overview, and other topics were all covered. The companies would have no command oversight over you or your fellow snipers; you follow battalion and regiment command orders and direction. You recognized several others from the course two years ago, the AC, or other tours. The group was of esteemed and reputable legionnaires, ranking as high as Sr. caporal. You felt small and insignificant.

The coxswain gives the alert to the caporal, thirty seconds! You carry very little other than two canteens of water and eight magazines of ammo, forty rounds, more than a sufficient amount to last the first hours of the assault. You wear a self-made, customized camouflage coverall-type smock, fitted with natural vegetation, neutral-coloured, cloth strips, a soft-cover Boonie hat, and your face is painted in a pattern of light green, tan, and brown. You are not expected to fire in a wild, excited, or undisciplined manner. Each of your shots is to be calculated, seeking out only important targets, no matter the situation around you. Leaders. The odds of your being killed in the deployment from the ALTC are 1:50. The enemy snipers are also observing and identifying potential important targets.

You feel the surge of the ALTC on the shore, the bumpy, grinding, abrupt change from a fluid motion to that of difficulty. You also identify the sensation of impact to the body of the armored carrier. The ALTC is taking fire. The standard practice of the assault craft crew is to navigate to a set line of disembarkation, offload assaulting forces, provide covering fire until the force is established, and then retreat to the FACS for the next assault group. That was the standard procedure. Your thoughts drift back to Lt. Commander JW Nowly as a young Shipman 2nd Class and her gallant action covering her offloaded assault force.

While the front of the ALTC with its reinforced heavy armor and the AP gun take the brunt of the incoming fire, the legionnaires exit the rear ramp, running to the sides of the ALTC and then move forward in a controlled and ordered maneuver. You run to the right side, crouching, and begin to follow a slight ravine, probably a natural drainage from the inland areas.

Scenario 1: With no fault of your own, you take a round clean through the heart. Your blood flows out and you drop to your knees and then fall face forward. An amphib beach assault is at a near three percent death casualty rate overall. You are dead.

Scenario 2: You are now alone and independent of 4th Platoon, Dog Company, 1/107. You slide into a depression and look for a target. You ignore the cries, screams, and pleas for help from the men and women of the platoon who just landed with you. You see a round strike a wounded legionnaire 10 yards from you, ripping his chest wide open. You scan for the possible source. There. A hole covered with *zalza* logs. You see the shooter. You take the shot. Another legionnaire falls, her cries buried in the sounds of ALTCs screeching in reverse to retreat back into the relative safety of the water.

On and on you make a target and then act. You are in this spot long enough. You cannot be marked or tracked to a definite spot or an artillery round or tube-grenade will find you. This is the hard part, moving up to cover the platoon and others. The beach doesn't look like the overview suggested in the orientation. The vegetation is not right; the colours and terrain are lighter. You are too dark. You move to a more covered position than you occupied during the past hour. You hurriedly change out the vegetation material that you can, rolling in the sandy soil, smearing your face with the sand of the hole, tossing handfuls onto your back. You creep up to the edge of the promenade, the morning in full bloom. An EFL AP gun rattles off a short burst, aiming at some equal position or sniper. You wait. The report echoes, the shot strikes the AP gunner in the throat, and you witness helplessly his spasm of death, with his partner, and the sniper that killed him. You shoot. You move on.

The morning grows hotter and more chaotic. The next wave lands and overruns the small advance of those before them, thinking they have won the advance, only to be struck down in greater numbers than the first wave. During the wild fighting you inch up, now even more cautious, if that were possible, of being mistaken by your own forces. An inexperienced, non-trained sniper of the next wave comes running by, momentarily looking at you, and then settles in at a destroyed log bunker. The available trained snipers were minimal, so they took from the ranks those that had high qualification scores and folded them in with the group during the six-day refresher. These legionnaires are good shots, but it takes more than that.

You watch him, wanting to yell at him to keep down, to go slow, but you can't. He is too impatient and slumps lifeless into the muddy water of the hole. After a few minutes, you crawl to his side, and take four of his magazines to replace the three you have used already. You pull his canteen from its pouch and drink the remainder of yours and slide his in. You peer through a crack in the logs. There he is, taking shots at will, behind a mini-gun team. His sudden silence alerts the AG and he bumps the gunner and the team sends a wild spray over the field to their front. The gunner's head jerks back and he half falls onto the AG. The man pushes his comrade off and takes the receiver, and never gets a burst off.

A fire-team of some squad runs up, a caporal yells at you, "Get moving! Get moving! Get out of that hole and shoot something! We got to take this beach!"

"Get the hell away from me," you reply, looking for another target from the crack.

Immediately he is shot in the leg and falls in the open. Another of his squad is hit in the groin. The other two drop in the hole with you, firing at nothing, wasting their ammo. One of them reaches out and attempts to drag the caporal in, and is hit.

Great, you muse, unwelcome company. The caporal is yelling in pain, the groin victim withering. The shooter is toying with them, trying to get another one to help.

"Come on Caporal Hughes, you can make it," the uninjured leg calls out.

"Don't move," you order. Another enemy team sets up on the mini-gun and begins firing.

The leg crawls to the caporal and tugs on his collar, half pulling him to the hole. The caporal is hit again, screaming out. You shoot the gunner. Another sniper is out there too, striking the groin victim in the arm, just for the pain and noise. You have to find him before he tires of this game and kills all of them. You ease back down into the mud and shift over to the right. There he is. You finish him and then the new AG.

"Pull them in. Stay away from me."

You crawl out of the hole, on a slant to the right, and up five yards and settle in. A few more moves and you can get to a small mound from the backside. The elevation is about six feet higher than the surrounding area. It takes you two hours to make it. The third wave hasn't even made it as far as the first wave and has stalled. A fourth wave is going to be needed just to secure the beachhead for the night.

Level Up – Dark, The First Night

The little knoll is an ideal spot, and had been manned at the beginning of the morning. The bunker contains four dead Chaloosa, killed by a grenade. The attack cost nearly a platoon, all scattered on the slope of the mound. The Chaloosa are going to want it back, and that will probably happen during the night. You find a Demo bag on one of the Sr. legs. You cannot rig a booby trap inside, the threat of your own forces setting it off is too great. You have to rig it against the enemy on their down hill side. That means crawling around in the open. That's dumb. There is no way you will be able to hold out during the night, you have to leave it. You rip the shirts off the bodies of the enemy and hang them on the log barricade facing your side with a rudimentary skull-and-crossbones etched in blood, a warning. You rig the Demo, in a step-series, hoping to get two hits before the knoll is taken. You leave and crawl to a pit. It turns out it is a slit trench and you move away but keep close to it for the smell to ward off possible scouts or search patrols.

During the night there are scattered bursts of firing, screams, and pleas from the wounded for water and rescue. The Chaloosa are crawling out of their holes and killing the wounded they find. The knoll explodes; there are screams of several men. A Chaloosa grenade is thrown in the bunker followed by shooting. Another explosion a few minutes later gives you peace of mind that your booby trap worked. There is not another attempt during the night. In the early dawn you watch as a three-man team edges up the mound dragging a mini-gun. They are cautious of more traps or even an EFL gun crew. You hit the lead man in the buttocks, *what's fair is fair*, you figure. That wound causes extreme pain and an inability to function. You shoot the second man through the neck and the third in the chest as he turns to shoot in your general direction. The three early dawn shots are not alone. Other targets of opportunity are waking up the weary combatants. The next wave of reinforcing legionnaires is beginning their landing.

Level Up – The Second Day

You have not slept now for over 24 hours. The sounds of the night, buzzing, chirping, croaking, rustling, squeals, all remind you of the Palanquin. The assaulting wave, the last of the remaining battalion, the 6/106th, drives hard into the outer fortifications, aided by the remnants of the first day. You crawl up, taking a good elevated position on a low roof of a command bunker. The outer perimeter is secured. At least on the beach side. There is another line of ditches and bunkers further inland. For now, at least, you are allowed a short break.

The commander of the assault, the under-corps commander, Brigadier General S. Renard, landed with the second wave the day before and was mortally wounded, dying after being evacuated to the hospital ship, *The Rosemary*. The 106th Regiment Commander, Colonel A. Pittman is now the invasion's ranking, and therefore, acting assault commander. None of that is any consequence to you. As the afternoon wanes to late day, you are summoned to the command post, a buried and heavily fortified bunker of zalza logs. The *zalza* is a tropical fruit-producing tree of a hard, encased nut the size of an adult male's head, with a white pulpy meat and a sweet, almost milky juice. The wood of the tree is hard and dense, the bark rough, segmented and patchy, nearly saw-toothed, like the fronds. There is no natural or outside ventilation in the bunker, only electric fans blowing the hot and humid air around, like an incubator or more accurately, a convection oven.

There are nearly two dozen other snipers from the 27 companies of the first three assault waves gathered in the cramped room. A mission brief is about to begin. You begin to realize, as the rest of those of your specialized skill set do, that of all the trained and untrained snipers of the assault, 72, this is all of you that remain. The truth is only roughly half, 30, of the first three waves were actual MCWS certified snipers. None of the fourth wave were, and none of those are casualties or present in the bunker for this brief. Of the 21 present, four are non-certified, instantly earning the respect from the rest of you. Their survival over the trained snipers and their unproven peers demonstrates their ability to perform at a higher operational level, no matter the individual circumstances of their ordeal.

The briefing begins.

Level Up – Reconnoiter the Enemy Position

Amphib Assault Mission #18 Brief

    Difficult 25 PP 60% success

    Character Summary

    Your Assigned Mission Is To Recon the Enemy Line and Stay Alive.

    Summary:

    Along with and separate from others of your group, you are to infiltrate and reconnoiter the enemy positions behind their forward lines. If the opportunity to destroy or incapacitate a strategic asset should arise, the freedom to make that decision is open. The primary mission objective is not one of physical destruction, but of Intel.

You are each assigned an area of operation, so as not to interfere with another. Your objective is a suspected AA and missile jamming station. As with all the area behind the lines and adjacent to the airstrip construction, a heavy number of anti-drone batteries exist. Whether there are anti-personnel, GSR, ground surveillance radar, or high intensity-low sound, auto-fire security guns along the perimeter is unknown. Each of the newly formed group, now known as *Sand Fleas*, are given the option of *bowing out,* with no negative notation to their record. Not one hesitated in telling the OIC to *bugger off.*

You walk out of the bunker and feel instantly cooler, the heat of the island has to be well above 100 degrees with as high humidity, but the bunker was worse. As the others of the group walk out one stops and stands next to you while lighting a stub of a cigar.

"Hey, I know you. You were with the Jungle Fox, 3/114. Right?" he opens.

"Yep. I think I remember you. You were 1st Platoon."

"That's right. We were patrolling with 3rd Platoon once when you *yokels* set off that seed pod mound. Ha-ha! That cloud floated for miles. You used to hang around the pavilion a lot, pass the days."

"Well, mate, I guess you were there too, doing the same thing. Baker," you hold out your hand.

"Winnon," he takes it and you shake. "I guess it's good we finally met and made acquaintance. Looks like this may be it. The end of the line for a pair of Palanquin Jungle Foxes."

You study him. He's a tempered veteran of many hard victories with what you suspect were low odds.

"I don't know. I'm not ready to fold just yet. Hey, I'll wager your last payout, where are you? Sr. leg? Hand me 42 summa."

He looks at you with a confounded expression. "What?"

"I'll bet you die out there tonight. I bet your last payout. Go ahead and hand it over now so I don't have to track down your body."

"You are out of your mind, Baker."

"You welching on a bet?"

"No! I'm not taking that bet!"

"What have you got to lose? You lose, well, it doesn't matter. You win, well I pay you back."

"Hahaha! You are insane." He laughs, suddenly seeing the stacked odds in your favor. "I'll tell you what, I'll buy the rounds. You meet me here in the morning, say 0800."

"I don't know. I like to sleep in, let's make it 0830."

"Deal. If you're late, you buy."

"It's a deal." You shake on it, pat the other on the back and turn to go your separate ways. The reality of the next meeting a painful acknowledgment of insurmountable odds. The challenge to succeed is more than a simple wish of good luck; it's a life-pact.

You stop at a supply point and find a case of GPXR. The QM caporal hesitates in releasing the rounds you request.

"What are you saying? You can't issue me the rounds I need because you need authorization to verify I am a specialized shooter? Are you serious? Look at me. Do I look like a regular leg? Am I carrying a GPS? I don't have time to play stupid games," you draw your GPC and aim it at his head.

"Issue me 15 rounds of GPXR, and let me move on. I'm tired."

The caporal quickly counts out the rounds and starts to place a RF on the table, then pulls it back.

"You can log it as Lance Caporal D. Baker. Dog, 1/107." You collect the rounds and fill an empty mag you retained from the night before. The remaining 10 rounds you slip in the large chest pocket of the smock you wear.

"Have you got a combat meal box?"

"Yes, Lance Caporal," he answers, even though he outranks you as he sets the box on the makeshift table.

You take the box and walk away, the small line moving aside.

"Did you see that?"

"That sniper just pulled a sidearm on the QM for rounds!"

"Are you serious?"

"That was the sniper I was in the hole with yesterday that saved Caporal Hughes! Shot four dead, Bam! Bam! Bam! Bam! Just like that. Holy cow! I'm sure that's the same one that rigged *Bunker Hill* last night and shot the crew this morning before it was retaken! *Skull and Crossbones!*"

You follow the direction from the briefing to the starting-off point. You look out over the area where you will advance later. There is a company of some battalion on the line, dug-in, several yards to your front. You check in with the company commander, a captain, and his sergent to let them know and to pass the word to their company that a sniper will be working to their front.

The captain nods his head and directs the sergent to pass the word. You sit down to eat and wait for dark then start out.

Level Up – Sand Fleas

Your passage through the 300 yards or more of broken jungle, bombed out craters, open rolling terrain, and a cultivated field is nothing less than a feat of great daring, impossible odds, and massive luck. It takes you almost five hours to reach the forward perimeter of trenches and fortified firing bunkers. Along the lines behind you, various companies are scheduled to initiate AP and GPS firing at specific times for 30 minutes and then halt. This will give the cover you and the other Sand Fleas need as a distraction. The company you are working in front of, India 4/107, began an hour after you went outside the wire. They will have two more sessions during the late night and early morning. With the time it took for you to achieve the enemy lines, you have very little room to waste before having to start back under the cloak of darkness.

During the night you hear the sharp crack, the distinctive gas expulsion of the GPXR in short but brief exchanges mixed with enemy firing, sometimes followed by a similar series of GPC shots. The only reason for that would be the unnerving reality that several of your fellow Sand Fleas ran into patrols and were found and possibly eliminated. You try not to dwell on that.

You work your way to a position to observe an AA/Jamming array along with a drone mini-gun battery. You have not seen any sign of GSR or HILS. The section of runway here is nearly complete with the repairs from the initial pre-landing missile assault three days ago. In the distance you can see several Marauders under their maintenance and security shrouds. The security in that area is high. If this drone battery and AA jamming station can be taken out, a shipborne missile barrage could play havoc on Marauders taking off from a still intact airstrip. That means having to extract from this location cleanly, giving the enemy no indication that this area has been surveyed. The journey back is harrowing, a patrol nearly spots you, searching and firing blindly into the jungle, attempting to pull you out. They finally continue on their way, deciding that there is nothing in the deep blackness of the night other than a stray animal. In the early morning, India Company's scheduled firing catches them. You keep low and crawl towards the line. With dawn, the sun comes up with 50 yards of jumbled open ground remaining. You are stuck in the open.

A round explodes to your left and you lay still. Another hits a zalza log at your feet. The sniper is too far away, trying to zero in on you. The ground dips to a slight depression here, the jungle foliage stripped away by the barrage days ago. The ground is littered with broken trees and splintered logs, a twisted muddy maze of obstacles. You can see the positions of India. A burst of fire comes from the line aimed into the jungle, providing you a momentary reprieve to seek cover. The log at your feet is the closest and you quickly slide beside it, taking a long position oriented at nearly a right angle to the jungle. The depression gives additional concealment. You begin to dig with your hands and knife, cutting a shallow half trench. The supporting fire shifts to the left and then stops. A round strikes the ground below your feet, the sniper unsure of your position now.

You remain in the shallow trench for the next two hours until a tropical downpour obscures the visibility in the immediate area for a few brief moments before passing. You slowly crawl to an uprooted stump, mixing in with the tangle of roots. The slick mud and ground vegetation aid in your disappearance. You orient facing the possible location of the shooter. And wait.

The rain lets off, the sun suddenly pops out, and the humidity soars along with the temperature. You have a canteen of water remaining from the night, but the movement now to retrieve it is too much risk. You will just have to endure the pain of thirst. The hole is partially filled with rainwater and the mud adheres to your body and uniform, creating a single, unified pattern of the surrounding ground environment. You wait and watch.

Your adversary is no doubt searching for you also, knowing that you had no time to crawl back to the lines and unsure how far you moved from the last known position. He waits. A mortar round explodes within five yards of the log you had been hiding behind, sending shards of hot jagged metal into the air. Another rocks the area to the left, down from the log. The shifted fire from India worked in creating a false course of direction. Your movement to the right was successfully masked. The mortar team is now enlarging a box, their own position behind or within the strip of jungle between the lines. The hunt is on. A micro Sat-link radio would have been ideal to have now, performing as a FO. Even last night, calling in the location of the drone battery would have been beneficial, allowing you to report and remain in position throughout the day. The enemy mortars are out of range to hit India. They would have to move forward to the edge of the jungle, which they dare not do until the EFL sniper is accounted for.

The afternoon drags on; the mortars ceased hours ago, finally giving up. You fight closing your eyes, even for a minute. The water in the hole is warm, tepid, thickening, the mud drying on you, along the length of your body. The GPXR is coated, all but the suppressor and the breach. A small protective balloon covers the muzzle, a quick wipe from your hand earlier taking away the thin layer of mud that had lightly covered it. Your mags are protected from the mud by their pouches, the wetness not so much. You have only four remaining, the others lost or discarded during the first day's operation and movement. You see movement in the foliage, a flicker of non-natural environment. A jacket, a hat, a pack. It could be a patrol or the sniper. You move your eyes to the left and right, not focusing on the spot. There. Again. Only a slight disturbance in the bushes and ground covering. Low to the ground. The position is sure now, the direction from your left to right. He had been to your left all along.

His decision to move to gain a better observation vantage point is costly; up to now, his position was unknown. Whether he believes you are still out here or he is unsure of your status shows that he is impatient. The mortars either killed you or they didn't. The rain allowed you to slip away or it didn't. The fact that your status is unknown is key. He moves again, settling in at the edge of the jungle and the ripped up open space. The range to effectively fire upon the India positions is too great; he needs 25 more yards. Your range is good, between 90 and a 100 yards. The late afternoon burns on, the heat saps your energy. You long for a drink of water. Not taking it pains you, yet you remain still.

He moves again after an hour, crawling to a clump of uprooted jumyal bushes, a waxy broad leaf ground vegetation that grows two feet high. You have a good shot and are about to put him down when you see additional movement to his rear. You wait. It's the mortar team! They begin to set up on the inside edge of the jungle, easily in range of India now. How much longer can you afford to wait? He is obviously going to move in closer to give them target coordinates. At the jumyal he cannot effectively observe India, so he will have to move again. You wait. The mortar team is set up and waiting, placing stakes at pre-marked degree headings. He remains still for another hour, while the mortar team establishes a secondary position. Suddenly you catch another movement and you realize this is the sniper, the first individual is a FO for the mortar team. If you had taken him out it would have given your position away. Your patience pays off.

The sniper, it is the second one, you are positive of it now, is much more careful than the FO. He selects a position where he can cover the FO and has a good field of fire on India's position. He is within your range and field without you having to adjust your position too much. You line him up and squeeze the trigger. He's out. The FO now is stuck in the void of the open ground with a good hour of light left and you let him be for the moment. He begins to direct the rounds onto you and you quickly and purposefully take out the *gunner*, not the *fire direction controller*, FDC. The two security riflemen lay down in the bushes, waiting to see what happens. The armorer/loader steps up to replace the gunner, the one who *drops* the round in the tube, and you wait until he *hangs the round* and then shoot him in the leg, which makes him miss the tube. The mortar round may or may not cook off, but the team scatters anyway and you nail the FDC. The security team begins firing wildly in your direction, but really have no idea where you are. The FO has you sighted in and attempts to finish you. He is a good marksman and gets close but loses the shootout.

You return your attention to the mortar team which has regrouped at the secondary position and begins to hang rounds once again.

Now the India positions have opened up along with the companies on either side, and a slugfest ensues, with EFL mortars and rockets ripping into the thin jungle strip. The whole of the day had seen sporadic firing on the line, with no major engagements or forward progress attempted. The entire line erupts now, minus missiles from off-shore due to the jamming. Mortars and rockets are lobbed from both sides. You put down the alternate loader and FDC and then the gunner as he runs away. An EFL round scores a hit on the site and the tube is destroyed. You ponder remaining in place and continuing your firing position, but regiment needs the Intel from your mission, and you carefully wiggle out of your mud encased cocoon and crawl back to the lines.

A hail for a challenge is given when you are finally spotted. You pause.

"Sand!" from the closest hole.

You respond quietly, "Flea."

"Come in."

You continue crawling and flop into the first hole you come to. The two legionnaires squatting in it look at you with alarm and even fear.

"You been out there all day? Since last night?" One asks.

"You got any water?" Your voice cracks dryly.

You take the offered canteen and give it a tip up, the hot water leaking around the side of your mouth and down your chin. You pour some over your head removing your hat, wiping your eyes.

"Baker?" A voice belonging to a colour sergent calls over the edge of the hole, the eyes of astonishment or admiration, awe.

"Yeah?" You manage with difficulty.

"Good grief, Lance Caporal. I watched you put down no less than eight men in two minutes! We lost you this morning after the rain, thought you were making your way back here slowly. You look just like the mud. Come on." He holds his hand over the hole and pulls you up.

Together you both walk past the India CP and down the line towards the Assault CP, the same bunker you met the day before for the briefing.

"How many of us made it back in already," you ask, not looking around, feeling the eyes of nearly everyone you pass upon you.

"Eleven so far, but we believe many are like you, stuck and waiting to come in after dark."

You nod your head, wanting to ask, but afraid to hear the report, hoping Winnon is one of those that made it in.

"I got a report yesterday passed down to me concerning a deadly threat with a GPC towards a QM over ammo issuance. I think that pretty much has been taken care of now, what do you think?"

"Yeah, I think that sort of thing won't be a problem anymore." Your answer is full of double meaning.

The colour sergent stares at you a moment and then laughs, "Ha-ha, I tell you what Lance Caporal, you got spunk. No, I guess not; that message has been sent loud and clear. But do me a favor. Try to be a little more low-key in the rear here. Col. Pittman wants to talk with you and then first sergent has something to add. Did you ever make it to their lines?"

You turn your head and give the colour sergent a glance and then smile, "Yeah, Colour Sergent, I got in."

"Yep, the way you operate, I figured as much. It was all quiet on your sector until they started hunting for you earlier this morning in the jungle. We weren't sure if they got you or not. Then we spotted you as the sniper was pinging you at that log. We never saw you up to that point and then lost you again in the rain. You're smooth, a real pro. Word is you were the one responsible for what they are calling *Bunker Hill*. That right?"

"No. The platoon around the hump took the bunker, getting the four inside. I just kept them out during the night. Those legs deserve that credit."

The colour sergent continues walking. "A Caporal Hughes reports you took out a mini-gun crew and a sniper earlier in the morning the first day, and there is documentation in that sector that confirm multiple kills along that corridor. You been a busy shooter."

You keep walking.

The CP is right ahead, the dusk coming on now and the excitement somewhere along the line as another Sand Flea returns to the nest.

"That's a good sign," The colour sergent says, hearing the noise. You enter the bunker and report to the command staff.

You are promptly taken to the intelligence chief. The colonel comes in and the debrief begins. As you are speaking, the new arrival walks in. To your complete surprise and utter joy, it is Winnon! The both of your show a relief in your face and physical attitude, gripping the other in an embrace.

"Oh, you made it!" he says, a broad smile crossing his otherwise exhausted face.

"You're late," you respond.

The command staff gaze at the two of you, caught in the personal emotion of seemingly two mates rejoining.

"You are old mates, I assume?" Col. Pittman inquires.

"No. I guess, maybe. We served in the same company back in Palanquin over two years ago, and only met yesterday after the briefing. Ha, strange reunion service you're running here Sir," you respond.

The bunker erupts in laughter and the dire mood lifts.

After the two of you complete your debrief, you are given time to rest, eat, and join the others of your group. Corps and Legion command are brought up to speed within hours with the valuable Intel from the returning snipers. Unfortunately, due to the status of the airstrip, the Sand Fleas are needed to once again venture out and take out the drone batteries so that offshore missiles can strike the targets. Three of the group have suffered wounds that require evacuation. Nerves are peaked, and two others break, not capable to go out again. It is now assumed that the remaining eight who have not returned are MIA, and presumed dead or captured, including three of the *uncerts*. This leaves only eight of the original 54.

As you prepare to go out again, silently checking over your weapons, reloading magazines, filling canteens, writing letters home, looking at the small group of you that remain, Col. Pittman enters the small bunker where you are housed.

"It has been decided at Legion level that this group is too important to lose any more of you in this operation. You are to stand down and get some sleep. I am pulling you off the beach and sending you back to the *Andover Hill* for the night. Get out of here." His smile tells you that he is glad of the decision, glad to have some of his legionnaires safe.

The first sergent of the 106th comes in and directs the group to the beach and to a waiting ALTC. The passage through the surf and waves, and then to the large ship seems short. Not a one of you have remorse for leaving the beach, knowing that the odds were pretty much stacked against your survival on the night's op. When you unload and the shipmen and ship's mates see your appearance and condition, they instantly realize that the battle on shore is different from others. The wounded have been steadily coming, heading to the hospital ship, *The Rosemary* and the rumors have been terrifying. You are taken to a smaller billet and fall straight upon the bunks without washing or barely removing your gear. You do not hear the sounds above you, even as an intense naval fight begins. You fall fast asleep.

Level Up – Return To Hell

The next morning the small group of Sand Fleas are instructed to report to the CP to receive new orders. No one takes a shower, choosing to decline a brief feeling of comfort in order to retain their camouflage. The ride in is nervous, a little joking and catching up of where everyone came from. There is no talk of the past days, or of any exploits. There is only one Sr. caporal left, two caporals, two lance caporals and three Sr. legs. The two that broke down were transported to *The Rosemary* for psych exams and will probably be shipped home. One of them barely escaped after being spotted early the first night and hunted for the next 20 hours, killing over a dozen and completely expending his ammo, never even getting close to his objective. The three wounded will probably not recover any time soon.

Once inside *The Oven*, as you all refer to the CP, you find coffee and sausage biscuits. Without asking or invitation, you help yourselves. The collective thought is *what can they do to me*? The mental attitude of being a survivor to this point is numbing, you all feel lucky to be alive and at the same time, feel guilty to be so. Nothing is real it seems.

You stand around and wait, looking over the maps and absorbing what little Intel you can from the scattered documents left about. There are several HQ staff working, including two or three leftenants or captains. They all avoid eye contact with you and give you space to roam free, as if they were afraid to challenge any of the Sand Fleas.

From a connecting room, First Sergent Romano, of the 106th Regiment, enters and announces Col. Pittman. Even as callous or nonchalant as you all seem to be, the pride of being a legionnaire and a structured life of strict discipline prompts you to show respect to this high command officer. Sr. Caporal Stranger salutes and reports for the group.

"As you were. Gather round. Let me fill you in as to where we are this morning," Col Pittman begins.

The group quickly assembles around the acting assault commander, an air of trust and mutual respect offered and received by two groups normally as far apart as a great gulf. The colonel lowering his walls of superiority and rank to a knot of filthy, smelly, crude, and junior rank NCOs not even at company level. His open-arm approach and strategy work, quickly gaining the approval of the otherwise guarded and suspicious junior noncoms.

"We sent out three recon teams last night on the three higher priority sites you all scouted the night before. As several of you suggested, they were equipped with micro Sat-links and remained in place. Team One is at the northwest main radar jamming station. Team Two is occupying a slit trench of all places, observing the centralized CP for the enemy HQ staff of the entire island. Team Three is on the southern airstrip next to a tri-threat battery of AP, Radar Jammer, and drone mini-gun placement. Each of you, as well as those that didn't make it back, gave us valuable Intel at great loss.

"Here is what we shall do," Colonel Pittman looks at First Sergent Romano and nods his head. First Sergent now quickly snaps his fingers and motions the room clear of only the colonel's personal staff and the remaining Sand Fleas.

"Sr. Caporal Stranger."

"Yes, Colonel!"

"For your dedicated and superior service and performance, you are hereby relieved, in good standing and gratitude from active field operations pertaining to all sniper assignments. Your promotion to Sergent is effective as to this date and you will commence training operations with Juno Company, Sand Flea Field Training Course, 125th Regiment V Corps, special attachment to 106th Regiment II Corps immediately."

The words were spoken with an air of such directness and authority that it hardly registered to you or any of the group, that there was no Juno Company in the EFL structure of unit organization. It only went up to India!

"Caporals Matzo and Bahtren."

"Aye, Colonel!" They each responded, still cloudy on the Juno Company.

"You are both promoted effective this date to Sr. Caporal and are now senior sniper team leaders. Your assignments will come directly from Juno Company command."

"Sir!" they reply with precision.

"Lance Caporals Baker, Smoot."

"Yes, Colonel!" The two of you answered in unison.

"I think you see the pattern here. You are promoted to Caporal. Caporal Baker, due to your esteemed and legendary exploits, not only here but back in the AC, with a documented kill record of over two dozen and an equal or greater of undocumented, you are assigned as chief instructor of Juno Company, Sand Flea Field Training Platoon. Caporal Smoot, you will continue as an operational sniper team member."

"Aye, Sir!"

"Sr. Legionnaires Winnon and Amber, you are promoted to Lance Caporal. Lance Caporal Amber you will continue in Sand Flea Sniper team operations. Lance Caporal Winnon, also per your lauded and highly acclaimed performance, almost a dozen confirmed kills and another dozen or so unconfirmed, most of those here on the first days of the operation, you are assigned as assistant instructor to Juno Company, Sand Flea Field Training Platoon. Not bad for a couple Jungle Foxes, eh?" The colonel's quick smile gives a hint to a shared past unit station.

"Yes Colonel Pittman, Sir!"

"Sr. Legionnaire Goffrey."

"Yes Sir!" The single remaining *uncert* sniper of the Sand Flea group answers.

"You are relieved from this command, promoted to Lance Caporal and will proceed, post haste, to new assignment MCWS and Mountain Sniper Course…"

There is an immediate shifting and air of discontent among the group. The attitude is not against newly promoted Lance Caporal Goffrey, rather, it is in favor of him and against a perceived sense of disrespect shown to him for his accomplishment while assigned to the newly esteemed Sand Flea Group. You are all survivors and suffered through tremendous odds and situations the past few days.

Sergent Stranger quickly looks at the rest of the group and speaks for all of you, "Pardon the insubordination, Colonel, but, Lance Caporal Goffrey is one of us, Sir. He stands as one of only eight in this Sand Flea Group of 54 that began three, four days ago. He don't need any certificate to say he stands, belongs with us. He's already earned that respect and privilege just standing here today."

"Aye,"

"Yep, that's right,"

"I agree, with Sergent, Sir,"

"One hundred percent,"

"He made it off the beach. That's his certificate,"

"Forty-six others, agree, I'm sure,"

Each of the remaining six voice support for Lance Caporal Goffrey.

"Sir, I, I. Thank you for the opportunity, Colonel. My scores were not high enough to qualify for Mountain Sniper Course and I am honored to be counted in with such a prestigious and esteemed group as my temporary fellows, but I..."

"This is intolerable and undisciplined behavior from a group of low rank noncoms..." First Sergent Romano starts.

Colonel Pittman waves him down, "Easy, Top."

"Sergent Stranger, you are now Sergent-chef, an old rank from past days, you command the whole of Juno Company and answer directly to me. I will take no excuses. Is that clear?"

"Yes, Colonel!"

"You run the company and will select your under-sergent from the company. This company, Juno, I am sure each of you have questioned the identity and organization of its status by now, is off ledger. Do you understand?"

The group stood still.

"You are a special assignment detail, company, platoon, only in service here on this archipelago. Only for this operation. No formal action reports to Corps or Legion. I require total commitment and results. This island group must be taken. Juno Company, Sand Flea

Field Training Platoon has a dual mission. First and foremost is the securement and complete control of the archipelago. Secondly, the forming of a standing platoon of field trained and competent sniper teams from existing personnel of the 106th and 107th Regiments. The on-site and cross-certificated graduates will play a significant role in accomplishing this objective. Without outside interference, Caporal Baker and Lance Caporal Winnon will develop, institute, and operate a course to train and provide capable and successful snipers for immediate field operational missions."

You heard the words but are still dumbfounded by the meaning. *What?* You have no experience, no training in advance training techniques or structure. You have no experience in running a class, let alone a course as significant and important or life-altering as a sniper course. How are you even to start? Where is it to be conducted? What facilities are available? Who is to choose applicants? Or where are they to come from? What standards of proficiency are to be achieved, and how? The massive complexity is only beginning to ripple through your conscience. Given just a little time, you are sure you can compile a much larger list of important questions and series of steps that will need to be completed prior to even organizing a sniper training course, yet alone operating from square one.

"Sergent-chef Stranger, Caporal Baker, Lance Caporals Winnon and Goffrey remain here, the rest of you are dismissed to Colour Sergent Brockmann. You are now Juno Company, 125th Regiment V Corps. Get cleaned up, refitted, and get some chow."

"Aye, Sir!" The group files out, led by the colour sergent that escorted you yesterday. Evidently, he is Brockmann.

"Caporal Baker."

"Yes, Colonel," you respond, the weight of the looming assignment more a direct obstacle than the audience of the regiment commander.

"I understand you may feel an overbearing sense of expectation, but let me break it down to a level in which I believe you can process the assignment. What skills were the most important to you that you took away from the Mountain Sniper Course? What was the first thing, the very first action you took upon hitting the beach? What kept you alive the first day? What was your personal goal that first night? How did you accomplish your mission the second night? What advice or skill would you want most desperately to pass on to another sniper? Why are you still alive, Caporal Baker? What makes you more successful than the other snipers that landed on the beach three days ago? We have lost eight more of the snipers from the fourth wave, those that are not included in your group. We are running out of marksmen, Caporal Baker. I need you to train them to survive."

You stand there in complete shock. This is too much responsibility.

"Sir, if I may interject on the caporal's behalf. I do not possess the top tier kills that the caporal has, but I have been successful and survived a few theaters," Stranger opens. "Baker has the knowledge, skill, and drive that few have. Let me sit and process the scope of this with the whole team. I believe we can formulate a rough and ready course that will be suitable and provide what is needed, while at the same time keep our assets alive. You have given me complete oversight of sniper team operations? Is that correct, Sir?"

"That is correct, as long as you provide results, Sergent-chef Stranger."

"Affirmative, Colonel. Where is the AO of Juno Company? I need to see the service folders of all legionnaires with a Sniper score."

"Your AO is where you request it to be Sergent-chef. As for now, Colour Sergent Brockmann has a burned out ALTC for you. All sniper qual candidates of the assault force from the 106th and 107th Regiments' have been exhausted. You will need to make a call for volunteers. I believe that is all you need for now to get started. I need competent, trained snipers within two weeks Sergent-chef Stranger."

You look up at the colonel. The others shift unsteadily. Two weeks? In a combat environment? Holy smokes! Mountain Sniper was three weeks in a semi-controlled environment. Here, where can the course even operate in a safe atmosphere? How would the final exam of a simulated drop occur and the approach to a mission objective? All the sniper score legionnaires of these two regiments have been expended? What was the pool to select from?

You are still in shock as Sergent-chef Stranger leads you out of The Oven to round up the others. You walk in a semi-state of distraction, still self-consciously aware of the hazards around you. Before you know it, you arrive at the burned out ALTC. This is home for the near future, you guess. The lances are tasked to quickly throw everything out of the back, including the discovered remains of a crew member, who is respectfully placed in a discarded poncho and marked for pick up by graves registration.

"Well, here we are. Comments? Questions? Concerns? I need a plan to take to Colonel Pittman by afternoon. We start in the morning. What you got?"

The discussions open up, each one of the eight voicing some opinion, concern or suggestion.

CHAPTER 13

Level Up – **Juno Company Sand Fleas**

Sniper Assault Mission #19 Brief

Difficult 25 PP 60% success

Character Summary

Your Assigned Mission Is To Establish the Sand Flea Sniper Course.

Summary:

With the remaining Sand Fleas, you are directed to organize, train and qualify successful sniper candidates for operations on the Sand Flea Archipelago.

"We gotta figure out where we can train these shooters. On the beach? The jungle? Along the crater strip?" offers Winnon, unafraid to speak out.

"What are we going to teach them? Who are we going to instruct? The colonel said all the sniper quals are gone."

"What! From the Corps?" Smoot replies, obviously shocked by the known casualty numbers.

"No, he said from the two regiments." Goffrey adds. He is still with the group, at least for now, his actual assignment unclear.

"Well, I think he meant from the assault force of the regiments," Stranger opts.

Sergent-chef Stranger turns to Goffrey now. "You got anything to add, Jules? How you made it?"

Jules Goffrey is a lanky, normal-height legionnaire, not overly impressive in any sort of manner, his presence in the room could be easily overlooked by those around him, particularly by Stranger or Matzo. Both of these legionnaires own the room not only in size but mannerism, professional EFLs.

"I'll be straight as I can with you all. I'm not that great a marksman, looking at you guys here, at Caporal Baker, Lance Caporal Winnon and you Sergent-chef Stranger. I only shot about 20 times. Four mags the first day and night, put out the lights of maybe half that. I didn't shoot at all during the recon."

"Did you make it to your assignment?" You ask, cutting in. The information that Jules is relaying is interesting to you. How he survived when all his peers did not.

"Yeah, I made it, Caporal-"

"Hold it. All of you, every one of us, let's get this straight right here and right now," Stranger was already standing, leaning against the rear ramp frame, but now he walks to the middle of the cramped cabin. "Forget rank, it gets in the way of what we got to say and what we already have no time to accomplish. I don't want to hear it in this group or with the legionnaires we'll be training. It seems we're going to be seeing some pretty young kids in here the next few weeks and there is more for them to figure out than what damn rank somebody is that is trying to keep them alive. All good?"

"Aye,"

"Yepper,"

"Clear,"

"Affirmative Chef!" Sr. Caporal Matzo jokes, the rest of you laugh heartily.

"Except you Matzo, you clown! You, you will not speak to me at all and that will make everyone's day better." The two evidently know each other and the tension is instantly gone from the group.

"Matz, you are my second, unless you are off on an op. Baker, I guess since you are senior instructor, of the two of you," he laughs, "you are next in command. This is all completely off the rails. Just all of you, figure it out. We have one mission, two really. First, train some snipers. Second, keep them alive. Where were we?"

"I asked Goffrey about the recon," you reply.

"Yeah, I made it there. It was just a part of the line, the perimeter. I sneaked inside and had a look around. Nothing along that sector other than firing positions and bunkers."

You stare at him in a quizzical manner a moment, then respond, "I'd say that was pretty damn impressive. You got in and out without being detected and without firing. I can't say that myself."

"Or me neither," Smoot retorts. "I had an identical assignment, and I got made on the way out. If it weren't for Quarles shooting up the entire night beside me, they would have been on me instead of him."

Quarles was one of those that broke the night before. Smoot looks at the ground, his inner demons no doubt casting guilt at his good fortune due to another's misfortune.

"Don't you fold on that legionnaire's sacrifice. Look up. Okay, we are getting somewhere, believe it or not. The mission was intelligence, and that's what we brought back," you speak now with new found confidence.

"I watched one of our guys the first day on the beach run up and barely take a covered position before he was popped. I was yelled at by at least two squad leaders to move up the beach, even as I was lining up the sniper that shot one of them. I laid in a slit trench the entire night and nailed a mini-gun team that tried to retake a bunker-" you are interrupted.

"That was you! *Bunker Hill, Skull and Crossbones*. You set the charges too, that right?" asks Stranger.

You nod your head and continue, "and the one thing I can point to is, patience. Cover and camouflage the next important."

"Yeah, that's what I took away from that little *training and orientation* we had before shipping out. Those few days with you guys saved my life," Goffrey is standing near the coxswain's pedestal nodding his head up and down.

"I see all of you found that the Intel on the ground cover was off, you made adjustments?" You ask, pointing to or touching their ragtag array of broken zalza or jumyal leaves, dried mud – a complete body transformation.

"Yep, almost right away."

"Uh, huh, took them damn cloth strips right off."

"This was a total nightmare coming straight from the AC here on my first cruise," Winnon minces.

"Same here," voices Goffrey. Everyone looks at him, "Well, I mean from the Xobian Desert..."

"Ahh ha-ha! We have a Salty Leg here, fellas!" Matzo hails and the rest of the cabin moves forward to touch the intrepid newly promoted lance caporal and a little more than gently.

"Alright, alright. Camouflage, move and cover, good cover, target acquisition. We're talking stealth, that right? Everyone agree? Is that the key?" Stranger puts it out.

"Yeah," the group unanimously agree.

"Great! We got the first couple days figured out. What's next?" he lightheartedly remarks.

"One shot. The only shot. It's just one shot at a time. That's the focus, put the next one out your mind. If the next shot is so important, that's the first shot. Right?" Winnon offers.

"I agree with that. You can't take the second shot until the first one, so, yeah, I agree with that." Bahtren speaks really for the first time. His accent reminds you of *The Xo*. He is from that region for sure.

"Next couple days, range time-" Stranger is cut off.

"No, I mean, yeah, it's important, so yeah, but that's not what I mean. I guess what I mean... I don't know that it's that important," Goffrey breaks in.

"I know what he means, Chef, let's get 'em close to the lines and pick off targets," Winnon fills in for the stammering Jules.

"What?" Smoot and Matzo both say at the same time.

"They got to shoot real targets," Winnon persists.

"You are out of your mind; we'll lose the class to mortars and rockets," Stranger is about half laughing.

"No, he's right, but not completely. My first caporal back in *The Xo* took me out one night and I couldn't come back to camp until I bagged 20 desert jumping-mice. Ha-ha! That ass. He dumped my water too. I humped the whole case of rounds and had to pay for all I used over 20, ha-ha!" You laugh recalling that moment so long and forgotten until now. Caporal Edmunds was, you just realized, your best mate from that time and the best mentor you ever had.

The group is all looking at you. "Yeah, okay, we'll compromise on the head hunting, and put a bounty on mice, rats or whatever else becomes a nuisance on this hellhole island. Where we going to do this?" Stranger looks to the group with open invitation.

"What is this, Landing Beach Orange?" Matzo suggests.

"No, that's north of here. This Is Blue Beach, the 4/107 put on here." Lance Caporal Amber finally puts in a word.

"Yeah, so did 1/107."

"It depends," Stranger responds. "All three beaches were used by each wave. It just depended what wave and battalion you were. I came on south of here on the first wave."

That made sense. What they all called Bunker Hill was a little down beach of here and that was where you watched 6/106 come ashore. So Stranger was in the same area as you were that first night.

"This looks like a good spot, we can rent a ALTC and drop them off on the break and have them get the beach," said Smoot.

"We already got the beach. That's a good tactic for sure, but not what we need at this point. We already have the beachhead, we got to get them inland," Winnon pushed.

"Right. The breakline of the zalza mess and the jungle strip. We need a secure strip," you muse.

"There's one. Far south end, we got the whole tip," Stranger says and the cabin erupts in laughter.

"Settle down!" Stranger laughs with the rest of the group, "I'm putting every one of you in for Port-side liberty when we reach *Key Esprada!*"

Ha-ha!

"Man, I'd take a Palanquin pavilion queen at this point!" jokes Matzo. The jeers are instantaneous, ah, not so familiar but fond memories all the same.

The heat is intense in the ALTC, the sweat dripping off the surviving members of the Sand Fleas.

"What about the other wave, the fourth wave? Are they in on this or on these sniper teams Matz and Bahtren are taking out?" asks Goffrey.

"Yeah, what about them? What'd the Ol' Man say?" inquires Smoot. He is beginning to take a lead in the entire discussion. He is a good legionnaire.

"I'll ask. I assume they are the recon teams out there now, and are probably cursing us."

"Hey, hey. We did our part. They came ashore the next day and didn't take part in the second night. We got nothin' to be ashamed of. But I do want to bring them in somehow." Matzo chimes.

"Exactly, they've lost eight now from their original 18. They're hurting as much as us. And all of them are uncerts." It is Goffrey that speaks, heralding a union between the two seemingly separate groups.

"Are they Sand Fleas?" asks Amber with no outward animosity.

The group looks around, each nodding their head, "Yeah, since the day they got their boots wet," Stranger adds.

"Here's the next task, I think. Crap, I was only a Sr. Caporal an hour ago and I'm running a company," he removes his boonie hat and rubs his bristled hair. High and tight, especially imperative for the start of a mission in a likely flea, lice or tick infested area. You marvel at the stark contrast of mostly clean, lightly tanned skin to that of the clearly defined mud line.

"Hey, if it is any consolation, the company only numbers eight including you, Chef!" hawks Matzo, bending over at the waist, having more fun than the rest of you.

"Ha-ha, ahh, shut-up, Matz. You go find that colour sergent, what was his name?"

"Brockmann, of the 1/107, I think," you add.

"Yeah, Brockmann. He seems to be the go-to guy for this operation. See if you can, in my name and position, put in for an open volunteer call of the standing battalions, of what guys? Expert? Marksmen? If all the sniper quals are gone, how many experts do you think will raise their hands?"

"Marksmen? Seriously? We can throw rocks and hit them with as much accuracy," Smoot lampoons.

"I don't know, I shot a 15 in BTC and then a 17 on my first range qual in Trahmel. They wouldn't look at me with a 19 on my application to MCWS." Goffrey says, shaking his head.

"You were in Trahmel?" Bahtren asks quietly. "That was my home."

He is a displaced indigent, an EFL Nationalized Citizen Applicant. He is the first you have ever met, but it doesn't matter. He is a legionnaire the same as you. His commitment for Summa citizenship was contingent on three years of meritorious service. As a caporal, now a Sr. caporal, he has long fulfilled his obligation and continued his service. Wow.

Goffrey looks at Bahtren a moment. The sudden tension between the two legionnaires is apparent. Would you feel the same way if a Wahti or Quepos was beside you now? Goffrey stretches his balled fist out toward Bahtren in a sign of solidarity, brotherhood.

"I liked it there. Maybe one day you will show me your village."

Bahtren bumps the fist and responds, "I am not welcome there. Maybe you will show me yours?"

They embrace, "You are welcome in my home wherever that may be, Legionnaire." The cabin is silent.

"So? What? Expert, Marksmen with a 15?"

"That's good, just put out a score of 15, don't differentiate the awards, doesn't matter at this point, who cares. We need shooters that can learn and become better. We can train shooters, hell, anyone can shoot better from that BT crap. This is real world. Anyone that is as close as we are to target can make the shot if they are actively shooting and not cowering behind a zalza log. If they raise their hand to step over here, they are shooting for keeps anyway. We just have to teach them to live out the time here." Smoot again adds his opinion.

You look at him and nod your head. "That's it, plain and simple. Get us some legionnaires that are actually shooting at a target, and we'll train them from there."

Matzo looks at Stranger, "Alright. That it?"

"No. See if he can get us an ALTC over on south beach, like this one, some water canisters, 12 GPXRs, ammo, lots of ammo, some chow, a supply of tropical smocks, four micro Sat-links, a couple pads of paper, some pens or pencils, and..." he pauses and looks at the group.

"We want the remaining Sand Fleas with us when they return from the op. Also," he opens a huge grin, "we need a unit patch, call it a Juno Company completion certificate." The group nods their heads and look around smiling at each other.

Every unit enjoys a simple banner, flag or sign outside their AO. Most battalions have a regiment patch. Yours from *The Xo* did, India 4/117. A round embroidered facsimile of the desert landscape with oil rigs protruding from the sand to the sky. The unit designation circled the outer edge.

You all step outside to the side of the ALTC. Smoot picks up a broken piece of charred zalza and marks on the broad, blank side of the vehicle.

"All of them are circles, let's be different," chimes Matzo.

"A triangle?"

"Sure, but why? I mean, it has to have meaning."

"Or not. It could be the group itself, say up one side – Juno Company, down the other – Sand Fleas," adds Amber.

"What's on the bottom?" Winnon questions.

"We can't say the unit, Col. Pittman says it's off ledger. And he may not approve anyway," Stranger says.

Smoot is busy tracing a triangle and the terms so far given.

"How 'bout EFL?"

"Nah, that's a given, of course it could be inside, like a wreath or scrolled banner," Winnon suggests.

"What's inside?"

"A Sand Flea! What else?" Smoot laughs, beginning a rough drawing of some monster.

"What the heck is that Smoot? A seal?" Laughs Matzo.

"It works. I'm sure the artist people among the fleet can look up a flea and impose the relief." Everyone looks at him.

"What? So I know a little about art design? Bugger off."

Ha-ha, you all laugh.

"What about Snipers?" says Goffrey.

"Or Pittman's Snipers," adds Bahtren.

"I like Hunters, keeps it a little less messy," Stranger suggests.

"Alright, how about Pittman's Hunters," you add.

"Yeah! Juno Company – Sand Fleas – Pittman's Hunters. With a flea in the triangle and a EFL banner. What colour? White base, red edge, a broken zalza tree in brown or tan." Smoot is scratching with the charcoal.

"That looks good. Put in an order for 60 or a 100. You got all that Matz?"

Sr. Caporal Matzo is quickly scribbling a rendition of the sketch on a scrap piece of a box of some trash, maybe an ammo case liner. He also scrawls the list of what Stranger had earlier rattled off.

"I got it. Where you gonna be?"

"Me, Baker, Winnon, and Bahtren are going to scout out the south beach. Smoot you, Goffrey and Amber stick around here and grab any replacement coming in that has a 15 or higher score and try to talk them into volunteering. Also talk to any guys that ask about the call up. We'll all meet back here and move together down there if the requisitions are approved. Don't push too hard on the patch, Matz, but we need the other stuff."

"I got it, Chef. Keep your head down."

"You too. We all have dinner together tonight."

"Juno." Winnon calls out.

You all respond, "Juno."

Level Up – South Beach

You watch over six apprentice volunteers as they work their way through the groundcover course. Winnon is downrange somewhere. You can't even spot him in the broken, deeply-advanced stages of decay and rot on the jungle strip. Sergent Stranger, *Chef*, is firing an AP close to the class, the rounds exploding so close you almost feel he is trying to hit them. You look up at the sun as it is only halfway to noon and already over 100 degrees. The tidal action and surf at the tip of the sand bar, only 100 yards or so away, is so violent you can see the sand being stripped away in the waves. The next tide cycle will dump another several tons of sand, coral, and other debris from somewhere, and the whole cycle will just begin again.

The 3rd Fleet has repositioned, all but a cruiser, an AHCS, FLSS and a couple of escorts, to the northwestern corner of the archipelago. The Chaloosa attempted to refortify, reinforce, and resupply their positions earlier on the fourth morning of the assault, sailing from mainland supply points and other established bases. The commander of 3rd Fleet moved at flank speed around the island cluster to cut off the mid-size armada and suffered crippling casualties but inflicted grave damage to the enemy fleet as well. Among the National Navy losses were a cruiser, a mid-size tanker, two frigates, and two escort ships. Your heart sank when hearing the news. More than a few legionnaires with prior OBSF assignments were likewise heartbroken to hear the reports, even without their former ship being counted in the causalities. Once you served with the National Navy on an OBSF detail, it was just like losing a fellow EFL.

The outcome of the First Sand Flea Archipelago Naval Battle was a dominating and decisive show of force by the allied forces in holding the Sand Flea Islands. The Second Sand Flea Archipelago Naval Battle, fought eight weeks to the day later, was a further testament to the limitless sacrifices that those in power were willing to offer without actually being involved in the fighting. The arrival of 2nd Fleet, with both Battalions of 2nd and 5th of the 106th and 107th Regiments, combined with the planned landing to reinforce and relieve those that had spearheaded the amphib assault was a long-awaited boost in morale. First Fleet with 1st and 4th Battalions of the 106th Regiment and 3rd and 6th Battalions of the 107th Regiment had landed three weeks before.

Legionnaires of the first landing were walking scarecrows. The remaining Imperial Marines of the Chaloosa forces were the same, fighting to the end, even when their destiny was sealed in defeat.

These were the last volunteers, coming from the other battalions of the regiments, but only marksmen quals. The battalion commanders wouldn't relinquish their better marksmen. That was understood. The volunteers were immediately immersed in the revolving and continuously evolving sniper course. You ran almost 80 volunteers through in the 12 weeks of the operation, turning out highly qualified snipers, a few of them top-notch. There was no failing grade; each legionnaire succeeded in gaining valuable knowledge and skills even if they were not selected as team operators. Not all of those selected made it off the islands. There was a 1:3 death rate, which never improved or changed. It was just what it was. You watched the six crawling towards twice-promoted Caporal Winnon and knew that two would never make it off. That realization was almost too much.

All of you had continued to patrol and run on teams. Finally Col. Pittman ordered the remaining five of you to remain within the AO of the course. You lost Amber, Matz, and Goffrey. Smoot had been hit and evacuated two weeks ago. After getting to know them, the other original Sand Fleas, the 10 from the fourth wave, were a great bunch of legionnaires too, and they all performed well and accomplished a fantastic kill record. All of them agreed to run through the course as guinea pigs and learn whatever they could from the notorious *Sand Fleas*, even though every one of you counted them as original members. Six remained and led active teams.

The rest of the course attendees continued through several missions before being pulled back to their original battalions. Col. Pittman was not promoted to brigadier general or given full credit for his success in taking the Sand Flea Island Archipelago. To this day, he continues his duties as the acting assault commander in an adjutant under-corps commander role.

You suddenly hear a ship's klaxon offshore. You have heard similar signals and communications before, but this seems different. You gaze out to the ocean at the little flotilla that guards your landing beaches against a rear-door counter-assault. The other ships join in, and a series of AP and mini-gun fire erupts, with no visible hostile air attack. You look on with dismay. What is going on?

Colour Sergent Brockmann rides up a few minutes later, honking his horn like a crazy man. He skids to a stop just on the edge of the training course and jumps out yelling, "That's it, Sand Fleas! That's it! Bring 'em in! We've taken this living waste heap. I want a full inventory of every piece of equipment and round issued to this miserable and unregulated, sorry excuse for an EFL unit ASAP, Sergent Stranger. I want the legionnaires under your command in regulation and proper duty uniforms. Be ready to stand-to for regiment formation in the morning at 0800 and ready for transport to FACS."

You are still standing among the sniper class members who do not respond to the news or react to the sudden outburst of a noncom they do not know and have had no contact with in the past ten days. Is it a trick, a ruse that they are to avoid if they live? The stories have circulated through the battalions and fleets of the non-official, non-regulatory sniper course and the cadre that conducts it. The tales are too immense to be accurate.

"That's it? No kidding? We're done here?" you address Brockmann.

"Yep, you return to a normal legionnaire in a few days."

"What about these guys? What do we do with them?" you ask inquisitively.

"They'll process back to their units as soon as we get word."

He turns and climbs back in his buggy and drives off.

"Come on in Winnon, Stranger, put that damn target shooting to rest. We got work to do. Colour Sergent wants a full accounting of all this stuff."

"All of what?" Stranger yells across the sand and broken zalza, standing up and collecting his weapon and rounds.

"All of everything."

"The hell you say! By when?"

"ASAP. We also have regiment review at 0800."

"Winnon!" Stranger calls out into the new growth encroaching the jungle edge.

"Aye, Chef!" Winnon responds from his still unknown hiding spot.

"Also, Colour Sergent says the unit must conform to regulations and proper uniform," you add, knowing that it is causing Stranger much consternation.

"Ah, for crying out loud," you hear from the very laid-back company sergent.

"Caporal Winnon!" he calls out again.

"Yes, Company Sergent-chef Stranger!" Winnon is playing along with the growing realization that this is the end of the combat action.

"Pull it in here. We got to gather our teams back in. Caporal Baker, assemble your class at the CP for mission debrief. We got work to do."

There are four teams out, with two sleeping in the bunker after their return from a mission last night. Two are preparing to go out. The teams are made up of three, a team leader, shooter, and spotter, and most members are capable of either role. The team leader is most often an experienced sniper from the original group, and the teams remain out for several days. They can operate anywhere on the islands, including across the narrow channels, straits, or inlets.

After almost three continuous months on the assault mission, the two regiments are at a dangerous level of nearly 50 percent. It will take a tremendous amount of rest and training to recoup.

By late afternoon all four teams out on patrol have been notified of the abort order and are making their way back to the Sand Flea AO, with explicit orders not to engage enemy forces unless attacked first. The news of the successful completion of the amphib assault mission is not divulged purposefully to maintain high alertness. The last thing Stranger wants is for one of his teams to be decimated by a Chaloosa patrol that has slipped through. Actually, it turns out, the archipelago is not completely taken, but is in such a progressed state of occupation that the National Army is tasked with the mop-up operation and garrisoning of the airstrip.

With the end of the day, the return of regular, daily EFL routine begins to reappear. Legionnaires that had been given some leeway in personal grooming and uniform appearance are quickly brought back to heightened standards. Uniforms are in pitiful condition after weeks in the tropical combat environment, and those that have been without proper allotment scrounge for what they can find. The uniform reissue will occur during the next few days before loading on the beach. The first Army forward units are already coming ashore and are moving inland to the old second perimeter positions that you and your fellow legionnaires had taken the first week. You stand with the others of your small group and watch the incoming train of supplies and personnel.

"Look at that, will you," comments a Sand Flea, his face still painted and filthy with camouflage.

"Yeah, they act like they're victors of some great deed, ha! A couple of weeks here, and they'll not look so pretty," another jests, sitting on an upturned pail eating rice and beans out of a mess pot.

The training course, and therefore the AO of the small Juno Company CP, is right off the beachhead on the southern tip of the landing beaches. The terrain and combination of the fractured jungle, with the broken zalza logs and sandy, wet, and exposed beach, was the ideal training area for the course, even as the occupation advanced further inland. The rear EFL supply and HQ bunkers and evac points remained where they were those first days, so the vantage point to observe the migratory influx of the new force is about as good as it gets.

"What can all that stuff be? I mean, they have the airfield. Why bring it ashore like that?" muses Winnon.

"I don't know. It doesn't matter to me, as long as they take the hand-off and we load outta here," Sergeant-chef Stranger replies.

Level Up – Beach Evac

During the night, which is one of the quietest that you have experienced in weeks with no shots or mortar explosions, the battalions reform and prepare to depart in the order in which they came ashore. You are still technically a member of Delta 1/107, even though you have had no contact with that company since you put ashore. The orders concerning established bunkers, positions, and fortifications are to leave everything as it is for the Army to occupy. All equipment and materials other than food, water, fuel, and furnishings are to be taken and loaded. The rest remains. That makes it easy. You have no extra food or water, and what furnishings there are for the course were made from what you scrounged in the jungle. Your uniforms were better than most, having scored a reissue of trousers and smocks only a few weeks past. The members of the company had resewn the Sand Flea patches on the right shoulder and worn them with pride.

The Sand Fleas are kept together during the regiment review, and the thought is that Juno will continue as a functioning unit. Beach debark points are assigned, and the planned exit from the beach is scheduled for the next three days. Companies of 3/107 will act as rearguard and final pullout units. Juno will also remain and hold final covering positions during the action. Sergent Stranger has less than 30 legionnaires to cover the last two debark points on the final day. The remaining two ALTCs will transport you to the FACS. There is no anticipated problem with the evacuation. The Army will be controlling the island and beach at that point. The pullout just has to be orderly and planned.

The first day, you watch the process of the platoons, companies, and battalions loading and returning to their ships. It is quite a view from the southern tip. On the second morning, Juno moves to beach points, occupying positions that had been overrun that first morning, so different now. Nine teams spread across a narrow strip of sand. Fox, Gulf, Hotel, and India companies of 3/107 are also repositioned during the day to the first hard-fought and contested perimeter. The next morning will be the last. The 3rd Fleet sailed the first day, 2nd today. First Fleet stands off-shore to take you on and return to home port. The regiments of II Corps are to be reorganized and made combat-ready as quickly as possible. The whole western Amphib/fleet schedule is disrupted.

On the third morning of the pullout, the four companies of 3/107 pass by your positions, looking for all the world as happy as they can be, even though they are racked with dysentery and malnutrition. Their uniforms are not the worst you have observed but still are not in a condition that will be salvageable. Yesterday, you and the others noticed that the Army and Navy had set up portable showers and uniform issue tents. Good; a shower and a clean uniform before loading will be great. There is a growing pile of discarded uniforms, and they are being incinerated right on the beach.

It is finally your turn. Juno and a command unit made up of the 107th to ensure the last EFL are accounted for. The Army and Special Flight Services now control the Sand Flea Archipelago. It is all theirs. As you and the rest of the company approach the tents and can more easily observe the activity, you find you are not to be treated to a shower as had been thought. Rather, a chemical delousing treatment, complete head-shaving, and stripping of all equipment except for weapons await you. Several soldiers search the discarded uniforms in a pile, collecting anything of value, including forgotten or displaced money, watches, rings, wallets, and patches. Quickly you turn to Bahtren beside you and put your arm out.

"Wait. They're stealing everything. Empty your pockets, Juno. Rip your patches off."

Most of you carry little of your remaining assault issue – equipment harness, body armor, butt-packs, ponchos or liners, softcover boonies, sniper smocks – whatever last possessions you own. Your duffle bags remain on your parent ship. None of you will see those until you make port. You tug at his patch, even as Stranger rips yours clean off. You bite at the thread and finally get enough of a space and tear the patch away, handing it to Bahtren.

You walk to the tent, and some sort of army attendant instructs you to strip down.

"Dump your equipment over there, uniforms on that side," he indicates.

"If you have ammo or explosives of any type, put it here," a stack of ammo cans, loose rounds, magazines of every caliber sprawl along the side. "You can only retain your personal weapons; that's it." He stares at the group.

You are sure that others have the same hesitation you feel, collecting weapons and personal effects for weeks. When you came ashore, your issued GPS was left on the *Andover Hill LC96*, carrying only your GPXR and GPC. But now, you not only have someone else's GPS but a different GPXR. Your GPC was lost several weeks ago, and you found another one. To give up ammo seems ridiculous, and there is no reason to part with personal effects. It all seems like a scam. The entire group carries sniper rifles along with an assortment of weapons, including enemy weapons, as you do.

"What are you guys? A platoon of snipers?" The question is too stupid to even answer.

"I have documents that I must retain for regiment records," Sergent Stranger states, holding a bundle of papers inside a file folder, including names and other operational details, kill records, and so forth. "Also, my legionnaires hold personal items that there is no way they are parting with."

The soldier gazes lazily at Stranger for a few moments and replies, "No clothing, no souvenirs, no ammo, no equipment."

"Well, you might have to take it from them then," Stranger offers.

"Let's go in there! What's the hold-up, Sergent?" an EFL major from regiment personnel pokes his head inside the tent from the outside.

Sergent Stranger looks at the major and then the clerk. The situation is strained.

"He's telling us we can't retain personal effects, Major. We watched them pull valuables out of the uniforms in the pile, Sir. It ain't right that we can't take it, and these lowlifes are stealing it."

The major looks at the group of you, "You're the company of snipers, Juno Company, that right, Sergent?"

"Yes, Sir."

"Take your weapons and butt-packs, no uniforms, clothing, ponchos, or liners," he pauses and notices the unfaded area where the patches were sewn, "take your unit patches; these guys here have no use for them. Let's go Sergent. They're holding our seats."

"Aye, Sir! Thank you, Sir!" you all respond while ripping off smocks, trousers, and disassembling fanny packs from the equipment harness.

The butt-pack or fanny pack contains mostly personal stuff anyway, or items needed while on patrol, including spare mags, water purifiers, cleaning kits, high-energy food bars, spare socks, maps of the islands, or whatever can be crammed into an eight by ten by six-inch pack that is worn on the back of the equipment belt and supported by the over-the-shoulder harness. The poncho and or liner is commonly attached to the pack or tucked between it and the butt of the legionnaire.

The group heads into the next tent and finds barbers waiting. You all receive a quick and clean haircut, even the females. The next tent is the chemical shower and each of you carrying a pack is asked to empty the contents and have the pack sprayed as well, then the items repacked. Several of you retain your boonie caps, and those are also treated, along with the patches. Finally, a pair of fresh, new white skivvies is issued, and then a body check ensures no fleas or other pests are attached to you. Without touching the beach's sand, you load into two ALTCs and head towards the awaiting fleet amphibious craft ship.

You are not the only one that begins to suddenly itch and feel nauseous, the chemicals making you sick. A Navy corpsman, a combat doctor, is on the ALTC with you, and she speaks.

"Don't worry. We'll get that stuff off of you as soon as we can. The chemicals are killing whatever parasites are on your body. We'll give you a short swim in the ocean and then a real shower onboard – new uniforms, some medications to treat your insides, and a meal. We have to manage your diet for a few days so that you don't get sick. You'll be pretty healthy by the time we reach port. Welcome to the *Moores Creek LC95*. Glad to have you guys back. It's been boring without you." She laughs.

Most of the company, not all, have experienced similar sanitizing procedures after extended amphib cruises. None have been treated at the beach in the manner you just were, though. Several are irate, including Stranger and another caporal that you know only vaguely.

"Well, we have had several bad cases of intestinal worms and severe flea infestation onboard after receiving some of you guys. I wouldn't press too hard on the chem-showers and equipment dump," the corpsman responded.

The company settles down and waits out the ride. Once reaching the ship and landing inside the cargo hold, you are offered an invitation to step off the giant ramp into the immense ocean. If a legionnaire is a little apprehensive of stepping into the deep, they can remain on the ramp and dunk under. The ocean's salt seems to settle the itch immediately, almost as therapeutic as the mineral baths back in the Palanquin after JWTS. It is soothing. You are all instructed to rub yourselves, wiping the chemicals off. After a few minutes of pleasure and relaxation that you have not enjoyed in months, you are ushered to Cargo Deck Five for showers and uniform issue.

The journey to homeport takes two solid weeks. First Fleet, which has only spent about six weeks on the assault, is only mid-way through their cruise, while 3rd Fleet is about two weeks early coming in. Second Fleet is nearly two months overdue. All 12 battalions of the 106th and 107th Regiments are exhausted, below strength, and weakened. You learn of a call for volunteers to form three battalions while sailing to port. The Corps commander is hoping to fill two downgraded battalions, and he gets almost four. They are designated the 100th All Volunteers Regiment and are split into four under-strength battalions of only six companies each, Alpha thru Fox.

CHAPTER 14

Level Up – **Bravo Company**

New Platoon Leadership #20 Brief

Medium 15 PP 80% success

Character Summary

Your Assigned Mission Is To Establish Command Of New Platoon.

Summary:

Assume command of the platoon.

You are assigned to Bravo Company, 2nd Battalion, 100th Regiment. The Sand Fleas of Juno Company are disbanded. Once you reach port, you are immediately ordered to report to the *Waxhaws LC105*, one of four FACS making up thrown-together Fleet Battle Group A. The operational battle group will be a small, fast attack force supported by two AHCSs, four cruisers, a single FLSS, a tender, one medium and one small tanker, four frigates, and another dozen escort frigates and corvettes. The fleet group needs to maintain a cruise for a two-month minimum while 3rd Fleet and the regiments repair, resupply, and retrain. Since 1st Fleet will return to a normal pattern and will be the last of the three to redeploy, the personnel of 100th Regiment will more than likely be reassigned to one of its normally attached battalions, the 1st and 4th of 106th or the 3rd and 6th of 107th.

After reporting to Bravo Company 2/100, you are assigned to 3rd Platoon as one of two caporals. With a shortage of Sr. caporals, platoons are being put together with well-seasoned and battle-wise newly-promoted caporals who are more than qualified to lead their own platoons. Most companies only have one or two Sr. caporals. Of the 24 companies of this abnormal regiment, the rank structure is pretty light at best. A real shortage of officers, NCOs, and upper-rank legionnaires is evident. None of the company, and you are sure that goes for the rest of the battalions, were issued proper or full gear during the new regiment formation.

As you walk through the platoon on an informal inspection within the bowels of the mid-deck *amphib berthing*, you can't help but notice that legionnaires don't even have proper tropical uniforms, wearing a mismatch of desert smocks and trousers, and training boots. Many are capless; some don't have equipment, harnesses or even campaign belts! None have water purifiers or tablets and possess only one canteen as opposed to two or the much recommended three. Each of them survived the Sand Flea Campaign, and all are volunteers, yet none are complaining about their lack of equipment. Many went without basic supplies for weeks; this is a treat to have clean, dry, and protected berthing and three squares a day. They all know that they could deploy at a moment's notice without a proper kit and will still fight to their utmost best. You can't help but be proud of the members of your new platoon. They are an odd mix from all 12 battalions of the two regiments.

You go to speak with the company sergent, Sergent Ragford. It doesn't matter what former battalion or regiment he came from; you are all 100th now.

"Hey Sergent, have you noticed that the platoons aren't fitted properly? I need to put in a-"

"Stand-to, Caporal. Where the hell did you wander in from? Don't ever *Hey Sergent* me, Caporal. You will address me with the proper respect and courtesies as you learned them, however many years ago that was. We may be on a cruise, but the dictum of regulations still applies. Stand at attention and readdress me properly."

You can't help but stare at him in a lost and uncomprehending way. This is a combat zone. You are at sea, patrolling for any trouble spots in the western ocean, a part of a hastily put together small force. He chooses to ignore deficiencies in his company's equipment issue and focus instead on proper reporting customs?

"I correct myself, Sergent Ragford. I wish to report to you the shortage of essential combat uniforms and equipment issue of my platoon."

"That's better, Caporal. Remember, unit discipline is linked to morale and conduct. I am aware of the lack of proper issue. The entire regiment is in the same predicament. Command is working on the refit. As you are well aware, the conditions of our pullout were less than ideal. I need a list of what equipment your legionnaires lack, a weapons inventory, and who has their assigned GPS and who doesn't. Pull the other platoon caporals together and pass those instructions on. Captain Hue wants a company meeting later in the afternoon after we shove off, and I'm sure the battalion commander will schedule his own in a couple of days. You're dismissed."

You find the other platoon caporals, which isn't too difficult. For the most part, they are performing their own inspections and talking with their legionnaires. You pass the word and introduce yourself to your co-caporal. The newness of command is strange yet not intimidating. Even though this is your first platoon command role, it is not your first command. Both the OBSF and the responsibility as lead instructor for the sniper course gave you incredible experience in dealing with under-ranks and higher chain of command. Sergent Ragford could decide to run the platoons by individual squads and direct the entire company through the caporals. Or he may wait to see which of his caporals were more independent and prone to taking their platoons. Either way, you just need to do your job and take care of your legionnaires.

"How's it going? I'm Wright, ha-ha, of course I am! A little joke I never get tired of." Caporal Wright is wide-shouldered yet still not filled out from the hardship of malnutrition and the effects of dysentery that probably dropped his weight by 20 pounds. His smile indicates that he is good-natured, well-liked, and a bit of a jokester.

"Baker. I guess we're together on this one. I took a walk through earlier; half the platoon is in BT boots and desert smocks."

"Yeah, we're a regular hand-me-down red-headed stepchild for sure. I didn't have much when we were pulled off the beach on the third day, but having to dump everything before the bleach wash didn't help." He watches you, gauging the information he shared against your reaction and what you give back. His openness reveals he was part of the last battalions to land, his self-worth measured by what another thought.

"You're right there. I watched those Army scavengers rifling through the uniforms, taking items others were forced to leave. Our Sergent forced the issue, and we carried our *butts* off. They even wanted our patches!"

"Huh, yeah, I guess they sell them to the collectors back home. I imagine a few of those battalions that were in the thick of it early on and that damn ghost company, Juno, you hear of them? The sniper teams? They are probably worth a pretty pence."

You take what he says and think about it, never realizing the value of unit patches in monetary value, only in *esprit de corps*. Occasionally, the bodies of sniper teams were found after ambushes or being overrun, brutally mutilated, much worse than the average EFL, and the Sand Flea patches were always taken as some sort of prize by the Chaloosa. Weeks ago, when performing an Intel search of an enemy sniper, you found Goffrey's patch in the breast pocket of the dead man. The habit of writing one's name on the backside of the patch before sewing it on came early, an ID if found later. You still had his stuffed in your pack. Stranger and you were the only ones who had control of the patches supply, awarding them to those who completed the course and reissuing them when a legionnaire lost his kit during a mission. The core of you, the team leaders and Winnon, voted to award the last six participants of the course their patch the last morning, and then you and

Stranger split the remaining ones to hold on to. You each had 12, the last unissued Juno patches.

"I guess so." You also managed to hold onto your boonie hat, heavily stained with paint, mud, and grease but completely disinfected and cleaned by the chemical wash, and sitting comfortably atop your head.

"It looks like we got a good mix of legs in the platoon. I talked to a couple of them as they drifted in from all the battalions this morning. I didn't know any of them, though. You?"

"No, I didn't see anyone I recognized. Maybe once we get their names on a list. Let's shake 'em up. How do you want to run it?" You offer.

"I guess get their names and cross-reference a basic kit list. I don't think any of them have more than the uniform on their back and a toothbrush."

"And their rifle," you add.

"Good point. Of course, some of them don't have that, from what I understand. How do you not have your issued weapon?" He looks at you with a grin, asking the rhetorical question in jest.

"Oh, there are reasons. My GPS is back on the *Andover Hill* with my duffle. I never took it ashore," you chuckle.

"What? What did you use? When did you go ashore?"

"Ha-ha, the first wave," you watch him.

His expression slowly changes from a happy-go-lucky to one that resembles someone who just discovered a dark secret. "Oh."

He hesitates and then asks, "So, any of them, uh, you know, part of that wave?"

"You mean the assault wave? I don't know. Could be. But I don't recognize any from Juno. Come on. Let's get these legs ready in case we're needed tomorrow."

"You bet, Baker." The two of you walk down the narrow passageway, talking and becoming instant mates.

Level Up – Battle of Blue Water Lagoon

The 100th Regiment and light Fleet Battle Group A's mission is simply to present a presence in the western ocean and contain or restrict any Chaloosa expansion while 3rd Fleet and her EFL contingent regroup. The Chaloosa are hurting just as badly as the allies in the western theater. However, they had not committed all of their fleets and imperial marines in the Sand Fleas. They decide to challenge the vacuum and launch a three-prong counter-balance thrust along the southern band of the equator, among a string of islands. The approach is brilliant, each island group giving cover and support to the other, thereby strengthening the whole. The easternmost group, Blue Water Atoll, forms a natural lagoon. The Chaloosa stage a protected carrier inside the lagoon to act as a temporary airstrip while hastily building the airfield and coastal air and naval defense batteries among the atoll. Simultaneously, they quickly construct the other two island bases in the plan. If they can complete the three bases, it will give them a controlling finger protruding out into the southern sea lanes. It is a daring move for the Chaloosa. The two westernmost bases are not yet capable of air support to Blue Water Atoll, and they take a great gamble that their naval support will not leave their assignment.

The assault plan is two-fold. While the main battle group with both ACHS, three cruisers, a frigate, and several escort class ships directly attack the lagoon-based carrier and its escorts from the northeast, the smaller landing force of the four FACS, a cruiser, two frigates, and six escorts will drive in fast and early at dawn from the east. The supporting craft will all remain with the main force to aid in offsetting the number of ships, and as soon as the attack is underway, they will fall back out of range of the carrier air umbrella.

During the night, the two groups split, and the landing force steams at flank speed to their designated dawn launch coordinates. There is no pre-assault bombardment, fooling the Chaloosa into thinking the assault is not imminent, the attackers waiting for additional forces.

The timing of the amphibious assault is to directly coincide with the rising of the sun, placing the bright ball in the defenders' eyes. The landing beach is not optimal; it is guarded by a shallow coral reef that rings the outer perimeter of the atoll and has a Chaloosa resupply cove on the lagoon side. Blue Water Atoll consists of five larger islands; the largest of these on the southeastern edge is five miles long and a mile and a half at the widest point. The atoll is no more than 15 miles across. This main island holds the airstrip but is not large enough to support the bulk of the Chaloosa Imperial Marine forces. Those are located on the adjoining island, which serves as the garrison, half a mile away across a shallow strait. If the EFL can take the main island and airstrip, the garrisoned forces will be slowly strangled and starved out even with the two other island bases offering support. Blue Water Atoll has to be taken.

The amphibious assault will be a quick, single, continuous wave for fear that the FACS will come under immediate attack by the lagoon-based carrier and escorts. The ships will withdraw and regroup with the main fleet battle group. Once the EFL land, they are on their own. You ready your platoon and load in the ALTC with 1st Squad and Platoon Leader Leftenant Lambert. Caporal Wright has 2nd Squad.

During the short cruise, the legionnaires of Bravo quickly learned of your exploits with Juno and respect your experience and leadership. Captain Hue designated you as the senior platoon caporal, and you and Wright worked together to ensure your platoon was as prepared as possible. Most still wear mixed uniforms, but they were finally issued the proper basic equipment.

The ALTCs will not return to the FACS, remaining instead with the legionnaires on the landing. They hold all of the supplies the legionnaires need for the first 48 hours of the offensive. Some planning officers do not feel that there is enough room on the small landing site for close to 4000 legionnaires and almost 200 ALTCs. If the landing area clogs up, the ALTCs loaded with EFL are sitting ducks if they can not off-load. At the last minute, they decide to hold back 4th Battalion and three companies of 3rd. That leaves 15 companies, 2400 on a first wave, and a second reserve wave of 1400. Will that be enough?

They are still reevaluating plans for the assault, even as the ALTCs are being loaded and launched. Confusion is so high that the invasion is in jeopardy of being postponed, but that would tip off the defenders, and the assault would never succeed with such low numbers. The entire regiment is smaller than a regular EFL Fleet Amphib force. Bravo Company 2/100 along with 1st Battalion receives the green light; the invasion is on.

The ALTCs race in the darkness of the predawn towards the atoll, low profiles bobbing on the rough seas. Behind them, the taller outlines of the FACS and their escorts blacken the sky. A forecasted storm cell will pass within 100 miles today but is not projected to adversely affect the operation. The sky is patchy, the swells rough. You feel the sudden jolt of the rocky bottom of the landing shore, but it is sooner than you expected. Before you know it, the craft is swimming again; it must have been a reef. A few minutes later, you make landfall. The ramp drops, and you quickly exit the ALTC, taking crates of ammo, food, water, and mortars with you. The ALTC coxswain has received orders to return to the FACS to make room on the beach for other craft. It quickly races back into the surf and is gone. You look around. It is still dark. The wind is increasing. The morning is silent. You caught them by surprise.

It takes a moment, and then you realize that there are a much smaller number of ALTCs landing than what should be. You look out into the waves and, to your horror, see a half dozen craft stuck on the outlying reef and floundering after making the mistake of dropping their ramps, therefore swamping and washing out their legionnaires into the ocean! Legionnaires are drowning. They are helpless with heavy gear, just 100 yards or more from the coastline. Leftenant Lambert watches it too. There is nothing either of you can do. Suddenly the main force begins their missile attack on the carrier. The surprise is over. You advance through the jungle carrying your supplies as far off the landing as you can, setting up a resupply point.

The 2nd Battalion CO, Major DePont, organizes his companies in a line to the right flank of 1st Battalion but quickly finds that he only has half his companies, three out of six, and two of those lost a total of three platoons on the reef. The other three companies, Delta, Echo, and Fox, evidently never launched, mistakenly ordered to remain as part of the reserve component along with all of 3rd and 4th Battalions! The reality is sinking in that a major blunder has occurred. The assault only consists of 1st Battalion and less than half of 2nd Battalion. A little more than 1000 legionnaires are on the beach, and the next wave is in danger of being destroyed in the water while landing. That's it. The smaller naval assault force pulls back and rejoins the main battle group, and waits for the lagoon carrier to be taken out. Meanwhile, the landed force has to cut across the half-mile of island and set up a defensive position across the strait from the Chaloosa

Marine garrison and keep them from reinforcing the main island.

The Battle of Blue Water Lagoon has begun.

Level Up – Lagoon Strait

You soon encounter light contact in the jungle along a work path that connects the strait with the airstrip construction site. Delta 1/100 engages what is probably an outpost that is assigned as OP off the beach from where you landed. Scattered skirmishes flare up, and Major DePont sends Charlie 2/100 around to the far-right flank to engage any marines coming from the airstrip. First Battalion now sends Alpha and Bravo companies to the south left flank to cut that tip, which forms a bulb, off from the strait. The fighting is heating up as the main garrison begins to react to the invasion, running to hidden shallow sandbars that cross the narrow channel.

Chaloosa mortars, rockets, and missiles rain in from ground, naval, and air positions. Legionnaires take cover where they can. The attack on the carrier is also heating up with air defense artillery, keeping Fleet Battle Group A helos at bay. A horseshoe position is quickly organized on the isthmus at the narrow neck of the main island, cutting a three-point intersection – the lower tip, the lagoon strait, and the airstrip – with the ocean to your back. Major DePont takes his three companies and seals the airstrip off. First Battalion orders Charlie to join Alpha and Bravo down in *the bulb* to clean it out and hold the southwestern coast from reinforcement. That leaves three companies, Delta, Echo, and Fox of 1st Battalion to hold off the garrison. The legionnaires dig-in and fight furiously.

Major DePont is missing 120 legionnaires from the get-go, the three platoons that perished on the reefs. Now, the morning sky is turning grey with the ominous sign of a tropical storm blowing in. There appears to be at least a battalion of Imperial Marines on the construction site along with construction workers. They have a network of bunkers and trenches linking the CP to perimeter defenses. The path through the jungle to the strait is more than a dirt trail; it is a crushed volcanic-stone-packed small road with inlaid fighting positions. No doubt there are tunnels too. Soon snipers begin to take shots from high points in the trees.

"Caporal Baker! Take them out! Clear this damn road!" Major DePont calls over the Sat-link.

Each company has designated snipers, and you are not one of them. Early on during the cruise, Captain Hue had discussed with you the role you would play and that he could not promise it would not include taking you away from your platoon responsibilities if needed. You understood and welcomed the ability to perform whatever task you were asked to do. One of the tasks you had been assigned during the cruise was to select and train the snipers of 2/100.

You carry the GPXR as your weapon. "Lance Caporal Schmidt, on me," you call the company sniper from down the line.

You crawl to a log, away from the line as he follows. The leaves are being ripped apart by mini-guns and individual rifle fire from Chaloosa hidden among the jungle. You quickly circle to the right flank; your uniform is not prepared for sniper duty but not clean by any means. You reach out and pull Schmidt down closer to the ground, covering his face, throwing dirt and mud upon him, then roll in it yourself, wiping your face. You both quickly snap leaves off and tuck them in your uniform, removing your harnesses and leaving them on the ground. You look at him, and he nods. You lead out.

You're back in the darkness of the hunt. The effort is not difficult, but a strange sensation envelops you nonetheless. You had thought maybe you could move on, that your career would move to the next step, but you are not bothered by this call. It is what you are called to do; it will help the mission. Schmidt follows your lead. You reviewed the team concept with the group as part of the orientation on ship, and he knows that he has a much higher chance of surviving with you than on his own.

Soon the two of you have worked around and flanked the jungle strip separating the airstrip from the ocean and then work back inside. You are behind the Chaloosa line and ignore a bunker for the moment. There is a nest in the trees along the work path. You see marines moving up to support the positions. You spot an officer as he crawls to a trench. He slumps to the ground. You keep moving and climb a slope. There is a natural defense from an ocean landing the further north the island goes, a crest or bluff eroded by the waves below. Atop this bluff, the jungle surrounds the airstrip at a higher elevation. The strait is lower than the southern tip, forming a saddle between the two higher points. The

Chaloosa not only have the jungle but the higher elevation as well.

    Schmidt is taking to the situation well. He is a second-enlistment, four-theater legionnaire on his third amphib cruise, like you, completing his 18 months. He has seen extensive combat and missed out on the AC sniper course by one point in his score. If he walks off this island, he should make caporal with a third enlistment for sure. If he walks off. There are no guarantees on this one; the odds are pretty stacked against the nine companies.

    Within an hour, both of you have scored several hits and are forced to take the bunker you passed earlier, wiping out six to gain the back door. Schmidt rigs a daisy chain in the trench servicing the bunker while you cover him. Sounds of EFL GPS and Chaloosa mini-gun and rifle fire mix in a cacophony of ferocious fighting towards the lagoon strait and along the path. Rain begins to fall, and the wind tears at the zalza fronds above. A concentrated effort by a squad-sized force to take back the bunker results in numerous casualties from their own captured mini-gun, so they fall back, setting off the mines that Schmidt rigged, killing the remainder.

    Eventually, a patrol from Charlie 2/100 creeps up to the bunker and prepares to storm it before realizing it is already in EFL control. The Sr. caporal of 2nd Platoon slides in with the rest of his squad and takes stock of the situation from the relative safety of the fortified position.

    "Where did y'all come from? Aren't you Bravo, Caporal?" he asks, taking a drink of water.

Ha-ha, you laugh, "From out there, Cap. Decided to get out of the rain. What took you so long?" The group of you laugh, taking a knee, reveling in the moment of the serenity of the storm.

"What's the situation on the lagoon? We were sent out to deal with the tree monkeys as soon as they opened up on us this morning. We got chased into here after a few hits," you answer.

"For now, it looks like 1st is keeping it closed. I don't know how the southern companies are faring," the Sr. caporal takes a peek out the back.

"It's time my spotter and I move along and do more work out there. You got a Sat-link?"

"No. Do you need to send a message to battalion? I can send a runner."

You think about it. Does DePont want you to continue or return to your platoon?

"Naw, we'll come in after dark or in the morning. Just, if you have a chance at some point, let the old man know you ran into us. We took four monkeys, another three on the ground, an officer early on, this hole, and the squad trying to retake it. I'm going to attempt to get the layout and what the force strength is."

The squad stares at you, and the Sr. caporal just grins, "Yeah, you're right. You need to stay out longer. You haven't done anything since you came ashore Caporal Baker. You fixed on everything?"

"You got any demo you want to be rid of?" you ask, patting your mag pouches, two of them empty. But they wouldn't have sniper rounds. You have 18 rounds left, Schmidt has less than 25.

You both acquired Chaloosa sniper rifles and use them at times to throw off the hunt.

"I can give you a pouch, but you have to put down a deposit. That thing cost me a heartache, and I require a co-signer," he laughs.

"I'm not signing for that thing if there's a clause about returning it *In Condition*," adds Schmidt in fun.

"Aw, forget it. Y'alls credit is probably no good anyway. Here, it's yours," he hands over a canvas pouch of explosives, Det-cord, primers, and detonators. "See you at chow."

"Hold our seats."

Schmidt waits for you to crawl out first and then follows. The afternoon rain blankets the thick jungle, and the bunker opens up with the mini-gun and rifle fire in a heavy cover for you. The Chaloosa have moved into a hold and defend strategy in a series of concealed positions along the crushed gravel path and in a line stretching clear across the jungle. DePont is concerned only with maintaining a foothold on the landing beach while 1st Battalion keeps the lagoon strait closed. The fleet must take out the carrier and then land reinforcements and supplies. And they must do it soon, or this tiny battalion will be overrun.

Schmidt sees movement in the trench to his right and tosses a grenade. The explosion rips through several unsuspecting Chaloosa. You both fire Chaloosa rifles to confuse the enemy, and the rain drowns out the cries. Rain beats down on the thick leaves of the trees and bushes, causing a loud and distorting drumming and cascading waterfall sound effect. Crawling on, you come to a path 100 yards or so behind the contested front. You are solidly inside the Chaloosa-controlled area. The construction clearing is not far. The aerial photos shown during briefings on the assault revealed that it is only several 100 yards past the cove used for resupply from the lagoon; the strait is south of that. There is nothing to keep the Chaloosa from landing their marines by the cove, and they will undoubtedly do that as soon as it is dark. There is also a pier or dock.

During the next two hours, the two of you scout the eastern side of the path after it breaks out of the jungle and continues to the group of buildings used for a CP, construction sheds, hangers, supplies, fuel depot, infirmary, and whatever else. You estimate there are no less than a battalion of marines and construction workers present and two operational ADA batteries on the eastern and northeastern promontories. Work on the airstrip is in full motion; the Chaloosa are wasting no time with the EFL tied up in the jungle amid the isthmus. They must understand the legionnaires only landed a small number before having to withdraw the smaller landing fleet. The trap is set.

As darkness creeps in and the storm continues to blow through to the north, you watch and contemplate a bold plan.

EXPEDITIONARY FOREIGN LEGION -The Xo

Level Up – Airfield Mission #21 Brief – A Bold Plan

___Difficult A 25 PP 60% success

___Difficult B 25 PP 60% success

Character Summary

You have selected Difficult Mission A.

Summary:

You realize that reporting the Intel you have gathered on enemy strength, positions of ADA, and the continuous work on the airstrip is vital to Major DePont. You and Lance Caporal Schmidt should make your way through the enemy lines and return to your company.

You have selected Difficult Mission B.

Summary:

You realize that reporting the Intel you have gathered on enemy strength, positions of ADA, and the continuous work on the airstrip is vital to Major DePont. You also see an opportunity to destroy the fuel depot, which would cause immense and immediate confusion, disruption, loss of valuable and hard-to-replace resources, possible casualties, and it would easily mark missile targets for nighttime drone attacks.

You discuss the options with Schmidt, and the two of you decide that the fuel depot is a rich target and will aid in delaying airfield completion. The escape plan is limited; the jungle is thin in this area, and the search will be fast and furious for the saboteurs. The only escape route is to the ocean off the cliff. The waters below are unknown. The current could sweep you out to sea, into the lagoon, against the coral reefs, beat you back against the cliff, or back down to the landing beach.

The aerial and naval fighting has not diminished throughout the day, both sides knowing the cost of victory or defeat. The Chaloosa are pushing harder from the garrison island across the strait, the tides working evidently to their advantage now in opening up the sandbars for crossing over. There's no time to waste. While Schmidt wires a covered bunker of barrels filled with fuel, you watch over him, ready to cover his retreat back to you. The sentry patrols are heavy, but there was a gap that you were able to take advantage of long enough for Schmidt to make it to the partially dug-out fuel dump. The Chaloosa are overconfident that their line is containing any advancement. You wonder if any other snipers or scouts have made it inside the camp perimeter.

Schmidt sets a timed fuse, really just a length of Det-cord with a simple pull-tube detonator. As soon as you pull the ring, you'll have less than a minute to get over the cliff before the dump goes up. You look at him, and he stares back, his face blackened, only his eyes giving a hint of life. You had no time to check the cliff. You don't even know if there are spider holes, hidden firing positions along rocks. The route you plan to take is between the two ADA guns, and you intend to take out a gunner or two before jumping over.

You motion to Schmidt to head out, and you flash your fingers twice, 10 seconds. He nods and moves on, almost blindly picking the path. You look up at the sky. Rain is still falling. Bright flashes of explosions and bursts from the naval guns interrupt the darkness. The night is full of noises, fighting all around this otherwise serene spot. Guards walk their posts, feeling lucky at the moment to be away from the area of fighting at the cove some two miles south.

Suddenly a sentry stops at the edge of the jungle strip between you and the fuel dump. He looks down at the mud and moves the toe of his boot. He's found the cord but doesn't know what it is yet. You pull the ring and set the Det-cord afire. Det-cord combines a strong plastic coating over a thin, explosive inner component that burns quickly and is nearly unstoppable once ignited. It cannot be halted by being stomped on, smothered, or extinguished. Only cutting it before it passes the desired spot will end it. Basically, it is a lit fuse, a rapid, high-temperature fuse. The guard shouts a warning and reaches down to pull the line even as the fire rushes past him, burning his hand. He looks towards the destination and then turns to trace the source. You drop him, then turn to follow Schmidt. The commotion sets off an immediate flurry of activity of yelling, shooting, and running in the direction of both the fallen guard and the fuel bunker.

"Come on, come on, come on, come on!" Schmidt is coaxing you in a loud whisper to his position in the dark. You slip in next to him and move to the right, facing south, towards the closer ADA gun.

Screams and shouts of orders proceed a frenzied rush out of the fuel dump right before the night explodes in a mix of fire, smoke, debris, bodies, and dirt. The shock wave is tremendous; the superheated air is so devoid of oxygen that it is hard to breathe. Hot gulps of air full of the taste of diesel and oil are all you can get. You feel the burning heat, even in the jungle, which is now on fire, splashed with fuel from the erupted and still falling barrels sent high into the air. Bodies lay all over. The buildings around the dump are mostly destroyed, and a section of the airstrip is lit by a lake of burning fuel on the northwestern infield. Pandemonium and shock are countering the efforts by at least one officer to gain control of the chaos.

"What about him?" Asks Schmidt.

"Yeah, take him."

The officer falls after two shots, never knowing the first one missed.

You shoot the crew manning the ADA position and then throw your last grenade.

"We got to go," and you quickly crawl to the edge of the zalza log boundary of the cliff.

Chaloosa rifle fire is now on you from several points along the short coastal watch wall and security positions. You return a shot and then another, taking down the Chaloosa shooters. Schmidt is working on the other side. Others now join the defenders after hearing the shouts and hails of the coastal lookouts.

"Climb over. Get to the water!" You order Schmidt, and he dives headlong over the wall and down the cliffside.

You take another couple of shots, dropping one more before changing your magazine and following Schmidt. The ground falls away, and you slide and roll, hardly able to control your speed or direction. Schmidt is in front of you, looking back up the slope, aiming and firing as you slide by, stopping a few feet past. You see the ocean, several more feet below, the white crests and breakers of rocks and sand. It is too shallow and rough. You'll never be able to swim out of the swells and will be pushed back in. You look to the south and then north. You'll have to move further south, under the coastal wall another 100 yards, before there is a spot that looks like you can jump into the sea.

You touch Schmidt on the leg and point the way. He slides down to you and starts crawling through the bushes. You fire several times to cover him and then wait. He has had time to set up, and you move. He switches to the Chaloosa rifle, and you pass him, setting up a few yards past. You both watch as a pair of missiles scream in from the fleet, finding targets on the lit-up northern tip. You find solace in the fact that the ADA batteries will now have to fight it out against a missile cruiser intent on silencing them.

After what feels like an eternity, and using up the Chaloosa rounds and most of your own ammo, you stare at the waves 12 feet below. It is not what you thought. The boil of the current rips against the undercliff, washing into a cavity or hole. Jumping in here will result in drowning for sure. There is a patrol to your front and another coming up behind. The Chaloosa know the conditions of the cliffs and the ocean that meets them.

There is no spot to enter the water; only a crazy person would attempt it.

"There!" Schmidt points to a rock a few feet further from the drowning hole. "If we jump to it and then time the outflow, we might can make it far enough out to swim away and catch a swell. See? The current is split right over there. This is the point break, the divide. We are maybe a couple miles from the landing beach at this point. The coral reef is out there 100 yards or so and is breaking the big swells. You ever swim in the ocean surf?"

"No, not really."

"We just need to swim to the south, don't fight the current, follow it along the coast. See. Look at the waves, how they form a ribbon moving at an angle to the shore. The trick is to get behind the breaking and stay in the current. Strip down. We can't swim with anything. Let's go." He quickly pulls off his smock, drops his equipment belt and pants, then puts his boots back on but keeps his rifle. You follow his lead.

With two last shots, Schmidt jumps to the next ledge and then the rock, slipping halfway into the surf before struggling back up. You move to the ledge, fire your last mag and then jump. Schmidt catches you and pulls you up.

The night is dark, the roar of the waves breaking fills your ears; the white of the crashing covers the two of you instantly with cold refreshing spray. "Watch it now. It's coming in, see, see?" The wave breaks against the rock and explodes. The current sweeps the water back momentarily before the next wave crashes.

"Okay, okay. This is how we do it. Right after it breaks, we jump as far out as possible, that way," he points south, "and swim like mad in that direction. Got it? Come on now, Caporal, you can't back out now," Schmidt says, no doubt seeing the concern on your face.

"The next one, ready, here it is! Jump!" Both of you fly into the air for what seems like a minuscule length and not at all far from the rock and into the ocean. You feel the tug of the current pushing you back with the next wave. You move your arms in an over-arm, windmilling manner, kicking your legs, ignoring the great amount of seawater you accidentally swallowed. Schmidt is in front of you, gracefully slicing through the water, even submerging at times. His power is amazing. He is using a breaststroke under the waves, effortlessly cutting the swells. He looks back and sees you struggling, swims back, and yells at you to turn on your back.

His arm grabs you around the chest, and he pulls you for a few strokes and then yells above the roar, "There, we're in the rip current taking us down the island. It's like a conveyor belt. We just have to get off of it before it sweeps us out to the ocean on the southern end."

You swim cautiously. You had always heard the rip current would kill you, drown you. The fear is intoxicating, you feel the strong current controlling you, moving you sideways, and it scares you that you are not in control. The waves in front of you move and form, stretching out and breaking upon the coastline. Time is forgotten and passes without regard; the ocean current has you and saps your energy. The water is surprisingly cold.

"There, up there! I see ALTCs, the ones that swamped. We got to be careful, keep away from them. Listen, it was a fun ride, but now we got to jump off, but she's not going to want to lose her riders. The top current is the wave action. The undertow is what has us. Swim at an angle, flat as you can on the surface, slice the angle to the beach, not too much. Once I get shot out, I won't be able to come back and get you. You got it? Swim!"

You watch him, and it is like he was shot out of a cannon. He is already 10 yards away, and you are further south, a wave pushing him in. You swim as hard as you can. The waves are tugging on you, but the current is still holding on, sweeping you further south. The panic is back. An ALTC is coming up, the waves pushing it, but it's stuck on something. Coral! Jagged, sharp rocks of coral. The ALTC spins slightly, the open ramp in your view. You see several bodies pinned inside. The swollen white faces of death staring lifelessly at you, bloated arms and legs mixed and hung up among the crates. You surge past and the coral cuts along your side and arm. Argh! The intense pain is unnerving. A wave catches you and sends you spiraling to the shallows; another topples you over as you attempt to gain your feet. A third spins you around and around, beating you against a jagged, broken piece of reef.

A hand grabs you and pulls you from the water, steadying you even as you belch out and bend over with spasms of retching, the saltwater burning your throat, mouth, and eyes. Your whole body stings. Sand has already worked itself into the deep cuts to your hands and knees and those along your sides, back, legs, and arms.

"Ha-ha! We made it! I'll be damned! Caporal Baker, we did it! Come on; we got to get off the beach and link up with battalion."

You sit back in the sand, "Thank you, Schmidt. I would have never made that without you."

"Come on, let's find some uniforms and get some water off some of these guys."

"Yeah, there ought to be weapons and some crates of ammo washed up by now. The battalion may already have sent a patrol down here to collect whatever they could. We'll have to be careful."

By dawn, you have made the rearguard of Echo 1/100 and are greeted with genuine surprise. You learn from the company sergent that no one has come up from the beach, surviving the costly mistake of those ALTCs that opened their ramps on the reef. Three entire platoons drowned. A team was sent to the beach before dark the night before to scrounge what they could find of what washed ashore, but they found little. You and Schmidt manage to equip yourselves with trousers, smocks, boots, and rifles from the bodies that did wash ashore. Schmidt bandaged your cuts as best he could. You found one case of ammo. You split the two boxes with Echo, giving them one, then moved on to find Bravo 2/100 and report to Major DePont.

DePont's reaction to seeing both of you is of surprise and elation. Your report is overshadowed by the revelation that the two of you were responsible for the explosion during the night. Your and Schmidt's physical condition, he is also cut up, and the news of your wild escape gives the whole battalion a morale boost. Casualties are high among the nine companies on the island. The Chaloosa have pushed several times over the strait, beaten back each time. There is no opportunity to evac wounded or allow those that can still fight to fall back. You wouldn't have anyway. The second day of fighting begins with a concentrated mortar attack by the Chaloosa that doesn't end until the early hours before dawn the following day.

With ammo stores depleted and magazines being collected off the dead and seriously wounded, the Chaloosa carrier is finally sunk on the third morning, and their air support is destroyed. At 0724, the first wave of reinforcements makes landfall and rushes to the beleaguered survivors of the 1st and 2nd Battalions. Of the original 1440 legionnaires that loaded for the beach assault three days prior, less than 500 are still standing with wounds. There are over 200 dead, the rest seriously wounded. That includes the three platoons, 120 that drowned. The Battle of Blue Water Lagoon is over, for you anyway. You are evacuated onto the *Waxhaws;* the hospital ship only takes the more seriously wounded.

Sergent Ragford and Caporal Wright both made it, as did Lance Caporal Schmidt. After three more weeks of fighting, 3rd Fleet, along with your old battalion, the 1/107, and the others of that group, arrived to continue the clean-up of the island garrison. Your coral wounds became infected, and it was touch and go for a few days with your own blood pretty much becoming a poisonous toxin in your body. The 100th Regiment returned home and was dissolved, the legionnaires absorbed back into the 106th and 107th.

With three months remaining on your enlistment, your next assignment is spent on the beach back in Port Summa in a quasi-instructor role attached to V Corps, training newcomers in Amphib Assault tactics and orientation. With one month to go before your EOS, you are sent for by the regiment first sergent. You have thought about what you are going to do. It is time to leave the EFL, return home, start a new life. You have put in six years in four theaters of war, achieved great success, and lived through several situations that others did not. To reenlist is tempting fate. You couldn't count the legionnaires you knew that died, good mates. No, you are done.

CHAPTER 15

Level Up – **Hard Decision**

A Farewell to the EFL #21 Brief

    Medium A 15 PP 80% success

    Medium B 15 PP 80% success

    Character Summary

    You must decide about reenlistment.

Summary:

    With only a month remaining of your second three-year service, you must decide on the course of your life. The regiment first sergent has sent for you and offers the next step to your EFL career, a four-year enlistment highlighting several milestones that, due to your high achievements and skills, you are already tagged to obtain in the near future, DI school, promotion to Sr. caporal in a year, the assignment of a training platoon, and hopefully sergent within the same enlistment. You stand in the position of *at ease* and listen thoughtfully, mulling over the offer.

You have selected Medium Mission A.

    Your mind is pretty well made up before entering the regiment HQ, having talked with several good mates and other caporals and sergents. Even listening to the first sergent, you are still not swayed by the offer of re-enlistment and inform the first sergent that you will EOS out at the end of the month, return home, and begin a new life. First sergent is a little surprised and, with a noticeable air of disappointment, ends the meeting with a comment that the offer will stand until the last day if you should reconsider. You thank him and exit the office.

Upon returning to your daily duty, you feel a sense of peace that you made the right decision. With the last week remaining, you begin your EOS process from the EFL, a checklist of various steps to separate from service. You have to visit personnel, finance, battalion, the regiment quartermaster to turn in all your gear other than personal uniforms, Regiment Intel and legal, the armorer, medical and dental, and even the mess sergent to ensure you have no outstanding fees for chit expenses while on leave! Several nuisance items pop up in strange places. You are being charged for an incomplete uniform turn-in on two occasions and a complete reissue of lost kit from your second cruise. Regiment legal is investigating a possible outstanding assault charge. Finance and food services question two chits submitted, one for a two-attendance *Field Games Admission/Concession* receipt and the other for a high-end restaurant. The quartermaster is declaring unsatisfactory condition on three equipment items. The armorer submitted an inquiry about the status of two GPXR sniper rifles you had in your possession on multiple occasions during your last tour. Regiment Intel is also seeking additional information concerning an incident in the AC when it was reported that you allowed a defeated enemy patrol to escape rather than capture or annihilate it. You are scheduled next week to meet with intelligence staff and answer questions, even though you only have two days remaining before your EOS!

On the day before your EOS, you are ordered to report to a new duty location with all your remaining kit and notified that your EOS has been extended another five weeks to complete unfulfilled enlistment obligations. The period between the conclusion of your first and second enlistment was not completely satisfied, and you owe the EFL that time. In addition, since your last promotion took place during a combat action in what is known as a *combat situational promotion* and your actual promotion eligibility to the next rank level was not met by either time and/or service or promotion points at the time of promotion, you are reduced to the rank of lance caporal. Further, the awarding of *Legion Cross 1st Class* for actions during the *Battle of Blue Water Atoll* has been rescinded to *LC 2nd Class,* and your two *Corps Action Recognition Ribbons* are reduced to *Regiment Commendation Ribbons.* That action alone, other than being a complete back-handed slap, also excludes you from obtaining an immediate senate seat, which is won by awarding of an *LC 1st Class* with a *CAR* ribbon.

You are delegated for the remainder of your service obligation to menial physical duty around post as if a common disciplinary offender. You are ordered to turn in your dress uniform to the QM. On your last day of service, you are expelled from the EFL in a manner consistent with a three-year draftee, not even given the benefit of a bus fare home. Your morale and emotions are unsteady as you gaze with longing at a life no more from outside the gates of the base. You are completely alone.

You hail a cab, return home in a few days, and restart your life. The memories and faces of mates eventually fade to obscurity, and you ease into a life of non-importance and normalcy. You eventually marry, have kids, raise a family, and rarely speak of your past or acknowledge your once adventurous and esteemed position among the highest level of professional warriors.

You have completed a baseline level of the game. Your overall standing, game ranking is __ with a score of __. You have achieved *Fraudulent Chancellor Nedib* ranking. Pitiful. Restart and play again.

You have selected Medium Mission B.

Even after talking with mates, lance caporals, other caporals, and Sr. caporals, you are still unsure of your decision. The last month of your enlistment rolls in, and one day, three weeks before your EOS, the regiment first sergent summons you to his office. You are now undecided even though you earlier decided to EOS and return home. You knock on the door and enter once the first sergent responds. You know him but only by brief meetings in the field and the occasional barracks inspection at the temporary barracks assigned to the battalions while in port. He is not of the same breed as Colour Sergent Willoughby, who made regiment first sergent several months ago and whom you served with on two separate tours. No, First Sergent Kristenson is, from all accounts, a repeat Amphib tour senior EFL NCO. He is dressed in Class I dress uniform, and you can plainly see and make out his awards and ribbons. You acutely notice the absence of both the Palanquin Jungle Theater Ribbon and the AC Theater Ribbon. He has multiple Amphib Cruise ribbons and two Xobian Desert Campaign Ribbons. Is he really a Salty Leg, as the rumor persists? How could he achieve such a rank position with only two theaters? You are drawn back to the present.

"I have reviewed your service record, Caporal Baker, and you are an outstanding legionnaire. What thoughts have you given to reenlisting? Hmm? I should point out to you that your achievements speak volumes, that your exploits are what legends are to be made of. I see here," he pauses and leafs through the open personnel folder in front of him, "you are credited for the destruction of the main fuel depot on the main island during the Blue Water Atoll operation, and..." He looks down to find the exact passage.

"Good grief! Caporal Baker! Your escape by way of the open ocean surrounding the atoll and further insistence on continuing in operational missions throughout the next day, despite your wounds, is paramount to hero status! You have more than three dozen confirmed kills and a score of unconfirmed, though highly likely, kills as a sniper. Additionally, Lt. Ashworth, the commander of the J*W Nowly*, also highly praised you during your first cruise as OBSF. He stated that you are the quote *'highest qualified OBSF detail leader I have ever had the pleasure of supervising or meeting'* end quote. I'd say that is a pretty good reference coming from the likes of a full lieutenant of an escort frigate, no, wait, from a corvette! Holy crap, Caporal! You pulled OBSF detail leader on your first amphib hitch on a corvette? As a lance caporal? Let me skip through all this report and service record bull-crap, Caporal Baker. You know your record better than anyone else. You are a top-notch, highly-trained and experienced, highly sought-after EFL asset. Your re-enlistment is tantamount to the EFL's further success and the competent training and survival of future legionnaires.

"Let me lay out what is available to you on your next enlistment. First, you will be rewarded with a two-year free choice theater of operations due to your record, successes and achievements. It is hoped that you would follow precedent and return to *The Xo* for that period and take on a new, fresh platoon straight out of BT, serving as the assistant platoon caporal under a confident and well-respected Sr. caporal that brought them out of BT. You would then serve the next 12 months in either the Palanquin or AC as a refresher of alternative combat tactics. Your last year will take you to DI school, a *close-out* company, and finally, the glory of all rising sergents, the promotion to Sr. caporal, and your assignment to a training BT platoon and your first platoon command."

You think about what he says. You have already experienced a first platoon command, even if it was briefly before being reassigned back to sniping. He sees your hesitation.

"Caporal Baker, your skills and experience greatly benefit the EFL and the young legionnaire cassum that weekly begin their three-year service. Sure, you could return home, start a wonderful life, find a spouse, and start anew. Let me ask you this – do you see those you knew or barely knew at night when you sleep? Do you find yourself speaking, acting or behaving peculiarly, more consistent to a military life than of the old and forgotten civilian life that has disappeared from your conscience? Baker, let me be perfectly honest with you, you have served six years in the EFL and seen things that most people back home cannot fathom. Only a few back there can relate, former EFL themselves. You will not fit in back in the place you called home. It will be a prison surrounded by unknowing and unappreciative strangers. Your true family will be here, fighting and celebrating the thrill of life together. You will be miserable anywhere else."

You stand at the front of his desk, swaying ever so slightly in an absent breeze that is just as powerful against your strength as if it were blowing off the fo'ward prow of the *JW Nowly* at flank speed in the open crests of the *Tripondorea Sea*. His words sink in. You know them to be true, if you are honest with yourself.

"Give it a day to think over. Go back to your quarters; take the day off. I'll send a message to your sergent. Think about it, Caporal Baker. Come back and see me in the morning."

Your decision is made with a strong and willful mind and thoughts as clear as they were three years earlier.

"That won't be necessary, First Sergent. Where do I sign?"

"Right here, Caporal. Let me buy you a beer. I want to know what that surf swim was like. Holy cow! I had an ALTC come apart on me once. The whole squad was in the water before we knew what was happening. By the greatest of luck, we…" his tale weaved into a night of revelry and lore that encompassed over 16 years of amphibious shenanigans and desert trickery! A host of navy ship's mates and senior mates found the table and shared tales along with a colour sergent or two.

Your first impression of First Sergent Kristenson was proved false by the end of the night. He was a well-respected and fervent ally of the National Navy and a staunch antagonist of the National Army.

Level Up – Return to Blue Water Atoll

The next morning when you are again summoned to the first sergent's office to complete a missed form or sign another contract, you thought Kristenson would be off-limits, stand-offish, a total stranger. You had no idea how wrong you could be.

"Good morning, Caporal Baker! Good night! I didn't expect to see you a part of the living. I, myself, have a jackhammer breaking rocks inside my head! I need to overfly the operation on Blue Water Atoll and submit an analysis to II Corps for additional EFL influx."

You stare at the first sergent in an unknowing, confused sort of glance.

"Simply, I need to verify we need an increase in troop strength."

You hold your stare.

"I want you to accompany me as my security team. You need to sign out a GPXR with ammo, and grab your gear. Just make it a light assault kit. We'll fly out at 0900 on a *HACI* to the airstrip on the *Douboo Archipelago,* then hot-seat an Ocean Stork to the AHCS

Fervent Wind, which is operating in support of the 2nd Fleet right now. It'll be a three-day trip. Don't forget your toothbrush. You have," he looked at his watch, "less than a half-hour. Make it happen."

You come to attention, perform an about-face, and exit the office hurriedly, breaking into a full run once you depart the HQ. What just happened? A flight on a *HACI*! That's a *high-altitude command insertion* jet that flew, by what you have heard, at supersonic speed and at the cusp of the atmosphere. And then a helo hop to an attack helo carrier!

Gathering your combat pack, you quickly repack for the mission that First Sergent Kristenson outlined. You won't need most of this. You take your poncho liner, butt-pack, equipment belt with harness, two canteens, water purifier, boonie cap, toothbrush, spare socks in a ziplock bag, and six empty GPXR mags with pouches. You start to change into a set of jungle cammies from the desert uniform that is the prescribed duty uniform on post. Several NCOs are watching you, and one Sr. caporal finally asks, "What gives? Where you going Baker?"

"First Sergent drafted me to accompany him on an Op. Can't say. Here, strip these off and replace these for me," you toss your equipment belt and harness to him to replace the regular GPS pouches with the GPXR magazine pouches.

Deftly the Sr. caporal accomplishes the switch over as you complete the uniform change.

"See you in a few days," you say as you run down the steps to the main level and the arms room to draw a rifle and a thirty-five box of rounds. You'll load the mags in-flight.

The first sergent is ready and steps out of the building even as you run up, not even out of breath. There were no issues with either drawing the rifle and rounds or with your company sergent you passed while intent on fulfilling your task. Evidently, First Sergent Kristenson had sent advance notice of your immediate and important pending mission, and there was to be no interference. A buggy is on the street waiting, and First Sergent loosely holds a less than half-filled seabag in his hand, the contents probably his change-out and personal effects. He wears a GPC on his hip with two magazine pouches and a canteen. He is the epitome of an operational small unit NCO commander. The buggy driver wastes no time getting to the base airfield, pulling right up to a sleek, light-blue painted jet after passing through three separate check points. Besides yourself, the buggy occupants include the first sergeant, a navy lieutenant commander, and an EFL captain. The buggy can seat five, and the space with various bags was tight but not overcrowded. All the others also wear a stripped-down equipment belt with a sidearm, one or two mag pouches, and a single canteen. Each is dressed in a simple duty uniform of khakis, the officer's casual day uniform.

Without a word, the small group grab their bags and climb the steps to the entry hatch on the underside of the fuselage aft of the wing struts. You barely have time to gaze at the spectacular craft, to view the airframe of the *HACI*, a plane that cruises at the edge of space! There is only one opening that you can see, a length of about eight feet by four feet. The rumor is that high-altitude para-jumps are made from this plane. *Kristenson did say you were landing on the Douboo airstrip and then taking a helo, right?*

After everyone settles in and changes uniform, the team gathers in a knot around a map affixed to the front bulkhead separating the cargo seating compartment from the flight deck. There are three rows of three seats in the middle of the compartment. Along the sides or bulkheads, there is space for four to sleep. The aft compartment, where the entry hatch is located, is a much smaller space with two opposing benches, seating four on each side facing inward to the hatch. That compartment is heavily insulated, and the door to the main compartment is similar to a ship's hatch. You can plainly see that this is not a regular airplane used for transport of personnel from one theater to another like the huge Galaxy Loadlifter that holds a company and their equipment, including four buggies or two ATCs.

The briefing goes over details of the campaign to date, losses, the territory won, projected enemy strengths, the status of the other two airbases and their projected completion profile, and what effect that will have on Blue Water Atoll and the legionnaires currently fighting there. You stand to the rear of Kristenson, your mouth shut and listening to everything. The lieutenant commander gives the briefing, and the others take in the information as if it were all new to them. Maybe it was. Most of it makes no sense to you, only the part of the estimated Chaloosa Marine numbers and that the enemy has been able to land and resupply the garrison somehow. An estimated 5000 Imperial Marines, nearly four battalions, are entrenched across the lagoon strait and continuously pound the airstrip and EFL positions. They seem to have an unending supply of mortar rounds and rockets. The coral reef protects the atoll, hence that garrisoned island. The Chaloosa had blocked the entrance to the lagoon with scuttled barges.

It finally dawns on you that the lieutenant commander is a fleet liaison to the EFL, and the captain is an intelligence officer of II Corps. First Sergent Kristenson is the highest-ranking and most experienced regiment NCO of the 106th and 107th. He knows both of these officers in a more than casual or office/work relationship. Your presence is not even a concern. You begin to wonder. If a first sergent requires security, would not a lieutenant commander, a commissioned naval officer O-4 level? The captain is an O-3, a company commander. Why, even Lt. Ashworth was an O-3 and had Senior Mate Oswella, an E-7, at his beck and call. So maybe First Sergent was the captain's security, and you were the team's third? Surely the lieutenant commander would pick up an escort detail once landing on the AHCS. More than likely, he would not even step off the AHCS, performing whatever Intel gathering from aboard ship.

Heck! First Sergent said that he would only overfly the operation and submit a report. First Sergent Kristenson wasn't landing on the island. Ha-ha! You are worried about nothing.

You gaze at the three men. They are each dressed in JCU and wear equipment belts with sidearms and a canteen. Their uniforms are not new or pressed, and you have never seen a naval officer in EFL jungle cammies, much less a boonie hat. Crap! This is a recon patrol. It hits you, no rank insignia, none of them.

"Baker, let me show you around," Kristenson turns to face you. The briefing is over.

"This is a HACI EF2021-9. You have probably heard a little about it. The EF stands for extended flight, and the nine is for the insertion capacity. Don't worry; we're not inserting on this mission. Ha-ha. The aft compartment is the insertion/jump chamber. The operational speed is around 550 miles per hour or 477 knots, with a range of 3500 miles. The insertion speed will drop to 150 miles or 130 knots at an altitude of around 35-40,000 AGL depending on the op. Special equipment and oxygen are required to make that sort of jump. Training is pretty intense. Here, you can see the benches the team uses before they deploy. The hatch opens, and the jumpmaster inspects each jumper before they exit."

He completes the tour, pointing to the aftmost hatch where a small head is located.

The flight will still take almost eight hours, and refueling is required mid-flight; the distance to Douboo is nearly 4200 miles to the south. Blue Water Atoll is another 1200 miles, but there is no friendly airstrip closer. The team finally settles down, and everyone tries to take a nap. After the night before with Kristenson, you welcome the chance to sleep a little more.

The transfer to the Ocean Stork is hectic but completed flawlessly. The Ocean Stork is a long-range rescue and cargo craft, adept at defending itself and skimming the water at such a low altitude that you can feel the spray from the waves. The doors can be closed but remain open unless environmental conditions force the crew chief to close them. The helo flies at a speed of 210 mph or 180 knots. The waist/door gunners are alert and scan for possible threats. The EWO scans for Chaloosa subs that the helo will attack if given the opportunity. The short, stubby arm-struts with a pod of five Air-to-Surface missiles each are a reminder that this lanky bird has teeth.

This leg will last another six hours. There is no more sleeping. Unless you were wracked with complete exhaustion, the noise, cold, and wind would eliminate any opportunity for sleep. Finally, after almost 15 total hours of flying, the Ocean Stork lands on the AHCS, and you are exhausted beyond belief. The thrill of being on board an AHCS is exhilarating, for a short time, as you look around at the flight deck operations, the non-stop landing and take-offs of helos, and the firing of missiles and AA guns. The fleet is several miles offshore of Blue Water Atoll, and it is the middle of the night. You can smell the cordite, diesel and aviation fuel, and the burning of explosives from expended ordnance. You are led to a small stateroom with six bunks and a basin by a ship's mate 3rd class. You are given instructions to get some sleep, and in two hours, you will be fed breakfast before you go ashore. You take off your boots and socks, strip off your smock, and hang your gear from a hook. The others arrived sometime after, but you had fallen asleep nearly instantly.

Level Up – Swimming Blue Water Lagoon

The landing is not the adrenaline rush that it was the other two times you came ashore on the atoll, but the early, predawn trip was not a sleeper either. The Chaloosa are holding on to the atoll with all their might. The plain simple truth is that they had fortified and prepared this group of islands better than previously thought. The garrison island is securely located inside the coral reef perimeter and is unapproachable from the ocean. The three smaller islands of the atoll group also hold entrenched and well-fortified marines plus ADA and anti-missile batteries. The two western island airfield groups are now up and operating. It seems the Chalossa have won the race. Blue Water Atoll is now a growing graveyard, even with control of the airstrip. If the EFL continue to pour legionnaires into the fight, they will again have to commit the entire two regiments of the western fleets.

The landing beach OP sent a message to their CP, and a security detail met your party at the beach, surprised to see such a small group and one with few supplies for disbursement. It is an unwritten code to always bring in ammo, food, medical or other supplies when landing from the ships offshore. You off-load what you personally carry, and the detail hurriedly collects what few crates or cases are for them. That three noticeably senior-rank and competent men are accompanied by a wet-behind-the-ears caporal is compelling evidence that something is amiss. None of the three wear rank, and each is clad in jungle cammies and camouflaged face paint. Besides their personal sidearms, they also have two micro Sat-links, five demo-bags, and four three-foot-long four-inch diameter tubes that are fairly heavy. They secured all of this equipment before joining you last night in the semi-private stateroom. First Sergent Kristenson is now also carrying a GPS. There is one last crate in the ALTC, which Kristenson calls for you to assist him in pulling out.

"Give me a hand here, Caporal. Grab that end there with the handle," he points.

The wooden crate is heavy at three feet by five feet. It is stenciled with military jargon which reads *Boat, Inflatable, Rubber; Light Surf, Two-Man, Limited Survival Duration; with Paddles and Pump*. The category or stock ID number and *National Navy Service* is also printed. A rubber raft? A small, two-person, coastal operations, with a short survival time-frame rating raft? What is going on? It is now almost four in the morning; you can see the pink of the sun rising from the east across the far-off horizon.

You feel a sense of hurry or rushed preparation among the officers and Kristenson. Lt. Cmdr Swenson and Captain Oroarha grab the loops at the opposite corners, and the four of you carry the crate down the beach, south. The small group divided up the equipment before breakfast. You carry two demo bags, a tube, your GPXR, another 15 additional rounds in your butt-pack, a GPC with two spare magazines, and a single case of combat rations of 10 meals in your free hand. The navy commander leads the way, and you find yourself on the opposite corner with him at the front of the crate. Kristenson and Oroarha are at the back. *What is going on?*

The four of you struggle with the load walking in the sand, and you remember this section. This is where you and Lance Caporal Schmidt made it to shore. Soon, the known beach is behind you, and the southern bulb of the island, which is covered in jungle, surrounds you. The trek now is in the surf, nearly to the knees. You feel like the current is tugging at you, almost sweeping you away. You remember Schmidt talking about the riptide. What would happen if you slipped and dropped the rations? Or lost the raft?

A sand bar or spit appears, separating the ocean from the jungle edge.

"Here. This is exactly where it showed on the reconnaissance photos. Kristenson, get this raft operational. We have an hour of darkness left. That should get us to *Manō Maku*, past *Hanu Maku*."

The words were of the western ocean people, the *Alelo*, which inhabited many island groups. Some had joined the allies, some the Chaloosa faction, and others remained neutral. Most of the islands were small atolls formed from lava flows from the *A'ā* volcano. You know only a couple of words, *Maku* is island, *Moana* is ocean. That was about it.

First Sergent Kristenson wastes no time knocking the boards off his end, "Get at it, Caporal. Be careful not to crush the crate inward, or you'll put a hole in the raft." He continues to rip the crate apart.

You kick awkwardly on the end in an outward thrust, partly missing and scraping the back of your leg, stumbling. Captain Oroarha is not amused and quips, "Move out of the way, Caporal."

Your initial reaction is to balk and offer an excuse, but quickly move out of the way and allow the captain to smash the wooden planking with a single blow at the middle of the end cap on the top edge. The four of you rip the crate apart, tossing the loose and broken packaging aside. Kristenson instructs you to grab hold of the inner protective bag and lay it out on the sand. The sand bar is not much bigger than the four of you standing upon it. Swenson, Lt. Cmdr Swenson, tosses the remaining crate package to the shoreside after ensuring all the components are accounted for – the pump, paddles, repair, and emergency kit.

Kristenson rips the bag away, and the two of you unfold and lay out the raft. It is no larger than three by four feet, nowhere big enough to hold the prescribed two men, yet alone four and all the equipment. He checks that all is clear and then opens a small plastic box, releasing a handle somewhat like a pull cord for a lawnmower. He pulls it, and the raft inflates in seconds by a compressed-air canister.

"Here's the situation Caporal Baker. I don't believe First Sergent Kristenson has briefed you fully. We are catching the current that sweeps past the tip of this *nui maku*, large island, and should sweep past *Hanu Maku* to the southern tip of *Manō Maku,* Shark Island. We'll land there and recon for an LZ. The Chaloosa are not purportedly as strongly fortified on *Manō*, only manning

ADA and missile batteries, relying on the outer coral reef as a defense barrier to a landing. The *maku* is hilly, uneven. If we can't find a suitable LZ, we will make for the next larger island north tonight. Are you in, Baker?"

Level Up – Recon *Manō Maku*

Raft Recon Mission #22 Brief

    Medium A 15 PP 80% success Return to OP

    Difficult B 25 PP 60% success Join the Patrol

    Character Summary

    You must decide whether to proceed with the recon patrol or return to the OP on the beach.

Summary:

    There is little time to dwell on the choice you must make; the horizon of the eastern ocean is already a thin line of lighter darkness with a tinge of pink. For the first time, you notice the night sky is darker with cloud cover of some gathering storm system. The waves break along the small sandbank; the current can clearly be seen just a few feet out, driving the tidal flow in a southerly direction. The three men are placing all their equipment in the raft and are preparing to enter the water. You look back the way you came and then towards the garrison island. What if the raft is spotted? Or is swept out to sea? There was no forewarning of this operation, only a thinly-veiled order to accompany the first sergent on a flyover.

You have selected Difficult Mission B.

You step to the raft and unshoulder your gear and unclasp your equipment belt, placing everything in the raft. There are four short lengths of rope with a loop attached to handles along the top edge of the raft. The others are slipping the loops over their head and around a shoulder. You do the same. The purpose of the raft was never to hold any of you; instead, it is for the equipment and as a support rest.

Before the group steps into the water, Swenson says, "The charts all show a strong current flowing around the atoll and converging on the western side. We need to stay off the waves pushing into *Hanu*, and avoid getting caught on the outside away from *Manō*. We'll need to pass *Hanu* then slant northwest. They'll be watching on the western side but not so much on the eastern shore. Let's go."

The current takes you right away. The sand bar is almost at the tip of the bulb of the island. The current is strong and pushes at a noticeable clip. Fear grips you, and you fight against the rope to swim back to the last point of shoreline.

"What are you doing? This way," Kristenson calls out.

You stop struggling and look around. The three men are holding onto the raft's side, peering at you over the edge. They are kicking with their feet and legs, pushing the raft in the general direction they wish to go. Your misdirected power fought against their propulsion. You swim to the raft and join them. Occasionally one or two along either side will stroke with their free arm, pushing or pulling the raft back on course.

You now can see the adjacent island rise above the waves. The jungle canopy appears first, then the glint of sand or black rock.

"Too close; push us out. We're being carried in," Swenson urges.

He is right. Less than 50 yards away, the island is quickly coming in.

"We're in a circling eddy. Oroarha, pull us out. Kris, you and Baker kick from the back," Swenson directs. The two officers drop off the edge and begin swimming in a near southern direction, pulling against the lead ropes while you and first sergent kick and pull with one arm. The exertion is intense, and progress is slow, but after a few minutes, the tip of *Hanu* slides by.

"Okay, now back in. We want to slip in between the two now." Again, the officers pull the raft back along the current and north.

You are exhausted. The morning's work of carrying the boat and gear in the tropical climate, the physical exertion in the cool water, and the stress and fear combine to drain you. The sun is now visible, a bright orb inching up, growing in diameter as it climbs, first a speck, then a beaming, piercing, blinding light. It grows as if a plate was held against the edge of a table and slowly pushed upward, its edges spreading further and further as it rises higher. The darkness of the night is being pushed back quickly, shrinking at an accelerating rate, as the orange, pink, red, yellow, and the lighter blue of dawn stretches ever faster westward. In less than 10 minutes, an observant eye will be able to trace the silhouette of the raft atop the waves.

The group is now somewhere between *Manō* and *Hanu Maku*, but just how far up the coast is not known. The current is a slip-stream, a swirling off-shoot of the main ocean current as it sweeps around the obstacle in the middle of the path. If you are not careful, this eddy current could take you straight into the lagoon, where the **Chaloosa** will quickly spot your presence.

"There it is. It looks like we are a couple hundred yards upshore. Swim." Lt. Commander Swenson has evidently studied the atoll at great length, not to mention the current and tide tables.

Just how a four-person patrol is to swim ashore with a rubber raft and not be noticed is foremost on your mind now. Thinking of how you are to extract had popped up earlier during the swim in but had been pushed out by the other more pressing and present concerns of the moment. Right now, it is all you can do to focus on landing undetected and locating a suitable LZ. You have been in the water for nearly an hour, traveling about seven miles of the approximate 15-mile length of the atoll. The dawn is here, burning away the light cloud cover. It will be hot and steamy on the island and in the jungle. You want a drink from your canteen; the splashing seawater has left your mouth agonizingly dry and salty, your eyes stinging, and your skin pruney.

"Shhh! Stay still. There's a missile boat in the slot," Swenson warns in a hushed voice.

It has to be one of only a few that have somehow survived the onslaught of the initial assault months ago. How it has eluded your forces or where it hides during the day is intriguing as there is no way they could have managed to sneak it in. There has to be a concealed cove, inlet, or cave along one of these other four islands. The morning is coming fast, but they have enough time to spot and destroy you or at least report your position to the shore batteries and coastal defenses. It seems to change course, turning towards you, and then, just as suddenly, it swerves to the port, east, and heads directly for the backside of garrison island or *Hanu Maku*. It is gone in the streaking light.

"Swim! We have to make the shore before light." There are breakers ahead, indicating a small formation of coral rimming this section of island. It just is not getting easier. The fractured channel current is such that it forms waves anywhere the shore shallows up to a beach or cliff face.

"Good night, Swen! I've done some crazy ops with you, but this is the hardest I've had to work to get in," First Sergent Kristenson says, holding onto the raft and kicking beside you.

"Ha-ha, Kris, you can thank me later. How's the rookie doing?"

Kristenson gives you a look, grins, and replies, "Oh, I think shooting any one of us has been entertained." The three laugh a quiet guff and continue swimming, pulling, pushing, and tugging the heavy raft in the now heavy, breaking surf.

The beach is not a beach, not even a sand bar, but a heaped-up pile of broken coral, sharp and jagged. The incline rises suddenly from some unknown depth to your knees and just as quickly to a shallow, barreling, wave-pounding shelf, barely a foot-and-a-half-wide. The sharp coral immediately slices your hands, knees, arms, and legs, and the intense pain knifing through your nerves is like an electric shock. You remember the month-long painful treatment you underwent with the last swim. This is much worse.

You crawl up on the shelf and pull on the raft, assisting in getting it landed and saving the team equipment. "Get on a covering position Baker. We'll get this," Swenson orders, struggling to disentangle his uniform from a piece of coral that rips through the blouse.

You reach out for your rifle and belt from the raft, the weight almost toppling you over from your fatigue. You hurry into the dense jungle, dismissing your own wounds, and set down in a hurried hide. This is your element; it takes little time for you to relax, settle your breathing, and quiet your pulse. You take stock of the lay of the land, the steep rise up from the shore, the dense jungle so much like the Palanquin. Not even the larger assault island was this thick. You listen for any noise, natural or man-made. You hear nothing other than insects, birds, and small mammals. Your position is only 10 yards out. Swenson only said to set up a covering position, but you know it's important to get a light recon of the area around the group.

After 10 minutes, you circle back to your starting point and find Kristenson set up, watching you as you crawl.

"What you see?"

"I only went out a little way. Quiet, no sign of any activity until 15 yards that way," you point to the north whispering. "A shore trail turns for whatever reason there and heads west a bit, completely skirting this spot right here, and then it goes back to the shore again."

The two of you are lying in a patch of thorny brush, and a giant termite mound is a few yards away. Maybe that was enough to send the trail in a detour? That and the fact that the point of shoreline where you came out of the water is so rough and uninviting, no one would think that an invasion would come from there.

"We'll sit here a bit and rest, check out the surrounding AO 50 yards out, and wait for the heat to build. Then we'll move."

The logic was backward but was also beneficial. The heat would build from midday until late afternoon, which traditionally was taken as a resting period while the tropical temperature climbed to over 100. Most sentries and guards would be more than predisposed to lay low out of the heat and limit work. If only the EFL would adopt such a practice. Many times in *The Xo* or the *Palanquin,* you could remember not only tactical practice and rehearsal occurring during this time but also heavy combat. It was one of the many standard practices that set the EFL apart from her enemies.

You observed that the raft now lay in the jungle, deflated from its operational pressure and hidden among the deadfall just at your feet. Lt. Cmdr Swenson and Captain Oroarha are busy studying a map that is protected in a waterproof case and discussing some issue. Kristenson holds out a pouch of something. Peanut butter.

"Eat this. It's the best energy food with less digestive time than anything else." You take the pouch, rip the corner away, squirt a stream in your mouth, and then offer it to Kristenson.

"Naw, I had mine; finish that." He lies there, scanning the perimeter.

"I understand if you're mad at me about this whole thing, but I couldn't tell you anything before getting underway. Security. I guess you figured out this is not a normal team or operation, huh?"

"Yay. I got that somewhere between the flight on the *HACI* and the swim. I'm not mad. I could have used a little more heads up on the op choice than the sink or swim back there on the sand bar, but I'm here."

"Good. I guess now is as good a time as any. If you're captured, at least you'll know why you are being beaten to talk. This is an ultra-sensitive, highly-classified covert recon team. Only a few are chosen. The number of teams is classified, and you won't know that level of Intel for some time. Four- and nine-man teams, mixed with Navy and EFL personnel. We're gonna locate and clear an LZ for an assault team to take control of this island, opening up a backdoor on the atoll. We'll take each of these islands in a domino, cutting off the garrison completely. Once that's done, the airstrip can be fully operational."

He never takes his eyes away from the scan. "You still in?"

You ponder the situation. There is no room for a complacent member of an understaffed team. "I guess so, First Sergent. There's nowhere to swim away to. Ha-ha."

"Yay, I get that. Col. Pittman vouched for you and Colour Sergent Brockmann. Those were some pretty good ops you ran with Juno. You stood out, as did the others. We don't lose those numbers here, though. These teams are well seasoned. When we get back, if you want to continue, we'll send you to V Corps and Special Operations Service training. It'll mold your future."

"Hmmm, well, First Sergent, let's complete this here and get off this island, and then I'll think about it."

"That's good—no hurry Baker. And call me Kris out here. The Commander is just Swen, and the Captain is, well...."

The two officers were just at your feet. They could surely hear the hushed whispers of your conversation, even as their low voices carried to you.

"Call me Hank, Baker, but I swear to you in front of these witnesses, you so much as stutter an 'H' in my presence back on the drill field, you will own the battalion lawn duty until the day you cycle out."

"Yes, Sir," you manage as the hushed laughter of the three fills the humid air.

"Here's the sit-rep. We are approximately here. This spine spans the island's entire length on a zero-six to one-nine-zero degree line. The ridge is steep and, from air surveillance photos, doesn't appear to offer much in terms of a perfect LZ, but I feel this location here, on the northwestern side, may give us the best shot." Swen circles the map with a finger.

"If they overshoot their DZ, they fall into the water or into rough jungle along here," Kristenson voices, tracing his finger on the map.

"It's all we got here; otherwise, it's over to *Kalo Maku*, which is larger, flatter, and also needs to be captured, but we were hoping to take *Manō* first."

"Second," you interject. The others look at you.

"The 100th Regiment took the first island on day three over five months ago." You will never allow the legionnaires that fought and died over this atoll to be wiped away, forgotten, or under-appreciated. Never.

"*Manu Maku*, Bird Island, Baker, and yes, you are right, the second island." Commander Swenson looks at you with a new appreciative respect. Even Captain Oroarha nods his head.

"We'll wait until 1300 and then start out. Baker, you have proved you are more than a capable spec-ops in the jungles. You'll take point. We are avoiding all contact if possible. Our mission is the LZ, nothing else. We make contact and announce our presence, and we fail the mission. Questions? Alright, Kris, take first watch, Baker second...."

Oroarha is evidently a medical doctor or specializes in wound care. He checks each team member for injuries from the coral, treating and bandaging the wounds as best as the situation allows. Each group member has cuts, some more serious than just a scratch, but there is no recourse; the mission has to proceed. Swenson's shoulder has a great gash that Capt. Oroarha stitches up and gives him a shot for. Each uniform is torn and cut up, offering little protection from mosquitoes and flies that harass the four of you. You have cuts, some deeper than others, on your hands, arms, knees, and legs, but you escaped the coral injuries to your chest and back that you incurred months before. You settle down for a nap.

Level Up – Shark Fin Ridge

The sun dips to the west. The terrain doesn't look suitable for a helo LZ at all. The group keeps to the eastern side of the range, the island only a half-mile at its widest, though nearly six miles long. That is deceiving. The ridge is very steep, rising nearly 600 feet from the ocean, cut with trails and OP stations. The work is hard, avoiding a few patrols and over-watch positions that are mainly concerned with the southern tip and the western approach. The effort of the team to enter the slot and land up from the southern tip kept you from being spotted. Now the objective to find a suitable LZ remains. You reach the northern tip at dusk and locate that foremost OP, a dug-out cave on a promontory rocky cliff, hewn straight from the lava flow that makes up this *maku*. There must be a labyrinth of caves and tunnels along and inside the ridge. You have only encountered a few roving patrols, all sticking to the paths.

There is no telling how many Imperial Marines are garrisoned here. There is only one way to find out, and it has to happen before the decision to land an assaulting force begins. Timing is critical. An LZ has to be selected and marked, rigged with explosives, and the tunnels scouted before the detonations, or the marines will be alerted. You understand that an assault group is standing ready for a green light to depart, and your team has not sent it yet. Finally, you find a marginal site; Kristenson and Oroarha evaluate it and lay out the demo plan. You will use a three-step clearing. The first two charges will clear the area of trees and portions of the ridge. Several seconds later, the third will detonate on the lower side to clear away the debris. Two OP's with radar dishes and ADA are on either end of the ridge adjacent to the demo area. You will rig them from above, and hopefully, that will close the openings.

The team goes to work; each member knows their assignment and performs their job flawlessly. It is close to 0430 when the last charge is placed over the final two OP Batteries of the six stations. That is all five demo bags. You lie just off the path of the 1st OP on the northern tip, ready to follow Kristenson into the cave. Swenson and Oroarha are each babysitting the 5th and 6th OPs. Swenson holds four of the igniters; Oroarha holds his. Kristenson crawls up to the edge of the cave and gives the signal, and you relay the cryptic message to Swenson that Kristenson is moving inside.

You watch as he takes out one, and then a second Chaloosa sentry with his *KIF* – you have to love the military for all its acronyms, even for a simple individual fighting knife! He disappears for half a minute, then reappears, waving you in. You close the short distance and straddle the short rock defensive wall. The bodies lay at your feet, neat, only the slightest puncture mark along the side of the neck offering a clue to their demise. Kristenson is stripping one of his blouse, soaked in blood and sweat. He pulls the body to a darkened spot in the small area. He is going in alone, the plan already detailed. You will remain in the dark and watch silently, neutralizing anyone that comes up the trail with your *KIF*. Kristenson will traverse the inner cavity as far as he dares and return, attempting to gain a feel for the actual number of defenders.

He's gone. Thoughts of various scenarios fill your head, from First Sergent Kristenson being captured, tortured, and interrogated to the four of you being trapped on the island and dying one at a time in a drawn-out, one-sided extermination. Within the hour, with less than half an hour to go of the observed two-hour rotation of the OP's, he emerges from the cave, soaking wet and looking 10 pounds lighter. The internal heat of the tunnels is obviously high.

"That's it, Baker. Signal for the demo and drop. We'll close this cave up with a *HEPR*." The *high explosive personal rocket* was the short tube you had carried since landing on the island. You have never seen or heard of it. You don't even know how to fire or prepare it for firing.

Kristenson leads the way back to the trail and takes a tube from you. Before entering the tunnel, he had left all of his gear except his GPC and a Chaloosa rifle with you. He demonstrates how to extend the tube and trigger mechanism, remove the front cover, and sight it in. You wait. It could be hours before receiving confirmation of the incoming assault. You can't blow the LZ too soon, or that will warn of an incoming flight that could easily be fended off by the island defenders or the supporting bases further west.

You wait. The Chaloosa will rotate the guard soon, find the dead sentries, and know that the enemy is present. What is the plan? It is almost dawn; the helos will be sitting ducks. The Sat-link clicks, and Kristenson instructs you to respond with a double click. Within seconds, you hear the explosion of the first charge, followed by a second explosion, and then 15 seconds later, a third one reverberates through the island. A few seconds later, you hear a rush of marines from the inner tunnel of your OP. Kristenson fires the *HEPR,* and a cascade of earth and rock falls on the small opening, not quite closing it up.

He fires his rifle and instructs you to find targets. Soon the hole is plugged with bodies, and he carefully steps forward and pulls rocks down by hand. "Watch the trail, nail 'em."

Two more explosions, smaller than the first three, tell you that the 5th and 6th OP Battery positions are now closed as well.

"Alright, keep this trail clear. I'm going up and over and light the way in for the *HACI* jumpers."

"What? I thought helos were coming in."

"No, two assault teams are in-bound now, 18 Spec-Ops. You'll see 'em floating in from the south in a few minutes. Hopefully." He takes the Sat-link and his pack and dashes up the ridge to the peak.

A body moves, pushed at first from inside and then pulled in. You wait until the marine is halfway out and do your job. It isn't in the least fair or civil or honorable. You take his rifle, collect the others you can, and toss them off the cliff, saving one. A patrol comes running up the trail, and you engage. There are at least five, and you hit two from the start. They take cover along the rock wall of the trail. They will soon attempt to flank you. Another group joins them, and you fire the Chaloosa rifle, emptying magazine after magazine from the retrieved ammo of the dead. Occasionally you fire the GPXR, scoring one-shot hits. Kristenson never said the estimated number of Chaloosa Imperial Marines within the tunnels. You guess there is at least a squad now at the trail, probably moving in a tactical flanking maneuver.

A strange apparition suddenly appears in the southern sky, not there a moment ago, and floats briefly before disappearing. There it is again, and another. They disappear just as quickly. You count five total. You hear a noise below you. This OP is on the island's northern tip; the trail the defenders are coming up winds from the eastern side traveling north. The trail converges here and then continues again around the western side and south. You shoot a marine working his way up behind you. He rolls down and falls from the cliff into the remaining dimness of the breaking dawn.

You are out of Chaloosa ammo and fire the last loaded magazine of the GPXR, digging into your pack for the 15 loose rounds, firing your GPC alternatively. How long are you expected to hold this trail? You take the HEPR from your shoulder and prepare to fire as you watched Kristenson do. You aim at the ledge above the trail where the Chaloosa have set up a defensive position and fire the hand-held rocket. The back-blast stretches behind you five feet in a flash of fire as the rocket ignites and roars to the cliff face, exploding and raining rock debris and burning phosphorous upon the Chaloosa. You load a magazine and fire three shots, each doing the job. You load the last two magazines and fire the last three rounds of the GPC. You are dangerously close to expending your remaining ammo.

Should you fall back? That will allow the Chaloosa to dig out the OP and strengthen the forces on the northern end. No, you still have ten rounds. That will give vital time to the jumpers to land, assemble, orient, develop a plan, rest a moment, and....

The sound of GPXR, GPS, grenades, and HEPRs rip the dawn along with flashes and explosions. The defensive position in front of you is cut off and decimated before you realize what has happened. Someone yells out a security call sign, and you are surprised at first. A predetermined call sign and challenge had been part of Swenson's briefing yesterday – *Angel–Dawn* – but you never thought you would need it.

"*Angel!*"

"*Dawn!*" you whisper loudly in response.

"Are you Baker? Stand up and walk forward."

"Who are you?" you reply, still unsure of what is happening.

"I will count to two and then blow you off this cliff with a *HEPR*! Walk this way now!"

You stand up uneasily and walk forward.

A dark green, black, and deep brown striped face appears from the shadows, throws you to the ground, and holds a KIF at your throat. Your body and your arms are pinned expertly, allowing no movement. You are defenseless and at the mercy of your assailant. The knife blade easily nicks a small incision; it's painful, but you dare not squirm.

"Who was your first platoon commander?"

The cobwebs disappear in a flash. *How the heck are you supposed to remember some green leftenant from The Xo you never spoke to or who never gave you the time of day?*

"We didn't have one. Second Platoon India 4/117 IV was commanded by an Adjutant Leftenant Pupello or Popullo, something, of 1st Platoon. Crap, Adjutant Leftenant Hue in the Palanquin was my first assigned platoon leader."

"Let 'em up, Sykes! Damn it, stop playing games. You know we got the damn *monkeys*."

Your tormentor moves the KIF away, then treats you to a knee to the abdomen. "Ugh.." your breath escapes.

"How are you fixed on ammo? You have any *Dem*?" the apparent team leader inquires.

"I have two magazines for the rifle. That's it."

"Pull whatever from these dead, all of you, quick! Let's keep moving, grab what you find. You're with us, Baker."

Now you see another figure stripping the dead of weapons, ammo, grenades, etc. You follow the lead, taking a single, short-stock, Chaloosa *TER-c*. The *tropical environment rifle* is a compact weapon similar in design to the EFL's GPS with a smaller caliber which offers a semi-automatic option along with full auto and takes a 20 or 30-round magazine. The Chaloosa have several model designs, unlike the EFL, for various theaters. It is your favorite weapon, second to the GPXR, with slightly less accuracy but more firepower than the GPS. You secure nine magazines and shove them in every pocket and pouch you can. There are no grenades or explosives among the dead.

"Baker, you know the layout of this *maku* pretty well? You humped the eastern slope?"

"I, yeah, I guess. From the landing site north three miles and then on the western face searching for an LZ."

"So, are you good to take us to the next OP or not?"

"You selected that leg-breaking, slide-for-life, mountain goat playground of an LZ? I oughta cut your throat just for that," the man named Sykes adds.

You ignore Sykes and answer the team leader, "I know where the 2nd OP is if that's what you need. How do you want to approach? Above or below?"

"Take us in from below. How many are on this side?"

"Counting this one, there are two more, then the 4th on the southern tip. Swenson and Oroarha should have closed the 5th and 6th."

"That's our assignment. Relieve you, seal up One, and take out number Two. Sykes, close it up. Let's move!"

You drop down off the trail to the jungle below, careful for more patrols and reinforcements coming to aid the force that was just wiped out. You are curious about Sykes now; will he be alright on his own? An explosion from the OP answers your question, and you hear the wayward and precocious member rejoin the patrol line a few minutes later.

You pause and check your bearings, sure that you have led the team to the proximity of the intended OP. This has to be it. The *shark fin* is nearly above you, observed through the jungle overgrowth. You learned, with much relief, that *Manō Maku*, Shark Island, was not named for the dangerous presence of sharks, which was your first inclination, but rather for the appearance of the *maku*, a high rock formation at the southern tip and a similar though shorter formation over halfway up. These evidently gave the semblance of a *manō*, shark, to the earlier voyagers and settlers of the atoll, the *Alelo*, the western ocean people. You hear the commotion and loud commands of officers and senior marines above you on the trail. In the distance, you can hear the din of fighting, small arms, AP, grenades, and missiles.

"Good job. Set up a nest. We'll do the main work. You take out any problems and high-profile assets. Got it?"

You nod your head and reply, "Understood."

You move up the steep slope quicker than you usually would under an isolated situation, but you realize time is critical to close up the remaining holes. There could be dozens more spider holes, secondary exits anywhere on the slope, or fighting positions that the recon team missed. The possibilities are endless, but you have to deal with the known first and then respond to the unknown or newly developed after.

The trail is right in front of you, heavily manned. At least 30 Imperial Marines are now hastily re-enforcing fortified defensive positions to the front of the OP entrance and the lone ADA battery on the eastern slope. Another relief patrol is forming to head north. Suddenly a fiery swoosh passes over your head and smashes the rock face above the tunnel. Another HEPR follows within seconds. The cave entrance collapses, and dust mingles with the now greying dawn. Weapons fire from both sides erupts. The relief patrol is caught in the open, cut down by what sounds like an AP, which is impossible with only a three-person team! A grenade scatters the remaining survivors. The surprise assault is danger-close to begin with, the Chaloosa Marines have nowhere to go.

You spot a low-grade officer and hold. He will look for direction from a superior momentarily. There. A glance, a simple sign of acknowledgment. You take the shot. The young junior officer is horrified as he realizes he is in command now; his face shows fear and uncertainty. He barks an order and turns his head to direct his *dux-sergent,* the highest-ranking enlisted marine of an Imperial Marine company. The non-commissioned, mid-grade enlisted marine, barely respected by the Chaloosa officer corps, is five yards down the line from the young sub-lieutenant and begins to organize a repulse but suddenly slumps back in the dust of the trail.

Young *Chaloosa Imperial Marine Sub-Lieutenant* still has not realized a sniper is working him, and points to his next ranking veteran after scanning the options. That marine yells a response back and fires blindly into the jungle, ignoring the officer. It is time to take the junior officer, and he lies still. The field of options is drying up, a pitiful collection of non-ranking, lower EM's with no apparent leadership. There are still many marines capable of mounting a counter-assault, but in the end, they remain and die one by one without effective leadership command. You move to the *TER-c* right after taking out the sub-lieutenant. The defenders only possess small arms and no crew-served weapons.

Quickly, Sykes scales the rock face above the entrance and sets up a demolition charge to bring down a fault-line crack. Shards of black glass lava fly through the air, even striking you, causing several minor cuts. The entrance is sealed. The ADA Battery personnel are among the victims of the assault and never regain a gunner team. The implication is clear. The Chaloosa never intended *Manō Maku* to be an amphibious defense position, only an outer-perimeter, moderately-manned air defense station supporting the airstrip and garrison islands of *Kalo, Hanu,* and *Manu.*

Smoke and dust waft through the air, and you lay among the thick bushes of jumyal and rutaceae, a small, yellow-green, citrus-fruit-bearing plant that brandishes sharp, two-inch thorns that are extremely painful. You wait for new orders and watch as Sykes and the third, as yet unknown and unnamed, team-member advance and probe the dead. The third individual is not big yet carries a modified and much smaller version of what appears to be an AP. Nothing you have read, studied, or seen indicates a model of an AP, anti-personnel, gun designed to be operated by a single person. Yet, there it is, deadly, heavy, bulky, and operational. You want a closer look.

The team leader now steps up to the trail and signals a rally point, circling his hand, finger extended, over his head several times, and then points to a spot close to your position.

"Stand fast, Baker, just in case," he says, squatting down on a knee and waiting for the other two to join four feet off the trail.

"We hold here. The initial reports are that all targets have been neutralized and are under control. Ninth SOSA Group is sweeping for spiders and monkeys now. Third SOSR is assisting with closing up all capped tunnels. Baker, you have been ordered to remain with 5th SOSA Group, Team 3, for now. I'm Navy Commander Hutchess. Call me Hutch or Three. I'm 5th Group Leader.

That's Ship's Mate 1st Class Sykes and Sergent Bolivar on the *SOAP*."

Your mind turns back-flips; the information and intelligence shared are overwhelming. You know vaguely of the Special Operations Service Branch. It is one of the six basic branches offered upon recruitment. You didn't qualify to enter that service branch six years ago when you filled out the recruitment questionnaire, but now, it seems, you are solidly entrenched in its ranks.

"Sykes, you and Baker set up on that rock there," Commander Hutchess says, pointing to a large rock that has slid at some point in history to a spot blocking the likely path and forcing a slight detour. It is an excellent blocking point. You rise to your feet and move to the rock slab, searching for a suitable nest even while 20 yards out.

Sykes joins you, quickly setting up a *channel-chute* 15 yards to the front, a great kill-zone entrapment ambush that was rarely used in the EFL, which preferred the *L* or *Head and Tail Ambush* setups. He makes his position just below yours and checks the trail.

"Nice shooting. It proves even an idiot can point a rifle."

Ship's Mate 1st Class Sykes is an above-average looking guy at almost five feet six, 200 pounds or so, and thickly muscled. He is arrayed in JCUs with at least three demo bags and two HEPRs among the dozen or more ammo pouches attached to either his equipment belt or equipment vest. He carries two canteens and a butt-pack. His face is painted in the diagonal pattern of dark green, black, and brown that you were introduced to earlier, and his aura is that of total control, being well-tuned and respected.

"I like the channel-chute, never had the opportunity to use it," you offer.

"Well, that's a given. Just don't pop the first guy that draws inside; you'll ruin it. The first guy at this point will either be a gung-ho veteran and might sniff it out or the latest replacement. The ridge is secured now, and the 9th is sweeping the boonies below us. The Chaloosa will bebop on down the trail here, or they may have figured out they need to defend their own future graves and stay in place."

You lay in a tangle of twisted vines and rice-grass, a sharp long-leaf prolific tropical grass that cuts through clothing to the skin. Your nest is in a slight gully that the rock gorged out on its evident slow descent, giving good cover from both above and to the front. The vegetation completely hides you. Your smock and face are matched to the surrounding environment as only an expert jungle instructor could pull off. Both weapons are at the ready, either one depending on the situation.

You hear the sounds of gunfire, explosions, and yelling interspersed throughout the morning, the exact location hard to determine, the sounds bouncing off the ridge and carried through the jungle. By midday, *Manō Maku* is taken, the tunnels sealed, and the captured ADA guns turned against their own aircraft. First Sergent Kristenson collects you. He shares that a new SOSR team, *Special Operations Service Recon*, as opposed to the *Special Operations Service Assault*, is already scouting *Kalo Maku*. Your team is heading out at dark in the raft to rendezvous with an Ocean Stork just past the reef. You are headed back to Regiment HQ.

Just before the team starts to recover the raft and haul it to the southern tip and ride the current, Sykes comes up to you and outstretches his hand.

"You did a pretty good job today. I hope to work with you again one day, Baker."

You take his hand and shake, "Thanks. You never know, Sykes. Keep it above the waterline."

He grins.

After a near-fatal swim through the coral reef, the helo spots the raft two miles out in the open ocean and recovers the team. The return to home port, a full meal with a uniform change, medical treatment, and a night's sleep are the beginning of a week's long recovery.

First Sergent Kristenson sends for you the morning of your planned departure from *Amphib Fleet West, Port Summa Naval Yard and Training Base*. You have said your goodbyes to your EFL mates you made over the past year and a half, missing the same to visit with your likewise old Navy crewmates. Your duffle bags are packed and rest against the wall in the hallway just outside Kristenson's office.

"You wanted to see me, First Sergent?"

"That's right, come in Caporal Baker. Have a seat," he waves to a chair at the end of his desk.

"Coffee? Spirited water?" he motions to the pot of coffee with an extra cup and a pitcher of freshly prepared water with ice and two glasses.

"Pour me a glass of that seltzer water too, Baker."

You pour two glasses and hand the other to him, taking a drink of yours. The boundary between the two of you is an easy one; he is not to be feared, and you know you can trust him. First Sergent Kristenson is a loyal ally to you now, still to be treated with proper professionalism and respect in an open environment, but here in his office, he has made you a close mate, one forged in mutual respect.

"What are your plans, Baker? Have you thought more of what I offered on the SOS training and assignment?"

"I have, First Sergent. I am interested, but I want to return to *The Xo* first and try to reacclimate to the EFL. Back to the basics. I had no idea I would miss the regular routine, the sands of the desert. Is that out of the plan?"

He stares at you with a tilted head and a blank face and then grins, shaking his head, "No, not at all Baker. There's plenty of time for Spec-ops, but you're right. You need to develop as a normal legionnaire, take a training platoon and mold them from your own experiences. I have two sets of orders for you here," he taps a folder on the desk. "One sends you back to the Xobian Desert as a well-trained, respected, and experienced caporal assisting the Sr. caporal of a freshly-trained and raw platoon of a BT company on their way to *The Xo*. Your tour of two years will see you complete a cycle that you surely remember and then transfer to a tour of the AC or Palanquin. In your last months, you will have a close-out company, DI school, promotion to Sr. Caporal, and a BTC platoon."

He pauses and watches you. Your thoughts are mixed.

"The second set of orders sends you directly to Special Operations Training School for 12 months, throughout every theater of operations. Each trainee is hand-picked, talented, and usually Sr. caporal or above. Rank is stalled for at least the first two years, and none of your achievements are recorded in your official service records. You will have no unit designation, no awards, no mention other than assignment to V Corps as a trainer. Some of the training courses you will undergo are HACI jumping, water ops, advanced combat skills, demolitions, sniper, and tropical insertion. You will hold key instructor ratings in nearly every basic course offered to caporal or below. Either choice is yours, no blow-back, and the door is open for the remaining option later."

He takes a drink of his water. You still hold yours in your hand; the condensation pauses in mid-drip off your fingers to your dress uniform pants in a time elapsed action. The clock on the wall ticks slowly in some slow-motion, time-frozen manner, a loud, drawn-out pause of continuum, even as the blood in your temples pumps in some bizarre, deafening, hollow drum sound. Both options are intriguing. One is a chance for adventure, specialized training, a little of everything. The other is a break, a return to the beginning, a chance to share what you have learned.

EXPEDITIONARY FOREIGN LEGION -The Xo

Level Up – Two Roads – One Less Traveled Mission #23

Difficult A 25 PP 60% success Return to *The Xo*

Difficult B 25 PP 60% success Special Operations Training School

Character Summary:

You must decide whether to return to *The Xo* or proceed to SOS Training and Spec-OP Unit Assignment.

CHAPTER 16

Level Up – **An Old, New Beginning**

You stand on a set of yellow, painted footprints and look around the *First Formation* grounds. The day is chilly, not what you remembered here that day so long ago. A slight mist wafts through the air. You never thought this place could be termed chilly, and even with your experience in the AC, the shiver you feel is somewhat unexpected, even coming from Port Summa the day before. Every month on average, twelve companies of IV Corps are closed out, deactivated. Every week, approximately three companies begin their arduous journey through BT at EFL Basic Training and Headquarters Base in Sahara, the Region of Del Rio.

You missed First Day of the newest cycle by three days, but that's not important. Your next company assignment is nearing graduation, less than three weeks away. You reported to Basic Training Command, 121st Regiment, V Corps. Each regiment of V Corps operates the training school units for the other four Corps. The 125th Regiment is earmarked as the quartermaster regiment, but you know 6th Battalion, 125th Regiment, V Corps is the parent unit of SOS. It came out in casual conversation on the flight back to Port Summa after the mission.

At any rate, you reported and received a checklist to complete. It includes a self-paced series of minor assignments, which consist of the following:

- a two-day orientation with the DI Course to observe an ongoing class,

- three one-day Training Platoon Observer days of any unit in Phase One Weeks 1-6,
- a full First Day from First Formation to Bed-Check,
- two 3-day Limited Activity with Training Companies in Phase Two Weeks 8-12,
- and a final assignment to meet with your Sr. Caporal before graduation.

The total days involved add up to 13 days! Two weeks. So, the caporal that shows initiative and hard work could be on their way in about two weeks or three, depending on when graduation falls. The first thing you decided to accomplish was to report to each projected HQ and request a scheduled day for each task. It soon became apparent that the logistics of such a feat were impossible to complete in two weeks.

You now stand on the First Formation pad and feel completely lost, overwhelmed, a failure due to your inept ability to circumnavigate a simple task sheet.

A legionnaire walks along the outer gravel walkway and stops.

"What the hell are you doing standing on my muster field? Come here."

You quickly obey, now remembering forming up here only one time, that first morning, and never again. It is as if the footprints and grounds are hallowed or special. You are quick to recognize the rank of the inquisitor, a sergent major! There are only five SM's in the entire EFL. You stand at attention and wait.

"Report."

"I am Caporal D. Baker, currently assigned to 121st Regiment, V Corps awaiting BT Company assignment to *The Xo*, Sergent Major!" You call out in a loud, clear, and concise manner.

He looks you over, taking in the *Class I Formal Dress Uniform* that you still wear from reporting earlier and did not take the time to change out of before engaging in your present activity after dumping your duffle bags in the temporary personnel barracks.

"Hmm... Impressive grill you have there, Caporal Baker. Very impressive. Are you always inclined to show off your achievements?"

"No, Sergent Major. I hate to wear the Class I's, but I wanted to complete my scheduling today and get going first thing tomorrow."

"Let me see your sheet," he reaches for the rolled sheaf of papers in your left hand, and you pass them over with no hesitation. He is a sergent major!

He takes the roll and unfurls the papers, shifting several until he finds what he is looking for.

"Why did you schedule the DI orientation for tomorrow and then a back-to-back Week 1-6 with a break for the Morning Formation?"

"I wanted to complete the list as quickly as possible and as close to the sequence given, Sergent Major."

"No. No, no, no. Have you identified the target company you wish to join, Caporal?" His frown is disapproving and direct.

"No, Sergent Major. I wanted to take the first available company that...."

He cuts you off, "Admirable, Caporal Baker, but stupid. You are, by first appearance, a highly motivated and successful legionnaire. Then I observe your rush to fulfill this status sheet, and I only see a blind mission objective. I don't know your record or you, but I sense you have served with some go-for-broke NCOs and units. Where did you start, which regiment?"

"I was with India, 4/117 during my first tour, Sergent Major."

"Well, the One-Eighteen, One-Nineteen, and the One-Twenty graduate in the next weeks. We like to keep caporals and Sr. caporals with their original regiments for familiarity and cohesion. Does that matter to you?"

You think about the revelation. It never occurred to you to return to the 117th; you always moved on to a new unit, new regiment, new corps. You never considered returning to the 117th.

"Sergent Major, I just want to go to the next available platoon. I want to help that platoon of legionnaires to survive the next three years of *The Xo* or

Palanquin. Just like my caporal and Sr. caporal did for me."

The sergent major remains in the same questioning and intuitive manner that he had begun. No indication that he has agreed or disagreed with your statement or logic. He scans your awards again and then your physical features, taking in the recent injuries from the coral to your hands and face paddling the outer reef.

"Report to my office in the morning, Caporal Baker. Continue your re-acquaintance with EFL Sahara and relive memories. Change out of those formals and into a desert uniform and boonie hat if that is your preference. If anyone challenges your being out-of-uniform, instruct them to contact me, Sergent Major Cordova. Dismissed Caporal Baker." He turns and continues his previous task, whatever that was before stepping into your world.

You stand there dumbfounded and then realize he retained the entire sheaf of papers you handed him. Nuts. He has everything, the status sheet, the map of the base, your barracks assignment and door code, the DI Course contact instructor's name. Crud! You have a scheduled observation day starting at 0500! What time are you supposed to meet the sergent major? You head back to the barracks, change, and prepare your bunk and locker. In the meantime, several other caporals return from their day's activities, and the group heads to dinner.

Level Up – The Wrong Way and the Right Way

At dinner the night before, the recently assigned caporals from all the regiments shared their insight into how the status sheet and timeline are best completed. Several are now only waiting on final platoon and company assignment and are the most informed on the matter. Yet, even they disagree on aspects of procedural strategy. Several others, like you, have only just arrived in the last couple of days and are running in circles to accomplish the tasks as if it were a race. That shows the mettle of a good caporal, hard-working, detail-oriented, objective-focused. Each of these caporals is the cream of the regiments they came from.

It is funny, each started here, just as you did, from the yellow footprints and two years in the Xobaian Desert with IV Corps. Hardly anyone knows another from a previous tour, so varied is the individual success rate and promotion schedule, but, as always, new mates are quickly made and stories shared. The influx of new arrivals is constant. As three raw companies of new cassum arrive each week and three companies of freshly trained legionnaires graduate, so also go 12 caporals and 12 Sr. caporals with them.

Your decision of scheduling a DI Orientation Day first thing is quickly debated and broken down by those caporals ready to depart. Pros and cons are thrown out, and in the end, it seems that an argument could be made either way for your strategy. There are 30 or so of you presently in the group, but that will change daily. Twelve are heading out Saturday, just four days away.

You are now standing outside the door of Sergent Major Cordova's office. It is 0730. Earlier in the predawn morning, when you reported to the DI Course Operations Room to inform the instructor that the Sergent Major had requested your presence first thing, you were the one to be informed that the Sergent Major himself had canceled your scheduled orientation. Colour Sergent Quincy stared at you with careful eyes while pausing in his first or tenth cup of coffee for the day.

"You some sorta butterfly, Caporal? You gonna be flutter'n round here for the next coupla weeks, makin' appointments and havin' Sergent Major wipin' your nose and reschedulin' them for you? I'm gonna give you one more shot, out of SNAFU, and then I'm done with you. Get outta here, Runt."

He is the epitome of a drill instructor. The Sr. caporals train their individual platoons, with assistance from caporals that are currently attending DI course. There are also senior DIs, most of them sergents, but also Sr. caporals that are permanently assigned duty as DIs. Colour Sergent Quincy runs the whole show.

By 0830 you feel something is amiss with the instructions given to you by Sergent Major Cordova, and you walk to the desk at the entrance. A lance caporal is busy wiping down the desk and computer.

"I've been waiting to see Sergent Major Cordova. He said to meet him this morning. Is he coming in later?"

The lance caporal looks at you, "Where did you come from? Sergent Major called at 0800 and asked if you were here yet. I told him I hadn't seen you."

Your face flushes with anger. When you arrived earlier, the lance caporal was not on duty and you were instructed to wait at the door just down the hall.

"Lance Caporal, I have been waiting outside his office since 0730. Surely you noticed me standing there on your way in."

"Sorry, Caporal, I didn't. Sergent Major Cordova is in a meeting with this week's graduating company staff. He'll be in at 0900, in just a few minutes. You can wait outside his office."

You truly want to choke him, but instead, without saying a word, you exit the reception office and return to the hallway.

When Sergent Major arrives at 0915, he barely acknowledges you, entering his office and saying he will get to you after taking care of a few matters. Finally, at 1000 he calls you, and you report.

"I guess *in the morning* to you is *later in the day*, Caporal Baker?"

"No excuse, Sergent Major."

"Stand at ease, Caporal. Let's look at this status sheet and discuss a proper sequence of effective mission success. I understand your eagerness to traverse the preliminary preparation steps to kick off the actual mission, but no team can go out partially prepared or ready. What is your aim, your goal? Huh? If you want a platoon right now, I can stick you in one that deploys Saturday morning, and we'll just throw this crap in the bin." He wads up the status sheet and throws it in the trashcan at his feet.

You are shocked, frightened even, the steeled temper of a man of his seniority and experience was giving you a class of instruction, and you had better grasp the lesson.

"Sergent Major, I may have implied that I was in a rush and felt the status sheet was a nuisance, but that is not what I meant or felt. I realize I need each of those experiences, the meetings, and time to readjust to a fresh company. The other caporals and I talked last night, and I have revised my plan. I most certainly would welcome whatever advice you have for me to succeed. No, Sergeant Major, I am not ready to take a platoon so soon."

He studies you. "I looked at your service file, both of them, and I believe your last statement is incorrect, Caporal Baker. I believe you are more than capable of not only taking out a platoon as junior platoon caporal, but as Sr. caporal if it came down to it. I also believe that for every day you spend here reacquainting yourself with normal, fresh EFL legionnaires and tactics, the more successful you will be. One of the underlying roles of this process is a selection process, selection of a caporal to a particular Sr. caporal and platoon that has attracted their attention, and selecting a Sr. caporal to his or her caporal. You and the other caporals may not realize it, but you are being evaluated and ranked. My advice? Take a few days and observe; go out to the drill fields, ranges, and CTTC. Walk in the company op rooms, talk with the DI's, and look at the status boards. Yeah, stand nearby, unofficially, this Saturday morning at First Formation. You'll probably get an invite to help out. Be there at 0230 for instructions. Here," he passes your papers back to you.

You take them and look at the trashcan. Sergent Major Cordova smiles, "That was a scrap piece of paper, for effect. You're dismissed."

You come to attention and respond with, "Thank you, Sergent Major," then take a step back and turn for the door.

"Oh, don't give Colour Sergent Quincy another bone to chew with you. Make damn sure you have your ducks in a row next time you meet him to schedule DI orientation. Get out of here. I'm busy."

You take Sergent Major's advice, and you spend the remainder of the week walking around the training areas, visiting the CTTCs, combat tactics training courses, the company areas, and the chow halls, avoiding the DI training course AO altogether. You start in the early morning, casually observing the training and talking with the DIs during breaks and even during sessions when the cassum are busy with some instruction or punishment. You eat hand-me-down combat rats when on the CTTC during meal breaks, and stand around in the chow hall in the evening. Saturday morning comes, and you are standing with another dozen or so of your fellow caporals, shuffling your feet in the rain, waiting for the buses.

That was the thing. Your bus ride took the whole day and night and arrived just a little before starting.

Others, you learned, had made the trip earlier and were housed in local hotels until that morning when they loaded up and rode the half-hour here. Either way, you didn't miss this experience, this moment, and were a little apprehensive concerning the cruel ritual that was about to take place.

A sergent approaches the group; he is a senior DI for the soon-to-arrive group of roughly 500 cassum that will be formed into three companies, twelve overfull platoons.

"I need volunteers to assist with First Formation. If you don't have the stomach for it, walk away. You will not strike any cassum or make threats of injury or any sexual innuendo. All of you are, I assume, awaiting platoon assignment. Well, these won't be yours, so don't get all wrapped around the axle for their ineffectiveness. I need you to yell repeated instructions, direct them to a set of yellow feet, verbally harass them, and move on. The DIs will latch onto the finer details. If you are struck, walk away if you can; if not, all of you have enough training to contain the situation until DIs respond. If a fight occurs, and they have, subdue with minimal force and step back when ordered by the DIs. I or one of the other senior drills will ask a few of you to continue through the day if we see potential or ask you to leave if we observe problems. Let me have your names." He quickly writes them down and walks away.

The buses start to arrive, and the anticipation and excitement grow, even in the now pouring rain. It feels empowering. You have experienced the rainy and dry seasons in the Palanquin, which is nearly the same.

Even in the jungle, it could be cold. This isn't cold, just wet. You have dressed for the rain, slipping on a wicking shirt and a light rain jacket with the hood cut-off under your blouse; a spare pair of socks with foot powder is in a baggie in your cargo pockets along with a small bottle of water and two packs of peanut butter. You wear your patrol cap, a soft cap with a front bill, instead of the boonie hat, pulled down to your nose and creased crown to form a ridge and bowl. It is the style of the career-minded leg. Most of the others are likewise fitted.

More buses, the engines idle, the occupants unaware of the looming chaos or even wondering if the activity is postponed due to the heavy rain. The DIs collect in the shadows, knowing exactly where the darkness falls. One of them glances at his watch and then counts the buses, checking a list. That must be all of them. He turns to the DIs, says something, and they emerge from the dark, quickly striding to a bus, each bus assigned a DI. They stand still, quiet. A whistle blows, and each raps on their bus door, immediately steps inside, and disappears.

"Oh, man! Of all the crap I have been through, I never want to go through this day again," one of the caporals offers. The rest of you give a laugh and a similar exhortation or agreement.

The buses begin to expel their cargo, and the group of you rush to the light, yelling, pointing, repeating directions, throwing items on the ground, intermingling with the DIs and senior drills, and basically welcoming the new cassum to the EFL.

You are all invited to remain, assisting with keeping the momentum and controlled chaos alive. The sergent that spoke to the group earlier comes up at one point in the midmorning during uniform issue and instructs the group to take a break in the company op room, get some coffee and a sandwich or soup, and dry out. He will need you during lunch. With that, the group ambles off to the ops room and finds exactly what he said, an endless urn of coffee, a large pot of tomato soup, and a container of sandwiches. You remove your soaking blouse and inner rain jacket, hang them on a chair and sit down to change your socks.

"What in the heck? You are bone dry, Baker! Where did you learn to do that with the rain jacket?" One of the others asks, touching your mostly dry shirt even as he is shaking from the cold.

"You got to be kidding? You did the Palanquin, right?" The others laugh.

"Yay, Baker loved that jungle, even on the islands." Another caporal adds.

You can't place him.

"You don't remember me, but I was in Echo 3/114, and we ran that JWTS Red Force together, ha-ha! I went Amphib you went to the AC. I was in Bravo 1/107 and went in with you on the first wave on the *Sand Fleas,* but you were part of that *Juno Company.*"

You are embarrassed, "Sorry, I don't recognize you." You feel bad. He knew your whole career practically.

"That's alright. I'm Waltz," he waves from the coffee pot.

One of the company staff is listening in, a lance caporal.

"You said you were part of Juno?" His face wrinkles in confusion or question. "There is no *Juno*."

Waltz looks at you, and you comically shake your head, laughing. "That's right. There's no Juno."

One of the other caporals then adds, "Wait, that was the *Sand Fleas*, the sniper teams. I was with 2nd Fleet, the 2/107. That's where I know you! It's been bugging the heck out of me; you were one of the instructors! For crying out loud, Baker! You put me in promotion line with that course! The ol' man, Pittman, ranked everyone who walked off with that course in their file. Where did you go? You disappeared. Rumor was you bought it right before we pulled out." His name is Klein.

"Ha-ha. I joined with the 100th to secure the airstrip on Blue Water Atoll."

"Now I know you guys are making this crap up," the lance caporal is now fully attentive to the conversation, eager to listen and learn deep secrets of the EFL's other war. "There's not a 100th Regiment. It's not on the organizational chart!" He points at one of the several educational posters along the walls of the ops room.

"That's right, Lance Caporal. There's no 100th Regiment. These guys are pulling your leg," you again side with the lance caporal looking around at the collection of wet, laughing caporals, sure that they are having fun at his expense.

He soon returns to his task of sorting through the names of the newly assigned cassum and formulating service files for each. After a few minutes, the group is sent for, a new round of tasks for the first day. The DIs also rotate off for rest, some leaving to return to other assignments; the core that will take the training companies through the end settles in. After dinner, the group of caporals is thanked and released. You return to your barracks, laughing and retelling funny moments from the day. The rest of the next two weeks pass, and you await your final assignment.

With the end of the fourth full week, you feel like you have been on vacation. This was much longer than you had initially anticipated for it to take, but you found that almost all the caporals take between three and four weeks. It is never a partial week. Graduation is on Saturday morning, the basic training companies' claim their new unit designation, a deactivated company reactivated, the ceremony of the colours being uncased, and the unit history read out. It is an exciting event, one that you understand better at this point but had no idea what was happening the first time you participated over six years ago.

The last week before your new company's graduation, you meet with the Sr. caporals, company commander, company sergent, and the other newly assigned caporals. There are two leftenants, an adjutant leftenant and full leftenant. There are now only 129 of the original 180 cassum that began BT 15 weeks ago. The remainder of the company, a full 164, including the CO, company sergent, and the two platoon leaders, will be filled out with legionnaires, Sr. legionnaires, and lance caporals either finishing up their mandatory service or on second enlistments once you arrive at 117th Regiment HQ.

The CO, the senior ranking officer of the company, commands the entire company on an overall, third-level sort of detached status. He is in charge, completely, just as Navy Lt. Ashworth was on the *JW Nowly*. His *second* is the company sergent, who repeats and carries out the orders or directives. The company sergent ensures that the four platoon Sr. caporals understand and accomplish the order or mission. The leftenants work solely for the CO and are mouth-puppets, also ensuring the orders are carried out, regular training is completed, and the platoon caporals are keeping discipline and high standards. Adjutant leftenants are almost totally useless, unless they are commissioned former NCOs that have *turned the corner*. These former colour sergents and first sergents held little chance to make sergent major before they retired or just wanted to command at a different level of challenge. Sr. caporals are pretty much left to run their platoons as they wish as long as it holds to EFL protocol, accomplishes the mission, and creates no undue problems.

You are now, or soon will be, the assistant or adjutant caporal of 4th Platoon, Gulf Company, 6th Battalion, 117th Regiment, IV Corps. The thrill is intoxicating. You have had many achievements, even leading small fire-team size units with a designation of platoon or company, but this is a real, fully organized regulation EFL platoon! Sr. Caporal Josef is giving you 2nd Squad, with half of the veterans and 16 of the cassum, soon to be minus nobilis, lower ranks. Ha-ha! You will be the first one to deal with any and all discipline infractions and punishments, track each nobilis on their climb to full legionnaire rank to achieve their Kepi blanc, monitor and encourage the achievement of senior gradum, Sr. legionnaires, maintain good discipline and provide encouragement to the whole of the platoon to re-enlist.

What approach will you use? What leadership or command style is comfortable for you? Can you pull off a reincarnation of Caporal Edmunds or Sr. Caporal Tollerson?

True to your memory and experience, the cassum of Gulf Company have no idea they are heading to the Xobian Desert as a complete unit comprised of their BTC. You and the other caporals, which include your now new mates of Caporals Waltz and Klein, stand separately waiting for the company colours' uncasing and join in with your assigned platoons. Each of the graduating companies holds their individual uncasing after the BTC DIs release them to their new COs and platoon leaders.

Almost immediately after the uncasing, Gulf Company double-times back to their assembly pavilion and gathers their duffle bags. They change out of the Formal Class I's and into newly issued DCUs, the same weight and material as the regulation duty basic combat uniform, but with a desert camouflage pattern. They are also now authorized to wear the coveted boonie hat. The

DIs and all the joining company staff are in formal dress, except wearing their Kepi blanc as opposed to the cassums' patrol caps, which, of course, look stupid with the dress uniform.

Sr. Caporal Josef had taken a strong interest in you as soon as he became aware of your presence in the rotation, sending a query after reading the *Caporal Availability List*. In conjunction with 121st Regiment V Corps, IV Corps drafts the list of potential caporals ready for assignment to fresh Xobian companies. They update the list every week. After their first week of making the list, several caporals are always hit with multiple queries by Sr. caporals. The COs and company sergents are completely out of the loop and hold no influence, not even receiving, officially, the CAL. You met with Josef and one other Sr. caporal Monday of your third full week, joining each of their platoons for a couple of days, observing the cassum and the Sr. caporals' attitude and personality. It was quickly apparent that Josef was exactly like Caporal Edmunds, dry humor, borderline punitive but always with an overshadowing reason, stand-offish to his cassum but personable at the most bizarre moments, and under all that, a funny and likable character. He was easy to talk to and pried open your thoughts and objectives for a soon-to-be deployed Xobian bound platoon. He noted a few countering items that were not on his list, was honest, and noted your extensive experience with sniping, commending you on such a successful skill. You both held similar tour experiences and passions, Field Games! After what was really an interview, his last comment was that he was in charge of the platoon and was preparing you to be an upcoming Sr. caporal as much as he was training his platoon. You dropped the other Sr. caporal that night and continued to increase your participation with what would become your new unit.

The CO orders the duffle bags and all newly acquired company gear or equipment to be loaded on four waiting ATCs and once again assembles her new company. She is EFL Captain Jacobowski, and she has six previous tours in the Xobian Desert. She is a former colour sergeant and has no tolerance for ineptitude or slackness. Her company staff is each highly trained and experienced officers and NCOs, and each holds the objective of ensuring the survival of every legionnaire of Gulf Company, 6/117 IV Corps. You stand in formation next to Josef and listen intently, even as scattered raindrops make one last appearance before the onset of spring. Soon, the normal 10-month dry season of the south-central desert region of Del Rio will return along with average daytime temps in the 90's.

"Company Sergent!"

"Yes, Ma'am!" he performs the obligatory sharp and loud response, quick steps to her front, and gives an appropriate salute.

"Move the company to the transition barracks and prepare for deployment!"

"By your order, Captain Jacobowski!" He then turns to face the assembled company and yells, "Company! Right face!"

The order is repeated by the platoon Sr. caporals at once.

"Company! Forward – march!" Each Sr. caporal repeats to their platoon.

With several short, quick change of direction commands, the company heads towards the transbarracks adjacent to the airfield five miles away.

"Quick time, march!"

The HQ staff takes their position at the front of the four-rank formation, the company sergent to the right side of the ranks, the ATCs follow behind the company.

The order is repeated.

"On the double-time! Run!"

The distance is five miles; the cassum each had to accomplish the four-mile run with light combat load, and a 15-mile march with normal combat load in the previous weeks prior to graduation. A five-mile run with LCL of one canteen, poncho with liner, butt-pack, and GPS is not excessively difficult; they aren't even carrying ammo. Still, minus noblis begin to fall out and straggle behind the formation at three miles. The CO becomes aware of the situation and sends word to the company sergent to entice the stragglers. The company sergent is running to the right of the formation. The Sr. caporals are each at the front of their platoons.

"I need a caporal to round up stragglers!" The sergent bellows.

You are right behind Josef and directly beside Waltz of 3rd Platoon with Klein and DePaul beside him. Immediately you each yell a response and cut off to join Sergent Camponello.

Level Up – Bringing Them In Mission #24

    __ Easy 10 PP 95% success

    __ Medium 15 PP 80% success

    __ Difficult 25 PP 60% success

Character Summary

You have selected Easy Mission.

    Summary:

You recognize that four highly experienced and competitive caporals are vying for early recognition. You want to establish your leadership style in the company, so you chose to treat the situation with gentle persuasion. You fall back to the lingering groups of stragglers and encourage the legionnaires to put in more effort and catch up to the main body.

You have selected Medium Mission.

    Summary:

With a sense of purpose and dedication to excel gained through extensive personal hardship, you prod the weaker and less dedicated to push harder, even taking weapons from three and challenging them to pass the next legionnaire in front of them.

EXPEDITIONARY FOREIGN LEGION -The Xo

You have selected Difficult Mission.

Summary:

Along with one other caporal, you physically strike several nobilis and push them forward, eventually achieving the assignment to bring the stragglers to the main group. Fear and discord among the company of minus nobilis set your reputation as a hard-nosed and feared caporal.

Mission Debrief

Character succeeds with Medium Mission. Easy Mission places you as a soft and easy caporal who will cajole and beg for performance. Difficult Mission shows you as an abusive caporal who resorts to physical violence to achieve objectives.

In the aftermath of Pass/Fail of the mission, your character summary is updated. You have gained/lost PP or no change.

Level Up –Time Off

Once the company reaches the barracks, orders are issued to set up rotational guard duty, unload the ATCs, remedial physical training of the stragglers, and individual platoon training. As night falls and the end of the first duty day for the newly formed company descends, you walk among the platoon, learning your new charges' names. Now that you have had an opportunity to work more closely with them you determine them to be a pitiful bunch. With the remaining hour before lights out, you give them options to choose from while on lockdown.

They can: (pick one)

　__Get a shower

　__Write a letter home

　__Read

　__Talk to their mates

Level Up – Xobian Reunion

　　With much anticipation mixed with a bit of apprehension, and after nearly a week of connecting flights and convoy travel, you arrive at IV Corps Headquarters and then onward to the 117th Regiment HQ. The desert seems calmer, not as harsh as you recall. The familiar sights and memories, the shabby, squalid towns, crude dirt roads, the oven-like heat, curious locals, the stench of burning human waste, the blank and lifeless stares of legionnaires all seem less bothersome to you after experiencing over six years in the EFL in multiple theaters. This is not as bad as you remembered it to be. You are greatly relieved as you realize your fears of not being able to cope with a challenging environment while leading your squad are quickly fading.

　　"Yeah, not as bad the second time around, huh, Caporal?" Josef grins at you from the burning sand of the Gulf Company CP once you finally arrive at the final destination.

　　"What was I remembering? This isn't any worse than the Palanquin or the islands. What's the drill, Sr. Caporal? We up on the mission roster yet?"

"Let's get them in their huts, introduce them to *Sand Drills*, and get the platoon properly motivated."

The next day 4th Platoon draws a simple patrol of the area 53 miles southwest of the battalion at an abandoned oil well facility. The drilling corporation decided that the wells were not producing the quota they were estimated to and closed the operation, capping the well-holes. The equipment was, for the most part, left to the elements. The platoon loads up on two ATCs and drives to the site.

Sr. Caporal Josef halts the vehicles two miles out, behind a large dune.

"Caporal Baker, take 2nd Squad and ease up the dune. Divide into two fire teams and move to the main entrance. I'll work around to the southeast and come up from the back side."

He moves out with his squad in both the ATCs. Now you are on your own with the responsibility of an entire squad. The full weight of command hits you. Your actions, from a compilation of experience, knowledge, and training, are now on display. Your four veterans are a lance caporal, a Sr. leg, and two rolled-over legionnaires that have less than a year left of their service. The remaining 16 of the squad are all fresh minus nobilis on their first mission in *The Xo;* each looks to you for their survival now. You split the lance caporal and Sr. legionnaire with one lower rank leg each to form the two fire teams.

There is sign of activity at the abandoned facility; whether it is a group of Bedouins or *Xobian Wahti* attempting to pump and refine raw crude is still unknown. You give the order to advance in a covering tactical leapfrog fashion. Your advance is sure to be noticed from far out. That's the idea, to give you the attention while 1st Squad moves to position.

Level Up – Action at Abandoned Well Mission #25

___ Easy (Light) Action 10 PP 95% success

___ Medium (Moderate) Action 15 PP 80% success

___ Difficult (Heavy) Action 25 PP 60% success

Character Summary

You Choose Easy Mission. You are involved in light action.

Summary:

As your squad moves closer, you are still unable to determine the identity of the occupants. With 200 yards before reaching the main entry to the compound, sporadic rifle fire erupts, and you order your squad to prepare holes. You move one team forward at a time, each preparing shallow holes to offer supporting fire. In this manner, you initiate strong contact with two forward OP or sentry positions, eventually overrunning them. The slow yet sustained movement allows Sr. Caporal Josef to maneuver with his squad and two ATCs to the rear and overtake the small number of drilling scroungers.

You Choose Medium Mission. You are involved in moderate action.

Summary.

EXPEDITIONARY FOREIGN LEGION -The Xo

As you move your squad in a pronged tactical road march up the dirt road, you come under fire as you close to 200 yards. Ordering your two fire teams up in a controlled cover-and-move quick pace, you overrun the lightly defended forward enemy positions and advance to 20 yards from the guarded entrance to the facility. You order your squad to prepare holes and set up for an assault. Sr. Caporal Josef arrives with his squad and two ATCs to support your assault. The two squads take the compound within half an hour of the first shots.

You Choose Difficult Mission. You are involved in heavy action.

Summary.

Wasting little time, you move your squad forward and annihilate the enemy forward positions guarding the entrance to the drilling compound. Out-pacing Sr. Caporal Josef's movement, you push your way inside the light defensive positions and force a standoff while taking your position in a mud-brick building with a low ceiling. The remaining squad arrives, and you force the enemy to surrender after an extended building-to-building eradication.

Mission Debrief.

You survive and receive an evaluation of how you chose to execute your orders. Sr. Caporal Josef points out areas for improvement in squad-handling but is generally pleased with your movement and tactics. Your squad and the platoon gain trust and confidence in you, and there are no casualties. All of the legionnaires of 4th Platoon performed well in their first operation together.

Fourth Platoon is ordered to remain in place and maintain security on the abandoned drilling site until relieved.

Level Up – Time Off

After spending three days on sentry detail at the compound, secluded and undermanned, 4th Platoon is recalled, never replaced, and returns to the battalion AO to rejoin the rest of Gulf Company. The platoon earns a 24-hour pass for their achievement and ventures hesitantly to the ramshackle outskirts of the battalion area, taking in the assorted offerings of the local inhabitants, small shops, traders, goat herders, foreign cuisine options, and entertainment, basically the 3Bs – Bazaars, Bars, and Brothels. The legionnaires can choose from a short list of activities offered on their first Day Pass:

__ Take a shower

__ Go to chow

__ Check out the sights

__ Talk to their mates

__ Play cards

Level Up – First Casualty

Fourth Platoon quickly sets a bar for the rest of the company to achieve. Sr. Caporal Josef and the other three Sr. caporals are virtually on the same standing, each first-time platoon Sr. caporals and having gone through DI course together, so the assignment of platoons from 1st through 4th was random, with no real seniority. The leftenants remain out of the way, and Captain Jacobowski reigns with a tight fist over the daily operation of any one platoon on any particular day. Today, the CO leaves Leftenant Roubere, a bullying officer and former first sergent in line to be promoted to captain after this tour, as the company's executive officer.

Once again attempting to push a spectacular battle scenario, Capt. Jacobowski assigns only 4th Platoon to patrol an area known to be controlled by the *Xobian Desert Regulars*. If needed, air and artillery support are lined up, and 1st and 2nd Platoons are in reserve. Third Platoon is assigned convoy duty to one of several pump station repair crews that travel from facility to facility in the vast desert. You remember that convoy duty, the day-long drive to Nahil Pump Station on the coast. Awful.

Sixth Battalion operates in a different area/region than 4th Battalion, your old unit. The scenery is pretty much the same, just different names of small villages, though there is no ocean anywhere within 500 miles in any direction. Any water is considered worth more than the crude oil which the EFL is out here to protect. Oases, as with all water sources, are controlled firmly by territorial and tribal means. Several underground subterranean rivers are known to exist in certain areas closer to the surface, then they disappear and are lost. The ancient Xobian Desert people know where to find water, and they guard the secrets. It is said that once a well is dug or a spring wets the sand the *maji* number the days and it will dry up to the exact proclamation. That is why the nomadic people of the desert, the real Desert Peoples, always move. The larger settlements and great metropolitan cities of the Xobian Confederation are far to the east and also to the north, along the borders of their allies the Chaloosa and *Aleihachu*. Water is not as scarce there.

The Xobian Confederation also have strongholds on their southwestern coast, farther south than Summa's influence and that of her allies.

It really isn't about oil control here; it's about water. The Xobian Confederation has oil; however, the deposits in the regions they control are not as rich. They push their influence into the middle desert not only to gain more oil, but also to prevent the free republics from getting it for nothing. To this end, water becomes the real quest. Water is life in the desert.

With just a month into the tour, none of 4th Platoon, or the company for that matter, realizes the implication too much. Sure, water is rationed; showers are allowed only once a week. No water is wasted; every drop is recycled and filtered. The water that you showered with yesterday may be the water you drink today. The combat kit for desert patrol is a minimum of three canteens, DCU with smock, an additional two-15 round magazines in the butt-pack aside from the six mag pouches on the harness equipment belt, boonie hat and helmet, BAC (just the chest armor, the rest is just too hot and heavy), a combat meal, water purifier, and *shemagh* or desert camouflage netting worn around the neck as a scarf, covering the head and upper shoulders. Most of the vets have already converted to a new back-carried water bladder that holds a gallon. It is worn outside of the BAC but under the smock. It is quickly becoming the new alternative canteen. You wish you had it in the Sand Fleas. The LCL is heavy and makes mobility difficult. But that's why you train so hard.

EXPEDITIONARY FOREIGN LEGION - The Xo

The *Aquifer Zone* is a one-and-a-half mile wide, sporadically appearing, erratically snaking, 652 mile long green thread in the middle desert. The Bedouins traverse the greenery lengthwise and across it, but never among it, fearing being swallowed up when and if it closed. Animals, wild and domestic, graze the lush, green grasses. Now, modern permanent settlements are even raised upon its boundaries. The majority of these, especially on the eastern edges, are of Xobian Confederation control or leaning. Water, in significant quantities, is pumped and transported in both hastily constructed pipelines and caravans to settlements aligned with the *XC*.

This is 6th Battalion's primary AO. The 118th Regiment is 300 miles north, and the 119th is 250 miles south, along the same AZ. This is the easternmost EFL position on the Xobian continent at close to 1500 miles from the coast. Other ally forces are also stretched along the AZ. Still, the border is so porous that blowing sand could not keep up with the XDR and numerous assorted Xobian militia and freedom fighters that cross at will. These enemy units quickly disappear in the wastelands and pop up anywhere to sabotage drilling facilities or ambush weak patrols. The 1st and 2nd Battalions are to the west, supporting the 4th and 5th Battalions of the 117th, keeping that apportioned desert and western coast open. Third Battalion lays beside 6th in a dual-support position.

Where is the National Army? The Army is purported to be four, five, or more times larger than the EFL. That question is raised a lot in off-duty discussions, around the card tables and bottles of beer. The only experience you have with the *NA* was when they took over the Sand Flea Islands. The Flight Special Services are observed on those occasions while utilizing their transport planes which ferry the EFL to various locations and theaters. The HACI you flew on, and the helos are all part of the National Navy's air wing squadrons. But the Army, what do they do? Your father served on the southern border in the Del Rio region his entire service. When you were home on leave, neighbors spoke of their sons or daughters attached to airbases in the western and eastern oceans, like *Douboo Archipelago* and others. Where is the Army? Why is the EFL always the branch to storm the beaches, fight in the cold and snow of the AC, swelter in the jungles of the Palanquin, and burn in the sands of the western and middle Xobian Desert?

Your world geography class in upper school was very general at best, lacking a *whole-world* perspective. There was never a complete, total, uninterrupted, whole-world overview. It was always odd and never fully explained. Most of the time, the student or students asking a question concerning this strange lack of information would be deterred, ignored, misdirected, or otherwise rebuked for some made-up disciplinary action or lose privileges, receive demerits, and in extreme cases, be suspended. A few of your closest friends took on a secret project to piece together a world map from various sources in your third year, revealing a wholly grotesque and unfitting sphere. Your father found it in the garage and promptly destroyed it, forbidding you to associate with the others. He argued that you could jeopardize your spot on the field games team.

You knew that the Eastern Ocean touched both the eastern coast of the Palanquin Rain Forest and also the western coast of the Great Xobian Desert Empire. The Western Ocean also touched the western edges of the Palanquin Rain Forest and the many islands of the *Moano Alelo,* the ocean people you had encountered. It also was the great ocean to the Chaloosa's eastern coast. From what you understood of the Chaloosa, they were not related to the Xobians, but held an ancestry line to the Alelo. The Xobians were related to the Aleihachu but not the Prangenua on the same continent. The Summarians held no direct ancestry line to the Chaloosa, Xobian, or Alelo yet were closely related to the Prangenuians, which were separated by a great ocean and the AC. To make it even more confusing, the Tamiarindos of the Palanquin had a genealogical connection to both the Alelo and the Aleihachu but not with Chaloosa or Xobians! That was the extent of your world knowledge. How or where did the Xobian Desert and the land of the Chaloosa then merge? Was there an empty, unknown realm or gulf between the two mighty civilizations? What did this landform look like? Is that where the absence of the National Army and Special Flight Services made sense?

    Captain Jacobowski elects to accompany 4th Platoon along with Sergent Camponello and a light fire team from 1st Platoon, four lower ranks, and a veteran Sr. leg, as her HQ detail. Sr. Caporal Josef leads off in the first ATC; 2nd Squad follows behind the two buggies with the HQ detail. Two ATCs and two buggies travel through the middle desert along an interconnecting system of village roads in the highly contested AZ. The dusty road immediately reduces visibility to poor conditions. You lose sight of the two buggies in the dust cloud so quickly that your driver has to back off 30 yards to avoid running over the top of them. The drivers and vehicles are attached to, and supported by, V Corps and are adept in operating in the conditions. You and your legionnaires are unaccustomed to this mode of travel other than the convoy escorts you performed years ago. Those were much different than this patrol dynamic.

The CO signals for a break two hours into the operation, stopping along a wadi where it follows and crosses the road. Sand and dust thickly coat the occupants of the buggies. When they lift their glasses or goggles, the dust is nearly a quarter-inch thick. Their mouths are dry; the shemaghs are as if they are the desert itself.

You order your squad out of the ATC and into a defensive position on the southern perimeter, giving instructions to drink some water and check their weapons. Josef gives a similar order to his squad, securing the north side.

"Here is our location, about four miles from the village of Zaphir on the western boundary of the AZ, along here," she traces her finger on the map.

You look to the low hills of the valley that surround you at this wadi. You do not like the crossing of the road and the dry riverbed. It is ripe for an ambush. Josef and Camponello also seem a little on edge, impatient to get back rolling again.

"We will enter the village on the southeast road, dismount, and conduct foot reconnaissance to the western road that leads through the AZ. Once inside the AZ, we will remount and fast-pace to the south three miles and exit here at the village of Kasish. We'll set up there for the night and then return to base tomorrow."

Sergent Camponello keeps his thoughts and reaction inside, as does Josef. You are stunned. This should be a company-level operation. You have never been inside the AZ but have heard stories of the immense beauty, opulence, and sheer change of environment from the outside desert. It is a vast oasis, cool, secluded, and dangerous.

Captain Jacobowski leads the way with both buggies, racing to the village in some unstated quest to arrive in a whirlwind. The ATCs lag behind, coughing and choking in the unsettled dust. Once again, your driver falls back due to low visibility and somehow runs off the road and into the dried-up riverbed of the wadi. You are stuck.

With all six wheels of the rear, three-axle, independent-suspension drive-train and the two front, separately-powered wheels spinning hopelessly, you again dismount and direct your squad to a defensive perimeter. You send a Sat-link message to Sr. Caporal Josef, who is unaware of your mishap and is attempting to stay in contact with the CO.

You are talking with the driver. Her experience and knowledge vastly outweigh yours in this particular situation. Suddenly, a *shoulder-fired missile*, much like the HEPR, streaks across the still dusty, shallow valley from the closest hill and strikes the ATC. The explosion rocks you, sending you sprawling into the sand. The destroyed vehicle is engulfed in fire. Your eyes burn from the fuel and explosives, yet you scramble to the door and pull the Sr. leg out, dragging her 10 yards beside one of your minus nobilis. The ambush is set, the isolation of a rear element. You immediately assess the situation. The placement is wrong. This was intended to be a Head-n-Tail Ambush separating the lead element and blocking in the rear and main body. The road crossing of the wadi was large enough. They had seen you approaching for some time, able to prepare the ambush. What messed it up, what confused the ambushers, was the deliberate stop of the convoy at the crossing. Before they could redirect, the CO sped off in front this time, forcing the first ATC to rush to maintain contact, leaving the lone ATC to fend for itself.

You react quickly, knowing that time is not on your side. You will never get out of the valley formed by the wadi and lower road. The enemy holds the higher ground. Your only defense is the wadi itself, to dig in and wait for reinforcements.

"Back, back, back! Senior Ladd, pull your team in line with that dry bank there! Dig in deep!" you direct Sr. Legionnaire Ladd, who instantly repeats the order.

"Do not fire, do not fire. Save your ammo, 4th Platoon," you calmly assert, even as several young lower ranks fire off rounds of no consequence.

"Lance Caporal!"

"Here, Caporal!" Lance Caporal Sebastian calls out, nearly at your foot.

"Draw your team to the southwestern bank. Keep 'em down. We will move along the wadi south and get out from under the direct fire from the northern hills."

"Copy, Caporal! A-team! Low crawl to the far side bank, Cordoba, bring your...."

You remain with the injured driver, who is burned and semi-conscious. Your GPS is slung on your back, but you also carry the GPXR. You lie down and look for a quick target, knowing the effect of a downed member of the ambushers will rattle them. You discovered, quite by accident, that the presence of qualified snipers in *The Xo* was abnormally low. The XDR have little experience with trained EFL snipers who prefer to remain in the Amphib and Palanquin theaters.

You drop two in a breath's time. The second is a caporal rank, a junior platoon member, unlike the EFL's caporal. The pause in the attack is noticeable. It is what you need. You quickly pull the injured driver the six yards to the near bank and drop to the lower dry streambed.

One minus nobilis stares at you, his face ashen, his eyes wide.

"Hey! Hey! Lower Rank Stephens, right?"

"Yes, Caporal," his response and momentary shock gone after being addressed.

"This driver is your responsibility. You will defend her with your very own life. You understand, Nobilis Stephens?"

You are already searching for another target, a silhouette along the hilltop.

"I... I... I... what am I to do, Caporal?"

You fire. The body **rolls several feet down the hill and into** the sand.

You look at the minus nobilis. "You took basic first aid, Stephens?"

"Yes, Caporal," he responds hesitantly.

"Well, then, treat for shock, bandage the wounds, monitor breathing. Come on. I'm busy. I need to do your job too?" You look up the hill and spot what you believe to be a senior commander directing several grenadiers forward.

You move to the left, inching along the slightly raised bank. The rippled **sand and dried, long-dead tumbleweed species** *Kali tragus*, or thistle, impedes your progress by making you take the time to work around it. You are moving north while Lance Caporal Sebastian is taking the squad south. He knows what is happening. He is a veteran of 2nd Battalion. He completed his second and third tours in the Palanquin and Amphib and is now back in *The Xo*. He's a good leg and will make caporal this tour for sure.

There he is again, rising on the back side of the hill, directing an XDR leader in what appears to be a circling or flanking maneuver. His next thought is interrupted as he stumbles back into a cloud of blackness, his body dropping to the dust. The XDR leader immediately drops to the ground, yelling orders and signaling that there is a sniper. The desert regulars, a mix of grenadiers and basic fighters and possibly a group of wahti, now are conscious of a change to the situation. They have only a short time before the main body, which was allowed to escape from the ambush, encircles them.

You gaze to the south toward your squad. Stephens is dragging the driver as best he can, lying beside her and pulling on the equipment harness a few inches at a time before having to reposition. He has taken the outside, unprotected edge of the stream bed, allowing the injured legionnaire to remain closer to the eroded bank. Lance Caporal Sebastian is now alternating the squad in returning fire, an ammo conservation tactic.

Ten yards ahead, the road veers away from the wadi and empties back out to the open desert. That would be the expected route of escape for a vehicle. The wadi follows the hills in a southerly direction. If you keep to the wadi, you will also continue to be entrapped by the hills. Conversely, you will have no cover if you attempt to break out into the desert utilizing the road. You chose to stay with the wadi.

You rejoin the squad as Sebastian reaches the split. He looks to you for your decision, trusting fully in your experience and rumored exploits.

"We'll keep moving with the wadi, Lance Caporal. Sr. Caporal Josef will know we kept moving south with the best cover option and will harass their rear from the east. Come dark, we can slip away."

"Yes, Caporal," he is relieved to hear what he was thinking himself.

You settle into a firing position as the rear guard and wait for the next target to materialize. The squad slowly progresses away from the ambush site. The XDR moves along with you, taking shots. This was not their plan. They gambled that the beleaguered legionnaires would either stay put and fight or attempt to break out at the road. Instead of locking down the wadi where the road broke away, they opted to place a good number on the eastern hills south of the road. You take advantage of their dilemma in repositioning their forces. Two grenadiers and a Xobian regular run across the road to reinforce the western hill. The lead man falls, while the second stumbles with the realization that they have been caught in the open. The regular continues to run, and you stop him with a three-round burst from the GPS. The second grenadier throws a grenade and falls behind his dead compatriot, tugging at the body to give him more cover. He lobs another grenade, hoping the explosions at best kill you or at least impede your hunt.

His wish is granted. Their grenades are lighter so that many can be carried and thrown with deadly accuracy by the specially trained, brave fighters who make up the elite grenadier companies. The explosions from the smaller-than-normal grenades cripple your ability to continue the hunt. Attention has now been taken of the small skirmish at the road junction. Several more grenadiers now come to the aid of one of their own caught on the road, two dead beside him as he fights to survive. Grenadiers, you have learned, will always come to the aid of one of their own. They are brave, taking chances that an average fighter would never do but will stop their assault to assist another. Their grenades are beginning to fall closer to your position; soon, one will get too close. You back off, turning to rejoin your squad.

As the sun weighs against the sky and beats a heavy and relentless assault upon the sands, the desert turns into an open convection oven of temperatures shimmering close to 112 degrees. The legionnaires of 2nd Squad continue to fight along the banks of the wadi as they slowly crawl south. **Two hundred yards after leaving the road**, the wadi changes course with a slow bend directly south. The hills become further away or simply disappear, but the bed is wide and shallow. Soon it is only several inches deep. The trade-off of a more open plain is a stream bed that empties into the desert. There is no sign of Josef and the rest of 4th Platoon. Where could they be?

With the last two hours of daylight remaining and the wadi all but gone, you order your squad to dig in. The sand is rich with runoff deposits, and the ground lends itself to good hole digging. Your legionnaires are low on water. The enemy is still out there, held to a distance that keeps them out of your range. They will either attempt to finish you off during the dark or fade away. Your plans are not as well-defined.

One of your legionnaires calls out to Lance Caporal Sebastian, saying he has hit rocks for the second time after moving his hole position. Your inclination is that rock debris has been washed down over the centuries, but you crawl over to see. No one else has hit any rock.

The first hole is only a few inches from the current one. The legionnaire is quite a digger; his first attempt was almost two and a half feet by three feet and two feet deep. All dug with his helmet and KIF. No one carries the short folding shovel. His second hole is almost the same dimension. Everyone else completed their hole while he was starting again. You gaze at the two holes, even as Sebastian crawls up next to you. His face is dirty and aged well beyond his 23 years. His smock is covered in thick dust, which hides the moisture of his sweat-soaked blouse underneath.

"You know what I think, Caporal?"

"A well?" you reply. Old, ancient wells were not that prevalent in the western desert where you spent your first tour, but you had seen them. This was long-buried. The rocks could be the outer edge or capstones.

"Yep. There might still be water down there. With the location on the end of this ancient stream, so close to the AZ, it's worth a shot."

"You've seen these before then?"

"Oh yeah, Caporal. The way it looks, it's about a four-foot-wide mouth. See how Nobilis Raisa has uncovered it dead center in his hole here, and then a few inches over, it curves to the back? If we dig back that way, we can see if it's open or been closed up."

You study the holes and surrounding area and then look out toward where Zaphir should be. Where are the rest of the platoon and the CO? There had been extra water in five-gallon cans on the ATC, but that was all destroyed along with spare ammo and food rations. Your legionnaires are dangerously low on water now, too young and inexperienced to self-ration. The injured driver is taking a large amount also to replace blood and body fluid loss from the burns. She will die by morning from dehydration if you can't get her more advanced medical care.

Level Up – The Retreat, The Well, and The Relief Mission #26

    __ Medium (Moderate) Action A 15 PP 80% success

    __ Medium (Moderate) Action B 15 PP 80% success

    __ Difficult (Heavy) Action C 25 PP 60% success

Character Summary

You have selected Medium Action A.

Summary:

With the ambushers' withdrawal, you decide that the best strategy is to exit from the AZ and lead your squad back to the company AO. If Sr. Caporal Josef is not here, that means he is, himself, under assault even closer to the AZ from larger XDR forces. You cannot risk your legionnaires in a wild and more-than-probable suicide mission. If you can make it back to the road on the western slope of the hills, there is higher probability that a patrol will pick you up as they search for the missing platoon.

All of the lower ranks and the two legs are relieved to hear the order to head west. Sr. Legionnaire Ladd and Lance Caporal Sebastian, not so much. They understand the numerical impracticality of attempting to find and reinforce the probably embattled remainder of the platoon and the CO. However, they are still heartbroken at the prospect of leaving fellow EFL to die in this desert. There should have been artillery and air support called in by the CO, and it was missing, as they are. They are already dead. It is the law of the desert; life is too vulnerable for those that make the mistake of not respecting the law.

Once the sun rises, if you are not found quickly, your survival chances are not great. It is well over 120 miles back to base.

The driver died the first morning. She screamed in pain before slipping into unconsciousness with spasms brought on by heat, swelling of the brain, and dehydration, dying a half-hour later. Three of the lower ranks gave up during the middle of the first afternoon, taking several steps into the hot sands and falling. You ordered a halt before sunrise to prepare holes and mediocre protection from the heat by draping the shemaghs as shrouds of canopy.

You and Lance Caporal Sebastian searched for water, even setting up a water still, soaking up what little dew you could find on plants. You collected all water the first night and began a ration of one cap-full every hour. At that rate, the water lasted until dark when you set out again.

When the patrol found you mid-morning the second day, two more nobilis had died, leaving you with 15 total in the squad and platoon. The news rocks you; the CO and the rest of the platoon were wiped-out on the outskirts of Zaphir. Sr. Caporal Josef had joined the relief effort only to be trapped himself in the open desert. Your decision to retreat saved the lives of your legionnaires. The Executive Officer, Leftenant Roubere, was promoted immediately to captain and now commands the company.

Upon arrival at Gulf Company, you are summoned to the CP for a debrief. Captain Roubere is a former first sergent and, therefore, a well-rounded legionnaire. He was a battle-hardened veteran NCO for many years before serving three years learning as a junior officer after *turning the corner*. He eyes you warily. He obviously distrusts you and questions your survival when the rest of your platoon perished along with the company commander, his entourage, and the company sergent. You stand at attention.

You have selected Medium Action B.

Summary:

With water at a dangerously low level, you decide that staying put for now and digging in an attempt to find water is the correct course of action. You directly spell Minus Nobilis Raisa and begin digging out the perimeter of the hidden well. Lance Caporal Sebastian digs from the opposite side, tracing only the stone buried in the sand and sediment layers as they reappear. Soon, Sr. Legionnaire Ladd takes over for you, and Legionnaire Abbott relieves Sebastian. In half an hour, the mouth of the well is exposed for the first time in over two centuries.

The outer hole is six feet in diameter and two feet deep. The digging is fairly easy after getting past the hard-baked crust. Each new rainfall and subsequent flooding stripped the hard crust away, leaving a new layer of sediment.

The squad all take turns digging, commendable in their self-delegation in relieving their mates. They also keep a constant watch, and you set up a little outside of the perimeter. Twenty legionnaires persist alone in the dark of the Xobian Desert, survivors of what should have been a deadly ambush. The well they have uncovered is four feet in diameter, inlaid with stone and mud bricks. It is, without a doubt, a previous Bedouin campsite, long dried up and forgotten by the desert tribes. Lance Caporal Sebastian takes charge of the excavation at this point. You are curious about the progress, but your priority remains your squad's safety and not getting in the way as an onlooker.

You hear an excited series of exclamations and oaths. The outer edge of the well debris collapses at several points. Sebastian orders everyone back and then to dig away the surrounding sand layers carefully. By early morning, all water reserves are gone. With dirty, salt- and sweat-stained blouses and undershirts, the entire squad sits and rests. They have lost all remaining hope. You are left with a massive hole two feet deep to the top of the well-mouth, eight feet across. The well itself has been dug out a mind-boggling eight feet by legionnaires working solo in the depth and then hoisted out by their mates. It is now too deep to continue since there is no way to pull the digger from any deeper, and too cramped to put two into the hole.

Lance Caporal Sebastian is so certain that only a few feet more will yield water that he volunteers to work alone in the depths. You forbid it. There is still hope that a patrol will find you as the search for the CO and missing platoon intensifies.

There has been no artillery or air support, meaning that the CO and the rest of the platoon were probably killed in their own ambush somewhere between the wadi and Zaphir. Surely, the company and battalion were searching by now. You look to the sunrise in the east, certain that no one else from 4th Platoon is alive. Your mind races to the obvious question, *Why hasn't a patrol been looking for you?* The destroyed ATC is proof that the platoon was ambushed at the junction. There are no bodies, so the survivors went somewhere. If the CO was able to get out a message, all efforts would be to locate and rescue her, but there should be air cover.

No, in her vanity and quest for a spectacular battle, the CO gave orders for no air presence until she called it in. With over 14 hours past a check-in, surely battalion was concerned about the situation; they would institute a search soon.

You are now committed to remaining in this location at least until dark. With no water, you will not get far in the desert. The afternoon sun bakes the sand and the bodies of the legionnaires. The driver is in and out of consciousness, the limited movement good for her. She rests in the shade beside the well. The rest of the squad is in the massive hole surrounding the well or adjacent holes. You have draped the shemaghs over the hole in an attempt to offer some relief from the hot sun.

A little after midday, you speak with Sebastian as he again volunteers to drop into the deep hole, "I won't be able to get you out; you'll die down there."

"I know we'll find water, Caporal, only a couple more feet," he asserts.

Grudgingly, you consent and lower him down yourself. You also lower a rope made of twisted shemagh to pull up the excavated dirt in a helmet. The squad is listless and on the verge of collapse after their long night of labor digging and no water.

"Sebastian?" you call down the hole after several minutes of inactivity and quiet. You fear he is dead, working himself to death in the tight and airless confines, the temperature soaring.

"I'm taking a rest, Caporal."

"I understand. Call me Baker, Lance Caporal," You are nearly weeping for this selfless legionnaire who is suffering above normal physical limits.

You hear a slight chuckle, "Only if you call me Sebastian, Baker."

"Deal, Sebastian. Come on, let me get you out of there."

"You can't. It's too deep. I dug another two feet, and believe it or not, it's cooler on the bottom. I'm sitting on the bottom, and I feel good for the first time in hours."

He was hallucinating, the early signs of despair and death. You had seen it before in nearly every theater in which you served. Legionnaires would see things that weren't there, water, food, loved ones, safety, paradise. Some would eat sand believing it was water or bread or walk straight into an enemy position thinking they were greeting family. It was always hard to watch men die, believing one thing and not realizing the danger.

You talk for several minutes, learning about his past. The others of the squad listen, their own lives soon to follow the course of their lance caporal, death from delirium.

"Hey, Baker, check this out. Pull up the helmet," as he tugs on the makeshift rope. A nobilis pulls up the helmet.

The visibility down in the 10 to 12-foot hole is poor, and therefore, Sebastian was unable to fully appreciate his find. It's a broken clay pitcher. You carve out the dirt and sand to find moisture in the cavity of the base! There is no way moisture would have survived in the hole for any amount of time! Water is close.

"Sebastian. Sebastian?"

"Yeah, Baker. I'm resting. Sorry, Caporal, I had to lie down. It's cooler on the bottom. I know you think I'm going crazy, but it's wet and feels good."

"Sebastian, I don't think you're crazy. You hit water, or at least a moisture line. We got to get you out of there and send down a fresh digger."

"Can't. Too tight now. I haven't dug all the way to the sides, only a hole on one side. Give me a few minutes to rest."

After what seems like an eternity, the rope tugs, and a nobilis hauls it up. A helmet of water! It is dirty, murky, cool.

"I found water, Baker! I found water," his call turns to somber sobs.

The laughter and cheering is instantaneous from all the squad. You soak a ripped undershirt and dapple the head of the driver, her response immediate to the cool touch. The remainder of the group share the water, each taking a cautious sip, only one, knowing others are just as eager for a small drink.

Someone lowers a canteen, and after a few minutes, it is retrieved, nearly full.

"You make sure you get some of this, Sebastian. Don't skip yourself," you order the lance caporal down in the well.

"I will. The smaller hole is leaching slowly but steadily. I figure maybe a quart every 10 minutes."

By evening you have figured out how to rig a sling to pull Lance Caporal Sebastian out of the hole and send down a rested and hydrated relief. You are dismayed by Sebastian's appearance when he reemerges from the pit. He is covered in drying mud, his eyes and mouth the only recognizable human feature. He removed his uniform down in the well except for skivvies and undershirt; the rest were either left behind or hauled up during the day. He has rehydrated, for the most part, drinking at will from the spring or aqueduct, but is horribly spent physically.

You sit him beside the driver, who is also improved, and order him to get some sleep.

In the morning, a heavily-manned patrol finds you and sends a message to Gulf Company and battalion that the ambushed squad has been found. You learn the fate of your Sr. caporal and company commander and the rest of 4th Platoon. The news rocks you; all of them are dead, caught in an ambush outside of the village of Zaphir.

The Executive Officer, Leftenant Roubere, was promoted immediately to captain and now commands the company.

Upon arrival at Gulf Company, you are summoned to the CP for a debrief. Captain Roubere is a former first sergent and, therefore, a well-rounded legionnaire. He was a battle-hardened veteran NCO for many years before serving three years learning as a junior officer after *turning the corner.* He eyes you warily. He obviously distrusts you and questions your survival when the rest of your platoon perished along with the company commander, his entourage, and the company sergent. You stand at attention.

You have selected Difficult Action C.

Summary:

You cannot fathom the thought of leaving legionnaires to their death without attempting to assist them. The village of Zaphir is some four or five miles away from where you are now. It is entirely feasible to cover the distance with a march at night by capable EFL legionnaires. Your water supply is dangerously low, and you collect all supplies and start a ration. You set Lance Caporal Sebastian upon digging out the well in hopes that he will find water soon.

The driver is in critical shape, and the allowance of water to a more than probable casualty is unwarranted in these circumstances. She has been receiving double the ordinary ration, but you cut it in half, allowing her only a normal amount. Now that cooler night air is upon you, the squad rests when not digging. The night is suddenly interrupted by artillery and air support in the direction of Zaphir. The rest of the platoon is under assault.

A little after the sun sets, with no water found, you lead out a group of volunteers, several minus nobilis, one leg, Sr. Legionnaire Ladd, and Lance Caporal Sebastian, nine total. The remainder stays at the wadi-well and care for the now comatose driver. What water remains is split evenly, less than a quarter canteen each, as is the ammunition. You start off towards the fight, recalling one of the general orders learned during BT. *My mission, my duty, is to relieve, in whatever manner possible, at any cost, the embattled position of another legionnaire.* The trek is not easy but well within physical limits. The five under ranks are keeping up admirably.

In a little over an hour, you reach the remnants of the beleaguered legionnaires outside the village's perimeter. The burned-out carcasses of the ATC and two buggies further down the road spell out the scene. The CO and her staff were destroyed probably instantly. Sr. Caporal Josef responded and was cut down by a similar SFM barrage. With communications cut to battalion and company HQ, they would not initialize support until a pre-established deadline, whatever that was.

Your arrival is just a sequence in time. Fighting to gain entry into the defensive perimeter, you watch as Lance Caporal Sebastian and Lower Rank Cordoba fall in a heavy rain of enemy fire. Sr. Legionnaire Ladd reaches the ATC perimeter, where the defensive line is now positioned under and around the burned-out hulk of the vehicle. He quickly administers first aid to a fellow mate.

You and Lower Rank Stephens fight to gain a hole at the front of the ATC. You put down as many targets as you can before depleting your specialized ammo for the GPXR. You switch to your GPS. In the bright starlit sky above, the drones are circling, detailing the battle, sending real-time footage back to HQ, where it is analyzed and categorized for further support. The artillery fire is non-specific, falling haphazardly, no trained FO to call in proper supporting fire. The CO or Sergent Camponello would have had that capability.

Beside you, Lower Rank Raisa and Legionnaire Pompano hold a shallow defensive hole along the right side of the ATC.

"We need ammo, Legionnaire Pompano! See if you can find some."

He drops his head, then answers, "Yes, Caporal Baker!" He backs out under the ATC and crawls to the rear, searching every corpse along the way.

EXPEDITIONARY FOREIGN LEGION -The Xo

Minutes turn to hours. Legionnaires die one by one. A stray missile from a drone-directed strike hits the ATC from above, killing most of who remain. At dawn, you watch a column of heavily-fortified EFL ATCs roll down the dusty road. The XDR withdraw to the AZ, escaping. Due to the *World Convention Civilian Population Abodement Agreement*, no habitation of civilian population can be assaulted without expressed, documented, and higher command authority, and only then with explicit evidence that combatants are residing within. The ambush occurred well outside the sanctioned perimeter of the village. The XDR retreated to the AZ, not the village of Zaphir, leaving the EFL and her allies flat-footed in the pursuit of the retreating enemy.

Legionnaires of Gulf Company and sister Hotel Company retrieve the remains of the botched AZ patrol out of the half-buried, defensive fighting holes around the shredded ATC. You and Lower Rank Stephens are buried under the collapsed engine block of the ATC and are unnoticed. Additionally, all of the survivors of the initial ambush that remained at the well are also unaccounted for. The official after-action report only states that several members of 2nd Squad, 4th Platoon were found KIA at the main ambush site; the rest are listed as MIA, possible POW, or DAC, *deserters in active combat.*

You are dead. Restart the game.

Game Summary:

You are ranked at __ out of __ active players. Your game score is __. You have reached General Patton level. Tough break. Poor decisions lead to poor endings.

Learn from your mistakes and become a better leader. Read on, Caporal!

Mission Debrief:

Character survives, Pass/Fail status update.

CHAPTER 17

Level Up – **The Middle Years**

Over and over, the lessons repeat, almost as a scratched disc, repeating the same song, verse, or scene. Through the past 20-some months, you have led 4th Platoon, Gulf Company into and out of what seem to be the same missions and scenarios of past operations. The greatest pain is not foreseeing the multitude of mistakes that cost legionnaires and your young mates their lives. It is shattering to see young, 17- and 18- year-old faces in the coffins to return home to their families. It cuts you to your very soul. The only consolation is that you are still trying to save as many as you can. And you do. Over and over.

It is no surprise or alarm when you receive the message to report to regiment this morning at 1030. Ha! Your best mate, Caporal Waltz, has an appointment this same morning at 0945, and Klien is at 0900! Gulf Company is about to be disbanded. The reality shakes you. It has been close to two years, and the company is well below forty-five percent, past time to *Case the Colours*. The objective of the meetings is to renegotiate previous contracts. What does the EFL want of you this time? They never offer extra summa or promotions, only postings, and reassignments as incentives. The advice of an old mentor comes to you. You haven't heard from him in years, it seems; he is probably retired or dead by now. *What are your plans, Baker?* First Sergent Kristenson asked you that in his office at Port Summa. You ponder that question as you now stand at the desk of the first sergent of 117th Regiment. Years have passed, lives ended, and friendships have begun and wilted. You have not busied yourself with the trivial posting assignments of Legion unit order. Yet now, standing at the desk of the Regiment First Sergent of 117th Regiment, there is a familiar face and name.

It is funny how things revolve; even seemingly unimportant moments, people, and places from your past revisit. Your memory of Sergent Stepanakert is not that monumental. He was the India Company Sergent of 4/117 during your first tour, your first posting. Because he was the company sergent, and you were only a minus nobilis working through the first two years of service, there was no real contact between the two of you. The only solid memory you have of him was right before you ranked up to Sr. Legionnaire. He stopped the *rite of passage* fight, even though he was impressed with your willingness to continue.

"I barely remember you, Caporal Baker. You have done well. I don't understand why you have not been promoted to Sr. caporal. Your record is above most of your peers. Your determination and drive are clearly evident, even to the present. I was not assigned to the regiment during the Zaphir Wadi Ambush, arriving a year ago. Do you feel that some blowback from that battle has affected your CO's recommendation?"

After being found at the wadi-well, when you arrived at Gulf Company, you were summoned to the CP for a debrief. Captain Roubere was a former first sergent and, therefore, a well-rounded legionnaire. He was a battle-hardened, tough veteran NCO for many years before *turning the corner,* or becoming a commissioned officer. He then served for three years, learning the ropes as a junior officer. He was immediately promoted to captain and given command of Gulf. He eyed you warily. It was understandable that he would question your survival when the rest of your platoon perished along with the company commander, her protection detail, and the company sergent. You stood at attention during the entire interview. It was clear to you that Captain Roubere did not like you and felt you were a coward. *Maybe you were?* After all the platoon survivors, including the driver when she was able, testified to your leadership, skill, cool-headiness under fire, and reasoning behind your decision to remain at the well, the CO kept you with 4th Platoon. He designated you as *caporal-chef*, and six lower ranks were shifted to fill out the platoon. The new company sergent, transferred in from another regiment, was cold to you at every opportunity. You lost a good mate and mentor in Sr. Caporal Josef. The second-guessing remains with you to this day.

"That's out of my judgment and understanding, First Sergent. I have continued to perform to all expectations and orders and am ready to continue with my next posting."

First Sergent Stepanakert continues to look you over, head to foot. He opens a one-inch-thick folder and flips through several pages; then, he opens a thin red folder. The service folder you carry with you in a sealed envelope to your next duty station. The red one you have never seen before.

"So, you operated with 'ol Kristenson, I see. You know he's Sergent Major of V Corps now. He sends word that he still has that spot," Stepanakert closes the red file.

"You are hereby promoted to Sr. Caporal, effective one year ago when I should have reviewed the Zaphir

Wadi Ambush report and findings and seen to the promotion myself. You have acted as the Sr. caporal of your platoon for 22 months! I am pissed! You are entitled to all back-pay and rank of service. Where do you want to go, Sr. Caporal Baker? Hmm? You still want that BTC platoon? We're going to skip all this other nonsense. You are a fully operational capable NCO that deserves credit for your own platoon, and, by the lights of the stars, I'm going to send you that way! Get your duffles packed and report back here at 1400. You're bound for *The Land of the Giant PX,* Sahara Del Rio! I'll have your orders and promotion packet all ready. Also, inform those three scruffy caporal mates of yours that there is a change to their orders as well. I'm sending the lot of you to DI course. You've gone through enough crap with this company. Get out of here." He waves you off and reaches for the phone.

"Get *Sergent-screw-your-legionnaires Humphreys* of Gulf 6/117 in here right now! I don't give a crap where he is! And see if the colonel has a minute to discuss a CO...."

Level Up – Fox BTC

You miss Sr. Caporal Josef more each day with every new problem that is thrown at you. His leadership style was so similar to Sr. Caporal Tollerson and Caporal Edmunds that it was comforting in a sense. Your own platoon, from fresh cassum to soon-to-be minus nobilis, reap the benefits of lessons learned from such masters of mental manipulation, hard discipline, physical conditioning, and tortured hardship. Today you are meeting with a caporal that you have watched for a few days. He arrived like all the rest, jumping through the hoops and completing all the preliminary status sheet check-offs. When you reviewed the CAL, you noted he was just from a two-year Palanquin, pulling the AC before that.

"You like the desert?"

"It suits me, Sr. Caporal. I was with 1st Battalion before. I don't like the cold. I'm from Del Rio."

"Why not try the Amphib tour?"

"Ehh, I had buddies that pulled it, said it was useless. Take an island, give it to the Army, then leave and have to retake it later. You liked it alright, Sr. Caporal?"

"Ha, yeah, that about sums it up, but it's worth the experience. What do you feel about discipline?"

He looks at the empty space above your head, tilts his, and muses on it for a moment. "I don't want you to take me wrong or anything, Sr. Caporal, but I feel unit morale is linked to a certain level of discipline. Not unwarranted or mean to be mean, but fair. Hard at first, but allow an ease up when earned. My dad was a retired, well, not fully-retired, colour sergeant, with 14 years. I know discipline."

You laugh, "I bet. Well, take a look around and feel free to ask any questions. Just let me know if you are looking strongly at another platoon. We got two and half weeks before graduation, and I want to take a strong caporal with me."

"Am I a strong caporal, Sr. Caporal?"

You look at him, gauging your answer.

"You're the only one I'm looking at so far, Caporal Chao."

"Well, Sr. Caporal Baker, I've looked into your record, and I can't think of a better mentor for me to learn from, other than my own Sr. Cap back in Charlie 1/117. I'd like to join the platoon as soon as possible, if you want me."

Ha-ha, you laugh, offering your hand, "I hope you read the unedited version, Chao, and got the whole picture, so you aren't disappointed."

"I did, and I think your record stands straight and tall."

You both laugh.

Graduation, the movement to *The Xo*, and first missions progress on schedule. Fox BTC is commissioned as Alpha 3/117, and you have 1st Platoon. Forty legionnaires are now your responsibility, and the weight is tremendous, but you handle it well. Caporal Chao is a good caporal, smart in the ways of the desert, and willing to learn all he can. At the same time, he takes a strong interest in developing the minus nobilis under his care.

As is the tradition, Alpha inherits a number of legs completing their three-year service who are prone not to reenlist. You spend considerable time and effort with them, coaxing them to a better outlook on the EFL. You, of course, also have Sr. legs and lance caporals to woo, which is not too difficult as they have already reenlisted once, but nothing is left to chance. Soon you become known throughout the battalion as *The Recruiter*, which is not the case at all. You also have a hushed reputation as a skilled sniper and excellent combat leader.

EXPEDITIONARY FOREIGN LEGION -The Xo

First Platoon and the rest of Alpha Company prepare for their *la marche Kepi blanc*, the march of the white cap. The 37-mile forced march, is two days in duration followed by the ceremony to receive the renowned desert hat of the Legion! You are as proud of this achievement for them as they are. You remember the still chaffing experience of 4th Platoon with Gulf 6/117; Captain Roubere and Sergent Humphreys regarded the surviving platoon members with questionable merit and disdain. During their *kepi* ceremony, your platoon was placed on sentry duty. It was an open slap in the face; the sentry detail was usually comprised of veteran legs and another company. They weren't even awarded their *kepis'* that day. The other platoons were dismayed at the treatment of their mates. Not a single leg was promoted to Sr. legionnaire from 4th Platoon, and none reenlisted.

Today was different! Today you are tearfully proud of your platoon. Every single minus nobilis completes *la marche,* and you and Caporal Chao clap them on the shoulder and shake their hands. The excitement is contagious; the new legs, nervous at first with the unexpected and very out of character behavior of their caporals, soon join in the revelry.

The CO and Sergent organize a wrestling match, and you remove your own *kepi* and blouse, a signal of non-rank recognition. You stand in the middle of the marked-off wrestling square and challenge any taker. The platoon, as well as the company, looks on in uncertainty. It is a trap! The Sr. caporal of 2nd Platoon, Urall, flings his *kepi* to one of his completely surprised legs, who barely catches it, and strips his blouse off, throwing it at another and yelling, "Second Platoon takes that challenge!"

The roar is instantaneous! As the antics and obvious fakeness become the showcase, Sr. Caporal Urall trips you and goes for the pin. Caporal Chao yells from the corner of the make-shift ring and reaches his hand out, even moving the cone inward! The other two Sr. caporals rush in and drag you and Urall to neutral corners. The mood in the desert twilight is festive and loud. With your tagging of Chao, Urall rushes to his corner only to find his caporal drinking a King Xobian Beer and watching with laughter, so he opts to tag, drag, an unsuspecting leg into the ring in his place! The matches continue for hours, slowly becoming more authentic, athletic, and competitive, with prizes awarded by the command staff.

You stand in the shadowy darkness, each of you still out of uniform, quietly sharing conversation and observing the scene around you. Leftenant Hays of 1st and 2nd Platoons, Company Sergent Maxton, Sr. Caporals Urall, Trey, and Kendel each have a bottle of beer and watch the company unwind and relax. A small group of newly promoted legs, a Sr. leg, and a lance caporal are sitting at a makeshift table of upturned crates, playing cards and drinking beer in the cool desert early morning. There is a partially-hidden, wooden 30-count *super-case* of King Xobian Beer, with water from the melting ice seeping into the sand under the lance caporal's boots. Undoubtedly, the beer was pilfered by the lance caporal himself.

"Man! I had no idea Sr. Caporal could be so cool and laid back," one of the legs says, his newly earned *kepi* sitting proudly on his head even as he slants alternately to the left, rear, and right on the metal ammo box, spinning in a slow, broken circle.

Leftenant Hays quietly chuckles, "Me neither!" Ha-ha, the command group laughs together in the shadows.

"Let me share this with you ignorant, drunk, mentally challenged, brain-deficit, soon-to-be colour sergent grass-detail, morning-sick, puking douches. I have never seen such an event in my four and a half years in the EFL. This here," he waves his finger in a circle in the air above his head, "this here, this is the land of – *make-believe*. Yeah! You better enjoy this while you can, because when you wake up with a splitting headache from dehydration in the morning, this will all have been a dream, and the Sr. caporals and caporals will be on fire, roasting your nimbies just like yesterday on *la marche*. Who's ready for another beer?"

It is evident they are a fire team of some squad in 3rd or 4th Platoon; you recognize a couple of the legs from BTC. The lance caporal was on target and attempting, in some small way, to steer his legionnaires into a coherent realization of the truth. Your group eases back into the darkness, and Sergent Maxton speaks.

"I'll suggest to the CO an early morning formation and a non-disclosed four-mile march with full combat load, followed after breakfast by a full-morning field layout inspection. We'll give them light duty to recover and lick their wounds in the afternoon. Normal patrol routine the next day. Sound good?"

"Yes, Sergent."

"Aye, Company Sergent."

"On target, Sergent Maxton."

That was exactly why a company-level sergent, enlisted rank-seven, has between nine and 12 years in service. The formula he just meted out is just the right amount of workload for a hung-over, confused, and unbalanced company of newly promoted legionnaires and an equally confused cluster of veteran upper-ranks. The early four-mile march would be difficult only due to their present physical condition, not overly arduous or too easy, especially with a full combat load. The unknown distance would serve as a mental disabler, a heart-breaker. The building heat of the day, coupled with the workout, would sweat out the alcohol that wasn't puked out. A full morning, physically easy, yet mentally stressful, including gear inspection, would break their remaining memory of a laid-back platoon command relationship. The menial duty for the remainder of the day would only rebuild the respect of rank that was expected, without punitive discipline.

The Sr. caporals disperse to locate their caporals and share the looming schedule, then turn in for the remaining two hours of sleep. The legionnaires of Alpha 3/117 will soon suffer the consequences of unguarded celebration.

The morning breaks early in the desert; the sun edges up over millennia-baked sands. The temperature fell overnight to 83 degrees, chilly, but that will soon rise. The young legionnaires of Alpha struggle to come to grips with the turn-about of their caporals. The sage upper-rank veterans are almost laughing, cursing at the situation, rousting up their squadmates, and repeating the shouted orders to fall out with full combat pack. The new legs are now completely confused and disoriented. They have only marched one time with a full pack during *la marche* in the desert. *Was this the new standard? Are they about to repeat that horrible distance?* As the first mile drags to the second and the cobwebs shake loose, muscles regain their stamina. By the third mile, their blouses under the BAC and smock are soaked, their muscles ache, and their hopes are dashed. Sergent Maxton has arranged for field chow to be waiting enroute, and the platoons quickly work through the line, pulling out mess kits and cups from their packs.

The mess line is quick and efficient. The intent is for the fare to be basic yet filling, with fried potatoes covered with morning gravy, a piece of bacon, and coffee. There is a single carton of milk or juice. A field sanitation station is at the end of the line to dip the kits in before repacking, and the march continues in less than half an hour total.

The CO modifies the suggested four miles to five-and-a-half, which pushes the time to a three-hour outing, plus the break for chow. Since the day began at 0500 with wake-up and the march commenced soon after, Alpha marches back into the battalion area before 0900. Orders are quickly relayed that the CO inspection of laid-out field gear will occur at 1030. Hearts and spirits completely break as the legionnaires dutifully prepare to break down their packs and lay out their equipment in the hard-packed, sand-blown formation area.

Following lunch, the legionnaires perform an assortment of duties for the rest of the day. These include repairing and whitewash/painting the mud-brick quarters, refilling sandbags and strengthening fortified positions, KP duty cleaning the field kitchen used for chow this morning, general area cleanup, disinfecting battalion water storage tanks, and sweeping the battalion parade grounds of sand.

The next day regular patrol routine falls back to normal.

Months later, 1st Platoon is assigned pump station repair convoy duty.

Level Up – The Kasish Wells Mission #27

    __ Light Action A 10 PP 95% success

    __ Moderate Action B 15 PP 80% success

    __ Heavy Action C 25 PP 60% success

Character Summary

You are involved in light action.

Summary:

Third Battalion 117th Regiment lays beside and serves in a dual support relationship with 6th Battalion, your most recent former unit. The patrol areas are similar but not duplicated. **Accordingly, you feel great trepidation when** your patrol assignment takes you to the *Oil Wells of Kasish*, the village three miles south of Zaphir. The wells themselves are not in Kasish, just named for the nearest settlement eight miles away. The AZ is less than 10 miles away. Echo and Fox Companies maintain rotational security of the well site facility. The pump repair convoy is setting out on a regular maintenance service schedule, with the assignment expected to last three days. The platoon loads up on two ATCs with Leftenant Hays in the lead buggy, and the four assorted service vehicles between the ATCs. Each service vehicle is equipped with an AP cupola, and the technicians are armed. Many techs are former EFL returning to *The Xo* as highly paid contractors completing two-year contracts but living a much better lifestyle. It is a source of contention among vets.

As the convoy approaches a range of hills, much like the hills around the wadi you experienced several years ago, you become more apprehensive. The hills are part of the same recurring range that follows the AZ all along the Xobian. The road crosses through much like it did in the Zaphir Wadi. This is a known ambush site. Leftenant Hays is well aware of this and pulls to a stop a mile from the entry point. As with every hill range in the desert, a wadi forms in the inner valley where rainwater collects and runs to the lower elevation. In this case, it runs north for three miles before the hills and, therefore, the wadi cease. The oil wells are another two miles southeast of the exit.

Leftenant Hays has precisely planned this very patrol exercise, tired of fooling around with the XDR at this particular location. He served a year as the adjutant leftenant of Fox Company before promotion to full leftenant and reassignment to Alpha. He positions the larger and more heavily armored service vehicle behind him, followed by the ATC and the remaining three trucks, then the last ATC. Hays is a competent and experienced officer, a former colour sergeant.

The convoy moves out, weaving and creating a thick dust cloud, essentially hiding the vehicles. Once the roadway narrows at the converging hills, the convoy reassembles and moves at a slowed pace to the inner valley. The buggy and lead vehicle continue, and the APs rip the hill summits on both sides of the road, stopping to allow the next three following vehicles to race through, a dust cloud forming. Both ATCs race up the side of the hills, and the squads dismount and scatter in a frenzied assault. The waiting ambushers are so overwhelmed by the fast-paced and unknown tactical maneuver that they are quickly routed and eliminated. The convoy quickly regroups and proceeds to the *Oil Wells of Kasish*. Thirty mixed forces of XDR and militia are left in the burning sands, stripped of weapons, placed in fetal positions with all of their water poured out, a strong, symbolic message. You suffer no injuries.

You are involved in moderate action.

Summary:

As the rearranged convoy approaches the entrance to the wadi, a premature SFM misses the buggy. Undoubtedly, a young, ill-trained XDR got too excited. The vehicles hastily form a line and begin an intense, saturating line of fire on the source of the missile while the two ATCs swing a wide flank and roll up the hill on either end. First Platoon dismounts and, in little time, ascends the rocky crest forcing the ambushers on the near side to retreat across the wadi or be swallowed up in the tightening net. The enemy forces on the far side now provide support for their fleeing fellows, exposing their positions. The line of vehicles now moves up the road to the summit of the hill overlooking the wadi and continues to pound the entrenched positions on the far side. Air cover is called in along with artillery. Leftenant Hays gives accurate *fire control coordinates*.

National Army mobile artillary drops a blanket of smoke on the far ridgeline, and you order your platoon to advance across the open wadi and up the hill. They advance in precise move-and-cover with Caporal Chao's co-leadership, and soon you are midway up the hill, assuming firing positions. The smoke lifts and Leftenant

Hays resumes FCC to the rear of the XDR and lays another blanket of smoke. The tactic is brilliant. While the enemy is caught in confusion, your legionnaires advance straight into their holes and wipe them out, taking seven prisoners with several light injuries in exchange.

You are involved in heavy action.

Summary:

Leftenant Hays' plan is working flawlessly as the lead, heavier vehicle preps the opposing ridgeline with AP. The buggy with Hays and the three following vehicles make their way up and out of the wadi. Suddenly the AP gun of the heavy service vehicle jams, and an SFM strikes the second service truck, only disabling it. The roadway is partially blocked. Hays must quickly decide whether to continue and abandon the vehicle and push it off the road with a heavy ATC, or to regroup and fight it out.

Before he can react, a second SFM hits the lead truck, taking out the AP turret. The enemy's strength is above normal. They were either assembling here for another mission further inside the desert or ordered to score a significant massacre. The forces on the western ridge are now closing the retreat roadway.

"North! North!" Hays yells and points the direction to the convoy drivers who immediately respond and race full-bore up the wadi. Whether there are landmines or not, sitting on the road caught between the two attacking, elevated positions is not healthy. It is three miles out of the wadi valley. The repair technicians scramble from the cover of their disabled truck and jump into the closest vehicle they can hitch a ride with. You collect two in your

ATC; Hays grabs another. One is missing. You look at the vehicle as it slips past. The larger service truck turns and races by.

"Who's missing? Who's missing?" you yell at one of the two men firing their rifles at the ridge positions.

"The other guy's dead," one of the techs answers back. The second one seems confused.

"Didn't two jump on the buggy?" he yells up to you.

"Slow down! Let me off," you order the driver, who looks at you with a shocked gaze.

You jump off and tumble to the ground as he slows, rolling. The buggy nearly runs you over in the cloud of dust. Hays stares at you with surprise and confusion as he passes; he assesses your dismounted predicament. The buggy continues to weave in and out before turning back, executing the same crazed maneuvering. You run to the truck as enemy fire strikes all around you. Your slide into the sand under the driver's side front wheel is nothing short of sensational, giving you immediate cover.

"Where are you? Where are you? Can you hear me? Are you hit?" You yell for the lost tech.

"Oh, for crying out loud, I thought you guys left me! I'm in the back on the floor. I got a broke leg and a through-and-through in the shoulder. They're rattlin' this baby good. I know there's another SFM with my name on it. Get me outta here, Leg!"

You crawl along the underside of the truck, which is oriented at an angle facing the eastern ridge. Neither side is well-protected from the opposing fire, but the driver's side offers a little more security.

"Which way are you facing? Please tell me the driver's side."

You hear a funny laugh, surprising under the situation, "Ah, now that would have been too easy, wouldn't it?"

"I don't guess you can turn, huh?"

"Sorry, no, it's too cramped in here. You're gonna have to...."

You quickly pop up, swing the door open, grab his boots, and yank him out onto the sand in one swift, powerful movement. His screams of pain, curses, and cries pleading for you to stop all mix together in an instantaneous moment of chaos. Together you fall back on the sand, and just as quickly, you both scramble to crawl back under the truck while rounds plunk the sand around you.

His cries intensify between the sobs of excruciating pain, "Oh, you son of a b...! Damn you! I told you my leg was broke, you freaking moron!" His face is nearly buried in the sand, resting on his folded arms. "This is exactly why I left the EFL, freaking crap like this! You damn legs are too freaking stupid to comprehend the simplest information." He lays there for a few seconds, in unbelievable pain, getting his composure.

You look around for the buggy and Leftenant Hays. He is circling, drawing the enemy fire, waiting for your signal to evacuate. The other tech is on the AP, rolling through the rounds. That was one thing; most of these techs were a bunch of mean-as-hell, spit-n-piss, fire-breathing, former legs.

"You got any water there, hero?" he calls out, shifting in the sand to turn on his side under the tight space and face you. His face is covered in sand, with wet patches around his eyes from tears. You are alongside him but facing outward watching the buggy.

"Yeah," you pull a canteen from the pouch on your side, passing it to him. You carry two canteens along with the bladder.

"I guess they all high-tailed it out here. What, you get left, too? Who's firing that AP?"

"The buggy is circling us, drawing fire, waiting for you to stop crying and get ready to run for it."

"What! Are you crazy?"

"Yep. You ready?"

"Ah, crap! You got to be one crazy, stupid Leg!"

"I'm going, you can come with me or stay here, but the train is pulling out of the station."

"Let's go," he starts to crawl towards you, and you pull him as you wiggle free from the undercarriage.

The Leftenant sees you, and they make a final crazy circle, changing direction and then swooping in close to the side, barely slowing down. You pick up the wounded tech and run for the tail of the buggy, throwing him in and jumping in almost on top of him. Hays turns and pulls the tech forward. The driver continues his wild weaving and zigzagging, racing to join the small column two miles ahead. Caporal Chao stopped the ATCs and dismounted the platoon to form a defensive position.

Soon the ambush is behind you, and the buggy reaches the platoon. Hays directs them to load up. You jump off and join your squad, and the convoy returns to the battalion area.

Level Up – Mission Debrief

Character survives, Pass/Fail status update.

Battalion and regiment are growing tired of the ambushes. The oil companies, facing personnel, equipment, and revenue losses, are applying pressure to protect their investment better. After 1st Platoon returns with one destroyed vehicle, another heavily damaged, and a seriously wounded technician, they turn up the heat.

The injured tech is scheduled to be flown out the next day; his injuries are not life-threatening. He left a message for you to stop by the infirmary. You are inclined not to until Leftenant Hays speaks to you.

"Man, what a piece of work that guy was! Wouldn't shut up, whining and complaining about the EFL. I mean, he truly hated his service from all that I could gather, but when he found out who you were, he shut up completely, didn't say another word. When they unloaded him, he made me swear to order you to go see him, Sr. Caporal. So, you need to see him."

"What's his name? Did he say he knew me?"

"Didn't say."

You enter the small infirmary, a dugout, sandbag fortified, mud-brick building in the center of the battalion AO. A generator is running on the backside of the building, and there are air conditioner units as well. Man, it feels good inside. A large canopy is rigged on the outside for those who can and choose to rest under it. You check in with the orderly saying only that you were summoned to visit the technician that was brought in today from the ambush. You are directed to the outside pavilion. The tech is there.

As you walk back out and turn to the shaded area, a voice calls out, "Over here Sr. Caporal, grab a chair and a water."

Several legs are lounging around with various injuries or ailments. You never chose to question a legionnaire who needed a few days of rest in the infirmary before returning to duty. The desert was hard.

The tech is sitting on a beach lounger of all things. His leg is out in front of him in a fresh cast, his shoulder bandaged, no shirt, cut off JCUs. He is wearing sunglasses, several days' beard growth, and his hair is unruly, blond, curly. He holds a sweating glass of spritzer water with a slice of lemon on the edge and another dunked inside. He is a large, sharply-muscled man. A pair of crutches lean against the mud wall behind him. He is grinning.

"Here's something I thought I would never say. It's good to see you again, Sr. Caporal Baker. You don't know who I am, do you? Don't remember? Maybe this will refresh your memory, 'Lance Caporal, you are relieved from the bridge.' Hahaha! Now I'll be honest, that scared the crap out of me. I knew you were furious. Hahaha! No hard feelings, Sr. Caporal. You saved my life."

You stand in astonishment; it is Sr. Legionnaire Juarez from the *JW Nowly*! He had been sent to the Palanquin for another two years.

"They told me what you did, jumping off the ATC to come back. I sure am glad you didn't know who I was! Hahaha! You've done well, Sr. Caporal."

You walk up and sit down, "No, I would have come back for you anyway, Juarez."

"I believe that, Sr. Caporal. I really do." He is showing respect for your rank even though, as a civilian, he was not obligated to. Maybe he was a different man.

"I hear you're the one to watch for as the future EFL Commandant."

Now you laugh, "Ha! I doubt that, Juarez."

"No, no, believe in yourself. Who would have thought a lance caporal would have been able to pull the strings you did? Heck, with that stunt today and what I heard you did on the rest of that tour in the Sand Fleas, you'll make company sergent inside of nine, maybe eight. Where are you now?"

He was wrong; you are standing close to nine now and still have a year with Alpha. Additionally, you still have to attend *Academe de Sergent*, a three-month course to prepare an NCO for a company-level command. No, it would be ten or more before you make sergent. That was okay and still within a good time frame. You are actually right on course.

You sit and talk for a while, laughing, telling, and listening to stories. Maybe under different circumstances, Sr. Legionnaire Juarez would have been a better legionnaire, if you had met him earlier in his service. Who knows?

You stand to leave. He reaches out and grabs your arm. Tears come to his eyes. "You saved my life, Sr. Caporal. Thank you. I'll never forget that."

You take his hand, and you both squeeze the other.

"*Ad legionem!*" he says.

"*Ad legionem!*" You respond, stepping back and giving him a salute.

You walk away feeling strange. You need to find a place to be alone.

Level Up – Sr. Legionnaries

It's hard to believe that two years have nearly come and gone, the time and events stacked against a wave of missions, actions, skirmishes, and deeds. Some are heroic, and others not so much, but each drifts on like the endless blowing sands of this formidable desert. You stand watching, not so much with anticipation or even fond memories of the looming activity. This is your third experience with this tradition, the first as a participant, the second as a non-involved observer, and now as a willing or rather, complacent accessory. The tradition is as old and storied as the EFL itself. That it is necessary or serves a purpose is not arguable, it does. That doesn't mean you agree with the brutality. The lance caporals are given the lead role and responsibility. Along with every other NCO, each of them has gone through this initiation, this rite of passage to become a Sr. legionnaire.

EXPEDITIONARY FOREIGN LEGION -The Xo

Out of the original Alpha Company BTC of 129 *minus nobilis*, only 75 remain, with a company total of 102. Alpha started with a full contingent of 164 officers, NCOs, and legionnaires. Today 33 legionnaires rank up to Sr. legionnaire, and most, you only know of three who are not, are transferring to the Palanquin or the AC in the next week. That leaves 72 in the company, less than 50 percent. Alpha is nearing her last days as an effective combat line company. Plans are already in place to combine the four platoons into two and use the company as a reinforcement or reactionary force.

You think back to Gulf 6/117 and the snub your platoon was given. Not a single legionnaire was ranked up even though eight earned it. The more you think back on the punitive and unprofessional behavior of Captain Roubere and Sergent Humphreys, the angrier you become. You heard from a mate back at 6th Battalion that Humphreys was busted down to caporal, and Roubere was forced to retire.

It seems none of the Sr. caporals of the company are fond of the initiation; each of you stands back from the activity. Sergent Maxton serves as the official observer to ensure it doesn't get out of hand. The four of you have become good mates, having gone through DI course and then Fox BTC together. Now, just as always, some of you will move on. *Academe de Sergent* will be next or another platoon and company or some other assignment like V Corps as instructors. The company caporals are excited, knowing that close-out assignments, new postings, or their promotion to Sr. Caporal are close. Caporal Chao has done exceptionally well, earning an R-Com as well as a Legion Cross 3rd Class for bravery in his own ambush situation, saving all of his squad and defeating a wahti patrol. You convinced him to return to the AC and attend the Mountain Sniper course. You made a call to V Corps and spoke to a certain sergent major to attain a spot for him; the rest of the discussion focused on your own future.

Three days later, 1st and 2nd Platoons merge into 1st Platoon, and 3rd and 4th become 2nd. Chao receives orders to MCWS for Sniper course. The rest of the caporals remain for the moment until Alpha is cased in the next few weeks. Your good mate Sr. Caporal Urall is reassigned to V Corps as a DI, returning only as an instructor and waiting on his promotion. Trey and Kendel will close out the company and then wait for new orders. Several of your legs have made known their intention to reenlist even without earning Sr. leg on the first round. They are good legionnaires. Nearly all your Sr. legs are nervous about what awaits them in the jungle and the icy northern territory. You were blessed with an above-average platoon of cassum. You lost nine in the two years, and each loss was hard.

"You ready?"

"Yeah," you answer, and the drivers start the ATCs. You jump in the buggy with Urall, a lance caporal, and a leg. The destination is the regiment HQ and then on to the airstrip. You have charge of the 30 Sr. legs catching the flight back to *The Land of the Giant PX*, Sahara Del Rio, for their first reassignments. The excitement is electrifying, if not sad in its own way. Mates part, a lifetime of memories of this desert etched into each one, not to be soon dislodged. Urall sits next to you in the back, a solemn yet knowing expression on his face. He, too, is leaving those in this vast sand that will never return home, his third tour also.

"*Ad legionem*," you both utter, removing your helmets and placing the kepis firmly upon your heads.

EFL
Rank Chart

Lvl/Yrs	Rank	Pay	Insignia
0	Nothing/Cassum	0	N/A
1/0-1	Lower Rank – minus nobilis	30	None
2/1-3	Legionnaire	35	V
3/1.5-6	Senior Rank – Sr. gradum (Sr. Leg)	42	V w/top bar
4/4-6	Lance Caporal	47	V w/2 top bars
5/5-7	Caporal	55	2 Vs
/6			
6/7-8	Senior Caporal	60	2 Vs 2 top bars
7/9-12	Sergent	67	3 Vs
/10			
8/12-15	Colour Sergent	75	3 Vs top bar
14			
9/15-17	First Sergent	82	3 Vs 2 bars
/17			
10/18-24	Sergent Major	95	3 Vs 3 bars
20			
11/20-25	Commandant		3 Vs 3 bars w/C inside
O1/14-20	Adjutant Leftenant	70 +100 adjustment	Small Disc
O2	Leftenant	85	Bar
O3	Captain	95	2 bars
O4	Major	105	2 bars and disc

EXPEDITIONARY FOREIGN LEGION -The Xo

EFL
Rank Chart

Promotion to next rank   Reenlist

0 Basic Training 69/92 B/A out of 111 total PP - Promotion Points
1 Complete 6 Missions at least 1 Chap with 150/115 PP

2 Complete 9 Missions 2 Chap __PP

3 Complete 12 Missions 3 Ch __PP Jungle School Demo/AP Course   3 yrs

4 Complete 18 Missions __PP AP/Demo course
5 Complete 21 Missions __PP Mountain School, Sniper course, DI School

4 yrs

6 Complete 24 Missions __PP Assign to BTC/take new platoon

7 *Academe de Sergent*

4 yrs

8 SNCO Command Course
Retirement with 50% benefits. Mandatory retirement E7 at 14 yrs   6 yrs
9
At this point, a senior NCO must look at their options. There are only 5 SM slots, and with remaining yrs to retirement they could crossover/attain O3-O4 with 25 yrs
10 A 5 yr extension is granted to SM

Normal Retirement 100% benefit. Mandatory below E10
11 There is only one Sergent Major-chef of the EFL
He can retire at any time
Cross-over to officer rank. A 5 yr extension is granted to retirement   5 yrs
O1 Any rank Colour Sergent and above may apply to crossover to officer
O2 Normal promotion to O2 after 1 yr
O3 2 yrs minimum O2
O4 This is the highest achievable rank of a crossover NCO

Mandatory retirement at 25 years 100% benefits at highest paid rank

G. VAN WALLACE

EFL Organizational Chart

Field Marshall   Legion – 216,000   Commandant

Maj/Brig Gen   Corps – 5/43,200   Sergent Major

I Corps   II Corps   III Corps   IV Corps   V Corps

Col/Adj Colonel   Regiment – 25/8640   First Sergent

101-105   106-110   111-115   116-120   121-125

Major   Battalion – 150/1440   Colour Sergent

1st Batt   2nd Batt   3rd Batt   4th Batt   5th Batt   6th Batt

Captain   Company – 1350/160   Sergent

Alpha–Bravo–Charlie–Delta–Echo–Fox–Gulf–Hotel–India

Leftenant/Adj Lft   Platoon – 5400/40   Sr. Caporal/Cpl

1st Plt   2nd Plt   3rd Plt   4th Plt

EXPEDITIONARY FOREIGN LEGION – The Xo

ABOUT THE AUTHOR

G. Van Wallace is a prolific writer and author of the highly acclaimed and action-packed military science fiction series, *NNP Fleet Marine*. His fifth published book, *EFL – The Xo*, firmly sets his place in the alternative history/military fiction genre.

G. Van Wallace is an Army veteran. He is married and has two daughters, and lives in Central Virginia.

Other books by G. Van Wallace/*Cross The Rubicon Publishing*

NNP Fleet Marine Series
    Book 1: Six Weeks
    Book 2: Colony Wars
    Book 3: Valhalla (in edit; coming 2023)
    Book 4: Syssistia (currently writing)

Cerpian's Massacre

Expeditionary Foreign Legion – EFL Series
    EFL – The Xo
    EFL – Ad Legionem (currently writing)

For Pre-Teens
Beautiful Seasons A Girl's Story

CROSS THE RUBICON PUBLISHING

On January 11, 705 AUC, when Julius Caesar crossed the Rubicon River into northern Italy, he quoted the now-famous words *Alea iacta est*, "let the die be cast." His crossing meant civil war, which he attempted to avoid, but the Roman Senate recalled Caesar, and he faced possible imprisonment, exile, and even death for his growing power and favor with the plebes.

His faithful *XIII Gemina Legio* followed him. There was no turning back. Once you pick up and read one of our titles, you too will *Cross The Rubicon*, and there is no turning back.

We believe in our constitutional freedom, support our Veterans, and have an unapologetic patriotic stance, all of which are integrated into our stories.

ABOUT THE BOOK

Expeditionary Foreign Legion – The Xo

It's only a three-year mandatory service, and many never even see combat. Of those that do, a majority come home. Then there is the *EFL*. Straight out of Basic Training, new EFL legionnaires are sent to the *Xobian Desert*. That's where the real training begins. If they survive that first tour and show some potential, they are given the opportunity to escape the heat, drudgery, smell, and death of *The Xo* and finish their service in another theater of operations. The pain is only just the beginning, as the EFL deploys to all major conflict hot spots worldwide. How long are three years when each day can be your last?

EFL is written in an exciting and rare format, placing the reader as a character in a computer game of sorts. Will you survive or die early in a few chapters? Will you be forced to *Restart* and live through all the trials and pain again or experience a new game, a different challenge?

The life-threatening and altering realities of combat are not to be taken lightly. Only those who have lived through it know its horrors, pain, deprivation, insanity, cruelty, and sorrow. Yet, each person who returns from combat also shares a deeper bond with those who stood by their side, forming a tight brother/sisterhood. There is also a lighter side: dark humor, fond memories of foreign places, smells, and sounds that trigger a moment experienced in youth many years past.

What choices will you make as the reader? Can you win the game?